Praise for the novels of Barbara Bretton . . .

"No one tells a story like Barbara Bretton."
—Meryl Sawyer, author of *Unforgettable*

"Ms. Bretton expertly weaves together second chances and affairs of the heart to form this delightful book. As always, a wonderful reading experience."
—*Romantic Times*

"Delightful characters . . . thoroughly enjoyable."
—*Heartland Critiques*

"Glamour, intrigue, and action."
—Nora Roberts

"A classic adult fairy tale."
—*Affaire de Coeur*

"[An] intricate plot . . . a sensuous read with well-defined characters."
—*Rendezvous*

"Seductive."
—*Publishers Weekly*

"Bretton's characters are always real and their conflicts believable."
—*Chicago Sun-Times*

Berkley Books by Barbara Bretton

SLEEPING ALONE

ONCE AROUND

THE DAY WE MET

THE DAY
WE MET

BARBARA BRETTON

BERKLEY BOOKS, NEW YORK

This is a work of fiction. Names, characters, places and incidents are either the product of the author's imagination or are used fictitiously, and any resemblance to actual persons, living or dead, business establishments, events or locales is entirely coincidental.

THE DAY WE MET

A Berkley Book / published by arrangement with the author

PRINTING HISTORY
Berkley edition / November 1999

The Penguin Putnam Inc. World Wide Web site address is http://www.penguinputnam.com

ISBN: 0-425-17190-6

BERKLEY®
Berkley Books are published by The Berkley Publishing Group, a division of Penguin Putnam Inc., 375 Hudson Street, New York, New York 10014.
BERKLEY and the "B" logo are trademarks belonging to Penguin Putnam Inc.

PRINTED IN THE UNITED STATES OF AMERICA

10 9 8 7 6 5 4 3 2 1

For Steven J. Axelrod, definitely
the world's best agent

The list is long. The gratitude is enduring. Thanks to:

Judith Palais—for her patience, understanding, and sense of humor. I have put all three attributes to the test many times.

Leslie Gelbman—for her support.

Tim Bowden, Reloj, Joyce Bradsher, Jim Selkirk, Kay Butler, Davis Morris, Gene Haldeman, Natalie Edwards, Susan Lacy, Dwayne Webb, Darwin and Barbara Holder, Martin Hughes, Beth Smarr, Sarah Hutton, Aida Cloutier, Annette Nunez, Bob Gouge, Jeff Donovan, Fritzi Lareau, Tom Isaacson, Benjamin Chee, Mark Kinney, Kali Amanda Browne, Julia Ramirez, Paul Schwartz—who are as generous as they are talented.

Laura Bretton—for being family.

Mel and Vi Fuller—for being not just family, but friends as well.

And, always and forever, for my husband, Roy—for being who he is. Nobody does it better, BDH!

THE DAY
WE MET

ONE

"Daddy's getting married."

Maggy O'Brien gripped the steering wheel and glanced at the dashboard clock. It was 7:08 on the morning of her thirty-fifth birthday, and she was in her pajamas and bunny slippers, driving her daughter to school. Up until that second, she hadn't thought things could get any worse. She met her daughter's eyes in the rearview mirror. "Would you say that again, Nicole?"

Nicole's gaze drifted away, and she disappeared behind a curtain of dark purple hair. Nicole was fifteen. Purple hair came with the territory. "Daddy's getting married."

"Today?" Maggy asked. He wouldn't get married on her birthday. He wouldn't do that to the mother of his children, even if the divorce had been finalized two years ago this past April.

Nicole made a sound of disgust. "Of course not today. Maybe Christmas."

"Well," said Maggy, and then she stopped. What was there to say beyond that? In a little over two months, there'd be a new Mrs. Charles O'Brien. "How long have you known?"

Nicole's slender shoulders rose and fell. "I dunno. Maybe a week."

A week. Maggy drew in a breath and forced herself to count to ten. "Why didn't you tell me?"

"I did tell you."

Count to twenty, Maggy. Thirty, even. Just don't let her push your buttons.

"You could have told me last week."

"I forgot."

"You forgot your father's getting married?"

Nicole sighed. "It's not like it's a big deal. He's been seeing Sally forever."

"Not a big—" She choked back the words. Her daughter was right. It wasn't a big deal. Ex-husbands remarried every day of the week. That's why they were ex-husbands, so they could find themselves new wives. "You're right," she said. "It's not a big deal at all. Your dad and I have been divorced for two years. If he wants to get married, he can get married. It's nothing to me." She flipped on her turn signal. "What he does is none of my business. I only care because it affects you and Charlie."

She made a right onto Main Street, drove two blocks, then pulled up in front of the high school.

"Oh, God," Nicole said, adding a groan for emphasis. "Don't park here! I don't want anyone to see you in your pajamas."

"You should've thought about that when you missed the bus."

"My hair wasn't dry yet."

"Then get up earlier, and you won't have these problems."

"I hate you!"

"I know you do," said Maggy. "Believe it or not, you'll grow out of it."

Nicole scrambled out of the car, slammed the door, then ran full speed toward the school as she tried to put as much distance between her and her mother as possible. Maggy used to do that, too, when she was a girl. She'd be out shopping with her mother and sisters and she and Claire and Eleanor would duck behind pillars every time they saw somebody they knew, because God forbid anybody should know that ditzy woman with the dyed red hair and too much blush was their mother. Funny how life can play tricks on you. These days, it was her sisters and her mother who pretended they didn't know her.

They meant well. At least Maggy liked to believe they meant well when they criticized everything from her haircut to her shoes and all stops in between. They worried about her. They said she stayed home too much, she worked too hard, she'd forgotten how to have fun. They told her she'd settled into a routine somewhere around 1982 and stayed there, and, try as she might, Maggy couldn't argue with that. Who had time for that nonsense anyway? God knows, she hadn't had time when she was a newlywed with a baby on the way or when she was following Charles from army base to army base with two toddlers, two dogs, one cat, and an irascible parrot, all of whom were her responsibility. Charles's responsibility was his career, and she understood that. It was her job to hold the family together, and if that meant learning how to pack up the old house overnight and turn the new house into a home the next morning, then that was what she did.

She could wrap, pack, and ship with the best of them. She knew how to open herself up to new experiences and make friends with people who would be important to her for the twelve months they'd be assigned there and forgotten the second they waved good-bye. She told herself she enjoyed the nomadic life of an army wife, but she enjoyed the fact that it came with an end date even more. Charles would retire when he hit twenty years, and then they'd buy themselves a real house in a real neighborhood, and the only time she'd pack a suitcase would be for their two-week vacation each July.

Of course, it didn't work out that way. What dream ever did? One night, Charles came home while she was packing them up for a move to Florida and told her that he'd decided to reenlist, that the opportunities presented to him were everything he'd ever wanted, and that he hoped she'd understand that he was only doing what was best for the family.

Six months later, she said those same words to Charles when she asked him for a divorce. There was no animosity between them. No screaming fights or bitter rages. Maybe it would have been better if there had been. Then there might have been something worth saving, some small remnant of the passion they'd once shared. Their good marriage had run its course, and it was time to divvy up the furniture and the savings account and get on with their lives. Charles had been assigned to a diplomatic position in London, and Maggy went home to New Jersey.

Home was a comfortable ranch house on three-quarters of an acre in the same neighborhood where she'd played as a little girl. Back then there hadn't been any houses, just lots of open space and woods where a kid could get lost with her dreams. Maggy's dreams had always been the same: home and family. With a home and a family to love, you could take pretty much anything life threw your way. Well, she had a home and she certainly had a family. Two kids, two sisters, a mother who'd suddenly discovered the fountain of youth, and enough aunts, uncles, and cousins to fill the Meadowlands. She also had a job and school, and if she didn't have love or passion or a man to hold her when the going got rough, she knew things could be a whole lot worse. At least her sisters didn't know Charles was getting married.

She stopped for the traffic light at the corner of Poplar and Sycamore and congratulated herself. One block away from home, and she hadn't been busted by any of Nicole's friends—or her own, for that matter. Another three minutes, and she'd pull into the garage, and nobody would ever know that she'd managed to sneak out again in her pajamas. It was a small victory, but she took them wherever she could find them. She flicked on her right-turn signal and angled onto Sycamore, then muttered a word she hadn't muttered since the day she got in between one of the cats and an angry skunk.

Her sisters' cars were parked at the curb in front of her house. Claire's Saab was angled toward the fire hydrant. The back wheel on the passenger's side was up on the curb. The front wheels looked dazed. Eleanor's gleaming black Lexus faced the wrong way. Its front bumper nosed against the fender of the Saab. This was nothing unusual. What was unusual was the fact that they were there at all.

Maggy's hands started to shake as she turned into her driveway and shifted into park. Something was wrong. Why else would they be there at seven in the morning? She knew it wasn't Nicole, but what about Charlie? She'd put him on the school bus over an hour ago. She'd noticed the substitute driver and made a mental note to call the school and ask for his name and qualifications. *Please God* . . .

She ran up the pathway, bunny slippers pounding against the slates. The door was slightly ajar, and she threw it open wide.

"Claire! Eleanor! What's wrong? Where are—"

"Happy birthday, Mags!" Her two impossibly elegant younger sisters popped out from the archway and enveloped Maggy in a pair of bear hugs. "Surprise!"

"Surprise?" She sagged against them in a mixture of relief and rage. "You almost gave me a heart attack!"

"You're getting old, Mags." Claire grinned. "Thirty-five must be a dangerous age."

Maggy's heart was beating so fast she found it hard to

breathe. "I thought something had happened to one of the kids. I thought the school had called you and—" She couldn't finish the sentence. No mother could.

Ellie, currently a blond, poked Claire in the upper arm with one French-manicured finger. "I told you she'd think something happened to the kids. We should've waited outside."

"Not to worry," said Claire, hugging Maggy again. "She'll live. Besides, any woman who goes outside in her pajamas and bunny slippers deserves whatever she gets." She made a show of looking Maggy over. "Good God, woman, what on earth were you thinking?"

"I wasn't thinking," Maggy said, sliding out of her oversized raincoat and hanging it from the curved oak hook to the left of the front door. "I was mothering."

"Nicole missed the bus again?" Ellie's naturally flinty voice always mellowed when she mentioned her niece.

Maggy struggled to hold back a sigh. She'd helped diaper both of her tall and elegant sisters. You would think that would give her an edge, but it didn't. Looking at them that morning made her feel dumpy and old and alone. "Nicole missed the bus. Charlie spilled orange juice on his shirt, and I had to iron another one. Tigger threw up on the sofa." *Take your pick, girls. Welcome to the exciting world of the single mother.* She reached back and adjusted her ponytail. "Besides, it's not like I make a habit of going out in my pajamas. This was an emergency."

"We know," said Claire, her perfectly mascaraed gray blue eyes wide with compassion. "Nic told us."

"Told you?" Maggy was puzzled. "Told you what?" No. Please don't let them know about Charles.

Another exchange of worried glances.

"About Charles." Ellie wasn't a toucher. She patted Maggy's forearm the same way she patted feral cats, quick little stabs with stiffly outstretched fingers.

"You know about Charles?" she asked. It wasn't even

eight in the morning, and already this qualified as the worst birthday of her life. "You can't possibly know about Charles. I just found out thirty minutes ago."

Claire and Ellie locked eyes.

"Stop that! If you two don't quit giving each other looks, I'm—"

"That's good," said Claire. "Let it out. That's the best way to get past the pain."

"Pain?" Maggy laughed. "What pain? Charles is getting married. I wish him well."

"You can level with us," said Ellie. "We're sisters. We understand."

"That's right," said Claire. "Everyone knows you don't marry your transitional lover. He'll learn."

"You remember that," Ellie said. "It's so easy to mistake loneliness for love."

They meant well. Maggy knew that. All of this patronizing talk about love and loneliness was meant to soothe her battered, divorced ego, to remind her that even though her ex-husband had found somebody new to love while Maggy stayed home with the cats and dogs and tended the home fires, there was still hope. Those two unmarried role models for success actually thought they understood how it felt to be the single mother of two, part-time student, part-time secretary, and full-time worrier that the road not taken was the one that led to the pot of gold. They loved her. It wasn't their fault that they didn't get it. How could they? Sometimes there was simply no substitute for experience.

"How did you find out about Charles?" she asked.

"Nic called me," Claire said. She looked slightly uncomfortable, although you had to have known her from birth to recognize the signs. Claire had always been good at concealing her feelings until it was too late.

A lump formed deep inside Maggy's throat. "When?"

"Right after she spoke to her father."

"Oh." Maggy knew her daughter and her sister were

very close, and she'd never been a bit jealous. The ugly
feeling in the center of her chest was a brand-new sensation, and she didn't like it. She wanted to go back to
the days when Nic was a sweet baby girl who needed
nothing more than her mother's love to make her happy.

"It wasn't that she wanted to tell me," Claire rushed
on. "It's just that you were out at school and—"

Maggy raised her right hand, palm out. "You're making it worse, Claire. Just let it go."

"You don't understand," her beautiful, clueless baby
sister said. "It was your school night and Nic was all
upset and she had to—"

"I know," Maggy interrupted, "and it's okay. You
and Nicole are good friends. I think it's great. Now, how
about some coffee? I don't know about you two, but I
could use some caffeine right about now."

"Not very subtle," Ellie observed. "If you want to
change the subject, just say so."

"I want to change the subject."

"Good," said Claire, "because you don't have time
for that caffeine anyway." She glanced at the man's
watch strapped to her left wrist. "What time is the appointment?" she asked Ellie.

"Eight-thirty," said Ellie, "and unless Maggy's going
out in her pajamas again, she'd better get moving."

They were up to something. No doubt about it. "Do
either one of you feel like telling me what in hell you're
talking about?"

"I don't need a makeover," Maggy said as they practi-
cally strapped her into the chair at Royal House of
Beauty an hour later. "All I need is a good night's
sleep."

The stylist, a tall black man named Andre, rolled his
eyes. "Rapunzel, you're not a day too soon." He held
her ponytail between his fingers and tsk-tsked. "We can't
pretend we're in high school any longer, can we . . . not

once those little gray hairs start coming in.''

"I do not have gray hair." It was hard to look fierce when you were wrapped in a pastel pink bib. "I'm too young for gray hair."

Andre pointed a comb in the direction of her sisters. "They're not too young for gray hair, girl, and neither are you. Now what to do about it . . ."

"Color all you like," said Maggy, "but don't cut an inch."

Andre rolled his eyes and turned to face Claire and Ellie, who were sprawled on chaise longues by the window. "The girl won't let me cut her hair, and you said I could cut her hair."

Claire leaped to her expensively shod feet. Manolo Blahniks. What else? Maggy couldn't even pronounce *Manolo Blahnik,* much less walk in them. "Of course you can cut her hair. That's part of the makeover, isn't it?"

"No, he can't cut my hair," Maggy said, growing annoyed. "Is this a makeover or an execution? Don't I have any say in what goes on?"

"No!" said the other three in unison.

"You're stuck in cement," Ellie said. "It isn't 1982 any longer, Mags, and you're not eighteen."

"Thanks for the reminder." Maggy watched as Andre removed the coated rubber band and brushed out her hair. It fell across her shoulders like a familiar dark blanket. Charles used to love her hair. Back when they were newlyweds with happily-ever-after stretching out before them, back before there was a future second Mrs. Charles O'Brien on the horizon, he used to bury his face in her hair, run his hands through it, tell her how much he loved her, and she'd whisper how they'd always be together, how there'd never be anyone else but the two of them while he took her hair between his hands and—

"Cut it," she said as her sisters and Andre stared back

at her through the salon mirror. "I want you to chop it off right now."

Andre's silver scissors glinted in the morning light. "Girl, once I snip, there's no going back."

"Good," said Maggy as she met the reflection of his eyes. "Cut it all off." She couldn't go back now if she wanted to.

The stretch limo was waiting at the curb when Maggy stepped out of the hair salon with her sisters.

"You didn't," she said, stopping dead in her tracks. "You wouldn't."

"Of course we did," said Claire, draping her arm around Maggy's shoulders. "You didn't think we'd just give you a haircut for your birthday, did you?"

"I don't know what I think anymore," Maggy said, running her fingers through her newly shorn, newly tinted hair. "I'm not sure I can think." Maybe Andre had snipped off her gray cells along with two feet of hair. She felt like a different person, as if thirty-five years of expectations had vanished along with her ponytail. She felt lighter, breezier, more capable, even though she knew that was giving a haircut an awful lot of credit.

"You don't have to think," Ellie said as the limo driver walked around the back of the car. "We did the thinking for you. Your bags are packed. We have an out-fit for you to change into for the trip. Nicole is staying with Claire. The Giordanos are taking Charlie. Yours truly will tend to the menagerie. All you have to do is have fun."

Her baby sisters had arranged for her to spend a week-end in Atlantic City. She'd be whisked down the shore in a cushy stretch limo, ensconced in a suite at one of the fancy-shmancy casino hotels, wined and dined and even gambled into pure and utter relaxation.

"You deserve this and more," Claire said, growing uncharacteristically teary-eyed with emotion. "After all you did for Mom last year—'' She stopped for a second. ''I mean, she wouldn't still be with us if you hadn't—''

''You've always been there for all of us to lean on,'' Ellie broke in, ''and it's time we showed you how much we appreciate you.''

Maggy made the right noises. She thanked them both and oohed and aahed over the limo and the little television and the fully stocked bar and the handsome driver, but the truth was, she would have been happier staying home. She'd planned to spend her day off in her pajamas, curled up on the love seat in the family room watching trashy videos and eating take-out Chinese.

The driver showed her how to work the television set, the radio, the heat, and the reading lights. He pointed out the bar, the ice buckets, and the pretty little glasses set up atop the burled wood ledge. The glasses had the hotel logo etched into the front. They sat on crisp white doilies that also bore the hotel logo. ''If you need anything else,'' the driver said, ''just push the button near the light switch, and I'm at your service.'' The Plexiglas partition whirred up between them, and they were on their way to the bright lights and spinning slot machines of Atlantic City.

Her most unfavorite city in the known universe. You'd think her sisters would know that simple thing about her. She wasn't a bright lights type. She wasn't comfortable in sequins and bugle beads. She hated crowds. She thought life was a big enough gamble and wasn't about to toss her hard-earned money into the mix.

She wasn't one of those mysterious women you saw in movies, the kind who dressed in black and smoked foreign cigarettes and spoke in hushed tones. All you had to do was look at her and you would know she'd be more at home behind the wheel of a minivan than in the back-seat of a stretch zipping down the Garden State Parkway.

She glanced at her reflection in the vanity mirror that folded into the rear door panel. The only thing left of her

old self was the look in her eyes. Everything else had
been cut and colored and shadowed and tinted and lip-
sticked and blushed into something as close to perfection
as Maggy had ever been. She hadn't looked this good on
her wedding day. It would have been fun to push a cart
through the ShopRite and watch her neighbors breeze
right past her in the frozen food aisle. "Hey, Marie,"
she'd call out. "You're not talking to me anymore?"
Marie's mouth would drop open when she realized who
was talking to her, and Maggy would live off that look
of amazement until the Christmas decorations came down
next year. What was the point of a makeover if you
couldn't make your friends green with envy?

What would Charles think if he saw her now? Now
there was a loaded question for you. Not that it mattered
anymore what he thought, but she couldn't help wondering if he'd feel a momentary pang for everything they
had shared. Maybe something like the pang she'd felt
when Nicole told her that he was getting married. She
didn't want to be married to him any longer, but the
thought of him marrying someone else made her feel like
weeping.

So many hopes and dreams ended with their marriage.
The small jokes at the end of a day. The shared concerns.
The vision of themselves, many years down the road,
surrounded by their children and grandchildren. She
knew that Charles would give his life for their children,
same as she would, and there was nobody else on earth
she could say that about.

Suddenly she wanted nothing more than to be home.
She supposed she could ask the driver to turn around. It
was her birthday, after all. Didn't Claire say she could
do anything she wanted? She'd have the driver take her
home, and she wouldn't tell her sisters. Charlie was staying overnight with his pals Kyle and Jeremy Giordano,
while Nicole would spend the night with Claire at her
fancy condo on the water. Nobody would have to know

that she was home with her TV and takeout. She'd say something at the next exit, she thought as they whizzed past Holmdel, heading south. The big car was as comfortable as her living room, and there was something hypnotic about the parade of blazing autumn color flashing by her window as they cut through what remained of long-ago forests and pine barrens. Another exit passed and then another. It was so easy to do nothing, to just lean back against the plush leather seat and let life happen.

She wasn't entirely sure she knew how to do that. She'd been the one with the lists and the schedules and the responsibility since she was ten years old. It was a tough habit to break. When the gods and goddesses of newborns doled out their gifts, they'd bestowed beauty on Claire, brains on Eleanor, and a sense of responsibility on Maggy. Okay, so maybe it sometimes seemed more like a chronic Catholic guilty conscience, but whatever you wanted to call it, it worked. If you needed someone to watch your kids, carpool for you on Tuesday, or pick up your dry cleaning, all you had to do was call Maggy. She'd never let you down. "Maggy's like Old Faithful," her ex said once in front of a group of colleagues at a boring cocktail party at the Officer's Club. "You can always count on her."

Her sisters said they wanted to thank her for all she did for the family, but Maggy knew there was more to it than that. They felt sorry for her. When they looked at her, all they saw was a thirty-five-year old divorcée with two kids, living in a tract house in central New Jersey. A soccer mom who took college classes at the community college two nights a week, who worked part-time for a priest of all things, and considered a trip to Pizza Hut a major night out. It wasn't conjecture. She knew that's what they thought because she'd heard them say it. Their mother had been recovering from the stroke at Maggy's house. Maggy was fresh from divorce court, struggling to set down roots for herself and her children in the town where she grew up. She'd been filled with fear and worry and the most ridiculously inappropriate sense of optimism imaginable. Ellie and Claire had come over for dinner, and Maggy overhead them talking in the kitchen. "Poor Mags," one of them said. "I feel so sorry for her. This isn't much of a life. Bet she wished she'd stayed with Charles."

She had laughed it off at the time, chalking the comment up to youth and inexperience, but as the months wore on, she'd found herself thinking about it again and again. Sometimes, when she was overworked and overtired, she wondered if she'd made a mistake when she divorced her husband. He was a good man. They'd had a good life. It was just that one day it stopped being the life they both wanted. By the time the divorce became final, she felt a sense of profound relief, and she suspected Charles felt it as well. Their time had come and gone, and she knew it, but still the news of her ex-husband's upcoming marriage made her feel as if a door had been shut and locked between them, a door that not even divorce had been able to close completely.

Conor Riley saw her as she stepped from the limo.

He'd handed over his car keys to the valet and was about to grab his duffel bag and head for the lobby where his brother was waiting for him when he heard a smoky female voice and a quiet laugh; he turned to his left and saw her. She had short dark hair shot through with red highlights and the kind of smile he used to dream about when he believed in such things. Her smile was wide and true, and it engulfed her whole face. He watched while she talked to the driver then shook his hand. Maybe a shade over five feet tall. Maybe a shade over one hundred pounds. Her eyes were a clear light blue, like a morning sky.

He caught himself and shook his head. Where the hell

did that morning sky crap come from? Female Caucasian, mid-thirties, brunette, blue eyes. Cold, hard facts. Anything else was a waste of time. If he didn't know that, he really was in the wrong line of work. Sixteen years on the force had taught him how to reduce a person to basics in twenty seconds, how to commit a face to memory in less time than it took to blink. How to take your emotions and stuff them in your back pocket where they couldn't hurt anyone. Emotions got in the way. They clouded your judgment. They made you see things that weren't there and miss the things that were.

Damn. He wasn't going down that road again. Not this weekend. He was going to roll some dice, play a little blackjack, maybe drink more than he should, and keep one step ahead of the memories. If he managed to get through this weekend, maybe there was a chance for him.

A bellman approached the blue-eyed woman and said something. She nodded, then the bellman took a garment bag from her limo driver and hung it on one of those rolling racks. The driver handed over two overnight suitcases that the bellman tossed on the shelf beneath.

Those suitcases reached out and grabbed Conor's attention. A pair of mismatched bags, one navy and the other a weathered tan, with scuff marks he could see from thirty yards away. The bags didn't fit the woman. Or the stretch for that matter. She was sleek and pampered and expensive. The bags weren't.

"Too rich for your blood," said a familiar voice. "She's either somebody's wife or a high roller. Either way, she's not for you."

Conor swung his bag over his shoulder and turned toward his younger brother Matt, who had joined him on the curb. "I thought we were meeting up in the lobby."

"We were," Matt said, "but after awhile, I began to wonder if you'd bailed on me. How long does it take to hand over the keys to the valet?"

"It's your hotel," he shot back. "Maybe you need a new efficiency expert."

Matt was the whiz kid in the Riley family, the one who'd broken out of the cops-and-firemen mold and found a job that didn't come with a uniform or a gun. The kid launched into a defense of his employer that lasted until Conor checked in at the main desk.

"Dinner at eight," Matt reminded him. "Nero's, on the third floor."

Conor was more the hamburger and fries type, but it was the kid's night to show off. "Eight o'clock, third floor," he said. "I'll be there."

They walked together toward the bank of elevators at the far end of the lobby, past a small room tucked into a quiet corner. He had a glimpse of dark paneling, lots of leather, oil paintings, and the dark-haired woman with the mismatched luggage sitting on the edge of a fancy brocade chair while one of the hotel assistants fielded a phone call.

"Told you she was out of your league," Matt said. "That's the VIP desk where the real players check in." He took another look. "Since when do you go for the waif type, anyway? I thought you liked big boobs and long legs and—"

"Shut up," Conor said good-naturedly. "You're not too old for me to deck you."

Matt was twenty-six years old, but that grin of his was only eight. "I've been telling one of the cocktail wait-resses about my big brother. Her name's Lisa. She's on tonight from four to midnight, and she's a hell of a lot more your type than the little brunette back there. Maybe—"

"Yeah," said Conor. "Maybe."

Maggy had first noticed the man in front of the hotel when she was talking with the bellman who took her bags. He was tall, big across the shoulders, with a few strands of silver threaded through his head of thick chestnut hair. Not that she'd been paying that much attention to him. It was just that the sunlight had managed to find him that second and draw her attention away from the bellman. A few strands of gray in a woman's hair, and her sisters gang up on her and send her out for a makeover. A few strands of gray in a man's hair, and he's on the cover of *People* magazine.

His gaze was deep, intense, and it didn't miss much. She looked back at him, almost daring him to acknowledge her, but a young man walked up behind him, and the man turned away. That was probably for the best, since she was easily the world's most inept flirt. She would have made a fool of herself and downright ruined the weekend before it had a chance to get started.

She hadn't thought about the man again until just this minute when he walked slowly past the VIP Check-in and smiled at her. At least she thought he smiled at her. She was reasonably sure she saw his eyes crinkle a little at the outer corners and his mouth edge upward in a smile that did little to soften his somewhat forbidding features. Then she saw that the same young man she'd noticed in the parking lot was at his side, and a rush of disappointment took her by surprise. The smile wasn't for her at all. It had nothing to do with her, and if she'd had the slightest bit of experience, she would have recognized that fact right off the bat.

Too bad Claire and Ellie weren't there with her to translate. When it came to the mysteries of the man/woman thing, Maggy was a newborn. Nicole knew more than she did, and Nicole was barely fifteen. Maggy was too literal, too down-to-earth, too busy to pay much attention to all of that nonsense. The last date she went on had ended badly when Maggy told the poor man that perhaps it was better if he didn't call again because the odds of a second date were maybe five million to one.

"You couldn't let him down gently?" Claire had

asked her the next day when she called Maggy for details.

"I did let him down gently," Maggy said. Why string him along when she had no intention of seeing him again?

Claire had told Ellie and Ellie told their mother and their mother told the aunts and the cousins, and before long the entire family was calling Maggy the Terminator. She laughed when they said it, but she still didn't understand what was so bad about telling the truth. What with school and work and the kids, she didn't have time for Mr. Right, much less for Mr. Absolutely Terrible.

"Here you go, Ms. O'Brien." The statuesque blond desk clerk handed Maggy a packet with a key inside. The packet was made of heavy, cream-colored vellum that was smooth to the touch. "Your suite is on the thirty-second floor. I'm sure you'll enjoy the view. You've been given access to the Augustus Club where members can stop for a complimentary drink or a bite to eat twenty-four hours a day."

She walked Maggy to the bank of elevators situated next to an obscenely expensive jewelry store whose sole purpose was to relieve lucky winners of some of that irksome money. Maggy tried to act nonchalant until the clerk walked away, then she all but pressed her nose against the storefront and gawked at the egg-sized diamonds and rubies on display. Garish, she thought. The jewels were ostentatious and vulgar and downright breathtaking, and she barely managed to control the impulse to step inside the shop and try on everything they had.

It turned out that the same adjectives could be used to describe her hotel suite. The bellman was waiting for her in the hallway. He smiled at her as if they were old friends as he unlocked the door and ushered her inside. He flipped on the lights, and she found herself wishing she hadn't tucked her sunglasses away in her purse. The windows faced the ocean, and the refracted sunlight bounced off the wall-to-wall smoked mirrors and almost blinded her. Louis XIV Meets Early Bordello with a touch of Vegas thrown in for good measure, all served up with an ancient Roman accent.

"This is the bar," the bellman said, pointing to a sleek curve of mahogany. She noticed gleaming gold taps and a row of glittering old-fashioned glasses. "Fully stocked. If it's not to your liking, just press five, and Stefan will be glad to help you." He showed her the pair of refrigerators—one in the parlor and the other in the bedroom—and the trio of closets, the huge jacuzzi, the steambath, the king-sized bed with the fur throw and explosion of pillows, the wine-colored velvet chaise longue turned to face the ocean.

He showed her the bathroom fixtures, the button for the living room draperies hidden behind the statue of Caesar and Cleopatra, the four separate phones, and the safe—and it wasn't until he started to show her everything all over again that she realized what he was doing and why. A tip. Of course, he wanted a tip. He carried her bags; he deserved a tip. She fumbled in her purse, praying she'd come up with the right amount. A dollar a bag? Five dollars for everything? Would he laugh in her face then call the front desk and tell them to toss her out on her ear? She settled on a ten-dollar bill. He thanked her and didn't slam the door behind him when he left, so she was reasonably certain she hadn't embarrassed either one of them.

"Now what?" she asked the statues of Caesar and Cleopatra near the window, but they had no answer for her. It was one o'clock on a Friday afternoon, and she hadn't a clue what to do with herself. Her dinner reservation, courtesy of Claire and Ellie, wasn't until eight at some place called Nero's. The thought made her shudder. Lots of tiny tables for two, with couples cooing over candlelight and champagne. Cooing, that is, when they weren't dancing to music soft enough to break what was left of your heart. Nothing like dinner alone in public on the night of your thirty-fifth birthday to lift a woman's spirits. Nothing like knowing your ex-husband wouldn't be eating dinner alone when his next birthday rolled around.

Two

"Lisa said you didn't call."

Conor drained his tumbler of Scotch and motioned for the waiter to bring him another one. "You're pushing, Matt," he said with as much good humor as he could muster. "I never said I would."

"I assumed—"

"Mistake number one." He broke a bread stick in half and popped it in his mouth. "Assumptions will get you into trouble every time."

"You don't know what you're missing. She's smart. Beautiful. Lots of fun." He polished off his own glass of wine. "You could do a lot worse."

"Listen," Conor said after the waiter deposited another Scotch in front of him, "she sounds like a great kid. Why don't you take her out?"

"I would," Matt said, "but I have to think of my job. Can't date the help."

Conor started to say something when she appeared in the doorway. Not Lisa. He didn't know this woman's name. She wore dark trousers, a pair of icy blue sweaters, and a string of pearls around her neck. No other jewelry except for a watch with a dark lizard strap. Her ears and fingers were bare. Her shoes were flat-heeled, and she carried a small, narrow purse tucked under her right arm. She looked expensive, he thought, like somebody who was accustomed to getting her way no matter how much it cost.

The maitre d' walked her past his table, and he caught the faintest scent of perfume, deep and rich and womanly. Womanly. That was the word he'd been searching for. She was tiny, but there was nothing girlish about her. She carried herself like a woman. She looked poised, sophisticated, perfect except for the tiny crease marks on her left cheek, telltale giveaway of an afternoon spent between the sheets.

The maitre d' removed one of her place settings, making it clear she was dining alone. Where was the guy she'd spent the afternoon with? She didn't look like the kind of woman who picked up talent in the casino for a quickie in her hotel room, but he knew enough about human nature to know that how people looked and how they really were deep inside rarely matched. She was probably sleeping with a married man, maybe some guy from Philly who needed deep cover, and the sex was good enough that she was willing to put up with eating alone.

"I can find out who she is." Matt sounded amused and slightly pissed off. He was the baby of the family and still thought he deserved undivided attention.

Conor shot him a look and addressed his attention to the towering salad in front of him.

"Or you could get off your ass and go talk to her," Matt continued, undeterred.

"Shove it," he said easily.

Matt shook his head. "Hope I don't get too old to take a shot when I see a woman I like."

"You're reading a hell of a lot into nothing."

"I saw your face, bro. Something about that brunette got your motor running."

Conor said nothing, just lifted a forkful of weird-looking lettuces to his mouth. Sometimes he thought he'd kill for a wedge of iceberg and some blue cheese dressing. Matt had a habit of saying whatever he thought, whenever he thought it, but every now and again, the kid managed to hit the nail on the head. The brunette did get his motor running. He wanted to know everything about her: her name, her phone number, why she was eating alone, why those big blue eyes looked like they were ready to cry, why he gave a damn about any of it.

Why didn't they just hang a spotlight over her head and a sign reading Table for One. It seemed to Maggy that everyone in the place turned to look when the waiter cleared away that pesky extra place setting.

"Would you like to see a wine list, madam?"

She shook her head. Eating alone was bad enough. Drinking alone was pathetic. "Mineral water, please."

He nodded and backed away like a courtier leaving the presence of the queen. She started to laugh, then remembered there was nobody to share the joke with and withdrew behind her menu instead. It wasn't as if she hadn't eaten her share of meals alone before. She grabbed a sandwich every Thursday night at the diner between work and school and she never felt uncomfortable, tucked away with tuna on rye and her textbook. Of course, the Cadillac Diner wasn't rigged up like an ancient Roman honeymoon resort with a dance floor, obsequious waiters, and music. Oh, God, the music. She felt as though the piano player knew all her secrets. She was a sucker for the old standards, always had been. She loved those lush lyrics about romance and heartbreak, about eyes across a crowded room, and happily ever after. All the things you grew up dreaming about as a kid.

"Oh, damn," she whispered, blinking back tears.

Maybe if she stuffed a twenty-dollar bill in the tip glass, the piano player would stop hammering on her heart-strings this way. She felt way too vulnerable tonight, too exposed to be sitting out there in public, pretending to be alone and happy about it.

She'd fallen asleep upstairs watching *General Hospital* and would have slept straight through dinner if house-keeping hadn't knocked on the door to see if she needed anything. The temptation to stay hidden away with a room service supper was strong, but it was her birthday after all, and her sisters would be devastated if she didn't take advantage of their gift to her. They were the kind who asked questions later, and there would be hell to pay if Maggy didn't have the right answers.

So there she was, adrift in a sea of sullen, middle-aged couples, lonely gray-haired widows spending their hus-bands' insurance money, and two guys who looked enough alike to be brothers. She recognized the older one from the parking lot earlier, and then from when she was checking into the hotel. He wasn't exactly handsome, not with that unruly head of hair and those rough features, but there was something so solid and male about him that she found him quite appealing. The younger one was a smaller, less battered version. They probably were broth-ers, she thought, peering at them over the top of the menu. They had a familial look of exasperation about them that reminded her of Claire and Ellie on a bad day.

The older of the two men looked up and met her eyes. He smiled slightly, the same off-center tilt to his wide mouth that she'd noticed when he walked past the VIP check-in earlier in the afternoon. The smile was shad-owed, shaded with sorrow she felt deep in her bones.

Right, she thought, and snapped shut her menu. Too many psych classes under her belt, that's what it was. She didn't know the first thing about the man, not his name or occupation or history, and the odds were she never would. A man looked at her across a room, and she was reading layers of back story into his smile. *Get over it, O'Brien. Stick with what you know: car pool, ShopRite, and mortgages. Leave the sad-eyed men for the women who specialize in that sort of thing.* She already had her hands full with her own sad-eyed little boy and a teenage daughter who'd forgotten how much she used to love her mother.

Maybe one day down the road she'd be able to smile back at a man in a restaurant and see what happened, but right now romance was at the bottom of her goals list.

"Looks like you struck out," Matt said as the brunette handed her menu to the waiter. "Gave her your best smile and everything. Use it or lose it, bro. I've been telling you that for years."

"Talk to me when you're old enough to shave more than twice a week," Conor said, pushing away his salad plate. Suddenly his appetite had gone south. "I don't need advice from a smart-mouthed kid I used to diaper."

"Save the big-brother rap for Eddie or Vince," Matt said, gesturing for another bottle of wine. "I'm not buying it." He grabbed a piece of salted flat bread from the basket between them. "You didn't even ground out. She struck you out at the plate."

"Can the baseball metaphors," he said, feeling less than brotherly, "and tell me how Sean looked when you were out there." His son was nineteen and a freshman at UCLA, attending on a football scholarship, and the reason Conor got up in the morning on a regular basis. Sean was a big, tall, strapping kid with a good mind and an even better heart, and every time Conor wondered why in hell he'd been put on this earth, he remembered the reason: to make Sean possible.

"He's struggling with the humanities but acing the sciences, as usual. One of his professors thinks he's wasting his time on football."

That got his attention. "Sean wouldn't be there if it

wasn't for football,'' he said. No way a New Jersey cop could afford a top-flight school. Not even with the help of his ex-wife and her husband.

"They think he has what it takes for premed," Matt said, slapping butter on an onion roll.

"Why didn't he tell me?"

Matt bit off a piece of roll and shrugged his shoulders. His expensive suit barely registered the movement. "You're his old man. Comes with the territory."

"Med school." He wouldn't have believed pride could make a make a man's chest ache, but it did. Right in the area of his heart. "Is he interested?"

"We talked about it over a few beers at a Mexican joint near the campus, some place where the jocks hang out. You should see how he fits in with them. He speaks their language. He's one of them. Still, I think he's flattered as all hell by the idea he might be doctor material."

"Flattered or interested enough to look into it?"

"Don't know," Matt said. "Ask him yourself when he comes back for Thanksgiving."

They both knew he'd ask Sean long before that. It wasn't every day a man heard that his jock son might have what it took to be a doctor. Sean was on the fast track to a career in the NFL, but it didn't take much for dreams like that to derail. A busted leg. Separated shoulder. One of those terrifying back injuries that reminded you why you never get too old to ask for God's help.

A doctor. Now that was something. The phone didn't ring at three A.M. with bad news about your son, the doctor. Doctors didn't leave thirty-year-old widows with two small kids. Doctors didn't kill.

Across the room, the brunette with the big blue eyes busied herself with something dark and leafy. He wondered if she had any kids of her own. If he told her about Sean, would she understand the painful pride inside his chest without being told or would she look at him, blank-eyed, while he tried to explain how sometimes Sean's future mattered more to Conor than his own future ever had. He wanted so much for his boy, to make right so many of the things he'd already screwed up along the way. The end of his marriage to Sean's mother Linda was the greatest failure of his life. She hated the idea of being a cop's wife. She came from a family of cops, same as he did, and she'd sworn she would never marry one. When he decided to enter law enforcement after graduation, she issued an ultimatum: "The police force or me." He tried to reason with her, but they were speaking different languages, and it occurred to him that maybe they always had. She remarried a few years after the divorce and went on to have three more beautiful, healthy kids. Her husband was an accountant.

"Listen," said Matt, "don't shoot me, but I asked Lisa to join us for dessert. She arranged to get off early."

"Forget it." He didn't even have to think about it. "Not interested."

"I told her we'd both be here."

"That's your problem, little brother. I'm hitting the casino after this. You want me, you know where to find me."

"She won't understand."

"You'll explain it to her."

"She'll think you weren't interested."

"I'm not."

"She'll think I set her up."

"Maybe she wouldn't be that far off the mark."

"Gimme a break," Matt said, dropping his Wharton School veneer. "I'll look like a schmuck if you're not here."

"Too late, pal. Unless I miss my guess, she's here."

A blond cheerleader type with a centerfold body was bouncing her way toward their table. She didn't need a name tag for Conor to know this was the legendary Lisa. He scraped back his chair and stood up. Matt was a split second behind him. The kid glowed as if he'd swallowed a hundred-watt bulb. So he was right. Little brother was in love with the wrong kind of girl.

Matt planted a friendly kiss on the girl's pink cheek. "Lisa, this is my big brother Conor."

Lisa's smile was a blaze of white. "You're the cop, right?"

Conor grinned and shook her hand. "Detective," he said. "Matty always forgets that fact."

It was clear Lisa wasn't one for fine distinctions either. At least not when it came to him. She beamed her smile at Conor then turned it on Matt, who pulled out a chair for her to sit down. "You wouldn't believe the terrible night I had," she said as she settled down between them. She wore a short black skirt, skimpy red sweater, and the highest pair of heels Conor had ever seen outside of a police lineup. "The daytrippers seem to think I'm working for love not money." If possible, her smile grew even brighter. He could almost see his brother losing ground to the inevitable. "I can't wait until I get my law degree. I'll be out of here so fast they won't know what hit 'em." She aimed one of her smiles at Conor. "The stories I could tell you about what goes on in this place." She rolled her eyes in mock exasperation. "I'm not even sure a cop would believe it."

Like he hadn't heard that line before from ten thousand other people with stories to tell. Conor smiled politely while she launched into a tale of two millionaire baccarat players, and he tried not to notice the way his brother was hanging on her every syllable.

I'm too old for this, he thought as he stared into his half-empty glass of Scotch. Cocktail party conversation. Big-eyed blonds with ultrabright smiles. Young men leaning across the table. Hope and hormones. That's what it was. Hope and hormones and the kind of innocence that life specialized in stripping away little by little, year after year, until there was nothing left but the bitter taste of regret.

He'd heard through the station grapevine that Denise and the twins were spending the week with her mother down in Florida. Everyone agreed it was better that she put as many miles as possible between herself and the memory of the night Bobby's luck ran out. They told him that he needed a break, that it was better for all of them if he took some vacation time and recharged his batteries. "It's been a shit year for all of us," the chief said when Conor protested. "You need to put it to rest once and for all."

So he took a break. He drove up to Maine for a few days and saw nothing but rocks and water. He drove into Pennsylvania and drove back out again. He considered flying out to California to see Sean, but the kid would be home for Thanksgiving before long. Besides, what nineteen-year-old jock needs his old man showing up uninvited? By the time Matty suggested a weekend in A.C., he jumped at it. Vegas without the charm. That's what his ex-wife used to call the place. They'd improved it a lot since those early days, hiding the harsher aspects of humanity away with greater care, building more and bigger and better and taller places to hide away your own sadness. Because that's why most of them came to A.C., wasn't it, the wired widows and the hollow-eyed widowers and the losers who'd never quite managed to grab a piece of the pie. You went to A.C. to be somebody else, to put your brain on hold, to lose it in front of the spinning Triple 7 machines. You went to A.C. because you didn't much like who you were at home, and you hoped that maybe you'd find out you were somebody better at Vegas by the Sea.

Maybe you even went to A.C. because you thought that maybe, just maybe, you'd find the one you'd been waiting for all your life perched on a stool in front of the Red, White, and Blue, popping dollar tokens in the slot like there was no tomorrow.

He pushed away the scotch and leaned back in his

chair. His little brother and the cocktail waitress/law student were still talking. Words swirled up and around them in a steamy fog of sexual awareness while they pretended they weren't interested in each other. Did they know what they were doing, or was it all blind instinct and denial? He didn't know if they were right for each other or all wrong, but there was no denying the chemistry or how old and alone it made him feel.

". . . dance?" The blond cocktail waitress was talking to him.

He frowned. "Dance?"

She grinned. She did it so well that he wondered how much time she spent practicing it in front of a mirror. "You know," she said, making a cute gesture with her fingers, "movement to music. It's an ancient concept but still viable."

He looked over at his brother who was an advertisement for misery.

"You're asking the wrong Riley," he said to Lisa. "Matty's the one with the talent."

"Can't dance with Matty," she said, tossing his brother an expertly sharpened look. "Might not be good for his career."

"Dance with the maitre d'," Matt said. "What the hell do I care?"

"Listen," Conor said, motioning for the waiter to bring the check, "why don't I pay up and leave the two of you to sort things out?"

"You could squeeze in one dance while you wait for the check," Lisa said, looking more like a schoolgirl than a femme fatale. "Please?"

It would be like refusing to push your little sister on her backyard swing. "Okay," he said, standing up and reaching for her hand, "but don't blame me for what happens to your feet."

"I'm sorry I came on so strong back there," Lisa said

as she stepped into his arms on the dance floor. "I didn't know any other way to get you alone."

Jesus. He didn't know which way to look except toward the exit. Matt was giving them one of those looks he used to reserve for opposing pitchers back in Little League days.

"Lisa, I don't know what Matt's told you, but—"

"I'm in love with him."

He missed a beat. "Did I step on your—"

She shook her head. "I'm fine." She met his eyes. "I'm in love with him, and he loves me, but he's too stubborn to admit it."

"You know he tried to set me up with you."

"I didn't say he wasn't a jerk." She threw Matt a look that would send most men heading for the hills. Not his brother. Matt shot one right back at her. "He's trying to discourage me because he's afraid being seen with a cocktail waitress will hurt his career."

"Will it?"

She hesitated. "I don't know. If he loves me, it shouldn't matter. I'm making enough to put myself through law school. You'd think that would mean something to him. Has he said anything to you?"

What the hell was he supposed to say to that? The chemistry between the two young people was undeniable, but love was something else entirely. Matt was dead serious about his career and his future, and a young woman could get seriously hurt if she got in the way.

"I shouldn't have asked that," she said. "I'm sorry. That was unfair. Whatever this is, it's between Matt and me, and we'll have to work it out."

"That sounds like a good game plan to me."

"You have a nice smile," she said, then kissed him on the cheek. "You should try it more often."

He couldn't help it. He glanced toward the woman with the short dark hair and big blue eyes and found that she was looking right back at him, and for a second the blond in his arms disappeared, and it was just the two of them out there on the dance floor, alone with the music and the candlelight and the long night still ahead of them.

There was nothing more pathetic than the sight of some middle-aged man trying to recapture his youth by sleeping with it. Maggy tried not to glare as the two of them danced near her table. The least he could do was hold the girl as if he meant it. What was it the nuns used to say back at high school dances? Leave some room for the Holy Ghost. That was the way he was dancing with the pretty young blond, as if he was leaving room for the Holy Ghost and most of the Apostles to walk between them. If he wasn't comfortable being seen with her in public, he should think twice about what they did in private.

The dance ended, and the blond kissed him on the cheek. He turned slightly toward Maggy, and she saw embarrassment in his glance. *Tough,* she thought, feeling unduly annoyed. *That's what you get when you date schoolchildren.*

She pushed away what was left of her crème brûlée and took another sip of coffee. Sometimes world-class people watchers saw more than they bargained on. She'd spent much of the evening trying to figure out the dynamics between those three very attractive people and just when she thought she had it all worked out, the older guy and the young blond got up to dance, and Maggy found herself back at square one. For most of the night the older of the two men had seemed separate from the group, brooding almost, as he sipped his drink and roamed the room with those sad, dark eyes. Once or twice their gazes had locked, and each time Maggy quickly looked away, feeling as though she'd been caught doing something vaguely illicit.

If his tastes ran toward miniskirted blonds with long legs, she must be downright invisible to him, sitting there with her short dark hair and twin set with pearls. She wasn't tall or glamorous or blond, and she especially wasn't young.

At least Charles wasn't marrying a high school cheer-leader. Sally was a graphic designer in her late thirties who didn't wear miniskirts. Sally was also a little hippy, a little loud, a little gray, and very affectionate—in other words, not at all the classic trophy wife most men looked for the second time around.

And Charles loved her. That was the biggest surprise of all. He beamed when he was around her, watched her every movement as if she were a combination of Mich-elle Pfeiffer and Pamela Anderson rolled up into one. Maggy looked at Sally and saw a pleasant, middle-aged woman. Charles looked at Sally and saw a goddess. He was marrying her because he loved her and wanted to spend the rest of his life with her, and suddenly Maggy wished with all her heart that the same thing had hap-pened to her.

She motioned for the check, then thought terrible things about the waiter for taking so long to bring it to her. There seemed to be some problem. Two waiters, the wine steward, and the maitre d' were conferring near the door to the kitchen and casting furtive looks in her di-rection.

Oh, wonderful. Something had probably gone wrong with the reservation, and instead of being comped for dinner, she was about to be presented with a bill that would make her monthly phone bill look small by com-parison. She sat there, fingers tightly laced together, hands in her lap, and waited. It was times like this when she wished she'd never given up smoking. Smokers al-ways looked in control of things. Stupid and foolhardy, yes, but composed. When she was nervous, her hands always gave her away. She tended to tap on tabletops, pick imaginary threads off her sleeves, drag her hand through her hair until she looked like an unkempt Shetland pony. Of course, that might not be a problem now that she was bald.

Could it get any worse?

Come on, come on. Bring me the bill so I can go back up to my room and watch Letterman. She didn't even like Letterman, but anything was better than this slow death at a table for one. She lifted her hand to signal again for the waiter when the kitchen doors flew open and an army of servers marched toward her.

"Happy Birthday to you . . . happy birthday to you . . . happy biiiirthday . . ."

The cake looked like a bouquet of Olympic torches. Did they have to light every single one of the thirty-five candles on it? She had never been self-conscious about her age, but the sight of all those flames flickering was enough to depress the most self-confident of women.

The servers gathered around her as the maitre d' presented the cake with a flourish. "To you, madame," he said with a slick professional smile. "Now the candles."

Human lungs aren't enough, she thought. A fire extinguisher was more like it. She drew in a deep breath, crossed her fingers under the table, and prayed that Jude, patron saint of lost causes, was watching over her tonight, because right now she needed all the help she could get.

The woman blew out all but three candles with one breath. Everyone applauded as she drew in another deep breath and finished the job. She smiled politely as the waiters wished her a happy birthday then disappeared back into the kitchen to cut the cake. She looked as if she wished she could disappear, too.

He wasn't exactly the sensitive type, but he would've made short work of anyone who tried a stunt like that on him. She didn't look like the kind of woman who made a living out of being second best, but he'd seen enough to know how deceptive appearances could be. When it came to love, smart women sometimes turned into fools.

That was the kind of thinking that drove his sister Siobhan crazy. Sexist garbage, she'd say. Neanderthal thinking. No argument there. Maybe the woman was some hotshot executive somewhere, a high roller like Matty said, who rated limos and fancy suites and comped dinners in the most overpriced restaurant in the place. Maybe she dropped a few Gs every weekend playing baccarat then limoed back up to Greenwich or down to D.C. and her real life.

He could get up and ask her. She was alone, and so was he. Matty and Lisa were locked in fierce conversation that anyone but his little brother would recognize as foreplay. So what was stopping him? He wasn't a kid anymore. That long walk across the room wouldn't kill him. Neither would the long walk back if she told him to get lost. You only regretted what you didn't do. He knew that better than most men his age. You only regretted the things you let slip away without a fight.

THREE

Maggy watched as he pushed back his chair and stood up. She waited, expecting the blond to stand up, too, and join him, but the girl didn't even glance his way. It seemed to Maggy that she was the only one on the planet who noticed him as he crossed the dance floor to say a few words to the piano player. Suddenly she knew what he was saying, same as if she'd heard his words herself. When the piano player glanced her way then nodded, she wasn't at all surprised.

She'd watched this scene in a thousand romantic movies, where the hero whispers something to the piano player, suddenly their song fills the air, the heroine spins into his arms, and they dance off into a happy ending. Maggy and her sisters had grown up with those movies. They'd dreamed away countless nights, watching strong, handsome men sweep beautiful women onto the dance floor and into a perfect life that couldn't possibly last beyond the final reel.

He walked quickly and with purpose, like a man who didn't waste time or motion in achieving his goal. She wondered how he was with the word *no*. She didn't feel like dancing, and she certainly didn't feel like being anyone's second best. If he thought he was going to throw the poor lonely birthday girl a bone in the form of a charity slow dance, he had another think coming.

Her chair scraped against the expensive carpet as she stood up. She reached for her envelope clutch and tucked it under her right arm. She felt a slight buzz, as if she'd been drinking. She turned to head for the door, but he easily cut her off before she moved more than a few feet.

"I've wanted to dance with you all night," he said. "Your birthday gives me the perfect excuse."

"Thank you," she said, "but I'd rather not."

His expression didn't change, but she sensed he was surprised and maybe a little hurt.

"Listen," she said, "it's nothing personal. It's just that I don't know you, and I'm afraid I'm not much of a dancer."

His smile was as quick as his walk and even more appealing. For such a rough-looking man, he had a surprisingly gentle smile. It was a dangerous combination, but she was good at resisting dangerous combinations. Especially when she wasn't looking for the complications they usually brought with them.

"I don't know you either," he said, "and I'm probably a worse dancer than you are."

She started to laugh. The sound surprised her. It seemed to surprise him as well. She liked that. He wasn't quite as sure of himself as he wanted to be.

"I'm not sure I believe you." *Listen to you, Maggy! You're flirting with the guy.* She was a half step away from batting her eyelashes at him.

He held out his hand. "You know how we can find out."

"You might regret it." She sounded like a giddy, foolish teenager without a care in the world.

"I'll take my chances."

She placed her purse down on the table and took his hand. "Then so will I."

It was foolish and romantic and utterly out of character for her, but he had no way of knowing she was practical Maggy O'Brien, mother of two and queen of the car pool. The last woman on earth you would find flirting with a stranger in some fancy hotel in Atlantic City. You were more likely to find her at ShopRite, talking to the produce manager about the sorry state of the romaine.

But he didn't know that. He didn't know anything about her, not her name, her occupation, her marital status, her taste in music, her taste in men. If she liked men at all or babies or puppies or chocolate. She could be anyone she wanted to be tonight. New hair, new clothes, new attitude. She was Cinderella with a limo instead of a pumpkin coach and no midnight curfew.

She melted into his arms as if she belonged there. The sense of recognition was so strong that she gasped, and when he asked what was wrong, she covered with a small cough. She told herself that it was just that it had been a long time since she'd been held by a man, but she knew there was more to the feeling than that. It hadn't been that long that she could forget the difference. When it was right, it was very very right, and nothing on earth came close to the feeling. It was his smell, the pressure of his hand at the small of her back, that they were both bad dancers but in the very same way.

"You're right," she said as they missed a step. "You're a terrible dancer."

"You're not so great yourself."

She smiled up at him. "Flatterer."

"Hell, no," he said as he led her into a turn. "I meant every word."

"I'm so bad I nearly closed down a dance school when I was a little girl."

"My old man used to say I gave clumsiness a bad name."

"Now that was cruel. You're not at all clumsy. You just can't dance."

He pretended to wince at her words. "Are you always that honest?"

"It's my major flaw," she said. "Except for that, I'm perfect."

He laughed and drew her closer. Not so close that it felt uncomfortable; just close enough that she became aware of the heat of his body. She felt drawn to him like a cat to sunshine, and it took all of her willpower to keep from molding herself to his contours and staying there for a year or two. The thought alone made her blush, and she was glad the height differential between them made it easy for her to hide her face until the heat faded. Her reaction to him went beyond mere attraction. She'd been attracted to scores of men over the last two years: dentists and sanitation workers and teachers and attorneys and professors and the guy who managed the local Blockbuster. The feelings were all transient and amusing; they didn't make her feel as if she were standing at the edge of a cliff in a strong wind and praying to fall.

She wasn't the kind of woman who courted danger. She liked to know where she was going and how to get there. She'd never made room in her life for the unplanned and the unexpected because she'd never needed to. Things like that never happened to her. Her life was as orderly as her kitchen cabinets and every bit as predictable, and if you had asked her twenty-four hours ago, she would have said orderly and predictable was a fine way to be.

She was no longer so sure about that.

"Your girlfriend's waving to you," she said.

"She's not my girlfriend."

"Then whose girlfriend is she?" *Listen to you, Maggy! Since when do you cut to the chase with a man?* The married Maggy used to circle her main point endlessly, so careful to pay proper attention to the care and feeding of the male ego that she never quite said what she wanted to say. The divorced Maggy shot from the hip.

"Nobody's," he said. "She's in love with my brother."

Maggy tilted her head toward the handsome young couple. "And that's your brother?"

"That's Matty."

"I take it he isn't in love with her."

"Jury's still out on that. Right now, Matty's in love with anything that keeps his career moving forward." He told her that his brother worked for the hotel and had his eye on moving up the ladder as quickly as possible. "Lisa's a cocktail waitress in the casino."

Maggy sighed. "And it's not good for his career to be seen dating a cocktail waitress."

"You caught on quicker than I did."

"She's beautiful." Suddenly she felt quite magnanimous.

"She's a kid."

"A beautiful kid."

"I prefer women."

Her breath caught. "You all say that but end up dating cheerleaders."

"You sound like you know something about that."

"Not personally, but I watch *Oprah*," she said. "I know what's going on out there."

He laughed, and she laughed with him. A man who got her jokes. This was too good to be true.

"So what birthday is it?" he asked. "It must be one of the milestones."

"Why do you say that?" Had she developed crow's feet during dinner?

"I had the same look on my face when I hit thirty and thirty-five."

"Thirty-five." She leaned back slightly within the circle of his arms and looked up at him. "This is where you say I don't look a day over thirty."

"You don't," he said, "but I figured you'd think I was handing you a line."

"I might have thought that yesterday when I was thirty-four but not anymore."

"Thirty-five's not so bad."

To her surprise, she found herself agreeing with that assessment. "So how many milestones have you celebrated?"

"Forty's on the horizon," he said, looking suitably pained. "Next September."

"This is where I say you don't look a day over thirty-five."

He laughed again, louder this time, and her spirits soared. Not even her sisters could have conjured up a better match. He was every bit as big a fantasy as the makeover and the clothes and the limo and—

Oh, no. She missed a step and thanked God that he was busy missing a step of his own and didn't notice. Don't let this man who actually laughed at her jokes be part of her birthday surprise. If he was, she'd never forgive her sisters as long as she lived. They could meddle with her makeup, her hair, the way she dressed, and how she ate, but if they tried to set her up as if she was some pathetic loser, she'd never talk to them again as long as she lived. Maybe even longer.

She decided to go straight to the heart of the matter. "Did Claire and Eleanor put you up to this?"

"Who are Claire and Eleanor?"

"My sisters," she said, her heart pounding with a high-octane mix of hope and trepidation. "They took care of everything else. I was afraid they'd arranged for this dance."

"You've seen me dance. Would you do that to somebody you loved?"

It was her turn to laugh out loud. "No," she said as relief washed over her. "Now that you mention it, I wouldn't."

You are too good to be true. Tall, handsome, and not afraid to poke fun at yourself.

Married. He had to be. Either that or a priest in civvies. One way or the other, he had to be unavailable, because men like this didn't suddenly walk into your life on the night of your thirty-fifth birthday except in the movies, and then he was usually the gay best friend.

"Your brother's leaving," she observed as she peered around his shoulder. "He doesn't look too happy."

"He'll get over it."

"Listen, I've enjoyed this dance, but if you have to go I'll—"

"Did I say I had to go?"

"No, but—"

"So why don't we start all over again." He looked down at her and their gazes met. "I'm Conor."

"Maggy."

"Are you involved with anyone?"

She shook her head. "How about you?"

"Nobody."

I'm glad, she thought as they moved a tiny bit closer together on the dance floor. She didn't know why exactly, but she was.

They gave up any pretense of dancing and swayed gently to the music while two other couples twirled past them in a flurry of skirts and aftershave. She could stay there forever, right where they were, with the candlelight flickering on the tabletops and the sweet music and the way she felt in his arms. He was taller than he'd looked from afar and broader of shoulder and chest. Although she thought of herself as short, not small, she was acutely aware of the differences between them. He made her feel vulnerable in a way that started a buzz moving along her nerve endings.

At home she was the strong one, the one who grabbed the baseball bat she kept under her bed and crept out into the hallway when Charlie heard a funny sound during the night. The one who captured the big brown spider in Nicole's room and set it free in the backyard because although they didn't want to kill unwelcome visitors, they didn't have to live with them either. The woman who did those things was an Amazon. She could leap tall buildings and bend microwavable Pop-Tarts with her bare hands.

She was still that woman tonight. She couldn't escape her if she tried. That woman was key to her survival. But she was also a woman she'd almost forgotten about, a woman who liked to be held close and flirted with by a man who knew how to do both things exceedingly well. No strings, no expectations. Just a dance.

The piano player chose that moment to close up shop for the night.

"Maybe if we tip him . . ." she said wistfully.

"I have a better idea," he said. "Why don't we go downstairs to Cleo's and raise a glass to your birthday."

She hesitated. Serendipity was one thing. Asking serendipity to follow you to the bar might be pushing it. The last few minutes had been so perfect, so magical, that asking for more was like asking for the stars to shine a little brighter just because you want to see if they can.

She was struggling for the right answer. If she'd asked him, Conor could have told her there was no right answer, only instinct and blind luck. Those two factors were at the heart of every great invention, every great battle, every act of heroism ever recorded.

Besides, if it took this long, maybe it wasn't meant to be.

She thought. He waited. She thought some more. He saw the handwriting on the wall. It was time for that long walk back across the dance floor.

"Listen," he said, "no problem." He placed his hand at the small of her back and led her toward her table. "Thanks for the dance."

"Thank you for not complaining when I stepped on your feet."

She had a disarming way of taking responsibility for things, a gentle way of poking fun at herself that he found endearing. It had been a long time since he'd found anything or anyone endearing, and he was sorry it had to end before he discovered where it might lead.

She quickly signed her tab, tucked her purse under her right arm, then they left the restaurant together. A bank of elevators lay dead ahead.

"If you change your mind, the offer still holds." He pressed the Down button.

"I'll remember that." She pressed the Up button.

Hotel elevators were notoriously slow, but not this time. The last elevator on the right shimmied almost immediately into position, and the doors slid open.

"Cleo's," he said as she stepped inside.

"Cleo's, " she repeated; then the doors began to slide shut, and whatever the hell was left of reason vanished. He placed his foot in the opening and held out his hand.

"Don't go," he said.

Her eyes widened.

"I'm not crazy," he said, feeling the pulse beating at the base of her thumb. "I'm not desperate or dangerous. All I know is that something is happening here, and we need to find out what it is."

She gave away so little. Except for the widening of her eyes, her expression didn't change. Was she afraid of him? Jesus, that's the last thing he wanted, but he still couldn't let go. Not yet. Not without laying it all on the line.

"Don't go, Maggy."

It was the sound of her name on his lips that did it. The intimate sound of her name spoken by a man who knew her only as the woman she was at that moment.

She knew the safe thing to do, the proper thing. She should smile and say good night again and go back to her room where she'd turn on the television and call her kids and watch the last few hours of her birthday tick away on the bedside clock. But it wasn't what she wanted to do. It wasn't what her heart was telling her to do, and maybe it was time she listened.

She took a deep breath and stepped out of the elevator, feeling shy and wild and alive. So alive it would have scared her if she'd been in her right mind. He didn't let go of her hand, and she didn't want him to. She wanted him to hold her forever or for however long it took for her to believe this was really happening, that magic in the form of a man with golden brown eyes could happen to a woman who'd quit believing it was possible.

Still holding hands, they walked through the lobby and down the escalator, past the glittering marble columns and frescoed ceiling and the enormous fountains and the knowing glances from the sad-eyed widows who made the casino their second home. Cleo's was dark and smoky, the way a good lounge should be. They claimed a tiny sofa near the back, far enough away from the jazz quartet for conversation but not so far that the mellow notes couldn't make her shiver with possibilities.

Possibilities. What a wonderful word.

For the last couple of years, she'd been so busy building a new life for herself and the kids that she'd packed away this part of her soul and stored it on ice, and there it had stayed. She had the kids to worry about and school and her job. Then when her mother had the stroke, she took over the day-to-day responsibility of caregiving, and it seemed that the next time she blinked, a year had gone by and she hadn't had time to notice.

"Champagne," Conor said to the cocktail waitress. "Two glasses."

"Any particular brand?" The young redhead was blatantly eyeing him. She had outsized breasts and a tiny waist, and she was young enough to be Maggy's daughter if Maggy had been precocious. The fact that she was

dressed in a short, white, one-shouldered Grecian goddess outfit didn't exactly help matters.

Conor turned toward Maggy. Every other man she
knew would have made a macho display of choosing a
wine. Not to mention the comments they would have
made about the waitress's ample charms. "Any sugges-
tions?" he asked.

"The only wine I buy comes in a box," she said. The
waitress frowned at her, but Conor laughed. "Whatever
you decide is fine."

"Dom," he said, then mentioned a few specifics. The
waitress nodded then hurried away.

"You know your wines," Maggy said, letting her
bones sink into the plush softness of the bordeaux-
colored sofa. "I'm impressed."

He leaned back and crossed his left leg over his right,
ankle to knee. "Price Club," he said. "White zin, ten
bucks."

"You know Price Club?"

"The South Jersey Neiman-Marcus."

It was her turn to laugh. "If you hit a sale, you can
get the mountain chablis for eight." *Damn it, Maggy.
What's wrong with you? Why don't you whip out your
ShopRite Price Plus card, too, while you're at it?*

She felt like a middle-aged teenager out on her first
date. Was it possible to feel both old and naive simul-
taneously? That's how she felt. She was aware of every
breath she took, the angle of her head, the slight pressure
of his right thigh against her left. *Touch me. Take my
hand in yours again. Kiss the side of my neck—*

The waitress appeared with the champagne, two
glasses, and a bucket filled with ice, then backed away
into the smoky recesses of the lounge. He knew his way
around a champagne bottle. No self-conscious jokes, no
wasted gestures. He eased out the cork with a resounding
pop, and they both laughed as a gorgeous froth of spar-
kling wine overflowed the bottle. Maggy grabbed for the

glasses and held them out for Conor to fill. For a second she thought he was going to be terribly corny and do one of those locked-arms toasts that lovers always used but he didn't. She was just the tiniest bit disappointed.

"To the unexpected," he said, raising his glass.

Her heartbeat all but drowned out her own words. "To the unexpected." *To magic and surprises and playing Cinderella for just one night.*

"Happy birthday, Maggy."

They clicked glasses, then each took a sip of champagne. The bubbles were round and full with a sweet bite that danced on the back of her tongue.

"Stars," she said, and he looked at her. "That's what they said when they created champagne. They said it was like swallowing stars."

Conor's last hold on reality slipped away with those words. He'd never met anyone like her. He'd known women who talked about the stock market, the situation in the Middle East, about the latest trends in criminal investigations, but he'd never met a woman who knew that champagne tasted like starlight. He leaned close to her and felt as if he'd breathed in a galaxy of stars.

"I saw you the minute you got out of your limo," he said. No bullshit. No games. "I could see your eyes were the color of bluebells from across the parking lot."

She couldn't catch her breath. His words, the sound of his voice as he said them, filled her with so much emotion she wondered that there was room for anything else.

"I remember," she said. "The bellman was taking my bags, and I turned and saw you standing there looking at me. I remember thinking what beautiful hair you had."

"I saw you in the VIP lounge."

"I was checking in."

"I smiled at you."

"I didn't know it was for me. I thought it was for your brother."

"You gave me the same look you gave me when I asked you to dance."

"That's my I-am-in-control look. It comes in very handy when I'm not."

He liked the way the real woman was beginning to peek out from behind the pearls and the sleek blue sweater. He wanted to know who she was when nobody was looking.

"I can't think of too many situations you couldn't handle," he said and meant it. She radiated warmth and strength, a lethal combination for a man in need of both.

"I can't handle this." Her voice was soft, not much above a whisper. "It's happening too fast."

"We can slow down," he said, elation racing through him like jet fuel. He wasn't crazy. She felt it, too. "We'll find our own speed."

She looked at him, and he saw himself reflected back in her big, china-blue eyes. The way he'd been once upon a time not that long ago.

"I can't do this," she said, her eyes welling with tears. "The rules have changed."

"We'll make our own rules."

"You don't understand."

"Tell me. Make me understand."

How do you tell a man that the woman he was looking at had nothing to do with the woman you were? The short hair, the fancy clothes, the makeup—it was all as fake as the pearls around her neck. She was a thirty-five-year-old mother of two with a job and classes and an ex-husband who had already found somebody new to share his life. She didn't know how to flirt or banter with a man, how to sip champagne as if it was Diet Coke, how to be something she wasn't, and she didn't have time to learn.

She stood up. "I'm sorry," she said. "I really have to go."

This time she didn't turn back.

FOUR

Maggy kicked off her shoes in the hallway, pulled off her sweaters in the living room, and stepped out of her trousers and undergarments on her way to the bath. She unclasped her necklace, unstrapped her watch, then laid them both on top of a precisely folded snowy-white face cloth on the pink marble vanity. She turned on the water full blast then stepped into the shower and tried to wash the stupidity away.

"Idiot," she said as she soaped her hair with lilac-scented shampoo.

"Cowardly jerk," as she squeezed a half-dollar of bath gel into the palm of her hand.

"Pathetic loser," followed the final rinse.

She called herself every nasty name she could think of as she dried off, and she invented a few new ones to fill in the blanks. She wielded the wall-mounted blow-dryer like a loaded .44 and then, when she was all done, she slid into the silky pair of unfamiliar pajamas her sisters had packed for her and sat on the edge of the bed and cried. Not weepy female he-done-me-wrong tears but the angry embarrassed kind that were as much about what you didn't do as what you did.

She should have stayed, that's what she should have done. She wasn't some naive little girl who knew nothing about life. She was a grown woman of thirty-five. She'd been married and divorced. She'd even dated on more than one occasion—fiascos she'd filed away in the Read at Your Own Risk file.

He'd been right when he said something was happening between them, some rare kind of chemical reaction that she'd never before experienced, not even with Charles. The second he said that, she'd experienced that fight-or-flight phenomenon that humans were prone to in times of danger. She had the feeling she'd broken a few speed limits in her race to get back to the safety of her suite.

She liked the way he spoke, the way he thought, the way he moved, the way he smelled. There wasn't one single thing she didn't like about him except for the fact that he put it right out there in plain English and expected her to deal with it.

She'd heard all the warnings about the dangers single women faced out there in the world. She'd probably lectured her sisters about them a thousand times. Listen to your instincts! Don't be afraid to say no! Drive your own car to the first few dates, carry enough money to see you through, remember you don't owe him anything but "thank you."

Her sisters should have warned her that the biggest danger of all was her own crazy heart. Who knew your heart could turn on you like that? After thirty-five years of steady and reliable emotion, it picked tonight to flex its muscles and start making demands.

She'd wanted to cup his face between her hands and press the tip of her tongue to the place where his lips met. She'd wanted to bury her face against the back of his neck, where his hair curled over his collar, and breathe deeply for a year or two. They didn't have to talk. He didn't have to listen to her stories or try to solve her problems. All he had to do was kiss her, and she'd never ask for anything else again.

She fell back against the pillows in an agony of remembering. She'd come so close to making a total fool of herself. The champagne had unlocked her tongue. A few sips, and she was ready to tell him that she'd been dreaming about kissing him for hours now, that while she toyed with her crème brûlée, she'd imagined the sweetness of his mouth on hers, of the way he would taste rich like wine and deep like chocolate. Thank God she didn't tell him that. She would have had to move to Siberia if she'd done something that stupid. She'd been one sip of champagne away from disaster.

At least he only knew her first name. There wasn't a chance he could track her down to her room, not unless his brother had access to the hotel registration list and—

The phone rang, and she nearly leaped off the bed in surprise.

"What are you doing in your room?" It was Claire, and she sounded indignant.

"Answering the phone," Maggy said, wishing she didn't feel quite so disappointed to hear her sister's voice. They'd had a difficult relationship over the years and had only begun to get along with each other since Maggy moved back to New Jersey.

"You're not supposed to be there," Claire said. "You should be downstairs in the casino having fun."

"I am having fun," Maggy said, feeling perverse and extremely older-sisterish. "I took a shower, and now I'm going to watch Letterman." She aimed the remote control at one of the suite's three televisions and watched as Letterman's face snapped into focus. "Why did you call if you didn't think I'd be here?"

Now Claire sounded huffy. "I called to leave you a voice mail. I was going to wish you one last happy birthday before midnight, but if I'm disturbing you . . ."

Maggy held back a sigh. Sometimes life was simply

too complicated. "Of course you're not disturbing me. I'm sprawled on the bed in my pajamas." *And thinking about a man I met at dinner. You'd like him, Claire. He's tall and strong and almost handsome. He laughs at my jokes because he actually gets them, not because he thinks laughing will score points. We danced, and he bought me champagne and told me my eyes were the color of bluebells and I got up and ran away like the hounds of hell were nipping at my heels.*

"You're having a wonderful time." It was a statement, the way Claire said it. She allowed no room at all for other options.

"Wonderful," Maggy said. She wasn't at all sure if she was telling the truth or lying through her teeth. "How are the kids?"

"I spoke to Jeremy's mom, and she said Charlie's sound asleep. Nic's fiddling around with my makeup."

"Don't let her go out tomorrow the way she did last time."

"She looked beautiful."

"She looked nineteen," Maggy said with a shudder. "Let's not rush things."

"You can't hold back time," Claire said. "Your baby girl's growing up."

"And a happy thirty-fifth birthday to you, too," Maggy mumbled under her breath.

"What was that?"

"I said the restaurant was terrific. You and Ellie were way too generous."

She could almost see her sister's lovely features reluctantly shifting gear to field Maggy's thanks.

"We can never repay you," Claire said simply. "You're the best, Mags."

Yeah, Maggy thought as she hung up the phone a few minutes later. *The best.* If she was so darned good, what was she doing alone? If she was so darned smart, why wasn't she downstairs drinking champagne with a man

named Conor who laughed at her jokes and didn't wince
when she stepped on his toes?

In the beginning he ran because it was run or kill somebody. Running helped him blow off steam, kept him from
drowning himself in a bottle of scotch when the going
got rough. You could go weeks without seeing a corpse
and then you kick in a door and find three babies curled
up dead by the window and the mother bleeding to death
on the sofa and the boyfriend smoking crack in a corner
with the gun resting across his lap. That was when you
thought about how it would feel to pick up that gun and
turn it on the son of a bitch. Later, when your shift was
over, you tried to make the transition from cop to human
being, and you noticed that it was getting harder to do.
Each year the transition took longer and was less suc-
cessful until the day came when you weren't sure anymore if you weren't the biggest son of a bitch of them
all.

So he ran. Every morning he got up, strapped on a
jock, pulled on his clothes, and he ran. Some days he
blistered the streets. Other days an old lady with a walker
could have passed him twice. He used to worry about
speed and distance but not anymore. The running was
part of him now. That first rush of morning air in his
lungs, the faintest hint of sunlight over the woods behind
his house, the rustle of birds high up in the trees. For a
little while each day, he could actually believe the world
wasn't such a bad place after all.

Then he'd get dressed, go to work, and run face-first
into reality.

There had been too much reality this past year. Things
he couldn't run away from or under or around. First thing
in the morning, last thing at night, he saw Bobby's face
and heard his voice when he said, ''It's not your fault,
bud,'' then ''Denise,'' and then nothing. The next second, Bobby went eyes-wide-open dead, and Conor didn't

have to look far to know where to place the blame.

He woke up around seven, and it took a few seconds to remember where he was. The hotel room bed was narrower than his bed at home and too soft. At home, he slept with the windows open. You couldn't do that in fancy casino hotels. The windows were permanently closed, and there were no balconies. He remembered hearing the stories about distraught gamblers who lost the family's savings then took the only way out left to them: a straight plunge from the twenty-second floor. Nowadays, if a gambler wanted to kill himself, first he had to get through three inches of reinforced glass.

A light rain tapped against his window and soaked into the sandy beach down below. The boardwalk had turned a darker gray, and wet seagulls swirled past, looking sullen. He dressed quickly, stuffed his room key in the back pocket of his sweats, then headed out. He was still tired, but he knew that would change as soon as he hit the cool October air and he started to move. In the elevator he congratulated himself on not thinking about the dark-haired woman named Maggy then laughed out loud. The irony wasn't lost on him, but then irony rarely was.

That was one of the things that had appealed to him about her, apart from her blue eyes and slightly off-center sense of humor. His instincts about people had been sharpened over sixteen years on the force, and he knew she saw the world around her clearly, with all of its faults and graces, and embraced it anyway. He'd decided long ago that that was the secret to it all. You knew a situation was imperfect and you worked within it; you didn't let the imperfections drag you down. She did that naturally. He couldn't say how he knew that, but he did, same as he'd known how she would feel in his arms. Too bad he hadn't known she would get up and walk away before she finished her first glass of champagne.

His timing had always been a bitch. A day too late, a minute too soon. Right woman, wrong time.

He exited the elevator at the boardwalk level and crossed the lobby toward the wall of revolving doors that led outside. The rain was cool against his face and arms. Perfect running conditions. The stretching took him a little longer with each birthday, but it was part of the deal.

A few rolling chairs were parked to the left of the doors. Their owners huddled under the awning, bent low over steaming cups of coffee, as they'd been doing for one hundred years on the boardwalk. The trumpet player wasn't there yet, but he would be. Rain or shine, he stood in the alleyway between the Plaza and Caesar's and played for change. He was a good-natured guy, and Conor always stuffed a few bills in the jar when he saw him. You never knew what life was going to throw at you, and he hoped he'd weather the storms with as much grace as the trumpet player did.

Matty had told him about some of the characters who frequented the boardwalk, the old men who sat on benches and looked out at the ocean for hours on end. The homeless ones who slept beneath the neon signs and hustled gamblers at the slot machines, bumming cigarettes and matches and spare coins. He came down for a weekend the first summer Matty was working, and he saw the woman with the shopping cart camped out near one of the schlocky tourist-trap shops. Mid-August, and she'd been covered with a pink and blue afghan. She was knitting another one, pulling lengths of gray yarn from a crumpled paper bag and twisting them around the fat wooden needles. When he saw her again that winter, she had a kitten sleeping under the afghan, its small white face peeking out from beneath the folds. He'd never forgotten that cracked optimism in the face of despair. It was what kept him going.

He jogged toward the railing to warm up and saw Maggy sitting on a bench not forty feet away from him. Once again, he experienced a jolt of recognition that rocked him to his core. The elegant clothes from the night before were gone. Today she wore sneakers, jeans, and a bright-red hooded sweatshirt. Her short, dark hair curled softly around her small face. Somehow she managed to look every bit as lovely and unapproachable in jeans as she had in pearls. She didn't see him. Her eyes were focused somewhere out on the horizon, and he was glad. Why embarrass either one of them with fake smiles and phony hellos? He turned away to head toward another more secluded part of the boardwalk when he noticed a rough-looking young man approach her.

The kid was maybe sixteen or seventeen, but he carried himself like someone a lot older and a hell of a lot more dangerous. Gut instincts counted for more than people realized, and Conor's gut instinct told him the kid was trouble.

The kid bent down and said something to Maggy. She shook her head and kept looking out toward the ocean. The kid said something else. She shook her head again, then angled her body slightly away from him. The kid stepped into her line of vision in a gesture of practiced aggression Conor was too damn familiar with. He knew where this was going, and there was no point in letting it proceed any further than it already had.

Maggy couldn't understand what he was saying. The boy was obviously drunk or stoned. His eyes were glazed, and he slurred his words together until you couldn't tell what language he was speaking. He wanted money. That much she knew. She also knew that she wasn't going to give him any. He was trying to intimidate her, and she was doing her best to make him believe he wasn't succeeding. She hoped he was too stoned to realize her hands were shaking and that tiny little twitch she got under her right eye when she was nervous had appeared.

She was about to get up and go back into the hotel when the kid stepped between her and the railing. He bent down and said something again, and she could smell the stink of beer and bad teeth. Her empty stomach seemed to tilt on its side. This wasn't what she'd hoped for when she set out to watch the sunrise.

"Why don't you take it somewhere else?"

The voice came from behind her and to the left, and she knew a moment of joy that had nothing to do with the situation at hand. It was the same voice that had told her that her eyes were the color of bluebells.

The kid's attention shifted to Conor. He said something in a belligerent tone. The sound of it made her knees weak. *Don't play hero,* she thought. Kids like this were trouble. If Conor pushed him, something terrible might happen. Conor, however, didn't back down. She looked up at him and was shocked to see he bore little resemblance to the romantic man who'd bought her champagne and flattered her shamelessly. His features had hardened. His expression was almost deadly. If she didn't know him, if she hadn't danced with him, she would have been terrified.

The kid said something else that Conor seemed to have no trouble understanding.

"Once more," he said, "and we'll be taking this over there to the security guard at the front door. You got me?"

The kid made a move toward the pocket of his billowy black jacket, and before Maggy had the chance to realize what was going on, Conor had him backed up against the railing. He pulled a small pistol from the kid's jacket pocket. It looked like a toy. A small but deadly toy.

"Tell security to call the cops," he said. He seemed calm and in perfect control. You would think he did this every day of his life. "Tell them we have a weapon."

The kid looked angry and embarrassed. He also looked dangerous.

"What about you?" Maggy asked Conor. "Can you handle this?"

"I think I can manage," he said, and unless she imagined it, there was a slight top spin on his words. She'd worry about that after she found help.

Maggy insisted on treating him to breakfast after it was all over. What could be more innocent, less romantic than breakfast? Especially when your hair was frizzing, your face was baby-bare of makeup, and you were wearing a sweatshirt and jeans. Caesar and Cleopatra themselves would have been hard-pressed to work up any decent chemistry under those conditions, but somewhere between the orange juice and the home fries she realized just how wrong she was.

She also realized her latent flirting gene had suddenly come to the fore. Both of her sisters were expert flirts, but Maggy had never exhibited the slightest talent for the sport. Apparently she was in the middle of a sea change.

"So now that the excitement has died down," she said, aware of the angle of her head, the timbre of her voice, the fact that she wasn't wearing any eye makeup, "I deserve an answer. You're either a cop or a major fan of *NYPD Blue*. So which is it?"

His smile was a sight to behold. That serious face, all angles and planes and deep shadows, seemed to ignite right in front of her, and she couldn't help but smile right back at him. They probably looked like two middle-aged fools, grinning over their breakfast specials, but she suddenly felt so incredibly joyful that her heart couldn't contain the emotion.

"I'm a cop," he said, dumping some sugar into his coffee.

"Right," she said, reaching for her cup of tea. "Seriously, how did you know what to do back there?"

"I'm a cop."

"No."

"Yes," he said, his smile widening. "Sixteen years on the force." He named one of the larger townships in central New Jersey.

"You're kidding," she said. "I live just two towns over."

"Montgomery?"

She choked on her tea. "You know the area."

"They sent me out there a few months ago to do a presentation at the high school on self-defense."

A little shiver of something silvery and bright ran up her spine as she remembered an afternoon not that long ago. "You were wonderful."

"You were there?"

She nodded and silently cursed herself for not keeping her big mouth shut. She wasn't ready yet to go back to being her regular self. She'd been standing in the hallway, waiting to deliver Nicole's gym clothes, and she'd heard much of what he'd had to say to the kids. Straight from the shoulder, practical advice delivered with humor and heart. She never saw his face, but she remembered the words.

"So you're a teacher." His inflection fell somewhere between statement and question.

She met his eyes. Time to face the music. "No, I'm not a teacher," she said. "I'm a mother. My daughter Nicole is a sophomore."

He didn't flinch. In fact, he looked interested. She was accustomed to a glaze of boredom whenever she mentioned her kids to strangers.

"My kid's a sophomore at UCLA," he said, not quite keeping the pride from his voice.

"UCLA?" She whistled. "I'm impressed. How'd you manage that on a small-town cop's salary?" *Oh, God, Maggy, what have you done? Now you've insulted the man and his ability to earn a living.* "I didn't mean that the way it sounded. What I meant was, colleges are so expensive and—"

"Football scholarship." His eyes seemed to twinkle with amusement. "My brother was telling me last night that Sean's been approached about premed."

She leaned back in her chair. "Now I'm really impressed, although premed and football don't exactly go hand in hand."

"Tell me about it. I tried to call Sean last night after you—" He stopped then changed direction. "Anyway, he wasn't in, and I decided that talk might be better face-to-face over Thanksgiving."

"Does it get any easier?" she asked him after a sip of tea. "I keep waiting for the real Nicole to show up, but she vanished the day I bought her her first bra, and I don't think she's coming back any time soon."

"Sean lived with his mother during the school year and with me during the summer," he said, "so I didn't get the full effect. It seemed like the first time his voice cracked, so did his personality. I'm seeing signs of the old Sean lately, so don't give up hope."

"How old is Sean?"

"Nineteen in February."

"Nicole's fifteen. Four more years of this and I'll be institutionalized."

"It gets better. At least that's what they keep telling me."

"They tell me the same thing, but so far, I'm not buying it."

He told her that he'd been divorced since Sean was a toddler. His wife had hated New Jersey, hated the fact he wanted to be a cop, and wanted to go back home to California. "We met in college," he said as they walked the rainswept boardwalk after breakfast, "fell in love, married right while we were still in school." He side-stepped a strolling pigeon. "We probably should've lived together, but we both wanted kids, and marriage was part of the bargain."

"I was in high school when I met Charles," she said as they walked past the Steel Pier. "He was the friend of a friend's older brother, and he walked into a party wearing his ROTC uniform, and I was done for."

"So what happened?"

"Not all that different from your story. I spent years following him around from assignment to assignment, thinking the end was in sight and we'd be able to settle down and have a house of our own, put down roots near our families, but he decided to extend."

"You left him because of that?"

She shook her head. "That's the reason I can point to. The rest are harder to explain." She thought for a moment. "We respected each other. We were a good team. It just wasn't enough. We loved each other, but we weren't in love anymore."

"That's more than some people get."

"I know," she said, "but it wasn't enough for either one of us."

"You wanted the whole package."

"Yes," she said, stopping in her tracks. "That's it. I wanted the whole package. We both did. We thought friendship and respect were enough, but they weren't."

"He remarried?"

"He's about to. Nicole told me yesterday morning."

"Nice birthday present," he observed.

"I thought so."

"Did you think there was a chance you'd get back together?"

She shook her head. "Anyone who's seen them together knows they're a perfect match. She's bright and warm and funny, and I even like her. Charles seems happier than I can ever remember seeing him. I guess it hurts that he's found something I might never have."

"A soul mate."

"Yes." Her voice was softer than she cared to hear it. "A soul mate."

"Isn't that what we're all looking for?"

"I don't know. It's the first time I've ever admitted it to myself." She looked up at him. "What about you? Did your wife remarry?" *Did you?*

"Linda took the kid back home to California and married the guy she should've married in the first place." The high school sweetheart she'd broken up with during freshman year of college. "They have three daughters together and a new son."

"Poor Sean," she said.

His brows drew together. "Why do you say that?"

"It's tough enough having a stepparent. How did he feel about his mother starting a new family?"

"Never an issue," Conor said. "Linda married a great guy. If I couldn't raise my son, I'm glad Pete could."

"It doesn't always work that way," she said as they stopped to buy a few pieces of saltwater taffy. The inside of the store smelled as sweet as bubble gum. "There's nothing tougher than blending families."

"You sound like you have some experience."

She thanked the clerk, and they left with their white paper bag filled with goodies. "Start with the vanilla," she said, handing him a piece wrapped in blue waxed paper. "You can work your way up to coconut and chocolate."

He took the piece of candy. "So how do you know so much about stepfamilies?" he asked again.

"Easy to see why you're a detective," she said, hoping her tone sounded light and breezy.

"You don't have to answer if you don't want to."

She wanted to. There was something about him, something about the way they were together, that made the impossible seem easy. "My father died when I was ten, and my mother was thrown from being a housewife to being our sole support. She had no education and no skills, and I can't blame her for marrying the first man who said he loved her and would take good care of her children. Unfortunately, he had a slightly different take on discipline. Her marriage didn't last, but it made quite an impression on my sisters and me."

He asked about her sisters, and she found herself talking easily about Claire's modeling career and Ellie's law practice, about their beauty and brains and accomplishments.

"They sound pretty impressive."

"They are impressive," she said. "Now I'm trying to catch up with them."

They talked about late bloomers and the difficulties inherent in returning to school as an adult.

"I started working on my master's a few years ago," he said, "but the timing wasn't right."

"I know what you mean," she said. "I'm almost twice as old as anyone else in the class. It doesn't do a whole lot for your confidence."

She talked easily about her classes and how strange it was to have your son ask if you'd done your homework yet. He laughed, but she sensed that there was something else going on, a vague air of sadness that had settled over him when he mentioned going for his master's.

By the time they reached their hotel, she had run out of anecdotes.

"Thank you again for what you did for me this morning," she said as they walked into the lobby. She held out her right hand. "I really appreciate it."

He clasped her hand in his, and they both jumped as if startled by the intensity of the connection.

Bellmen bustled around them. Guests wheeled overnight bags across the polished marble. Security guards eyed them with a combination of curiosity and envy. They saw nothing but each other.

"I'm not big on daytime gambling," he said.

"Neither am I."

"We could drive down to Cape May for lunch."

"I've never been there," she said.

"We can change that today."

The old Maggy would have spent at least an hour debating the fine points of his suggestion. She would have whipped out paper and pen and drawn up a list of the pros and cons. She didn't need the list to know that she'd lost her mind to even consider going off with a man she'd just met, but it felt right. It felt better than right. It felt like the only possible thing she could do that made any sense at all.

FIVE

Conor turned the shower on full blast and stepped inside. Maggy said she'd meet him downstairs in the lobby in forty-five minutes, and there was no way in hell he'd keep her waiting.

He'd been better at this when he was sixteen and ruled by his hormones. When he was sixteen, he would've taken that opportunity down there in the lobby and kissed her. His thirty-nine-year-old self had been too stupid. He'd been so content to stare at her lovely, rainy-day face, so galvanized by the touch of her hand, that all he could think of was how to keep her near him the rest of the day.

Should've kissed her, pal. You might not have another chance.

There's optimism for you. He'd have an entire day with her in beautiful, highly romantic Cape May. There would be lots of chances for that first kiss.

Yeah? This little afternoon of yours comes with a guarantee?

They'd be together. That was the most important thing. Once that was established, the kiss—whenever it happened—was inevitable. The pull between them was that strong. Chemistry. Kismet. Attraction. Whatever you wanted to call it, they were in the middle of it now.

What if she doesn't meet you in the lobby, hot shot? What then?

He soaped, rinsed, then stepped back out of the shower. He didn't have an answer for that one. He could still see her elegant back as she walked out of Cleo's last night. He knew she was the kind of woman who could say no, if that was what she wanted or needed to do. She wouldn't hesitate to stay away.

"But she'll be there," he muttered as he toweled off. "She said she'll be there, and she will."

Unless she wasn't.

Maggy sat on the floor in front of her closet and almost wept with frustration. She was bundled up in a terry robe with the hotel logo emblazoned on the breast pocket. Her wet hair dripped down her forehead and over her cheeks. She looked like a study in confusion. What do you wear on a drive to Cape May in the rain with a man you don't know but wish had kissed you senseless in the lobby? She bet not even a fashionista like Claire would have an answer for that. Obviously the jeans and sweatshirt combo was too grubby for a stroll through the late Victorian town. She couldn't wear what she wore last night, which left the other outfit her sisters had surprised her with yesterday morning. A skirt, of all things. She wasn't sure she even remembered what her legs looked like. She wore jeans to school, sweats around the house, and nice slacks to work at the church office. Skirts meant thigh upkeep. Skirts meant a serious investment in pantyhose. Skirts reminded a woman that, like it or not, she wasn't sixteen any longer.

He'd already seen her without makeup, she reminded herself. Could it get much worse than that?

Obviously, the man was crazy. First she walked out

on him in the bar, then she popped up this morning bare-faced and wet-haired and in need of minor rescuing, and he kept coming back for more.

You're being courted, Maggy. What do you think of that?

"I love it," she said to the pile of clothes strewn across the bed. "I absolutely love it." When he took her hand in the lobby, she'd felt giddier than she ever had while drinking champagne. The touch of his hand was enough to send her heart spiraling skyward. She was a practical woman who prided herself on being level-headed and responsible, the kind of woman who saw *Titanic* and couldn't quite understand why Jack sacrificed himself so Rose could live. A mother would sacrifice herself for her children. That was a given. But the kind of huge, Technicolor romantic love other women flocked to the theaters to enjoy seemed as improbable to Maggy as the adventures of Luke Skywalker. Maybe even more so.

Still, there she was, a grown woman and mother of two, worrying about her hair and her makeup and whether her legs would look too skinny in the little navy blue pleated skirt her crazy sisters thought was so appealing. With the crisp white shirt and patterned sweater, she was afraid she'd end up looking like a Catholic schoolgirl many years after the fact. Hardly the way to a man's—

Whatever. She wasn't about to pursue that line of thought. Way too dangerous.

Use your own instincts, Maggy. Stop worrying about what other people think and start thinking for yourself.

Then again, Claire was as gorgeous and well-turned-out as they come, and Ellie was known for both her great courtroom technique and her great courtroom clothes; if they both thought this outfit worked, then maybe it was worth a shot.

•   •   •

He paced the lobby from front desk to exit to elevator bank, then paced it again. He reminded himself that she wasn't late; he was ten minutes early. That fact probably said more about his state of mind than a half-dozen love songs from his youth ever could.

His timing was way off. The Jeep was already idling at the curb, watched over by a well-compensated parking valet. She didn't look like the Jeep type. No matter she had two kids and a regular life. He saw her in a little Miata maybe, or a Porsche, something small and as finely made as she was. He wondered if it was too late to rent some late model, sleek and worthy of her. Then he kicked himself for being a bigger jackass than usual.

He wasn't the sports car type. He drove a Jeep that had seen some rough miles, same as its owner. If she hadn't already figured out that much about him, she'd know it as soon as she climbed into the passenger seat.

"I didn't figure you for the Jeep type," Maggy said as she buckled her seat belt. "I figured you drove one of those sexy little foreign jobs with no backseat and a trunk the size of my overnight bag."

"That's how I saw you."

"Me?" She stared at him in surprise. "I have two kids, remember? I'm your typical minivan-driving soccer mom."

"So far I don't see anything typical about you."

She ducked her head, feeling a tad more pleased than the statement warranted. "Thank you. I don't care for the description, but it pretty much sums up my life."

He shifted into first and merged into the Saturday-morning traffic.

"I love this Jeep," she said, running her hand along the console between them. "It's so . . . clean."

He laughed out loud. "I've heard this heap called a lot of things before but never clean."

"You should see my car," she said, grinning at him.

"Empty Happy Meals carriers, tissues, soccer gear, ice skates, ballet slippers, the occasional rogue french fry. I'm a traveling yard sale." Her teeth were small and white and even. Her lips were full and deep rose. The contrast of dark hair, light blue eyes, and fair skin was dazzling. No doubt about it. He had it bad.

He gestured toward the backseat and the area behind it. "I use the truck as a rolling file cabinet. It used to drive—" . . . *my partner crazy.* No. Not today. Today was about her smile.

If she noticed he changed course, she didn't let on. She laughed when he described the time he found a memo at the bottom of a mountain of clutter when his anal-retentive commanding officer couldn't find his own nicely filed copy.

"I wish I could say the same thing." She shook her head, and he watched, mesmerized, as the soft curls shimmered with the movement. "I try to check the back every week or so since I found the school hamster nesting under my library notes."

"I missed all of that with Sean," he said as they joined the highway heading south. "I'd see him every few months, and the changes in him would blow me away."

She reached out and lightly rested her hand on his forearm. She had no idea how much power there was in her touch. She couldn't, because if she did she'd rule the world.

"Did you ever think about moving to California to be near him?"

"Sure, I thought about it," he said, "but Sean seemed happy and healthy. My ex and her new husband are good parents, and they were building a new family together. I figured I'd only get in the way."

"I'll admit you don't seem much like a California type to me."

"LAPD didn't think so, either." He'd interviewed one summer, but the mismatch was of legendary proportions.

"You're a Jersey boy," she said with certainty. "Born and bred." She turned slightly in her seat and pretended to check him out for signs of the Garden State. "Am I right?"

"Would you believe me if I said no?"

"Not a chance."

"You're right," he said. "South Jersey, down near Great Adventure. Most of my brothers and sisters are still there."

"Brothers and sisters. How many of them do you have?"

"Three of the former, two of the latter. How about you?"

"Two sisters and one bathroom."

"Two bathrooms," he said, changing lanes, "but it wasn't close to enough."

"I can imagine."

"So where did you and those two sisters grow up?" he asked. "I'd say Greenwich or maybe the Upper East Side."

The look of surprise on her face made him laugh. "Remember the high school we talked about, the one where my daughter's a sophomore? I graduated from there eighteen years ago."

"What brought you back to Montgomery?"

"Do you know how many people have asked me that since Charles and I broke up?" She pretended to count them off. "How can you stand it here after living in Italy and Japan and all those other fabulous places? This place is nothing but a dead end with green lawns. I think I've just about heard it all and even agreed with some of it, but the truth is, Montgomery's the only place that's ever felt like home to me. If my kids are half as happy here as I was, I'll know I did the right thing."

"And how about you? Are you happy?" He never asked questions like that. He wasn't even sure he knew how to define the concept of happy.

"I'm content," she said after a moment.

"But are you happy?"

"I'm not unhappy."

"There's a difference."

"Maybe I'm too busy to know the difference." There was a bite to her words, a sharpness in her tone that wasn't there before.

"Sorry," he said, and he meant it. "I forget sometimes that life isn't an interrogation room."

She nodded, but she didn't back down. "That was a very personal question. Do I get to ask one in return?"

"Will that get me off the hook?"

"It might," she said. "Depends on the answer."

"Shoot," he said. "I'll take my chances."

He saw her elegant breasts lift slightly as she drew in a breath. She clasped her hands in her lap, and he suspected it was to keep them from trembling. This was going to be one hell of a question.

"Somebody hurt you," she said. "I can see it in your eyes. You started to say something a little while ago, and you stopped yourself, back when you were talking about your truck. I want to know what you were going to say."

"Any question but that," he said without looking at her. "Someday I'll answer that, but not today."

A woman, she thought as they settled into an awkward silence. Some woman broke his heart and not all that long ago. She hated the way that knowledge made her feel. Small, somehow, and diminished, as if the day had lost much of its glow.

You're better off finding out now, Maggy. You were about to go off the deep end for the guy, and he isn't even really available.

Not emotionally, where it counted.

The land flattened out south of Atlantic City. The air smelled cool and beachy as they drove past Egg Harbor, and she marveled that such heavy woodlands could thrive so close to the ocean. It was no longer raining, and the faintest rays of sun were struggling to pierce the heavy cloud cover. Two painfully young optimists in a red convertible whizzed by, their wheat-blond hair flowing wildly in the wind.

"I guess that proves I'm doomed to think like somebody's mother," she said as the sports car zoomed away from them. "All I could think about was how they should put the top up so they don't catch cold."

"Now try thinking like a cop. Nothing like two rich kids in a red convertible to bring out the worst in some people." He didn't enumerate the problems, but suddenly Maggy saw everything short of pestilence and plague hurled in the direction of the hapless kids. "They might as well paint targets on their heads," he added.

"Not down here," she said as she spotted a pair of fawns grazing along the side of the road. "Nothing bad could possibly happen in such a beautiful place."

"You're right," he said. "Nothing bad ever happens here."

She heard the touch of sadness in his voice, and her anger disappeared as quickly as it had come. Her emotions weren't always this close to the surface. Her sisters had hair-trigger tempers and easy access to tears, but not Maggy. Maybe it was because she was the oldest sister and had been almost a surrogate mother to them when they were little. She'd never had the luxury of acting out her feelings, so she learned to subdue them. That intense flare-up of irrational jealousy wasn't like her at all.

"It's not a woman," he said, and her head snapped toward him.

"What?"

"Your question." He met her eyes for a moment. "It's not about a woman."

"I'm that transparent?"

"No," he said. "I wanted you to know."

They whizzed past Sea Isle City then left the highway

to begin making their way down local roads toward Cape May. The Anchorage Inn. Dock Mike's Pancake House. The Riverboat with the monkey-vomit yellow siding. She started to comment about The Riverboat then caught herself. Too maternal. "Monkey-vomit yellow" was how her son Charlie had described their house when he first saw it, and the term had become a family catch phrase for ugly on a grand scale.

Docks lined both sides of the narrow road. It seemed as if every slip had been claimed by fishing boats, party boats, and brightly painted sightseeing boats that promised dolphin and whale sightings or your money back.

"I had one of those," he said, gesturing toward a largish sailboat bobbing happily on their left.

"Had?"

"You know that old saying: the two happiest days of your life are the day you buy your boat and the day you sell your boat. I spent more time repairing her than I did sailing her."

"You don't look like the sailing type to me," she said. "I can see you with a little plane."

"You wouldn't say that if you knew how I feel about flying."

"You, too?" she said. "I've tried everything from hypnosis to headphones to a pair of double martinis, and I'm still your basic white-knuckle passenger."

They exchanged a few airborne war stories then fell into a more comfortable silence, if you could call the silence between two strangers who were almost painfully attracted to each other comfortable. She felt by turns excited and terrified, elated and totally unnerved. She'd taken a giant step out of her normal life and didn't quite know which way to turn without a road map. This sort of spontaneous adventure came naturally to her sisters. For Maggy it was akin to walking on the dark side of the moon.

The last time she went out with a man, she'd insisted

they take separate cars and meet at the restaurant where they'd be having dinner, and she was reasonably sure she'd dated him once or twice way back in high school.

Next thing she knew, they were whipping into a parking spot at what wasn't exactly the picturesque spot she'd been expecting. She looked over at him and said, "Conor?"

"This is the other Cape May," he said. "The one Mother Nature put together before the architects found the place."

He jumped out of the truck then walked around to her side to open the door for her. The only other man to do that for her in recent memory was yesterday's limo driver, and she'd had to tip him.

The parking area was flanked by a pair of what could be charitably called shacks. A half dozen sightseers huddled by the one with the 'Eats' sign nailed over the walk-up window. The other one bore a sign marked Souvenirs, although she couldn't imagine what such a ramshackle building could offer up for sale. A brisk wind had kicked up, carrying with it a stinging rain that quickly had Maggy wishing she'd brought a jacket along with her.

"Wait a minute." Conor opened up the back of the Jeep and pulled out a heavy, hooded sweatshirt with the Rutgers University logo on the back. "You look like you need this."

"You're a mind reader," she said and slipped her arms gratefully into its warmth. There was something very sensual about wearing his clothing. The sweatshirt carried the faintest essence of his scent, and she barely managed to resist the urge to bury her nose deep into the folds.

"A little big on you," he said as she let the sleeves fall far below her fingertips.

"I love it," she said, pulling the zipper tab up as far as it would go. "Thank you."

He loved seeing her in his sweatshirt, knowing that the next time he pulled it on it would carry the memory of her perfumed skin, the shape of her breasts. They walked out onto the beach, and he pointed out the concrete boat *Atlantus*, which had been slowly sinking since World War I. He felt like a tour guide and a bad one at that. *Shut up. Let her look around on her own. You sound like a nervous teenager.*

He wanted to fill the silences with sound so she wouldn't hear the loud pounding of his heart every time her hand brushed his or he caught the sweet smell of her hair.

Say something, Maggy thought as she listened to him explain why the U.S. Navy ever thought a concrete boat was a great idea. *He must think you're dumb as a plank. It wasn't every day somebody told you about a cement boat. Ask a question. Make a comment. Don't just stand there, staring up at him as if he could part the Atlantic.* She loved listening to the sound of his voice, his words, the beating of her heart hidden away in the rush of wind. She was afraid if she opened her mouth to speak, her heart would tumble at his feet.

Their fingers brushed as they strolled up the beach, and it seemed natural to join hands. Her hand was very small in his. Bones as fine as a bird's wing, but strong. Surprisingly strong. She'd carved a life for herself and her children, and his admiration was boundless.

He had no rose petals to toss at her feet, no glittering Cape May diamonds to spill into her waiting hands. All he had were his words and so he told her about the tides and the phases of the moon, about the marsh grass and the rocky shore and the low dunes sliding down into the sea, and when he ran out of words, there was nothing left to do but kiss her.

S I X

"Maggy."

Her eyes closed at the sound of her name on his lips. She was afraid she'd break apart into a thousand pieces if she looked at him. Her emotions were right there at the surface, all of them, waiting to see what he would do next.

"Look at me, Maggy."

He urged her, and she resisted. She knew she wouldn't be able to hide her heart once he looked deep into her eyes, and with each second that went by she became less sure why she might want to. She had never fallen so far, so fast. Not even with Charles. This sense of passionate recognition was the stuff of dreams. There was no turning back from this.

He cupped her face between his hands. His fingertips lightly grazed her temples. His thumbs caressed her chin then followed the curve of her jaw.She opened her eyes, and her next breath was slow in coming. How could she breathe when he was so close to her? His eyes were more beautiful than she'd realized, the color of melted caramels shot through with gold. He was bent low over her, shielding her from the winds whipping off the ocean, creating an intimate hideaway where anything could happen.

He had fine lines at the outer corners of his eyes and thick, dark lashes that bristled rather than curled. His nose had been broken a time or two, but somehow that only intensified his appeal. She'd never been drawn to pretty boys who looked as if they had been born on the pages of a magazine. His jaw was wide and strong, and she could see the faintest shadows beginning to appear. It was a lived-in face, very male and attractive, but his eyes held her attention most. Sad eyes filled with secret sorrows she could only guess at.

He watched her steadily, scarcely blinking, and the intensity of his gaze was almost overwhelming. She tried to look away, but he held her face tenderly between his hands, and there was nothing she could do but let him look deep into her soul, to the secret place she hid from the world.

She was more than beautiful to Conor. She was strong and lovely and intelligent and womanly. It was in everything she did. The way she spoke, the graceful way she moved, the way she radiated kindness like a healing force. He was drawn to her on so many levels it scared him. He had the feeling he could spend the rest of his life getting to know her and never come close to discovering all of her colors.

She watched him closely. He felt her gaze as it moved across his face, studying his jaw, his cheekbones, his brow bone, his eyes. She wasn't flirtatious or coy. She didn't have to be. The sheer female power in her serious gaze did more to buckle his knees than a full frontal assault by another woman ever could. He knew all about sex and the way it could turn your brain inside out, and it wasn't until it was over that you realized what the whole thing had been about.

Not this time. He knew just by looking in her eyes.

Her wide, bright blue eyes dominated her small face. Her lashes were long and curly, and they cast shadows on her cheeks when she blinked. They would feel feathery against his chest and shoulder, like small secret wishes coming true.

She placed her hands against his chest, not to push him away but to draw his essence in through her skin. She no longer had any sense of time or place. They were suspended in a fragile soap bubble, floating gently above their real selves, their real lives.

She moved her palms across his chest until they came to rest above his heart, and she knew that quick, deep thudding of the blood belonged to her.

The kiss only confirmed what they already knew.

He tasted like sunshine and hot coffee.

She tasted like orange juice and stars.

The kiss was sweet, lips pressed to lips, eyes open, fingers entwined. It was both promise and fulfillment, less exploration than a kind of coming home.

Maggy was trembling when the kiss ended. She leaned her forehead against his chest and waited for the world to stop spinning, hoping it never would. She was a practical woman who'd found herself face to face with magic, and the collision left her reeling.

Conor wanted to make love to her right there on the sand. He wanted to cover her perfect body with his own, pleasure her and protect her and pledge to her a future he hadn't believed in until their lips met. He wasn't a romantic man, never had been, but suddenly he understood the meaning of roses.

They walked back to the car with their arms around each other. Less than an hour ago they had been two separate people, a man and a woman who were strangers to each other. Now they were a couple. That kiss, that gentle, innocent kiss, had changed everything. He opened the door of the Jeep for her, and she leaned across to open his door. A small thing, but it signified.

A steady rain slanted against the windshield as he drove slowly back into the heart of town, but not even rain dimmed the beauty of the place. Maggy was enchanted by the huge Victorian mansions that gracefully rose above the tree-lined streets. Most of the houses boasted wide front porches that invited you to sit awhile and watch the world go by. Cape May was less than an hour away from Atlantic City, but it might as well have been on another planet.

"Different life forms," he said as he angled the Jeep into a tiny parking spot across from the Walking Mall.

"That's exactly what I was thinking," she said as an elderly couple walked by, cozily sharing a bright red umbrella. "I feel as though I should be wearing a long dress and high-button shoes." For all that the beach was right there at the doorstep, there was something quaintly formal and stately about the town that made Maggy feel as if she should work a little harder to live up to its standards.

The Pilot House was around the corner and up the block. Conor offered her an umbrella, but she refused.

"Now that I've been shorn," she said, touching her hand to the unfamiliar short haircut, "I don't have to worry about getting caught in a little rain."

"You had long hair?" He took her hand, and they dashed across the street ahead of a horse-drawn carriage on its way back to shelter.

She nodded. "Very long." She told him about Andre and the rush of freedom she'd experienced when he lifted the heavy ponytail from her shoulders and sliced it right off with one snip of his scissors. "I felt like I was flying," she said. Like someone had set her free.

"One of my sisters did that a few years ago," he said as they rounded the corner and were surprised by a brisk sea breeze. "She started growing it back the next day."

"Not me. I feel like a new woman." The symbolism hadn't been lost on her yesterday when she made the decision to let Andre go ahead. That long mane of hair had been the last link to the old Maggy, the woman who was the first Mrs. Charles O'Brien.

He liked her with short hair. Yesterday he would have said he preferred long hair on women, but that was before he met her. He liked the way the dark curls hugged her head and drew attention to her lovely face and those wide blue eyes.

They were shown to a table on the closed-in patio where they sat surrounded by bright red and orange and yellow autumn flowers and watched the rain slide down the wall of glass. They held hands across the tabletop and talked of many things, none of which Maggy remembered later on. Words were unimportant. The sound of his voice, the timbre, the rhythms—that was more than enough.

The restaurant had a nautical theme. A mounted swordfish decorated the wall near the entrance. Model schooners sailed across the ceiling-level shelves. Casablanca fans whirred lazily overhead. Fat hurricane lamps graced every table. Weathered rigging from long-forgotten vessels was nailed to the dark wood walls.

"So, folks, what'll it be?" The waitress, a tall athletic redhead with triple piercings in her ears, approached the table. Her gaze landed for a second on their clasped hands. She didn't exactly smile, but she thought about it. "We have some great specials if you'd like to hear about them." They nodded, and the waitress pulled in a comically deep breath and launched into her spiel. "We have a baconlettucetomato on freshly baked focaccio with our special homemade mayonnaise. We have a grilled swordfish served on a bed of lemon risotto with a light remoulade. We have grilled chicken laced with pesto and served with homemade tagliatelle." She paused. "Oh, and we have liverwurst and onions on rye."

Maggy couldn't help it. The contrast was so absurd that she burst into laughter. Conor wasn't far behind. The waitress simply waited until they composed themselves long enough to order clam chowder and BLTs on plain white toast, then strode off in the direction of the kitchen.

"She thinks we're nuts," Maggy said, wiping her eyes with the paper napkin at her place.

"The menu probably sounds normal to her."

"I hate cute food," she said. "It's like somebody came along when we weren't looking and outlawed all the foods we grew up on."

"You're describing my brother Matty," Conor said, tracing the outer edge of her wrist with his thumb. "He eats to impress people."

"So does my sister Ellie. You should hear her theories on the hierarchy of lettuces." She started to laugh again. "She claims the way to a full partnership is through power ordering at business lunches."

"And your other sister?"

"Claire's a model," Maggy said. "She doesn't eat at all." She told him about growing up in a family of elegant swans, the practical older sister who watched her little siblings shoot up until they towered over her before they were twelve years old. "I made up for it, though. I was the one in charge when Ma was at work." Before their mother found out what she was up to and put a stop to it, she'd had Ellie and Claire doing all the cooking and cleaning while she stretched out on the sofa and watched *General Hospital.*

He had no trouble imagining her bossing around her little sisters. She was strong and self-confident. He wouldn't be surprised if she'd been class president and voted most likely to succeed.

She asked for his family secrets, and he soon had her laughing at his stories about the intricacies of family dinners that had to accommodate vegetarians, vegans, carnivores, Weight Watchers, Sugar Busters, and parents with an extreme love of grease and carbohydrates.

"Your family sounds wonderful," she said. "I keep wishing Claire and Ellie would get married and have a few kids. I'm looking forward to being an aunt." She missed being around babies. If she and Charles had stayed together, she would have loved at least one more child.

"Five nephews, eight nieces," he said. "Two more in the works that I know of."

"Claire said she's never getting married. So far, she hasn't liked what she's seen of it. Ellie won't marry unless Axel agrees to a twenty-nine-page prenup."

"And he won't sign?"

"Axel's a lawyer, too," Maggy said. "He countered with a forty-page prenup of his own."

"That's the good thing about being a cop your whole life. You don't have to worry about anyone marrying you for your money. There isn't any."

He owned a house and the Jeep, paid his bills on time, took vacations when he needed to. He wasn't rich, but he was comfortable, and that counted for plenty.

"I know what you mean," she said, sprinkling pepper into her bowl of steaming Manhattan clam chowder. "I don't drive a Saab or a Porsche, but I'm doing okay." She took a sip of soup then blotted her mouth with the paper napkin. "Better than okay." She owned her car. She owned her furniture. The bank owned most of the house, but she was working on that.

They agreed the soup was good and the sandwich even better. Her appetite surprised him. She ate with an appealing combination of enthusiasm and delicacy. Her movements were graceful and precise as she navigated the thick sandwich. She didn't so much as lose a lettuce leaf while he had mayo sliding down his wrist and under his shirt cuff.

Outside, the skies darkened and the wind kicked up in earnest. They watched as other tourists raced for the shel-

ter of the cozy restaurant, shaking off the rain like enthusiastic puppies. Maggy excused herself to use the
ladies' room and found herself side by side at the mirror
with an elderly woman whose heavily sprayed snow-
white hair was beaded with rain, and an intense dark-
haired young woman who had Maggy's idea of New
York Editor written all over her. The girl was dressed in
black with a man's jacket draped over her shoulders. Her
hair was the color of eggplant, glossy and deep purple.

The girl checked her teeth, smoothed her hair. She
practiced a smile in the mirror. She gave no indication
that she realized there was anyone else in the room with
her. Most likely she didn't care. Maggy and the old
woman were invisible, the way anyone over thirty is invisible to anyone who hasn't yet reached that plateau.

The old woman watched the stylish New York prototype as she left the bathroom. Her eyes met Maggy's
reflection in the mirror. "Never grow old, dear," she said
as she repaired her own lip color. "The upkeep is terrible. Stay as young and lovely as you are right now."

The woman added a bittersweet laugh, her fingertips
lightly touching the lines and wrinkles around her mouth.

Maggy smiled but said nothing. It wasn't the kind of
statement that lent itself to comment.

"I blinked my eyes and I was alone," the woman said,
sliding the cap back on the silvery tube. "It all goes by
so fast. One day you'll know just how fast."

It was an odd thing to say to a stranger. The result,
most likely, of one too many margaritas with lunch. Still,
there was a sharp reminder in the woman's words, a nugget of truth Maggy couldn't ignore.

The waitress returned and asked them about dessert.
Neither one of them could resist a towering chocolate
construction called Dark Side of the Moon, which they
decided to share. "Now, there's a surprise," said the
waitress as she wandered off.

"She thinks we're lovers," he said when the kitchen

door swung shut behind the waitress. The hand-holding, the long looks, and the private jokes—a blind man could see where they were headed.

Maggy felt hot, as if someone had raised the temperature a degree or ten. "Let her think it," she said, loving the way her hand felt enveloped by his. *Let her think whatever she wants to think.*

"You're blushing."

"Irish skin," she said as her cheeks burned hotter. "You should know something about that."

He wasn't buying it, and she was glad. He raised her hand slowly to his lips then pressed a kiss into the palm, folding her fingers one by one over the spot where his lips had been. It was far and away the most tender, most deeply romantic thing any man had ever done for her. That simple gesture made her feel cherished. Tears sprang to her eyes, but she didn't look away. This time the heat wasn't limited to her face; it spread down her throat and over her shoulders and burned fiercely behind her breast bone.

You shouldn't have this power over me, she thought. *I barely know you.*

Not that it mattered. It seemed the decision had been made for her, and there was nothing left to do but give over to the inevitable.

"I want to be alone with you," he said, and she nodded. It was what she wanted, too.

He tossed down a flurry of bills on the table, and they raced from restaurant to car. They laughed at the rain, blowing hard and horizontal now like movie rain, as it soaked their clothes and hair. Nothing mattered . . . and everything did.

"Where are we going?" she asked as the engine roared to life.

He had in mind one of the beautiful B and Bs that lined each street of that postcard town. Maybe a big four-poster with a view of the Atlantic, a clawfoot tub, and her body warm and wet in his arms.

It took three tries before they found the right place, a tiny cottage adjacent to the main building of a charming B and B that overlooked the beach. "You're very lucky." The owner was somewhere in his mid-fifties, bearded, and very affable. "We had a cancellation because of the weather. The Honeymoon Cottage is usually booked fifty-two weekends a year."

Conor signed the register then pocketed the room key.

"Do you need help with your bags?" the owner asked.

"We're fine, thanks," said Conor while Maggy gave herself away with another blush. He took her hand, and they made their way across the sandy yard to the tiny cottage tucked into a stand of bare maple trees.

A motel room would be better, she thought as he unlocked the door and motioned for her to step inside. A bare and ugly motel room with an unshaded lightbulb dangling overhead. A narrow bed with a cheap cotton spread that had seen better days. A bathroom with rusted fixtures and a stall shower. Not this wonder of gleaming brass and faded quilts and firelight. You could lose yourself forever in a place like this.

"Check your heart at the door." She turned to face him. The door to the cottage was still open. "The deck is stacked."

"The choice is still ours." His voice was low; his eyes never left hers.

She hesitated, but only because the life she'd led up until that moment hadn't lent itself to choices like these. *This is right, Maggy. Everything about this is right. Everything about him.* "I think you should close the door."

When she hesitated, he'd been sure she was about to change her mind. In that smallest of time spans, he'd seen

his future without her, and the emptiness he felt scared
the hell out of him.

She was standing near the foot of the bed. Her fingers
worried the hem of her sweater. She watched him closely
as he walked toward her, eyes wide and very blue. He
wondered what she was thinking, if she was thinking at
all or running on pure emotion same as he was.

She sighed softly when he drew her into his arms, then
pressed her lips to his throat. He swept her up into his
arms and carried her to the bed. The curve of her bottom
felt round and full against his palm, surprisingly sensual.
A jolt of heat joined the sense of wonder.

They fell together to the bed in a tangle of arms and
legs. Her skirt rode up her thighs, and she instinctively
reached to pull it back into place, but he clasped her wrist
to stop her. She met his eyes, and for a moment he saw
a flicker of fear. Before he could react, that widening of
her eyes was replaced by a growing sensual awareness
that shot him straight into full arousal. He'd never met a
woman before who could match his hunger, a woman
who understood the full range of experience possible between a man and a woman. Not until now.

She leaned back against the pillows. Her dark hair was
wet with rain. Her legs and thighs were exposed. The
only thing between him and paradise was a thin pair of
navy tights. Her breasts were round and surprisingly full
beneath the rain-soaked sweater and shirt. He knelt between her legs and removed her shoes, then tossed them
to the polished wood floor. Her knees were pressed
against his thighs, and he felt both resistance and surrender. He stroked the line of her leg with the index finger
of his right hand. Over the outside of her calf, inward at
the knee, over the supple length of her thigh and the
round swell of her hip. Her eyes were half closed as she
watched him, as if she were shutting out everything in
the room but the sight of him.

He drew his finger back to her ankle then stroked her

again, long, silky strokes, along the inside of her leg. Up
the calf, inward at the knee, over the trembling firmness
of her inner thigh until he reached the warm and succu-
lent center of her being. She made a sound, low and
exciting, deep in her throat. A cross between a moan and
a sigh that made him harder than before. Her head
dropped back, and her lips parted as he cupped her with
his hand. Her fierce female heat branded his palm even
through the layer of clothing. He pressed lightly against
her mound with the heel of his hand, quick touches that
made her hips rise up from the mattress to meet him. He
could feel her growing wet and ready, and only the fact
that he wanted her to remember this night for the rest of
her life kept him from taking her then and there.

He lifted her sweater and shirt then drew his tongue
across the quivering flatness of her abdomen, faint silvery
tracings that proved she'd borne two children. She wore
a sheer white bra with a lace design that didn't hide her
pale rose nipples. He took one nipple gently between his
lips then sucked through the delicate fabric until the nipple turned hard against his tongue and teeth. He did the
same thing to her other nipple as she moved beneath him,
her hands clutching his shoulders as she urged him to do
more and then more again.

He fumbled with the button and zipper to her skirt. His
fingers felt huge and clumsy as he tried to work the tiny
fastenings. She helped him, and a second later, he slid
the skirt over her hips and legs and tossed it to the floor.
The navy blue tights followed right behind. He buried
his face against her heat, sucked her through the damp,
sheer fabric of her panties, using lips and tongue and
teeth to make her wetter and harder and hungrier than
she'd ever been before.

She came alive each place he touched, a series of tiny
sensual explosions that brought her closer and closer to
where she wanted to be. She felt deliciously wanton as
he urged her to rest her legs over his shoulders. The angle

made her cry out with surprised pleasure. The sensations built one upon another, sometimes hard, sometimes so soft she thought she had imagined them, never stopping, never ever stopping. She wanted to feel his tongue against her bare skin, wanted him to taste her and know her as deeply as it was possible to know a woman. She wanted to reach down and rip off that foolish little scrap of lace.

He stopped suddenly, and she whimpered. The sound embarrassed her. So sexual. So hungry. The secret she'd tried so hard to keep, the part of herself that she couldn't control but worked so hard to hide.

And now he knew. This stranger. Her lover.

He seemed to know her body's secrets as if he'd been handed a sensual roadmap. Where to touch. How to touch. The unanswerable question of why it was all so important, so life-affirming, so terrifying. She didn't have to tell him because he knew.

Maybe he read her mind somehow, tapped into her most private dreams, Somehow he knew that she was going crazy, losing her mind, and he skimmed her panties over her hips and down her legs and pierced her with the supple blade of his tongue again and again until she bit down hard on the inside of her hand to keep from screaming.

He told her not to hold back. He told her with words and touch, and suddenly she heard a cry rise up from the center of her soul as she came violently against him, without shame, without holding back, crashing like the waves against the rain-soaked beach beyond the window.

SEVEN

Time passed in a sweet haze of kisses and touches and laughter. The laughter surprised them both. Each time the wild surges of passion abated, laughter rose up from a wellspring of joy and drew them closer together. They were clumsy sometimes, awkward now and again, never shy. There was no reason to be shy because they had been together before. Both felt it although they didn't talk about it. The sense of homecoming, of reunion, was in everything they did, every word they uttered, every kiss.

Rain tapped its knuckles hard against the windows. Wind buffeted the small cottage. Their bed was shelter from the storm.

Darkness fell, and they floated back to earth long enough to realize they were hungry.

"There's no phone in here," Maggy pointed out from the haven of his arms. "Guess we'll have to starve." She didn't care. She was drunk on the smell of his skin, sated on his touch.

He began to slowly, sensually, disengage his limbs from hers. "You stay here," he said as she protested. "I'll bring us back a pizza."

"I don't need a pizza," she said, aware of how empty the bed was without him there beside her. "I need you."

He leaned over the bed, cupped her face in his big warm hands, and kissed her. He was a great kisser, a world-class kisser. He drank from her mouth as if it were a goblet of wine, engaging all of her senses in the moment. She swore she could feel her bones melting. She could go on kissing him forever and would have tried if he didn't break away.

"Pepperoni," she said, sulking against the pillows. "None of those nasty anchovies."

He feigned horror. "An anchovy pizza's the only way to go."

"Bring back an anchovy pizza, mister, and it's all over."

"You drive a hard bargain." He pulled on his pants, then yanked his sweater over his head. "Pepperoni it is."

She smiled when he wasn't looking. Who knew feminine wiles were this much fun? She watched as he put on his shoes, dragged his fingers through his thick chestnut hair, then shrugged on his jacket.

"Don't move," he said, kissing her again. Kissing her until she felt dizzy with longing. "That's where I want you when I get back."

"Maybe," she said, offering up a mock salute. "Then again, maybe not."

He told her why he wanted to find her in that bed, naked beneath the faded quilt, and her eyes closed for a moment on that delicious image.

"I'll give it my consideration," she said, but they both knew where she'd be when he returned.

A fire crackled merrily in the grate and cast both shadow and light across the bed. Maggy considered rousing herself from comfort and using this time to repair whatever damage their passionate lovemaking had wrought in her appearance, but the bed was so deeply comfortable, and the intoxicating smell of his skin was everywhere. Instead, she curved her body around his pillow and watched the flames dance like pagan worshipers.

She knew she should be thinking deep and serious thoughts, but she was too profoundly satisfied to muster up even a moderately serious one. The rest of the world seemed very far away, as if she'd dreamed a house in the suburbs and two kids and an ex-husband who'd found himself a new bride. What would they think if they knew she'd spent the afternoon making wildly inventive love with a man she'd only met the night before?

The thought was too delicious to contemplate. Not that they'd ever find out. The only person on earth who knew Maggy and Conor were in Cape May was the owner of the B and B. She doubted if Claire and Ellie had had this in mind when they put her in the limo bound for Atlantic City yesterday morning.

It seemed as if her whole life up until today had been public property. Her sisters had always broken the rules while Maggy worried about them and started supper. As a young girl, it wouldn't have occurred to her to kick up her heels, because it wasn't in her nature. She knew her mother depended on her to help keep the household running while she worked double shifts, and, being an old soul, Maggy fell in line. Marriage was much of the same. She became pregnant with Nicole on her honeymoon and went from newlywed to new mother in nine short months. She filled notebook after notebook with endless lists of baby names, nursery decor choices, top-ten favorite bedtime stories. Army life was filled with uncertainty, and Maggy took it upon herself to make sure she provided her family with as much stability as she could possibly manage. Never out of touch. Never out of sight. A twenty-four/seven wife and mother who didn't so much as take a hot bath without telling her family where she was, then setting the cordless on the ledge of the tub "just in case."

She'd taken a giant step outside her own life, and if

she thought about it too long, she might gather up her
clothes and disappear before he came back. She felt as
if she'd been set down in the middle of some other
woman's life, a woman who didn't have to worry about
bad hair days or car pools or the midterms that were
coming up. If you'd asked her this time yesterday, she
would have said she didn't have time to take a lover, and
she would have meant every word.

Her family teased her mercilessly about her love of
order and organization. The Maggy they knew was calm
and always in control. The kind of woman whose sweat-
shirts hung neatly in the closet, arranged according to
color. Okay, so maybe she ran car pool now and again
in her pajamas, but it was always by choice, not by accident. They hadn't the foggiest notion that beneath the
cool exterior, a whole other woman existed.

Conor knew. That pool of clothing on the floor was
all the proof she needed of that fact. Her skirt, the tights,
those little scraps of lace masquerading as bra and panties
lay in a tangle a few feet from the bed. What was more,
she had no desire to get up and neatly fold each item and
place them on the chair near the fireplace. She loved
looking at them, loved thinking about the touches and
sounds that came before. Their lovemaking had been
wildly exciting, lovemaking with no boundaries and no
limits, but always—always—with a deeply sweet current
of tenderness that brought her close to tears more than
once.

*It's been a long time for you, Maggy. Maybe you're
not thinking straight.*

She knew the difference between having sex and making love.

*You think you do, but how can you be sure? You've
only been with two other men in your life.*

Two or two thousand. What did it matter? Magic
didn't arrive on schedule or on demand. If you could

wish magic into being, she would have found Conor a long time ago.

So how do you know he's coming back?

Her heartbeat lurched forward. Of course he was coming back. He was out looking for food, that was all. He'd be back any minute. She made a point of avoiding the clock on the nightstand.

Seems to me he's been gone a long time. He got what he wanted, and now he's headed back up to A.C. Wouldn't be the first time a man walked out on a woman after the party was over.

Ridiculous. Completely absurd. The man she'd made love with wouldn't leave her stranded down in Cape May without food or a car or an explanation.

Looks like you made a fool of yourself this time, Maggy, throwing yourself at a stranger just because it was your birthday and you were all alone.

It wasn't anything like that. He approached her. She had been perfectly happy to sit there and finish dinner without male companionship. Besides, how could she call him a stranger when she'd told him things she hadn't told her own sisters, secret fears and longings that nobody else on earth knew anything about?

And what do you know about him?

She hesitated. Not very much. She knew he loved his son, his family, respected his ex-wife, worked hard at his job. What more was there?

You weren't very careful, Maggy. You let yourself get carried away. You lecture your kids night and day about taking responsibility. Maybe you should start paying more attention. It isn't so easy to think clearly when you're on fire, is it?

She didn't have an answer for that one.

The rain was coming down so hard it was like driving through a car wash. Conor was glad there was no Saturday night traffic to speak of out there, because he was having a hell of a time finding his way back to the B and B where he'd left Maggy. He drove slowly, peering out through the rain at street signs, wishing the damn wiper blades actually did something more than smear water and dirt across the windshield. A pepperoni pizza occupied the place of honor next to him. An enormous bouquet of flowers lay across the backseat, accompanied by a bottle of champagne and chocolates. If more stores had been open, he would have bought her a silk scarf to drape across her shoulders, a silver chain, the sun and the moon and the stars, and anything else he could gather up. The small gift shop near the florist was about to close its doors when he stepped over the threshold. The owner took pity on him and showed him a rack of soft, silky robes in smoky blues and grays, and he picked one the color of Maggy's eyes.

You're losing it, pal. The only thing you know about her is the way she feels in your arms.

That was enough, he told himself as he pulled the Jeep into the flooded driveway to the B and B. When you came down to it, what was more real than that? Stripped to the skin, vulnerable, no place left to hide. You could know a person for ten or twenty years and not have any idea what made him tick. Sometimes you had to shut down your brain and go with that first sharp gut instinct, the one that was never wrong.

Oh, yeah, hotshot? What about when Bobby took that bullet for you? Where was your gut instinct that time? Got any answers for that?

He swore out loud, an ugly biting sound in the quiet truck. Not tonight. He wasn't going to wrestle demons tonight. Tonight he was going to lie by the fire with a beautiful and willing woman in his arms, a woman whose passion was more than a match for his own, and pretend he lived in a world where the good guys won and guys like him always made the right choices.

He gathered up the pizza and the flowers and the

glossy white box with the robe inside it and ran up the slope to the cottage. It was cold and stormy outside, but inside it would be warm from the fire, and an even warmer woman, naked and glorious, would be waiting for him in the bed where he'd left her. If you were looking for a one-sentence definition of heaven, that would pretty much be it.

He swung open the door to the cottage and found her sitting at the foot of the bed. She was fully dressed. Her makeup was perfect. Tights, skirt, blouse and sweater, all perfect. Her hair curled sweetly around her face. She bore little resemblance to the woman he'd last seen reclining against the pillows, her face flushed with passion, nipples rosy and still hard.

"It's hell out there," he said, putting the pizza down on the small round table to the left of the fireplace. "The fog's rolling in on top of everything else. You can't see two feet in front of you."

"I've been thinking," she said, and from the tone of her voice he knew he wasn't going to like whatever it was that she'd been thinking about.

"Too late to change your mind," he said, striving to keep his own tone light and easy. "I told you anchovy was the way to go."

She smiled a little. Just enough to let him know she got the joke. "Maybe we should get back to Atlantic City." She said something about her children, what if they called and she wasn't there, something false and brittle-sounding to his ears. She was trying to pretend she didn't see the huge bouquet of roses that suddenly looked garish in the firelight.

He said something about how they wouldn't be able to reach her anyway if she'd spent the day down in the casino, but the words rang false. This wasn't about her kids. This was about what happened between them.

"If that's what you want," he said, "then we'll go back to A.C."

Her huge blue eyes shimmered with tears. "It's not that I want to go back—"

He tossed the box with the robe in it onto the chair. "Then what is it? Are you sorry we're here? Having second thoughts about what we did?"

"I don't do things like this," she said, her voice soft. "I've never done anything like this in my life. I have two kids, a job, school—" She sank back down onto the bed and buried her face in her hands. "I think I've lost my mind."

The bed dipped as he sat down next to her. He smelled like cold rain and sea air. She wanted to bury her nose in the hollow of his throat and stay there for a lifetime or two.

"Nothing like this has ever happened to me, either."

She peered at him from between her fingers. "Don't patronize me."

"I get up, go to work, arrest some felons, come home. Not much room there for miracles, Maggy."

"Don't tell me there haven't been any women."

"Not for a long time." He'd told her that in the middle of lovemaking, that one brief moment when her rational brain kicked in and she made a quick run at reality. "And never anything like this."

"I'm a cautious woman," she said. "I'm careful about things. I look both ways before I cross the street. I carry a bag of Halite in the trunk every winter. I always keep my cell phone charged up." She met his eyes. "I don't sleep with strangers."

"Until today."

"I don't even talk to strangers as a rule."

"We didn't talk that much."

The words sat there for a moment, and then she started to laugh. He looked so big, so male, so serious that she couldn't help herself.

At first he stared at her, too surprised to laugh, but then he saw the look in her eyes, that wide-open look of wonder and terror that matched the feelings inside him; he started to laugh with her because, really, what else was there to do?

They stayed the night. They told themselves it was safer that way, what with the rain and the fog and the crazy Saturday night drivers out there, but they both knew they were lying. There was nothing safe about what they were doing. Staying there alone together in that little cottage with the pizza and the champagne and the rose petals and the silk robe caressing their naked bodies while the fire-light cast long shadows across them was the most dangerous thing they could do.

She slept in his arms and when she dreamed, she dreamed that it never had to end.

He awoke before she did, and when she opened her eyes, she found him watching her. Nobody had ever looked at her before with such a combination of tenderness and longing and wonder. She wondered what he saw in her eyes when she looked at him, if she was revealing half as much of her heart as he seemed to be. The thought terrified her. She'd always been one to hold her emotions close, to keep them her own private business. It seemed as if those days might be gone.

"What time does the car come for you?" he asked, his voice husky with sleep.

She leaned up on one elbow. "Noon."

"It's after seven now. The rain stopped. We could go to the Walking Mall and have breakfast at the Pilot House."

"I'd like that."

He nuzzled against the side of her throat. "Know what I'd like?" He told her and then he showed her and then it was after eight o'clock and they were in the shower together with the warm water sliding over their shoulders and even warmer hands sliding everywhere else. She dropped to her knees and cradled him in her hand, ran her wet cheek against his erection, then drew him slowly into her mouth. Nobody had ever taken him that way before, with such sensual deliberation, such obvious delight. She moaned as she took in more of his length, as if this were as much for her pleasure as for his. That realization was almost enough to push him over the edge. Fingers, hands, lips, teeth, tongue, rushing water, the sweet smell of a woman in heat, and then the rush of wild sensation he'd been looking for. He sagged against the wall of the shower, drained of everything but joy. She looked up at him, eyes glittering, her mouth rosy and swollen, and he knew that image would stay with him for the rest of his life. He helped her to her feet, her body sliding up his torso, then he found her with his hand, the warm creamy wetness between her thighs, stroked her slowly because there was nothing else in the world that mattered to him, caressed her deeply until she shuddered against him on a sigh he would never forget.

Breakfast went untouched. They sat across the table from each other and held hands. She had a dim memory of sipping some orange juice. He vaguely recalled gulping down some coffee. Neither one was ready for the idyll to end.

They didn't talk on the drive back to Atlantic City. When you came down to it, what was there to say? The real world had a gravitational pull they couldn't deny.

"No regrets," he said as they walked back into the hotel, past the fake temple and phony gods and goddesses bearing mimosas and hot cups of coffee. The sound of slot machines almost drowned out the Muzak.

"No regrets," she said.

They paused between two banks of elevators.

"I'm Centurion Tower," she said. "Remember?"

"Right," he said. He was Augustus Tower.

She pushed back his sleeve and looked at his watch. "Eleven forty-five. I'd better hurry."

"The limo will wait for you," he said. "That's what they're paid for."

But they both knew that would just be delaying the inevitable. She scribbled her phone number on the back of a cocktail napkin snagged from a passing drinks goddess. He wrote his on a matchbook cover. She said maybe they should let a full week go by before they spoke to each other. If what they had was real, it would still be burning brightly; if it wasn't, better to know now before it went too far.

He pulled her behind a marble column and kissed her. She felt sixteen, filled with hope and happiness. He felt like he could rule the world.

"A week?" he said, touching his thumb to her chin.

She kissed his finger. "It will be over before you know it."

"The hell it will." Then he kissed her again, and it was her turn to wonder just how long seven days really were.

The message light was blinking when he stepped inside his room. Six messages, all of them the same. He picked up the phone and dialed his brother Matt's home number.

"Where the hell have you been?" Matt barked at him. "I've been calling you since yesterday morning."

"I didn't know I had to check in with you, little brother. This was supposed to be a vacation."

"I snagged tickets for you for last night's show. You blew a chance to see Barry Manilow."

Conor blinked. This from the kid who'd lived for Duran Duran and U2?

"I'll live," Conor said, not surprised at all when Matt didn't catch the spin he put on the words. "Is that it?"

"You still haven't told me where you've been."

"Out," he said.

"Out where?"

"What the hell business is that of yours?"

"I fixed up this trip for you. The least you can do is put in some gambling time."

"So that's what this is about? I haven't clocked enough time at the tables to suit you."

"I didn't say that."

"Sure as hell sounded like it."

He could almost hear the wheels spinning in Matty's head. "They keep track," Matty said. "Play has to be up to a certain standard or you lose the comps."

"I don't get any comps, so what difference does that make?"

"You got the room, didn't you? That's a comp."

"But I'm paying for it." Handsomely, too. "What kind of comp is that?"

Matty explained a very arcane ritual involving gambling percentages, hours spent on the floor, and how much your slot host liked you.

"Let me see if I've got this straight," he said. "Because I was comped for $100 on the room, I now have to gamble $500 to pay for it."

"That's right."

"Why don't I repay the $100 comp?"

"It doesn't work that way."

"You left six messages to tell me that."

Silence on Matty's end, then, "You were with that woman from the restaurant, weren't you?"

It was Conor's turn to play the silences. "Not your business, little bro."

"Be careful," Matty said, sounding like their father. "She's not in your league."

He thought of her lovely face, her gentle smile, the fierce hunger she brought to their lovemaking, the unflinching honesty. "You're right, Matty," he said. "She's not in my league at all."

With a little luck, they'd be together twenty years before she figured it out.

EIGHT

"Nicole!" Aunt Claire's voice floated through the closed door to the bathroom. "Hurry up in there! We leave in fifteen minutes."

Nicole looked at her reflection in the makeup mirror. Her right eye looked pretty good, but her left eye still needed work. Claire had shown her how to use the two shades of brown shadow to give her eyes depth, but that blending stuff was giving her trouble. Why blend it until nobody even knew you were wearing any eye makeup? Aunt Claire said that was the point of it, but that didn't make any sense. Why bother if nobody could see it?

She leaned forward and dabbed on another layer of taupe then examined the results. Better, she thought. Now you could at least see something was going on there.

"Nicole! Did you hear me?"

"Fifteen minutes!" she shouted back. "I'll be ready."

You could sure tell Claire was one of the Halloran girls. They were all bossy, although Claire only pulled rank on Nicole now and then. Still, it bugged her. All of that clock-watching seemed silly. It wasn't like they had a plane to catch or something. All they were doing was taking her home, which wasn't exactly a big deal.

The thought of going home made her sigh. She was having so much fun. Being with Aunt Claire was like playing Barbie when you were a little girl. The only difference was now you were Barbie, and Claire's apartment was your Dream House and there was a closet filled with every beautiful outfit you could possibly imagine right there for you to try on and pretend you were a beautiful model, too.

Melissa and Stacey were emerald with jealousy. "Ask her if we could come next time," Melissa had begged her. Nicole knew she kept a scrapbook of Claire's magazine covers even though she thought nobody realized it. Nicole just smiled and said her aunt was terribly busy and maybe someday but not now. The truth was, Claire would have been happy to open up her sunny and spacious condo to Nicole and her girlfriends, but Nicole didn't want to share her with anybody. She loved it that they adored her aunt and wanted to be part of her life. It made Nicole feel special.

Why did she have to go home anyway? It wasn't as if her mother would notice she wasn't there. She was always running to that stupid job at the rectory or going to school, which was so dumb that it boggled the mind. Imagine going to school if you didn't have to. You'd think her mother would be embarrassed to sit there with all those young kids. Sometimes Nicole wanted to die when she had Stacey and Melissa over and her mother made one of those lame jokes about all of them doing their homework together at the kitchen table. Yeah. There was a good idea for you.

If she never heard stupid remarks like that again, it would be too soon. At least Aunt Claire remembered how it felt to be almost fifteen. Maybe it was because Claire was almost ten years younger than Nicole's mother. Grandma Halloran said having a few kids would shape Claire up, but Nicole didn't see what that had to do with anything. She couldn't imagine her aunt being any other way but the magical and exciting way she was.

Back home she had to share a bathroom with that idiot brother of hers and listen to her mother's endless yapping about homework and college and responsibility. Aunt Claire never talked about any of that stuff. Her aunt talked about makeup and fashion and told stories like the one about what happened on her latest photo shoot when the stylist brought the wrong shoes and the designer pitched a fit and shredded the clothes to ribbons with a Swiss Army knife.

She leaned closer to the mirror so she could get a better look at her face. Aunt Claire said she had what it took to be a model, but she wasn't so sure. When she looked at herself, all she saw was a big-eyed girl who was too tall and too skinny to rate a second glance from any of the guys at school. She was all arms and legs, always tumbling over herself like some stupid puppy looking to be liked.

"All you need to do is make a few changes," Claire had said to her last night while they were curled up on opposite ends of the couch watching *Titanic* for the thousandth time. Claire reached for a piece of dry popcorn from the small bowl on her lap and snarfed it up. The popcorn in Nicole's bowl glistened with melted butter. So did her fingers. "Lose a few things."

"Like the butter?" Nicole asked with a grin.

Claire tossed a kernel of air-popped in Nicole's direction and grinned back at her. "I was thinking more like the purple hair."

Nicole frowned. "I like my hair."

"You look like an eggplant."

"You sound like my mother."

Claire made a face and pretended to shudder. "Now that's a terrible thing to say! I love your mom, but we both know she isn't the most adventurous woman around."

Nicole hated it when Claire said things like that. It always left her feeling like a real creep if she laughed with her aunt and a phony if she didn't. Her mom was kind of a stick-in-the-mud, certainly nothing like Claire, who jumped from airplanes and wore backless evening dresses with five-inch high heels. She wasn't much like her other sister either, for that matter. Ellie dressed like Ally McBeal and stalked the courtroom like Johnny Cochran or one of those other lawyers who knew how to charm the jury into coming up with the right verdict. "There's nothing wrong with flirting if it gets you where you need to be," Ellie said once during an argument with Nicole's mom. "The point is to win the case for my client. I'll do whatever I have to, to get the job done."

Nicole had to sit through a long lecture from her mom after that, one of those "I'm glad you love your aunt Ellie but you shouldn't pay attention to some of the things she says" kind of lectures that made her feel like she was trapped in a room with her little brother and his smelly friends. Her mom was a real Girl Scout about most things. As far as Nicole knew, she'd only dated one guy since divorcing Daddy, and that didn't work out for long. Big surprise there. Her mother wasn't exactly great date material, going around in jeans and a sweatshirt all the time with her hair in that stupid ponytail that made her look fifteen same as her daughter. Sometimes she wanted to throw herself under a truck rather than admit that was her mother driving car pool in her pajamas. Maybe if parents had a clue how much they were embarrassing their kids, they'd think twice before they did stupid things.

"Nicole!" Claire rapped on the door again. "Five minutes!"

"I'll be there!"

She balanced out her eyes by adding more shadow to both of them and then another coat of mascara and a little kohl along the lashes. She liked the way all that smoky

darkness made her blue eyes jump out like that. Her hair
didn't look so good though, hanging all limp thanks to
the rain. She pulled one of Claire's curling irons from
under the vanity and plugged it in. It took forever to heat
up. She could hear her aunts out there talking, probably
staring at the clock and wondering if they'd have to send
a rescue party in there to get her. There! The indicator
light went off. She twirled a section of hair around the
curling iron, pressed it hard for a few seconds, then
moved on to another section and then another. Nobody
would mistake it for a professional job, but it sure looked
better than it had before. She unplugged the iron, laid it
across the ceramic rest, then pouffed it out with her fingers until she thought she looked almost as glamorous as
her aunts.

Perfect, she thought as she turned to leave the bathroom. She looked at least eighteen.

You were fifteen yourself once, Claire reminded herself
as she caught a glimpse of her niece in the rearview mirror of her Porsche. Subtlety wasn't part of a fifteen-year-
old girl's vocabulary. Excess was. Nic would probably
beam if Claire told her that she looked like a teenage
streetwalker with all that gloppy makeup on her eyes and
the big hair and short skirt. She was a beautiful young
woman with real potential, and the urge to wash her face
and comb out her hair was almost irresistible.

I'm glad I'm not your mother, she thought as she and
Ellie exchanged meaningful glances. An aunt could shrug
her shoulders and wait for the storms to pass; a mother
had to get in there and bail water. Neither one of them
had the slightest idea how Maggy managed to keep the
high-strung young girl in line without going totally mad.
Nic was a good kid, but since the divorce she'd been
moody and argumentative and convinced that her mother
was easily the most backward woman on the planet.
Claire might have her problems with Maggy's fashion

sense, but she couldn't fault her mothering, especially the way she handled Nicole. Nic was a daddy's girl. Everybody knew that. Although she didn't say much, it was clear that she missed her father. The last two years had been rough on her and, as a result, very rough on her mother.

Claire didn't understand the whole daddy's girl concept. Her own father had died when she was a toddler, and she had no clear-cut memories of him at all. Unfortunately, she did have memories of the man to whom her mother was briefly married not long after her father's death, and those memories made it difficult for her to understand what the fuss was about. They'd been much better off without that loser in their lives. She'd never missed having a father. Between her mother and Maggy, she'd enjoyed more love and support than any three daddy's girls of her acquaintance. A father would have been as unnecessary as air-conditioning in winter.

Sometimes she wondered if a father, a real father, would have made a difference, but she couldn't quite wrap her brain around the idea. A father couldn't have stopped her from pursuing her own life in her own way. He couldn't have kept her from making mistakes. Nobody could have. Mistakes were what she was best at.

She glanced again at the rearview mirror. Nic was listening to music on her portable CD player. Her head bobbed along with the beat. Claire turned to her sister at the next stoplight.

"I wish Maggy hadn't found out about Charles before she left."

"She had to find out sometime," Ellie said. "Besides, what difference does it make? They're divorced. Sooner or later one of them was bound to remarry. He just got there first."

"Very logical," Claire said. "I'm impressed. Now forget you're a lawyer for ten seconds and think like a woman."

Ellie grinned. "The two aren't mutually exclusive."

"I wish you'd remember that," Claire said. "Nic is hurting about her dad's engagement, and I'll just bet Maggy's been crying her eyes out alone in her hotel room."

"What have you been reading lately anyway? You sound like one of those old romance comic books we used to read under the covers when we were kids. Maggy's fine about Charles. Nic's the one we have to worry about."

"I suppose you're right," Claire said reluctantly.

"Of course I'm right. Just because you live with your emotions hanging out there in the breeze doesn't mean everyone else does. Some people just get on with it."

Ellie's remark hurt, although she probably didn't mean it to. Claire's life had been a roller-coaster ride that included running away from home, success too early and too little, and a bout with drugs that almost destroyed the family. She often had the feeling that she'd be playing catch-up for the rest of her life, trying to make up for all the trouble she'd caused.

"Sorry if I came on like I was in a courtroom," Ellie said. She'd always been good at seeing both sides of a situation, even if the situation dealt with her own shortcomings. It was a trait Claire admired more than she would ever admit to her sister. "Sometimes courtroom skills come in very handy in this family." She leaned back in her seat and slid off her right Manolo Blahnik pump with the toe of her left one. "Besides, I really don't think this is that big a deal. It's more important to Nicole and Charlie than to Maggy any day."

Ellie had a way of slicing through the layers of emotion surrounding a situation and zeroing in on the core. That method worked well for her in a courtroom, but she often missed important emotional nuances that tripped her up in real life.

Claire's whole life was built upon a foundation of

emotional nuances. She supposed she should be grateful Ellie's wasn't, because a more astute sister might have noticed that Claire was keeping a secret. Hidden away in a portfolio in the trunk of her car were a series of photos a photographer friend of hers had taken of Nicole last month. Stunning head shots, great action poses, moody portraits that gave you a glimpse of the woman she was on her way to becoming.

No doubt about it, her niece was the real thing. Claire's own gifts paled to nothingness alongside her niece. The camera loved Claire, but it adored Nic. The lens softened angles, shadowed curves, added a dimension of complexity and maturity that wasn't quite there yet in real life.

Claire would never be anything but a mid-level model, but Nic could be something special. She'd shown the photos to her agent, and right away Leah had wanted to sign her to an exclusive contract, which only made Claire more convinced than ever that her niece might have a shot at the big time. Leah wasn't the right woman for the job, however. She was too aggressive, too sharp-tempered and bottom-line. Great for Claire but terrible for a vulnerable young girl. If only someone had realized that fifteen years ago when there was still time to make a difference in her own life.

She hadn't shown the photos to Nicole yet. She knew the girl would go completely crazy, want to throw aside school and move to New York and become another Cindy Crawford. As if Maggy didn't have enough on her hands as it was. So the photos had stayed where they were, stashed in the trunk, while Claire tried to figure out what to do. Sure, the world could live without another teenage model, but was that being fair to Nicole? It was her life, after all. A year or two of part-time work could put an end to worries about how to pay for a college education. A year or two of superstardom could bankroll the rest of her life and maybe, if she was very lucky, help Claire as well.

She missed him. It was so ridiculous that even Maggy had trouble believing it. She'd only known him for forty-eight hours, and she missed him so much it hurt. A dull ache had settled somewhere in the vicinity of her heart, and it grew stronger the closer she got to home. What on earth had she been thinking when she suggested they wait a week before contacting each other? She must have been out of her head, totally mad, to think she'd be able to last seven days without the sound of his voice.

That's why you have to do it, Maggy. Let things cool down a little and see what you have once the fog clears.

Good advice. She knew it was good advice, but she'd never imagined she would feel his absence so strongly. Was it possible to lose your heart so quickly? To fall so completely? This was the kind of thing that happened to her sisters, not to reliable, dependable Maggy.

But it had happened. She couldn't deny that. Whoever it was she used to be, whoever that Maggy O'Brien was, that woman no longer existed. A new one had taken her place, less confident maybe and definitely more vulnerable but happier than she'd been in a very long time. Now all she had to do was keep her delicious secret close to her heart until she found out if he still felt the same way once the week came to an end. Once she knew the answer to that question, she'd worry about how to tell her family. Until then, she was going to keep her mouth closed and her secrets all to herself.

Nicole screamed when she saw her. Maggy had barely stepped out of the car when her daughter let out a high-pitched wail and screamed, "You cut your haaiiiirr!" with the same tone of voice somebody else might use to announce the approach of the four horsemen of the Apocalypse.

Maggy counted silently to ten then threw her arms wide. "Come here and give me a kiss," she said, forcing a big smile. "We'll talk about my hair later." *Not to mention that hideous makeup you're wearing.* She shot her sister Claire a long and deadly look. Claire shot back a look of her own that said, *Don't blame me. I told her to blend.*

"Pearls?" Nicole rolled her eyes. "Mother, really . . ."

Three words, five syllables, and Maggy's day took a nosedive.

"Purple hair?" Maggy shot back. "Triple-pierced ears?"

Nicole stiffened in her arms. Maggy didn't blame her one bit. They hadn't been together thirty seconds and already they were in full mother-daughter battle positions.

Thank God the driver asked her something about her bags, and then Ellie came racing down the driveway to greet her, lobbing questions at her like tennis balls, then tossing more her way before she had a chance to answer.

"I knew that skirt would be perfect on you," Ellie said as they strolled arm in arm up to the house. "You look absolutely terrific."

"I feel terrific," Maggy said.

"You had a good time?" Claire asked. She and Nicole were bringing up the rear.

"Better than good," Maggy said. "The best."

She tried to ignore the sniff of disdain that sounded from her daughter. Kids didn't like their parents to have fun. That was a fact of life. Parents, especially mothers, were supposed to stay home and behave themselves. Getting upset about it was like telling a bird to stop flying. She reminded herself that in ten years this would be an amusing anecdote that she and Nicole would giggle over at lunch.

Either that or they'd kill each other.

"I tried to call you last night," Nicole said, "but you weren't in your room."

Ripples of guilt washed over Maggy, but she refused to let them get the better of her. "Of course I wasn't in my room," she said. "What fun would that be in Atlantic City?"

Nicole reached out and touched Maggy's hair then made a face.

"It's too short," she said in the petulant teenage tone of voice that set Maggy's teeth on edge. "Makes your ears look big."

"I like it," Maggy said calmly with a glance over her shoulder at her daughter. "It was time for a change."

"Nobody's wearing tights this year," the girl went on.

Claire stepped in before the conversation degenerated any further. "Everybody's wearing tights in New York. Short hair, too. I'd cut my hair off in a second if it wasn't a breach of contract."

Ellie, who wore her long hair in a low chignon, nodded. "I'm thinking of following Maggy's lead before I leave on vacation."

This led to a breezy discussion of long hair versus short hair, the pros and cons of each, both physically and emotionally, until Nicole sighed loudly and took her overnight bag up to her room.

Maggy shook her head sadly. "If there isn't a patron saint for mothers of teenagers, there should be."

"I nominate you," Ellie said, patting her on the shoulder. "Tell me we weren't like that when we were growing up."

"We were worse," Maggy said, flinging open her suitcase so she could drop her laundry in the washing machine next to the kitchen. "I remember Ma threatening to bundle us all up and leave us at the convent for the sisters to take care of."

"I almost forgot," Claire said as she watched Maggy take the small hotel laundry bag from her suitcase.

"Joanne called. She said she'd keep Charlie for supper then bring him home around eight o'clock."

"Sounds great," Maggy said, wondering if all little boys were as easy as hers or if it was just by comparison to his teenage sister. "Why don't we call out for pizza?"

"Oh!" Ellie lifted the slate blue silk robe from the suitcase and held it up. "This is gorgeous, Claire. Where'd you find it?"

"I didn't." Claire turned a suspicious eye on Maggy. "You bought that for yourself?"

"Don't sound so shocked," Maggy said as a telltale blush began moving upward from her throat.

"Do you know how much this would cost at one of the hotel boutiques?" Claire went on. "You wouldn't spend that much on a used car."

Maggy snatched the robe from Ellie and quickly changed the subject. "Why don't I run upstairs and change while you call Domino's?" She tucked the robe under her arm and made a run for the hallway. "Make it one pepperoni and one mushroom. Don't forget the soda."

"Maggy!" It was Claire, using that prison-matron tone of voice she'd picked up in drama classes and trotted out to annoy her sisters. "You met a man!"

Nicole hadn't set out to eavesdrop on her mother and aunts. It just happened. She'd been on her way back to her room after using the bathroom when her Aunt Claire's words seemed to fly right up the staircase and grab her by the ankles. It was like she couldn't move if she wanted to.

"You met a man."

The thought made her feel like hurling.

No way. Not her mother. Claire must be on drugs or something. Her mother didn't even think about things like that, which was fine with Nicole. It was bad enough that her father had gone out and found himself somebody new. Sally was nice and all that, but it just felt really weird, seeing her father with somebody else. They might even have a baby if Sally wasn't already too old.

Nicole knew exactly what that meant. Men went off and started new families, and once they did, the old families were forgotten. She'd seen it happen to her friend Stacey. Stacey's dad had twin baby daughters with his third wife, and you would think Stacey was some stranger knocking on his door to sell Girl Scout cookies. Last year he forgot her birthday. He wrote Stacey a note and said it was only because Margot was in premature labor and the date slipped by him. Stacey wrote back and said it was okay, but it really wasn't. How could it be okay for your own father to forget the day you were born?

Nothing made sense anymore. Sometimes she dreamed that it was all a big mistake and that she'd wake up one morning and come downstairs for breakfast and Daddy would be sitting at the kitchen table with his newspaper propped up against the sugar bowl and his coffee cup balanced on his knee, and everything would be the way it used to be. Not that everything was always perfect, but it sure was better than the way things were now.

Maggy stopped dead in her tracks, clutching the evidence. She was afraid to turn around because she knew the second Claire saw her face, it would be all over.

"Oh, my God!" Claire's shriek could be heard in Trenton. "You did!"

Ellie, who'd been dialing up Domino's, dropped her cell phone to the floor with a crash and ran into the foyer. How she managed to break land speed records in those teetery heels of hers was one of the secrets of the universe. "You met a man?"

"You don't have to sound so surprised," Maggy said, a bit annoyed at the note of shock in Ellie's voice. "It's been known to happen."

"Yes," said Ellie, wide-eyed, "but not to you."

"Keep your voice down," Maggy said, motioning them back toward the living room. "I don't want Nic hearing this."

"You met him at the roulette wheel," Claire, ever the romantic, said. "You put your money on noir, he put his money on rouge and—"

"Actually we saw each other in the parking lot then bumped into each other at dinner."

Claire pouted. "I like my story better."

"And—?" Ellie prodded. She reached out and fingered the luscious silk robe. "He bought this for you, didn't he?"

"None of your business." A part of her wanted to tell them absolutely everything, if only for the satisfaction of watching the look of shock on their faces. That would almost be worth the loss of the one tiny bit of privacy she'd managed to wrest from their grasp.

"You might as well tell us," Ellie said, "because we'll get it out of you sooner or later."

"I'll tell you," Maggy said, "but not now." She didn't feel like fielding the inevitable questions and opinions that would turn her story into something vaguely tawdry and ridiculous. Her sisters were young and single. They hadn't a clue about her real life, about being a wife and a mother and an ex-wife and a student and so lonely you thought your heart might stop beating. Their lives were crammed with friends and trips and important career decisions and wondering about the best way to shelter the money that was pouring in.

"You were careful, weren't you?" Claire asked. "I thought about putting a few condoms in your overnight bag, but I really didn't think you'd—"

"Claire!" Maggy was shocked. The whole thing had gone way too far. "I'm not going to talk about this with you."

Claire's jaw dropped open. "Please tell me you didn't sleep with him."

Ellie gasped. "It's written all over your face! Maggy, have you lost your mind? You don't pick up strange guys in Atlantic City and sleep with them."

Something inside Maggy snapped, and she whirled on her sisters like a crazy woman. "I didn't sleep with him in Atlantic City. I slept with him in Cape May, and if you're looking for details, go home and read the Kama Sutra, because I think we about covered everything in there."

NINE

For a second the room was dead quiet, but then they started to laugh, both of them, big huge whoops of laughter that made Maggy want to hit them over their heads with a rolled-up newspaper.

"Is the thought of me having a fling so hilarious?" she demanded.

"Y-yes," Claire said, wiping her eyes. "I don't know what I was th-thinking! I'm sorry, Mags!" She collapsed again into gales of laughter and had to grip the back of a chair for support.

Ellie was no better. Her serious sister was doubled over with mirth. "Thanks for the Kama Sutra remark," she said. "That's what brought me down to earth."

"You had me going for a minute there," Claire said, struggling to recover her composure. "You looked so serious."

"I am serious."

The room went quiet again. She could hear Nicole talking on the telephone upstairs and the sound of one of the cats snoring in the next room.

"Quit looking at me like that!" She smoothed the robe

with nervous, guilty fingers. "I haven't committed a crime."

"I'm sorry," Claire said, "but I just can't believe it. You'd never have a one-night stand."

"It's not against the law, is it?" Maggy shot back. Suddenly she was in the mood for a fight. From the moment she stepped foot from the limo, it seemed as if her entire family had been conspiring to stomp every last vestige of happiness from her body.

"She's kidding," Ellie said, looking greatly relieved. "Maggy's too level-headed to do something like that. Can you just imagine her going off with a stranger?" She looked ready to start laughing again, which infuriated Maggy.

"Look at her face," Claire said. "I don't think she's kidding. You can see she's keeping a secret. Look at her eyes!"

"I told you this Atlantic City thing was a terrible idea," Ellie said.

"Puh-leeze," said Claire, totally ignoring Maggy. "You wanted to send her to visit the Amish. There's excitement for you."

"I think I know my own sister," Ellie said. "She—"

"Neither one of you knows the first thing about me," Maggy interrupted. "You have no idea what I would or wouldn't do, and if you don't quit talking about me as if I'm not here, I'm going to scream."

"Will you listen to her!" Claire said. "She's lost her mind."

"I haven't lost my mind," Maggy said, clutching the silk robe against her chest. *But I think I might have found my heart.* "I'm just getting a bit tired of being thought of as some poor little innocent out there among the wolves."

"Do you have any idea what it's like out there?" Claire went on. "Promise me if you ever do something like that, you'll use condoms."

Maggy was engulfed by a full-body blush. "What makes you so sure I haven't already done something like that?"

"You're a terrible liar," Ellie observed. "One look at you, and we both knew you'd been up to something."

Maggy laughed out loud. "You didn't know one single thing until you saw the robe. As a matter of fact, you still don't know anything. You're only guessing. Make up your mind, ladies: Did I have a weekend fling or not?"

"You're not being funny," Claire said. "We're just concerned about you. After all, we're the ones who sent you to Atlantic City."

"Just tell us who gave you the robe," Ellie said, in the deceptively sweet tone of voice that had lured many a plaintiff to an early demise, "then we'll drop the whole thing."

Maggy was not about to be so easily swayed. "Maybe I decided to splurge on something silky and beautiful. Did you ever think of that?"

"No," her sisters said in unison.

"No offense, Mags," said Ellie, "but you're a tad frugal."

"Cheap," said Claire.

"You two are unbelievable," Maggy said, shaking her head. "I can't believe this is what you think of me." *Cheap, boring, and sexless.*

"Then tell us what's going on," Claire demanded. "We feel responsible. My God, what if you'd taken up with some crazed lunatic and the cops found your body at the bottom of a bog? How do you think we'd feel, knowing it was all our fault?" Claire had always tended toward melodrama.

"I'm thirty-five years old. I absolve you of all responsibility. I think I'm capable of making my own decisions."

Claire and Ellie exchanged looks.

"I saw that," Maggy said. "Do you think I'm blind?"

"No," said Ellie, "but you've been married most of your life. It's the millennium, honey. Things have changed."

"I think I know that."

"So where did the robe come from?" Claire asked. "Tell us that, and I promise we'll leave you alone."

Her sisters watched, open-mouthed, as Maggy draped the gorgeous robe over her shoulders and let it slide down to her ankles. She wrapped it around her body and breathed in the memory of his skin. "Kmart," she said with a smile. "It came from Kmart."

"I'm sure she's lying," Claire said to Ellie as she drove her sister home.

"Of course she's lying," Ellie said. "You don't find robes like that at Kmart."

Claire sighed in exasperation. "I'm not just talking about the robe. I think she's hiding something. You did notice she didn't touch her pizza, and pepperoni's her favorite."

"She did seem distracted," Ellie said, "but I just don't think Maggy would know how to keep this kind of secret."

Claire shot her sister a withering look. "You'd be surprised how well you can lie when you're embarrassed."

"She didn't look embarrassed to me."

"Of course she was embarrassed," said Claire. "Didn't you see the way she blushed when we noticed that new silk robe?"

Ellie sighed deeply. She had a lifelong love affair with beautiful clothes. "That certainly was one gorgeous piece of cloth, wasn't it?"

"Kmart," Claire said, shaking her head. "Does she think we were born yesterday? You don't find robes like that at Kmart." Or, for that matter, at any store with the word *mart* in it.

"She was going to tell us everything," Ellie said. "I don't know what stopped her."

"Think about it," Claire said as they came to a stop at the intersection near Ellie's house. "We found her that morning in a ratty bathrobe and pajamas. Now she turns up with that silk wonder. I think the meaning's pretty clear, don't you?"

Ellie started to laugh. "Maybe she bought it to drive car pool."

Claire laughed despite herself. "That does sound like Mags, doesn't it?"

"Let's face it," Ellie said, "our big sister just isn't the secret lover type. I think we jumped to the wrong conclusion."

"That still doesn't explain the robe."

Ellie thought for a moment. "She was in A.C., after all. She probably won a few bucks at a slot machine and decided to splurge."

"And bought the robe with her winnings?" Claire asked.

"Exactly. You know there's no way Mags would feed those coins back into the machine. She'd go and use them to buy something that would last."

Claire had to agree that the idea made sense, but she couldn't help feeling disappointed. It had been a long time since she believed in fairy tales. It would have been nice to see one up close and personal.

Charlie burst into the house at eight o'clock sharp. Maggy was in the kitchen, wrapping leftover pizza for the freezer when she heard the dogs start barking the joyous canine chorus that meant her son was home. She wiped her hands on a dish towel then called out, "I'm in here, honey!"

He bounded into the room then threw himself at her like a human cannonball. He was nine years old going on ninety, and she never knew if he was going to strangle her in a bear hug or push her away with an embarrassed, "Aw, Ma . . ."

"Missed you," she said, ruffling his thick, dark blond hair with her fingers. "You look like you grew while I was gone."

"Mrs. G. made lasagna for supper," he said, sniffing the air. "Did you bring in pizza?"

"I know how much you like Mrs. G's lasagna," Maggy said. "Don't tell me you still have room for pizza!"

"One slice," he said, hopping around in front of her the way he did when he was a very little boy. "Pepperoni, right?"

"Of course pepperoni," she said, and they high-fived each other. "Is there any other kind?" She nuked him a slice, poured a small glass of milk, then sat down opposite him at the kitchen table. How she loved this sweet, uncomplicated little boy of hers. She knew that in a few years he would turn into a sullen stranger who was forced to live under her roof and obey the rules she set up specifically to torture him, but right now he was the light of her life. "So did you have fun with Kyle and Jeremy?"

He shrugged. "Yeah, I guess." She resisted the urge to lean across the table and dab at his milk moustache with a napkin. "We played with Kyle's trains, but mostly we watched videos."

"Anything good?"

"*Jurassic Park, Lost World,* and *Godzilla,*" he said, big blue eyes shining at the memory. "Kyle owns all three of them!"

"Wow," said Maggy. "That's one lucky boy." Charlie owned *Jurassic Park* and *Godzilla,* but she still hadn't bought him a copy of *Lost World.* The look on his face made her decide to add it to the Christmas list.

He gobbled the pizza and drank some milk. She set out a plate of chocolate chip cookies for the two of them. She nibbled at the edges of one while he told her all about Kyle's electric train setup in the basement. She had the feeling Kyle's father was the one who got the most use out of the elaborate and quite sophisticated setup, but she kept that observation to herself.

"So," she said, patting her hair, "do you notice anything different?"

He squinted at her over his bright red drinking glass. "Yeah," he said. "You cut off your hair. Can I have some more milk, Ma?"

Maggy took the dogs out for a walk around nine o'clock. The rain had finally stopped, and the pavement glistened beneath the street lamps. Here and there a plume of woodsmoke curled up into the creamy night sky, reminding her that winter wasn't far away. Tigger and Data weren't much interested in getting their paws wet. They stepped cautiously, casting aggrieved looks back at Maggy, who only laughed.

"You weigh more than I do," she said as they rounded the corner. "A little rain won't hurt you."

She enjoyed these evening walks. Sometimes she thought that was why she'd always loved dogs, so she'd have an excuse to go out after supper and let her mind roam. Charles had never been much of an evening walker. Neither were her children. So it had become a solitary pleasure for Maggy, a time to reflect on her day. She missed the walks terribly on Tuesday and Thursday nights when she was at school and the kids cared for Tigger and Data; sometimes those walks were all that kept her sane.

Tonight, however, not even her walk was enough to calm her. She felt unsettled, restless inside herself, as if she'd been gone for years rather than a weekend. Her sisters' remarks had gotten under her skin and made her wonder if anyone on earth had the slightest idea what she was about. If tonight was any indication, it didn't seem as if they did. Both of them had had their share of romantic flings. They'd fallen in love, made mistakes, wept a lot, then gotten over it. Why couldn't she have the same rights and privileges?

Maggy was the only one who chose to marry and raise children, and when she came back home after the divorce, they'd treated her like a returning warrior coming home from battle, tired but triumphant. Just like old times, they said, gathering around Maggy's kitchen table for cheap wine and great talk. Then when the wine and the talk were over, Claire and Ellie would dance back into their exciting lives, happy in the knowledge that Maggy would be waiting right where they left her.

She'd tried to tell them about Conor, but they weren't listening. She hadn't meant to spill the beans, but they'd looked so shocked when they saw her beautiful silk robe that she couldn't hold herself back. She blurted out the truth—that Kama Sutra remark still made her blush— and wouldn't you know it? They hadn't believed a word. They thought she was making it all up simply to get under their skins. For a moment there, she thought Claire believed her. The talk of condoms had been both sweet and vaguely annoying. Then *poof!* She was back to being boring Maggy in their eyes, the only living, breathing, virgin mother of two in the state of New Jersey.

She thought of Conor, how in two days he had uncovered more about her true self than her sisters had discovered in a lifetime. Oh, she knew that Claire and Ellie loved her. Love was never in question. It was just that there were some people in the world who demanded to be noticed and others who seemed to be just this side of invisible, and she knew she belonged to the latter group, not by choice but by circumstance. She'd always been willing to take a step back so her little sisters could step forward into the spotlight; that ability translated well to marriage and motherhood. After awhile, you forgot there was any other way to live.

When she and Charles divorced, she could no longer

pretend that was true. Her life would never be the same again, and if she wanted that new life to be a good one, she would have to create it herself. Moving back to Montgomery was the first step. Buying a house. Getting a job. Going back to school.

Taking a lover.

The words alone flooded her with urgent heat. She had been fine, just fine, as she was. With the way things were. Her days were busy, and so were her nights. Not with splendor, perhaps, but with books and study and the on-going work of motherhood. She was a warm and passionate woman by nature, but she'd learned to do without. After awhile, she even convinced herself that doing without wasn't that bad, that when you didn't have all the messy emotions associated with sex and love to worry about, you could focus much better on the things that were really important.

Now that she'd met Conor, she couldn't remember what those things might be.

She felt connected to her body in a way she hadn't in ages. All of one piece. The sensual and the intellectual and the spiritual all working together to make her feel as if she could conquer the world. She hadn't known what she was missing until she found him, and now she couldn't imagine why on earth she'd said they should wait seven days before they saw or spoke to each other again. She must have been temporarily insane to suggest such a ridiculous thing.

You're in a fog, Maggy. You need time to regain your perspective.

Time wouldn't change the way she felt about him. It would only make her long for him more.

Besides, for all you know, he's already forgotten all about you.

Impossible. She'd seen the look in his eyes when they said good-bye, and she knew he shared her feelings.

You don't know that for a fact. Cape May weekends aren't real life.

Tigger sneezed.

Data scratched.

Maggy sighed.

Real life. No doubt about it.

She turned and headed for home.

"Get out of here!" Nicole screamed at her little brother as he ran from the room. "If you so much as breathe on me again, I'll kill you!"

She considered throwing the cordless phone at him, but it might break and then she couldn't finish telling Melissa about her weekend with Aunt Claire, which was what she had been doing before that moron she was related to snuck in and tried to steal her diary.

"So, as I was saying"—she threw herself across the bed and put her feet up on the headboard—"Aunt Claire thought I should maybe lose the purple hair and go auburn."

"Nooooo!" Melissa sounded like she was having a cow. "I love your purple hair!"

"Me, too," said Nicole, pulling a strand across her face so she could inspect the ends for splits, "but Aunt Claire says purple stopped making a statement last winter."

"Huh?" She could just imagine Melissa's little face all scrunched up in a puzzled frown. "I don't get it."

Melissa didn't read the fashion magazines the way Nicole did, so she didn't know all about how everything you put on, every choice you made, said something about who you were and what you believed in. Purple hair might be a statement in tired old middle-of-nowhere New Jersey, but it was a big yawn in New York.

"Aunt Claire knows this stuff," she said. "She—oh, wait a sec, Missy. Call waiting!" Her heart started to pound like crazy. Maybe it was Steve DeVito. Her mom had forgotten to leave the answering machine on all weekend, so maybe he'd been calling and calling and nobody was home and now he was calling one last time and there was no way she'd miss that, not even for Melissa who was most definitely her best friend in the known universe. She took a deep breath then said, "Hello?" in the sexiest voice she could muster.

"I couldn't wait, Maggy." It was a man, and it wasn't Daddy. "Seven days was six and a half too many."

"Who is this?" she demanded, sitting straight up. And what was all that seven days stuff?

He took a second to answer. "Sorry," he said. He sounded like he was forcing himself to smile. "This is Conor Riley. I'm calling for Maggy. Is she there?"

"No, she isn't," Nicole said in the snippy voice her mother hated. Conor Riley. What kind of dumb name was that, anyway? Puh-leeze. You couldn't get more Irish if you tried.

"Do you know when she'll be back?"

"She's walking the dogs." *Like it's any of your business.*

He got real quiet. *Fine,* she thought. *I don't want to talk to you, either.*

"Okay," he said finally. "Tell her I called and that I'll call her back."

She mumbled something, he thanked her, then she clicked over to Melissa.

"Where'd you go?" Missy demanded. "I fell asleep waiting for you."

"Some guy calling for my mom," she said.

"A guy!" She could almost imagine Missy's brown eyes popping out of her head. "Your mom's got a boyfriend?"

The idea made Nicole shiver. "Yuck. He's probably some loser from school who wants to borrow her homework." Although that seven days stuff didn't sound like he was talking schoolwork. She remembered what Aunt

Claire had said downstairs, something about her mom meeting a man, but they teased her mom like that all the time, mainly because there wasn't a man anywhere on the horizon. Like her mom would go off and be with some guy and hide it from the rest of them. No way that would happen. Her mom would probably call a family meeting before she held his hand.

"So what about your hair? I don't get it. Why can't you make a purple statement?"

Nicole stretched back out on the bed and settled down to explain the facts of fashion life to her innocent best friend. That was much more fun than thinking about her mom any day.

TEN

"Now, stay off the sofas," Maggy warned Data and Tigger as she unclipped their leashes. "At least until your paws are dry."

She knew it was borderline crazy, speaking to dogs that way, but she figured she had at least as good a chance of getting Data and Tigger to obey her as she had of getting a similar response from her kids. Or so it sometimes seemed.

The pups showed no interest in the sofas. They jostled her playfully and bumped cold wet noses against her hands and arms until she gave each of them a huge hug. They were baby giants, and sometimes she forgot that inside those huge bodies beat hearts just past puppyhood.

"At least you're glad I'm home," she said as she kicked off her shoes and started for the staircase. Nicole's chilly reception still hurt. She told herself it didn't matter, that her daughter was fifteen, and fifteen was a volatile age, but that did nothing to take away the sting. She loved her daughter without reservation, but there was nothing easy about their relationship. Not at all the way it was between Maggy and her son. Charlie was bright and sunny and uncomplicated, everything his sister wasn't.

"Par for the course," her mother said every time Maggy broached the topic. "Little boys love their mothers. Little girls' hearts belong to their daddies."

She closed her eyes for a second, trying to conjure up an image of her father. Don Halloran had been dead twenty-five years, yet she could still remember the way he smelled of cigar smoke and lemony aftershave, the way his dark brown hair gleamed with auburn highlights in the sun just like her Nicole's hair did.

Each year, it grew a little harder to remember his face, and she knew that before long, the day would come when she would know him only through photographs and even then just barely.

But, oh, how she remembered the day he died. She'd turned ten the week before and she was feeling her oats. That morning she'd planted herself in the middle of the kitchen and stated in no uncertain terms that there were quite enough babies in that house and she didn't want to see any more come along. Her sisters were two and three years old at the time, and Maggy could see which way the wind blew. The little ones were taking over the place, and it was time to take a stand before it was too late. Her father had been sitting at the kitchen table, nursing a second cup of coffee, and he looked over at her mother. She could still see that look. His eyes crinkled when he laughed, and his lean cheeks suddenly grew very round. The look he gave her mother was so filled with love and joy that Maggy could see it right now as if it were yesterday.

It wasn't yesterday, of course. It was a very long time ago, the last time she saw her father alive. Sister Mary Aloysius came into history class that afternoon and whispered something to Sister Mary Benedetta. They turned toward Maggy, and she started to cry. The other little girls started to cry, too, even though they didn't know what was going on.

"Your dear daddy was in an accident," Sister Benedetta said as the two nuns led a crying Maggy from the classroom. "We're going to take you home so you can be a comfort to your momma and sisters."

Maggy didn't know how she was supposed to do that, but she would try her best if they thought that was the right thing to do. Twenty-five years later, she was still trying.

She paused on the landing in front of Nicole's closed bedroom door. Not her favorite memory. She had been a daddy's girl, same as Nicole, and she'd missed him so much she thought her heart would break in two. Nicole's father, thank God, was still alive, but they were apart, and she wondered if her little girl's heart felt like it was breaking apart.

"Nic?" She tapped lightly on the door. "Can I come in?"

No answer.

"Nic?"

"Come in if you want."

It wasn't exactly an engraved invitation, but Maggy knew it was as close as she would get to one at the moment. Nicole was sitting cross-legged in the middle of the bed. A half-dozen fashion magazines were scattered across the mint green and white quilt, along with a tube of mascara, a handful of eye shadows, and an eyelash curler. Nicole was writing something in a looseleaf binder.

"Mind if I sit down?"

Nicole shrugged. "It's a free country."

How many times had she said the same thing to her own mother? She sat down at the foot of the bed next to a copy of *Elle*. A lovely young woman smiled up at her. "You know," said Maggy, "she looks a little bit like you."

Nicole's head shot up. "You think?"

"Yes," Maggy said. "The eyes and nose. Definitely a resemblance."

Nicole ducked her head, and a curtain of purple drifted across her cheek. *Keep your mouth shut, Maggy. Just once don't say a thing about her purple hair.*

"There's leftover pizza in the fridge," she said, yearning to lean forward and smooth the hair from her daughter's face the way she did when she was a baby.

"What kind?"

"Pepperoni and mushroom."

Nicole wrinkled her nose. "Together?"

Maggy laughed. "Separately. I know you don't want anything else touching your pepperoni." She waited for her daughter to laugh. It was an old family joke that apparently was no longer funny. "Did Daddy call this weekend?"

"How would I know?" Nicole shot back. "I wasn't here, and you forgot to turn on the answering machine."

"Sorry, honey. If you like, you can give him a call tomorrow after school." *I know how much you miss him. I missed my own father, too.*

Nicole shrugged. Maggy hadn't the slightest idea what that shrug meant. She stood up. "Well," she said, "I think it's time for me to get some sleep." She reached over and stroked her daughter's hair. So soft. So silky. So purple. "Don't forget to set your clock."

"I won't."

It was probably the longest conversation they'd had in at least six months. Maggy hated for it to end, but she knew the dangers of prolonging contact with an unpredictable teenage girl. She opened her mouth and was about to say good night when the phone rang. She frowned. "You know what I told you about phone calls after nine o'clock." Sometimes the rules sounded arbitrary, but structure and boundaries were important. Still, she hated always feeling like the heavy, something that was unavoidable in a single-parent home.

Nicole rolled her eyes and reached for the cordless. "It's for you," she said, pushing the phone toward Maggy. "Same guy who called before."

"Somebody called before?" *Calm down, Maggy. It can't be him.*

"Yeah," said Nicole. "Sorry. I forgot to tell you."

Maggy's heart was beating so fast that she felt dizzy. Silly. Foolish. She was behaving like one of Nicole's friends. Suddenly, she became aware of her daughter's curiosity, and she gathered her composure and took the phone.

"I couldn't wait." Conor's voice, deep and thrilling, spun through the wires.

"So I see." She had to work very hard to sound friendly but casual.

"I take it that was your daughter who answered."

"Yes, it was."

"And that she's right there, listening."

"Absolutely. Why don't you hold on a second, and I'll take it in another room." She pressed the hold button, then stood up. "Don't go to bed too late, honey," she said, leaning over and kissing the top of her baby girl's eggplant head.

Nicole pointed toward the phone cradled against Maggy's chest. "Do you know him from school?"

"No," Maggy said. "He's a new friend." She wouldn't lie to her daughter, but she also wasn't ready for total disclosure.

Nicole said nothing.

"Lights out by midnight, okay?"

She affected a casual attitude but secretly thought it miraculous that the fireworks and shooting stars going off inside her heart weren't visible to the naked eye.

"I'm sorry I took so long," she said to Conor as she

curled up on the window seat in the corner of her bedroom.

"No problem," Conor said. "If this is a bad time, I—"

"No!" She caught herself, then laughed and lowered her voice. "I mean, I'm so glad you called."

"I didn't wait the seven days."

"I would have been disappointed if you had." She leaned back against the pillows, smiling like the silly romantic fool she apparently was.

"I had to call and see if you were real."

"Oh, I'm real enough," she said, cradling the phone closer. "You should have seen the look on Nicole's face when she handed me the cordless."

"Hope I didn't cause any trouble."

"Of course not. She's at that age where everything I do is either uncool, embarrassing, or downright stupid."

"Where does this fit in?"

"This might be off the chart."

"I miss you," he said.

Her breath caught. "I miss you, too."

"I shouldn't have let you go."

His words hit her like champagne, bubbling and cartwheeling through her veins. "I had to leave," she said. "I have this whole other life . . ." And so did he, even if she knew very little about his day-to-day life as a cop.

"I want to see you again."

She laughed softly. Definitely champagne. "I feel the same way."

She told him her schedule, and he whistled low. He made light of his own commitments and said he would meet her any place, any time that worked for her.

"Why don't I pick you up tomorrow morning and we'll catch breakfast before you go to work?"

"No!" *Good grief, Maggy, you sound downright hysterical.* "I mean, I don't have much time in the morning, and this is car pool week and all . . ." She let her words drift away and hoped he would understand.

"Too close to home."

She exhaled on a sigh. "Yes," she said. "I'm not ready to share you just yet with anybody." *Listen to you. You sound like you believe there's a future here.*

"I'll take you however I can get you."

"Me, too," she whispered. "I feel the same way."

"There's a lot I want to say to you, Maggy."

She closed her eyes and saw the cottage in Cape May, the roaring fire in the fireplace, that magical bed. She felt his hands on her body, his breath hot and moist against her inner thighs, the sound of intense·pleasure he made when he entered her that sent her straight over the edge into ecstasy.

"Tomorrow," she said, feeling dizzy with remembered pleasure. "I have two free hours in the afternoon between work and car pool."

There was a diner on Route 18 they both knew and loved.

"The Cadillac," he said. She could almost see him grinning.

"The only diner in New Jersey with big pink tail fins suspended over the front door." She was grinning herself.

"Twelve-thirty?" he asked.

"Noon," she said. She doubted she could wait any longer to see him again.

"A booth," Conor said to the hostess of the Cadillac Diner the next morning, "no smoking section, near the back, by the window." He wanted to be able to see Maggy when she pulled into the parking lot, watch her as she walked into the restaurant. They had one hundred and twenty minutes to spend together, and he wasn't going to waste a second.

"How many?" The hostess had a swirl of platinum blond hair that reminded him of cotton candy at the circus but without the pink dye. He ate at the Cadillac at least once a week, and he'd never seen her hair move.

"Two," he said.

She plucked two enormous menus from the stack near the coat rack. "Follow me."

Her hair never moved, and she never smiled. Hostesses were supposed to smile and be friendly. That was part of the job description for every other diner hostess in the state. She had to be one of the owners. There was no other explanation for her continued employment.

She stopped in front of a booth halfway up the aisle. "How's this?"

He pointed toward the last booth in the row. "That one would be better."

No reaction from the hostess. She flatfooted her way to the designated spot. She tossed the two heavy menus down on the table. "Enjoy your meal." All done without ever once making eye contact.

He shrugged out of his leather jacket and hung it from the hook behind his seat. He knew exactly what she was doing. Hell, he did it all the time himself. You had to do it in some jobs or lose what was left of your sanity. There was a way to be there without being there, and the hostess with the cotton candy hair had mastered the technique. That was how you managed to do what you needed to do without giving away any more of yourself than you had to.

Sometimes he wondered if somewhere along the way he'd gotten too fucking good at it, and it had cost Bobby his life. At the meeting this morning, his lawyer had told him that kind of thinking was counterproductive. "Nobody's accusing you of anything," Glenn had said, rubbing the bridge of his nose with index finger and thumb. "All the prosecution is looking for is a recitation of events as you saw them. This is as close to an open-and-shut case against the Walker kid as it could possibly be."

Everyone told him that. Other cops. The shoe store

owner who'd been at the scene. Hell, even Walker himself had confessed to EMS workers, only to recant as soon as he was put into the hands of a good attorney. There wasn't a doubt in anybody's mind that Allen Walker shot Detective Bobby DiCarlo and killed him on the night of October 15, one year ago.

So why couldn't he let go? Why couldn't he make his peace with the whole fucking deal and get on with it and quit beating himself up? "You did everything you could," the shoe store owner had told him time and again. "I saw you. I know what happened."

Bullshit, he thought as he looked out the window and waited. There was one piece of the equation that they all kept getting wrong. You don't let your partner take a bullet meant for you.

Maggy blinked and realized Father Roarke was saying something to her. "I'm sorry, Father. What was that again?"

"Is something wrong, Maggy?" he asked. "Mrs. Martinez and I were asking your opinion of the menu for the Saint Jude's Golden Anniversary Dinner, and you looked right through us."

"Will you look at that," said Eileen Martinez with a sly smile. "Our Maggy's blushing."

"I am not," Maggy protested. "I was distracted by—" Distracted by what? The rectory was silent as the grave. There wasn't so much as a bird chirping outside. *Oh, wait! What was that ungodly racket?* "That noise!" Bless you, she thought as the furnace, which was pretty close to celebrating a golden anniversary of its own, hissed and sputtered and clanked up a storm down in the basement. "I think that furnace is on its last legs."

"All the more reason to consider mounting a fundraiser next year," said Father Roarke. "We'll need a strong proposal to convince the bishop to give us his approval." He looked over at Maggy, who was still trying to gather her wits about her. "I think you're the one to handle it, Maggy."

She almost cried. The last thing she needed with her schedule was one of these long-term, free-form projects that depended almost solely on her facility with the written word. Sure, she was majoring in journalism, but that didn't mean she knew how to put together the kind of proposal Father Roarke was looking for. She had half a mind to tell him that maybe this time he needed to look elsewhere for assistance. Remind him that she was only a part-time employee, and an underpaid one at that, and she simply didn't have the time to put into such a demanding project. Of course, if she did that, Father Roarke would turn on his charm—and after eighty years of practice, his charm was considerable—and she'd give in anyway. Why not save them both the trouble and give in right up-front?

"You know I'll do my best," she said, then pushed back her chair and stood up. "I know it's a few minutes early, but would you mind terribly if I left? I'd be happy to come in at eight tomorrow to make up the difference."

"I hope there's no problem at home," Father Roarke said. He was such a happy, cherubic sort that it took enormous effort for him to look serious. His occasionally edgy sermons were often at odds with his rosy countenance.

"No problem at all," she said, "just an appointment on Route 18, and with traffic and all . . ." She told herself she wasn't lying; she simply wasn't volunteering any information, something she seemed to be doing a lot of lately.

The priest's smile returned. "We want the best for you, Margaret," he said, and she winced at the sound of her given name. "We want you to be happy."

She felt a tad guilty as she hurried to her car. Father Roarke had been part of her life for as long as she could remember. People talked about the impersonal nature of most organized religions, how the men and women in positions of power cared for nothing but money. You couldn't prove it by Saint Jude's. When her father died, it seemed the entire parish rallied around to help her mother. Father Roarke became a member of the family, offering a male perspective on life that was sorely missing in their all-female household. He was a dear man, and she loved him. Anytime somebody asked her why she worked so hard for so little money, she told them that it was a privilege to work for Father Roarke, and that if she didn't have children to support, she'd work there for nothing. Talk like that always made Ellie roll her eyes. "Better enroll in a few business courses," she had said the last time she overheard that particular remark.

She slid open the door to her minivan and climbed in. She had an hour to make the half-hour drive, which meant she could afford to spend a few minutes touching up her makeup and brushing her hair and thanking God that Claire had picked out some clothes for her birthday. She'd fallen back on the icy-blue sweater set again but this time with the navy blue pleated skirt and sheer hose. She peered at her reflection in the rearview mirror.

Oh, no. Nicole was right. Her ears looked huge without all of that hair to cover them up. What had possessed her to let Andre hack it all off? She looked like a wombat. She wondered if it was too late to stop at the mall and buy a wig. The thought was so absurd that she burst into laughter as she started the engine. This wasn't a blind date. He knew what she looked like. He knew what every part of her looked like, for that matter. He'd never seen her with anything but seriously short hair. There was no reason to go crazy.

Still, her eye makeup seemed to lack pizzazz. Her skin tone wasn't as even as she might have liked. A trip to the dentist for a bleaching and cleaning wouldn't have hurt and, while she was at it, an exfoliation, a facial, bikini waxing, and breast implants. "Why don't you just hire Winona Ryder to go in your place?" she asked the woman who looked back at her.

She told herself there was no reason to feel so nervous, but that didn't stop her hands from shaking as she drove toward the Caddy Diner. What if the magic was gone? Things like that happened all the time. A man and a woman meet, there's instant attraction, they have a red hot few days, and then *pow!* It's over as fast as it had begun. They might take a look at each other by the harsh fluorescent light of the diner and wonder what on earth they'd been thinking.

By the time she pulled into a parking spot in front of the diner, she had convinced herself that the weekend had been an aberration brought on by poor judgment and insufficient lighting. Her sisters were right. She wasn't the kind of woman who went off to Atlantic City and had a fling with a total stranger. Her sisters knew that. Her mother knew that. Everyone who'd ever met her knew that.

Everyone except for Conor. Oh, God. What if he thought she made a habit of picking up guys at hotels and spending the weekend with them? She wasn't sure if the thought made her want to laugh or weep. The whole thing was so far from her own personal reality that it was hard to get a handle on it.

Can't be that far away from your reality, Maggy, or that weekend in Cape May would never have happened.

She hated that little voice. It popped up every time she tried to rationalize her way out of a sticky situation. What she did wasn't wrong; it was simply out of character. So far out of character as to seem downright surreal.

Maybe it wasn't out of character. Maybe it's a part of you that you never allowed to exist.

Sex with Charles had always been good. She'd never had the slightest complaint on that score. When they first divorced, it took some doing to adjust to a more monastic

life. She threw herself into work and school and being
the world's best mother to her kids, and after awhile, she
was too busy and too tired to remember how it used to
be. She was reasonably sure that how it used to be didn't
come close to how it was with Conor. Explosive, vol-
canic—name your own fiery adjective—and it was all
heightened by a sense of tenderness that breached her
defenses before she had a chance to take a deep breath.

She didn't imagine that. She couldn't have, since nothing remotely like it was in her emotional vocabulary.
This was uncharted territory, and she was thrilled and
terrified and everything in between.

Traffic on Route 18 was heavy but moving. She
whizzed past a huge Border's Bookstore, three Mexican
restaurants, at least six fast-food joints, a cluster of movie
theaters, and more strip malls than you could count on
an abacus. She passed the world's biggest Chinese restaurant, the one that looked like a converted bowling
alley, then felt a wave of dizziness wash over her. The
diner was just ahead, at the point where the road widened
and the stores gave way to trees. The thought of seeing
him again made her mouth water.

She'd never seen the parking lot when it wasn't
crowded, but the goddess of lovestruck women was
watching over her, a spot in front of the window opened
up as she pulled in the driveway. She couldn't help smiling as she whipped into the spot next to a Mazda the
color of her daughter's hair. The dashboard clock read
11:50. Should she sit there in the car and wait until the
stroke of twelve before she went in so he wouldn't know
she was early, or should she go in anyway and claim a
booth for them?

For all she knew, he might already be in there, watching her from a window table, wondering why she was
still sitting in the car, staring at her hands trembling on
the wheel.

This isn't a lifetime commitment, she told herself as

she stepped into the lobby, which was lined with phones and arcade games and real estate promotions. *If you see it's not going well, you can make an excuse and leave.*

She was greeted by the deadpan hostess with a froth of meringue-white, Marie Antoinette hair piled high atop her head. She tried not to notice the kohl-rimmed eyes or the chewing gum. It was always a losing battle.

"Table for one?"

"Two," Maggy said, trying hard not to gloat. "I don't know if he's here yet."

"We got a single in no smoking. Big, lots of hair, leather jacket."

Maggy nodded. "That sounds like him."

"He's been waiting back there over an hour." The hostess gave her a quick once-over then said, "This way."

He'd been waiting for her since before eleven. It hardly seemed possible. Nobody ever waited for her. They never had to. She was the one who showed up early for appointments, who had a clock in her bathroom so she wouldn't lose track of time in the tub and get to classes late.

Don't go reading anything into it, Maggy. Maybe he was between appointments and had some time to kill.

Maybe, maybe not. All she knew was that he was somewhere in this room, and any second, any moment, she'd blink and there he would be.

They walked swiftly past an elderly couple who were entertaining a halfhearted argument about poached eggs, a middle-aged man and woman who seemed to have nothing to say to each other, and a young mother with three children, all of whom were intent upon pummeling the nearest sibling. The woman looked up at her, and Maggy couldn't help but smile in sympathy. She knew how it felt to be overwhelmed to the point of tears by it all, ashamed of the fact that the ones you loved most in the world could drive you totally mad in less time than it took to sneeze.

Then she saw him, and everything else dropped away.

He saw her the moment she pulled into the parking lot. The minivan came as a surprise. That she was as lovely as he remembered didn't.

She sat behind the wheel for what seemed a long time, and he had an ugly moment when he thought she was about to change her mind and wheel out of the parking lot. He wanted to bang on the window like Dustin Hoffman in *The Graduate* and yell out her name, but before he had a chance to make an ass out of himself, she stepped from the vehicle and started for the door. She wore blue and she walked like a queen. Those were the two things he noticed through his intense relief.

The hostess with the towering white helmet of hair dwarfed Maggy as she led her toward his booth. He glimpsed an arm, a graceful hand, a fleeting peek at her shiny dark brown hair, which seemed to glow with highlights of auburn and gold. Maggy paused for a second, and he caught sight of her smile. He didn't know who she was smiling at or why, and the hot stab of jealousy that ripped through his midsection shocked the hell out of him. He wasn't the jealous type. Never had been. This was a whole new ballgame.

She didn't realize he was watching her. She looked a little nervous, a little scared, too young to be the mother of a teenager. Her gaze darted toward the kitchen, the dining room, the teenagers at the booth across the aisle, the parking lot, and then landed directly on him.

Everything stopped. The diner noises disappeared. The smells of bacon frying and hot coffee vanished. The entire room seemed to grow dark, pitching him forward into a black void, and then a split second before he fell, she smiled, and it was like the sun coming out for the first time on the first day and he was there to see it shine.

ELEVEN

She smiled with her whole face. Mouth, eyes, cheekbones, lashes, everything. Conor didn't know any other
way to describe it. She radiated joy, and he actually believed that some of that joy might have to do with him.

He leaped to his feet, almost toppling the hostess.

"You're here!" Maggy said, sounding so happy that
he felt like throwing back his head and laughing out loud.
Another woman might have feigned indifference, waited
for him to set the tone, but not her. She jumped right in
and said what was on her mind.

"I got here a little early," he said. He felt more like
a teenager than he had when he actually was one.

"I know," she said. "A whole hour early." She looked
so dazzled and pleased that he wished he'd spent the
night there waiting for her. Anything, if it meant seeing
her so happy.

They stood in the center of the aisle, smiling at each
other. He wasn't sure how it happened, but one moment
they were on opposite sides of the table, and the next she
was in his arms. He couldn't be near her and not kiss
her. Their lips touched briefly, sweetly, and his senses

reeled at the fragrant smell of her hair and skin. He wanted to slide his hand under her skirt and cup her against his palm and watch those wide blue eyes grow wider with pleasure and delight.

She blushed slightly, and he wondered if he had said something or had she simply read his mind. Nothing would surprise him. The connection between them was unlike anything he'd ever experienced.

They sat down across from each other. He wondered how it would feel to sit across from her every day. Would he ever get used to that sweet face, or would every morning feel like Christmas?

"I hate couples who sit all scrunched up together on the same side of the table," she said, wrinkling her nose in distaste. She had the faintest dusting of freckles across the bridge. He'd never noticed that before. "I'd much rather be able to see your face."

He reached across the table and covered her hands with his. "I'm glad you're here."

That world-class smile of hers was back. "So am I."

"I saw you pull in," he said. "For a second there I was afraid you were going to pull back out again."

"I thought about it. I was afraid I'd find out it had all been a dream and there was nothing between us after all."

"I don't know what it is, but it isn't a dream."

She met his gaze head-on. "I'm glad."

"I missed you," he said.

"I missed you, too. Isn't that ridiculous? This time last week we were strangers, and now . . ." She let her words trail away.

"We're lovers." He finished the sentence for her.

"Yes," she said. "Lovers."

They both laughed softly.

"I saw you leave Sunday," he told her. "I almost drove after you."

"I wish you had. You could have flagged down the limo."

"Probably ended up arrested," he said with a grin.

"You have friends in high places," she said, grinning back. "I'm sure they'd understand."

"One hundred eleven," he said, glancing at his watch.

"One hundred eleven what?"

"Minutes until we have to say good-bye."

Her breath caught. "I wish you hadn't said that. I want to pretend we have all day and all night."

So did he. He wanted to leave behind another unfinished meal and take her home with him. He wanted to lock the door behind them, build a fire in the fireplace, pour some wine, hold her, make love to her, sleep with her, listen to her stories, tell her some of his own, and then do it all over again. Maybe after a year or two, he might actually believe it was real, that she was real, because right now he wouldn't be surprised to wake up and discover he'd dreamed the entire thing.

Maggy felt the same way. High on emotion, excited, terrified because it was happening so hard and so fast and so real. It felt like fantasy, but it wasn't. He made her burn for him with all the fiery thrill of discovery, but he also felt like home. That was the strangest thing of all. Being with him felt familiar in the best possible way, as if they'd finally returned to the place where they were meant to be.

They both ordered western egg sandwiches and coffee. Destiny, they decided. Fate working her magic. If she'd needed further proof that they were meant for each other, she found it at the Cadillac Diner.

She told him about Saint Jude's while they drank their coffee and waited for the food. "I thought I'd just be typing letters and keeping up with Father Roarke's filing," she said, while he traced her wrist bone with the roughened tip of his right index finger, "but it's mushroomed into a good deal more than that.'' Saint Jude's sister parish in Honduras had been devastated by Hurricane Mitch in 1998, and the Saint Jude's parishioners had been working tirelessly to supply food, medicine, money, and most important of all, human power to help begin the slow process of rebuilding the area's infrastructure. ''When you don't see the suffering right in front of you on the nightly news, you forget.''

''That's human nature,'' he said. ''We're not hard-wired to dwell on pain.''

''Exactly. That's why we have to work very hard to maintain enthusiasm for this project.'' Thirty years, she told him. That's how long it would take to bring those areas back to where they'd been before Hurricane Mitch found them.

''And you'll still be here in thirty years?'' he asked her.

''I hope so,'' she said. ''I've spent my entire adult life packing and unpacking. I'm ready to put down roots again and stay awhile.''

They fell silent for a moment while the waitress delivered their coffee and sandwiches.

''They forgot your pickles,'' Maggy said. ''Here. Why don't you take one of mine?'' He gave her a funny look, and she groaned. ''Sorry. I'm so used to mediating food problems with the kids that I—''

He reached across the table and grabbed one of the two pickle slices. ''Hey,'' he said. ''You didn't hear me complaining, did you?''

She still felt foolish. ''It's so hard to shift gears,'' she said. ''Back when the kids were little, we were stationed in D.C., and it seemed there was always some fancy dinner we were required to attend. Once they made the mistake of seating me next to Charles's C.O., and I leaned right over and cut his filet for him.''

''What did he do?''

''He was a lovely man. When I finished cutting, he

reached for his fork and said sweetly, 'I can take it from here.' " She shook her head at the memory. "I wanted to crawl under the banquette and never come out."

"My sister Siobhan was so busy talking politics a few Thanksgivings ago that she cut my turkey and fed it to my ear before she realized what she was doing."

The image delighted Maggy, and she laughed. "How many kids does Siobhan have?"

"Six. The baby, Caitlin, was a fortieth birthday surprise."

Maggy's eyes widened, but then she realized she wasn't all that far away from turning forty herself. "I always wanted a big family," she said, fiddling with a packet of sugar. "With all the moving around we did, two was about as many as we were able to handle."

"I wanted my own basketball team," he said. "I didn't care if they were boys or girls, just so they had a great jump shot."

She pretended to frame him between her hands. "I can see you out there in the driveway with your crew. You'd be a tough coach."

"The toughest."

"But with a heart of gold."

He grinned at her. "Don't tell anyone. It'll blow the image."

"Your secret's safe with me." A gorgeous, sexy man who wasn't crazy and who wanted a big family. She whispered a prayer of thanks to Saint Jude, patron saint of the impossible. "My sisters used to say I was born in the wrong era. They think I should have been a rancher's wife, cooking for a big brood of strapping sons and sewing party dresses for my beautiful daughters."

"And what do you think?"

She drew in a deep breath and met his eyes. "I think that I was meant to be part of a family. I'm at my best when I'm near the people I love most in all the world." *This is who I am. This is what matters to me.*

He didn't say anything for what felt to Maggy like the longest silence in recorded history. She told herself it was better to know these things now, before they went any further, because this one was a deal-breaker.

"We all stuck pretty close to the old neighborhood, too," he said, and Maggy felt herself go weak with relief.

"Both of my sisters live within five minutes of the folks, and the rest of us aren't that far away, either."

"We're a dying breed. Most families are scattered from one end of the country to the other." His expression darkened, and she was instantly contrite. "Oh, God," she said. "I'm so sorry. Your son is in California."

"Maybe that's why I'm sticking close to the rest of them," he said.

"My ex didn't understand that."

"Neither did mine."

They forgot about their sandwiches and coffee. They forgot about the time. They forgot about everything but each other. They held hands across the tabletop and whispered to each other so the other patrons wouldn't hear. Twice the waitress walked by and pointedly glared at the unpaid check, but they ignored her. They'd make up for her inconvenience with a great tip.

Finally, Maggy forced herself to push back his sleeve and glance at his watch.

"Oh, God! It's after two o'clock. I have a meeting at school at three, and I'll never make it." Her usual school days were Tuesday and Thursday nights, but she'd asked for a special study date with some classmates, and she owed it to them to try to be on time.

He paid the bill, left an eye-popping tip that Maggy added to, then walked her to her van.

"I don't want you to leave," he said.

She slipped her key into the lock. "Believe me, I don't want to leave, but I have to."

He put his hands on her shoulders and turned her to face him. "Have dinner with me on Friday."

She hesitated. "I don't know if I should. I mean, I just went away for the weekend and—" *Nicole is fifteen, Maggy, and Charlie isn't that far behind. You have friends and family who'll watch them for an evening.* "Yes," she said, then "Yes," again. She threw back her head and said, "Yesyesyesyesyes!" until they were laughing too hard to speak.

"We'll make this work," he said as he drew her into his arms. "We'll find a way."

"You talk too much," she said. "Let's kiss."

He made an event out of kissing, a four-star, world-class Olympic gold medal event. Some men treated kissing as something they were forced to do, but not Conor. With him kissing was as slow and juicy and sensual and exciting as any of the other delights they'd shared. His lips were full and deliciously soft. She caught the lower one gently between her teeth and laughed at the way his eyes popped open in surprise. They were so close their lashes tangled. So close they were breathing the same breaths.

How unbearably sexy to watch your lover as you kissed him, to see that erotic haze soften his face and make his eyes glow like stirred embers. She wanted him so much that she was tempted to say to hell with school, to hell with her meeting, and drag him into the back of her minivan and have her way with him on a bed of Happy Meal containers and psychology texts.

"Your meeting," he said, his lips moving against hers in a way that made it hard for her to think clearly. "You'll be late."

"I don't care," she said, then pulled him close for another deeply delicious kiss, which unfortunately had to end because she was at heart the most dependable woman on earth.

"I'll call you tonight," he said as she settled herself in the driver's seat and buckled up. "What time's good for you?"

She thought for a second. Charlie surfed the Web for a while after supper every night, and Nicole usually fielded a half dozen calls before lights out. "Ten-thirty," she said. "Everyone will have had a shot at the phone by then, and I can claim a few parental privileges without facing an uprising."

"Ten-thirty," he said, kissed her one last time, then stepped back as she started the engine.

He watched her as she exited the parking lot and kept watching until she disappeared around the curve of Route 18.

She knew because she was watching him in the rearview mirror.

"What are you doing here?" Joe Wojtowicz said when Conor walked through the front door of the station house an hour later. "Thought you were off on some fancy-schmancy vacation."

"Nah," said Conor, shaking hands with the veteran cop he'd known since his first day with the squad. "A few days in A.C., that's all." A few days that had changed his life, but he wasn't about to share that, not even with an old pal.

"So how'd you do?" Joe asked.

Conor made a win some/lose some gesture with his right hand.

"That's better than Lady Luck treats me down there," Joe said with a laugh. "I told Patty I might as well hand over my wallet at the front desk and call us even. I can't catch myself a break."

Conor made sympathetic noises but didn't say much. He'd met Maggy down there. Lady Luck didn't get much better than that.

"So what brings you here today?" Joe asked when they ran out of A.C. talk.

I needed to touch base, Joe. I'm starting to feel as if

the doors are swinging shut on me. "I was in the area, so I figured I'd stop by and pick up my messages, maybe make a few calls while I was here."

"Wouldn't catch me here on my vacation."

"I'm not on vacation, Joe. Remember?" This sabbatical had been the suggestion of the chief of police, who timed it with the beginning of the murder trial.

"Listen," Joe said, "I'm not sure this is such a hot idea. Maybe you should put those phone calls off for another couple of weeks."

"Are you telling me I'm not welcome around here?" He tried to back his anger down a notch or two. This had nothing to do with Joe. Joe was only trying to help him.

"I'm not saying that." Joe looked so uncomfortable that Conor almost felt sorry for him. "I'm just saying the wind's not blowing in your favor right now. Denise was in on Friday. They had a little ceremony in Guttman's office. Gave her a plaque to commemorate Bobby's . . ."

"Death," Conor said. "You can say it. I was there. I know what happened."

Joe's hangdog face hung even lower. "You're not the only one missing Bobby, pal," he said. "We loved him, too."

Joe's words tore at his heart. He had a habit of forgetting other people hurt, too, that he wasn't the only one whose world stopped spinning when Bobby DiCarlo drew his last breath.

"So how was Denise?" he asked. It was as close to an apology as either man expected. "Did she bring the kids?"

"She left the kids with her mother," Joe said, "but she looked good. Smiled a little." *Not like at the funeral,* he was saying without saying it. *Not like that time when she screamed and called you a coward and a murderer.*

"So that's why the captain cut me out of the mix for

a few weeks," he said. "Didn't want me bumping into Denise."

"You'd have to ask him, man. I'm not gonna even guess what the captain was thinking."

Back when Bobby was alive, Denise had included him in all the family occasions from birthdays to Christmas. He was even godfather to their second child, Jennifer Marie. He hadn't seen Jenny in at least eight months.

"It hurts too much," Denise's mother had told him when he asked. "She can't look at you and not think about Bobby. Every time she sees you, she expects to see Bobby bringing up the rear like he always did. She just can't do it anymore, Conor."

So he backed away. There was nothing else he could do. She'd made her position clear, and he respected both her and Bobby's memory enough to comply with her wishes. Denise and the kids had been his link to Bobby, and without them, he felt guiltier and more alone than ever.

They all said they didn't blame him for Bobby's death. They all claimed they believed the reports that said Conor hadn't had a prayer in hell of getting to Bobby before that bullet did. You couldn't have saved Bobby, they'd told him. Not with the kid holding the gun at almost point-blank range. But as Conor walked back to his cube, he clearly saw what Joe was talking about. Something had changed. Old friends turned the other way when he walked past. The greetings he did get were perfunctory. The sense of anger and betrayal was everywhere. It used to be directed toward the kid who'd held the gun, but now it seemed it was aimed at him.

It surprised him. It shouldn't have, but it did. He'd failed when it mattered most, and that failure had cost his partner his life. There was no penance for that, no punishment beyond living with that failure every day for the rest of your life.

Detective Bobby DiCarlo's death had hit the township

hard. He was the first officer to die in the line of duty in the town's one-hundred-ten-year history. There was a sense of community outrage that such a thing could happen in their safe little town, followed by a deeper sense of sadness that now they were just like everyone else. Danger had their zip code and a road map, and nothing would ever be the same again.

Reporters had been dogging the story for the last year, and he knew there was some statewide interest in the case, too. Bobby's face would be plastered all over the six o'clock news again, along with the ugly details of the afternoon he was murdered. Conor dreaded the invasion of the cameras, the questions screamed at him by ambitious reporters, his own face plastered across the front page of the local papers for everyone to see.

Maggy. A cold sweat broke out on the back of his neck. She didn't know a thing about any of this. Or if she did, she hadn't yet associated any of it with him. She'd sensed his sadness. She'd thrown a stunner of a question his way that first day, and he'd come close to telling her everything, but he couldn't find the way to tell her that he'd let his partner die.

"Maggy!" Janine's voice was sharp. "If you're not going to pay attention, what's the point?"

Maggy blinked and struggled to bring her mind back to the subject at hand. "I'm sorry," she said, although she really wasn't. "I guess I'm a little distracted today." She'd been reliving Conor's kiss in lush and erotic detail, a far more fascinating subject than Principles of Crisis Management.

"If you're distracted, why don't we call it a day?" Janine suggested. "I don't know about you, but there's plenty of other stuff I could be doing."

"No," Maggy said, "I really appreciate the tutoring, Janine. I'll concentrate. I promise I will."

Janine looked extremely skeptical—and with good reason—but said she'd give Maggy another half hour before she had to leave.

Maggy swore she would make good use of the time and forced herself not only to pay attention, but to ask intelligent questions as well. As it turned out, that was asking quite a lot of her that day, because her normally agile brain was happily sitting in a corner playing "loves me, loves me not" with a fistful of daisies. Janine must think she was a total idiot for setting up the study date then flaking on her. She didn't blame the girl for being annoyed. Who wouldn't be? Still, she wondered what Janine would do if she sat her down and said, "I met a man this weekend, and we made love all night while the rain tapped against the windows and the fire roared in the grate. I can't eat, I can't sleep, I can't stop thinking about him."

"That's it!" Janine closed her textbook and stood up. "This is ridiculous, Maggy. You haven't heard one word I said."

"You're right," she said, too shocked to dissemble. "I haven't heard a single word."

"Is something wrong?" Janine softened just the tiniest bit. "This isn't like you at all."

"I know," said Maggy. "Isn't it wonderful? All because I met a man."

Janine's expression went from gloom to downright ecstatic. "Oh, Maggy!" She threw her arms around her. "Who? Where? When did this happen? Spill the beans, girl!"

"I met him this weekend," she said. "He's a cop. We saw each other in the parking lot and then in the lobby and finally in the restaurant. He came over and asked me to dance and . . ." She sighed happily. "What can I say? We fit."

"He's not married, is he? Please tell me he isn't married."

Maggy grinned. "He isn't married."

Janine hugged her again. "I'm so happy for you! A fling is exactly what you need to put a spring in your step."

I think it's more than a fling, Janine, she thought as she walked to her car a little later. *I think I'm falling in love.*

How she wished she could tell somebody, but her mother and sisters had no patience with romance.

It wasn't that the Halloran women didn't believe in love. They did. They just didn't believe it lasted more than forty-five minutes at any one time.

Rita, Maggy's mother, had made one good and one terrible marriage, and that was quite enough for her. Her second marriage had been brief and horrific, and the experience had soured her on the institution forever. Oh, she liked men well enough, but only on a temporary basis. Men, she said, were like library books: you didn't have to own one to enjoy him.

Claire and Eleanor were their mother's daughters. Ellie used her legal background to keep her relationship from progressing, hiding behind endless prenup language and arguments. Claire used her beauty, both as a shield and a weapon. Neither one believed happy marriages were possible. At least, not for women. They'd watched their mother and older sister very carefully, and the one thing they both agreed on was that they'd never make those mistakes. Maggy tried hard to explain that her marriage to Charles had been a good one that had amicably run its course, but she couldn't make them understand the difference between having a good husband and having a soul mate.

And she wanted a soul mate.

She believed in marriage and family and happy endings and maybe, just maybe, she'd met a man who believed in all of those things, too.

Maybe she'd met her soul mate.

TWELVE

"My own phone?" Nicole stared at her mother as if she'd double-pierced her nose and shaved her head for good measure. "Are you serious?"

Her mother reached out and ruffled her bangs, something Nicole usually hated. This time she put up with it. "Of course I'm serious. You and Charlie will have to share it, but I think it's time we became a two-phone family." She said something about getting the teen phone rate on it, but Nicole quit listening after the first few words. Her own phone! Now she could talk to Missy and Stacey for hours, and nobody could tell her it was time to hang up.

She threw her arms around her mom, which wasn't all that easy since she was five-foot-ten, and her mom barely tipped five feet. "This is better than Christmas," she said. "I can't believe I'm getting my own phone!"

Her mother hugged her back, and for a second Nicole remembered how much she used to love that feeling of being little and knowing that nothing bad could ever happen as long as her mom was around. She didn't feel that way much anymore, not since the divorce. Mostly she just felt scared, like she used to feel on the first day in a new school.

"Remember, you have to share the phone with your brother. I'm sure you can work that out between the two of you without any help from me." Her mom looked happy and kind of silly, like one of Nicole's friends, instead of a middle-aged woman.

"This is so exciting! I'm gonna call Missy and tell her right now."

Her mom glanced at the clock on the nightstand. "It's almost ten-thirty. You can tell her tomorrow at school."

"It's not too late. Missy'll be up for hours." Her mom had a funny look on her face, kind of happy and guilty at the same time. Nicole had never seen her look that way before, and it made her feel a little scared, even though she didn't exactly know why.

"Not tonight, honey. I need the phone for a while."

Suddenly Nicole knew the answer. "It's all because of that guy who called Sunday night, isn't it?" So that was the reason for the new phone. It wasn't like she cared about making her daughter happy. She wanted a phone all to herself so she could talk to some old spaz.

"Yes, it is, honey."

"Who is he?"

"His name is Conor."

"You go to school with him?" Stupid question. It wasn't like she hung out in singles bars or burned up the chat rooms.

"No, I don't."

Nicole tried not to look surprised, but she was. "So where'd you meet him?" The woman worked in a rectory, so it wasn't like she could meet a guy on the job.

Her mom didn't answer right away. She kind of looked away for a second, like she was thinking about what to say, then took one of those deep breaths that made your shirt flutter. "I met him last weekend."

At first, Nicole couldn't figure out what her mom was

talking about, but then she remembered. "You picked up some strange guy in Atlantic City?" Her voice climbed so high that she sounded like the cartoon characters on *Nickolodeon*.

"Yes, I met him in Atlantic City," her mom said, sounding a little bit annoyed. "Is there something wrong with that?"

"I can't believe this! You don't even know this guy, and you gave him our home phone number. You'd kill me if I ever did something like that."

"I don't like that tone of voice, Nicole."

"I don't care! Daddy wouldn't want you giving out our number to a stranger."

"This isn't your father's business; it's mine. I think you can trust me not to put any of us in danger."

Her mother's voice shook, a sure sign that Nicole had pissed her off big time. She looked hurt, but that was just too bad. Nicole was hurt too, not that anybody cared. Nobody ever asked her how she felt about the divorce or moving to New Jersey or Daddy marrying Sally or just about anything else she could think of. Things just happened all around her, and it seemed like there was nothing she could do to stop any of it.

Conor and Maggy spent four hours on the telephone Monday night, then seven hours on Tuesday. Maggy's decision to invest in a second phone line had been a stroke of genius. These calls were their courtship. They told each other about their childhoods, their triumphs, and their humiliations. Conor told her about the time he asked the class beauty queen to the senior prom and couldn't believe his good luck when she said yes without a moment's hesitation. Two weeks later, he couldn't believe his bad luck when she backed out on him in favor of the quarterback. Maggy told him about being the last girl to be asked to dance at the church youth center socials and how badly she'd wanted to hide in the coatroom until it was all over. He told her he would have asked her to dance the second he saw her. She told him she would never have backed out on the prom. Small things in the framework of two lives, silly promises, but with each shared memory, their hearts grew more entwined.

"Meet me for coffee," he said as the first rays of sun gilded the trees in front of her house on Wednesday morning.

"I can't," she said, curling her body around the phone. "Car pool day."

"Meet me now," he said. She loved that he wouldn't take no for an answer. Nobody had ever pursued her before, and his lusty enthusiasm delighted her.

"I shouldn't."

"Why not?"

"My mom came home last night from her Caribbean cruise. This is her first morning back, and I know she plans to show me all of her pictures over breakfast. The least I can do is be here when she wakes up."

"Leave now," he said. "We'll have coffee and donuts, neck a little, and you'll be home before anybody knows you were gone."

It was a crazy thing to do, almost as crazy as the fact that she was wide awake at five in the morning, talking to a man who made her tingle from head to toe with every shade of excitement in the erotic rainbow.

It was so crazy that it was irresistible.

They met at the Dunkin' Donuts near the mall at sunrise. The sight of him leaning against his Jeep made her feel like dancing. She did an awkward but exuberant soft shoe right there in the parking lot, and he swept her into his arms and led her to the door in an exaggerated, impromptu tango that left her weak with a dangerous combination of desire and laughter.

The place was empty. Maggy claimed a tiny round table near the window while Conor placed their order. He hadn't asked what she wanted, but she had the utmost confidence that he somehow knew she loved raspberry donuts.

"Raspberry," he said, placing three donuts on a plate in front of them. She wasn't at all surprised. The gods, after all, had been watching out for them from the very start.

They fed each other bits of donut and stared deep into each other's eyes, and neither one noticed when the front door opened and a tall, skinny blond woman stepped inside.

"Maggy O'Brien?" The woman sounded incredulous as she said the name. "Is that you?"

Oh, God. Amy Weintraub, only the biggest gossip in the tristate area. Maggy wanted to sink beneath the shiny floor tiles and stay there.

Instead, she laughed nervously and patted her short hair. "It's me all right, minus about two feet of hair."

"Oh, wow!" Amy made a show of inspecting Maggy's new short hair, but it was clear she was really inspecting Conor. "I love it, but what on earth possessed you?"

Maggy gave her a brief description of her sisters' birthday surprise while Amy oohed and aahed over Maggy's new look. Not to mention the new man by her side.

"You look great." Amy turned to Conor who'd been observing the exchange. She put out her right hand, and Maggy winced. She hadn't even thought about introducing them. "Amy Weintraub."

He shook her hand. "Conor Riley."

Riley, thought Maggy. They'd spent the last three nights talking on the phone until two in the morning, and this was the first time she'd heard his last name. She put out her own right hand and grinned at him. "Maggy O'Brien," she said. "Nice to meet you."

He started to laugh. "O'Brien, huh?"

"Riley, is it?" she said, laughing back.

"Weintraub," said Amy, looking from one to the

other, "although I think this just might be an Irish joke."

Maggy fumbled around for a believable explanation for their laughter, preferably an explanation that went nowhere near the truth. Amy nodded good-naturedly. She didn't seem at all put out by their silliness, but Maggy knew that behind those big brown eyes the gossip wheels were spinning madly.

"Uh, oh," Maggy said as Amy whipped her Mazda out of the parking lot. "Everybody in town's going to know about us now."

"I don't mind if you don't," Conor said.

"Easy for you to say. You didn't grow up here."

"That's the point, Maggy. You did grow up. It doesn't matter what any of them thinks."

But it did matter, and it continued to nip at Maggy. The whole thing was moving at supersonic speed, and she wasn't ready to bring her family into the equation. The thought of Conor being subjected to the scrutiny of her mother, her sisters, and her children was enough to make her dizzy. Better to be dizzy on champagne and flowers and the sheer giddy excitement of discovery for as long as possible.

"I wish we could hide just a little bit longer," she said as they finished their coffee. "I never had a secret love affair before. I want to enjoy it a little longer before we have to share it with anyone."

"You can't stop people from finding out, Maggy," he said, touching the tip of his index finger to one of the golden hoops dangling from her ears.

"Sure we can," she said, kissing his fingertip when nobody was looking. "We can create a secret world that belongs to only us."

Of course he was right even if she did hate to admit it. She wasn't a secretive woman by nature. A woman who understood the chemistry of secret liaisons and rendezvous and all those luscious French words for the magic that happens between the right man and the right woman wouldn't be sitting there in the local donut shop with her lover, holding hands and staring into his eyes. The idea of sneaking around was alien to her. The kids, especially Nicole, already knew something was up, and sooner or later she would have to come clean.

But not quite yet.

Her mother was awake and sitting at the kitchen table when Maggy let herself in the back door. The air smelled of freshly brewed coffee and the faintest hint of cigarette smoke. Under normal circumstances, Maggy would have said something about the cigarette smoke, but she was feeling a bit like a guilty teenager herself and decided to limit her criticism to a raised eyebrow.

"Don't say it," her mother said, raising her right hand in the air. "I forgot your ban on cigarettes." She pointed toward the open window over the sink. "See? Give it five minutes and you'll never know I sinned."

Rita was a tall and beautiful sixty-year-old woman with artfully dyed red hair, enormous blue eyes, and more energy than her three daughters combined. She'd been a redhead almost as long as Maggy could remember and had adopted many of the stereotypical redhead traits as her own. Her early life as a demure blonde sounded more like urban legend to Maggy than fact. The Rita she knew was a fighter, a woman with the courage to survive widowhood and a disastrous remarriage and keep her family together. A stroke last year had set Rita back, but after lengthy rehabilitation and much hard work on her part and Maggy's, only a slight hesitation over certain words remained to remind them of that terrifying experience.

"So where were you?" Rita asked as Maggy slipped off her coat and draped it over the back of a chair. "I heard the car around five-thirty."

Maggy placed a bag of donuts on the table. "Would you believe me if I told you I had some errands to run?"

Rita stirred some sugar into her coffee and looked at her daughter. "Would you want me to?"

Maggy sat down and poured herself a half cup of coffee. "I would if it meant you wouldn't ask me any questions about where I was."

Rita placed a gentle hand on Maggy's forearm. "Honey, if you're in any kind of trouble . . ."

The one thing she couldn't do was let her mother worry needlessly. She took a bracing sip of coffee—which probably sent her caffeine level over the top—then blurted, "I met someone, Ma. His name is Conor, and I think it's serious."

Rita was quiet for a long time. Maggy was fairly sure she knew what her mother was thinking and why.

"Out of my three girls," Rita said at last, "you're the one I worry most about."

"Me?" Maggy was amazed. "I'm the one who never got into any trouble, remember?" She was the sister who obeyed curfew, kept her room clean, produced grandchildren. Ellie was the hard-headed, ambitious one; Claire, the self-destructive wild child.

"You're the one who had the biggest dreams," her mother said.

Maggy laughed. "I think you're confusing me with my overachieving baby sisters, Ma. I'm the housewife. They're the ones with dreams of the Supreme Court and the cover of *Vogue*. All I ever wanted was a good marriage and a happy family."

"Exactly," said her mother. "The Supreme Court can't break your heart the way a bad marriage can."

Maggy shifted in her seat. She felt as if her clothing had suddenly grown a size too small for her frame. "I don't think I'm in any danger of a broken heart."

"Ellie and Claire told me about your trip to Atlantic City, honey. I know all about how exciting a whirlwind romance can be." Maggy opened her mouth to protest, but her mother was having none of it. "I also know how easy it is to make a terrible mistake."

"I don't know what Ellie and Claire said but I think you're all jumping to conclusions."

"You might have fooled your sisters with your story about the robe, but you can't fool me." Rita pointed to the shiny surface of the toaster oven resting on the countertop. "Look at your face," she said, "and tell me I'm jumping to conclusions."

Maggy averted her eyes. She knew exactly what she would see: the dazed look of a woman on the verge of love. "I know what I'm doing," she said. "You don't have to worry."

"I thought I knew what I was doing when I married Cal, and see where that landed us."

"You can't compare our situations," Maggy said. "You were left alone with three little girls when Daddy died. Cal seemed like a gift from the gods."

"And what do you have?" her mother countered. "Two kids who'll be in college before you know what hit you, a part-time job, no prospects—"

"Mother." Maggy's voice held an edge that wasn't there before. "There's no comparison between our situations," she said again. "Charles is still the children's father. He has never shirked his responsibilities, financial or otherwise. Maybe I can't afford to dress the kids from the Gap, but we're doing fine." Besides, she was back in school, and sooner or later that would pay dividends in the form of a bigger paycheck. It stung that she would have to explain any of this to her own mother.

"You can't tell about a man until you marry him," Rita said. "Everything before that is dress rehearsal."

"Lots of women make mistakes," Maggy pointed out. "Cal was a bastard, but you got him out of our lives."

"Not soon enough."

"You got him out of our lives in time," Maggy repeated. "That's what matters."

Much of Rita's natural ebullience dimmed at the memory. "I would do anything for you girls," she said. "I'd give my life to keep you safe."

"I know that," Maggy said, her eyes filling with tears. "We all know it."

"Every time I think that my mistake put you in danger—"

She took her mother's hand in hers and squeezed gently. "You never did anything but love us and look out for us. If I can be half as good a mother as you are, I'll be proud."

Rita's eyes swam with tears, but she managed to smile and squeeze Maggy's hand in return. "Nobody will ever love your children the way you do, Maggy. Nobody could."

Matt called late on Thursday night with an invitation. "Listen," he said to Conor, "I nailed a quartet of tickets for the Holyfield fight tomorrow night. Pop and Eddie will swing by and pick you up around six-thirty and—"

"Sounds great," Conor said, staring into his bare refrigerator, "but I've got something on for tomorrow." Maggy was coming over for dinner, and he was in need of a culinary miracle.

"So cancel it," Matt ordered. "We're talking Holyfield here, man. Heavyweight cham-peen of the world. You don't want to miss that."

"Thanks for the offer, but I'm gonna have to."

Matt was quiet for a moment. "What is it—you got to work tomorrow or something?"

"Or something," Conor said.

"You're passing up Holyfield tickets? Evander Holyfield tickets?"

"You heard it here."

Matt rapped on the receiver with his knuckles. The scratchy tapping sound made Conor wince. "Gotta be something wrong with this phone. No way my brother would pass on ringside.''

"I'm passing on ringside."

"So you gonna tell me why?"

"I hadn't planned to."

"Is it a woman?"

Suddenly Conor had a brand-new understanding of why Maggy wanted to keep their relationship under wraps just a little bit longer. Relatives were downright scary. "Yeah," he said, searching for the can of beer he thought he'd spotted behind the dangerously old container of milk. "It's a woman." No reason to lie, but there was also no reason to volunteer any more than he had to.

"Anyone I know?"

"Nope." *And nobody you're going to know either.* At least not right now.

Matt was the runt of the litter and scrappy as all hell. Being the baby in a big family, he'd been spoiled rotten from the cradle and he still expected the bunch of them to fall all over themselves to grant his fondest wishes. This little dose of reality would have the kid muttering for a week. Unfortunately it would also have him phoning home to spread the news that Conor was seeing somebody so special that he'd passed on Holyfield tickets.

So maybe he and Maggy weren't meant to be secret lovers. Maybe they were meant to be thrown kicking and screaming into the middle of family life so they could discover if what they'd found was the real thing. Every time he saw her, every time he heard her voice, he felt himself falling deeper into something that seemed a hell of a lot like love. If you'd asked him this time last week, he would've laughed in your face. He would've said he didn't believe in love at first sight or eyes across a crowded room or any of the hundred other romantic clichés people had invented to disguise pure unadulterated lust. Not that there was anything wrong with lust. You didn't have to pin flowers to it and call it something it wasn't to make it acceptable. It was fine just the way it was.

Except for the fact that when it came to how he felt about Maggy, lust didn't even come close. Lust was a poor relation, a watered-down impostor compared to the urgent, powerful, downright magical emotions she brought to life inside him. Every time he thought he'd managed to find a label that neatly described the way she made him feel, she made him feel something else, something newer and more profound, something that made it impossible for him to see a future without her right there at the center of it.

She made him forget all the ways he'd failed. When he held her in his arms he could forget about Bobby and Deni and those two little girls. When he made love to her, he was at peace, something he hadn't been since the night when it all went horribly wrong.

If he had his way he'd declare himself right now. Tonight. Pick up the damn phone and tell her what was in his heart, tell her everything, and take his chances. Life didn't come with a timetable. He'd had a firsthand lesson in that when Bobby was killed. One minute you're living your life, making plans, dreaming of the things you wanted to do some day, and the next they're laying you out in a casket. The blink of an eye. The snap of your fingers. All of it over before you even got started.

The last day of Bobby's life had seemed like any other. There wasn't a lot of excitement in detective work, not the kind of detective work they usually did. They'd spent the afternoon out at a horse farm on River Road, interviewing the owner about the theft of an Arabian stud. The owner was distraught. She wasn't just in the business for the money. She genuinely loved the animals and felt the loss keenly.

"What do you think?" Conor asked his partner as they climbed back into their unmarked sedan.

"I think I feel like Columbo," Bobby said. "This is the best gig we've come across in a long time."

Neither one knew squat about the world of race horses, but it was a welcome diversion from the run of burglaries and assaults they usually ran up against.

"I need to stop by Toys R Us," Bobby said as they headed back to the station. "They're holding Tina's birthday Barbie for me until five o'clock."

Conor teased him mercilessly as they drove toward the mall. Birthday Barbie. Detective Ken. The kind of pointed gibes partners specialized in. Bobby took it all with good grace. He always did. "What can I tell ya," he said with a shrug of his boxer's shoulders. "I'm a family man." He was and he loved it. Bobby DiCarlo's world revolved around his wife and kids. They were the reason for everything he did. Bobby loved being a cop, but he looked forward to the day when he logged in his full twenty years and could retire early and spend 24/7 with Deni and whoever was left at home at that point. Bobby DiCarlo didn't want a hell of a lot from life.

Conor hung around the edges of Bobby's life. Deni always included him at family gatherings. He was god-father to their youngest daughter. Bobby taught Conor's son Sean how to fly-fish one summer. They were planning a fishing trip to the Adirondacks to celebrate Sean's graduation from high school.

Conor pulled up in front of the toy store. "Gimme five minutes," Bobby said. "This won't take long."

"Go get your Barbie doll," Conor said in mock exasperation. "Just don't make me get a ticket out here waiting for you."

Bobby leaped out and jogged toward the entrance. Motown blared from the radio, and Conor leaned his head against the seat and closed his eyes. Sun sizzled through the window glass, and he was thinking how glad he was the department had sprung for air conditioning when he felt a thump against the car. He shot up, instantly alert, and saw Bobby barreling across the half-empty parking lot.

Conor flung open the car door and jumped out. He heard a woman's high-pitched screams for help, Bobby's pounding footsteps, a man's angry words. A carjacking. Shit. He took off after Bobby. A teacher had been murdered in an adjacent township a few years earlier in a similar situation. This woman was a hell of a lot luckier. No way that would happen this time. They knew how to handle this.

Too slow. Crank it up, Riley. Move!

Bobby knew how to mediate, how to step between the perp and the victim, how to play for time while Conor got an angle on him. They had it down cold.

What the hell's the matter with you, old man? Push it.

He was out of breath, struggling to put one foot in front of the other. What the hell was wrong with him? When did he get so out of shape he couldn't tear across a parking lot?

Come on . . . come on . . .

The woman was crouched on the ground near the front of her Blazer. Bobby was wrestling with a skinny guy in a gray jacket. Sunlight bounced off the gun in the guy's hand.

Don't sit there, lady, move it! Make a run for it. The guy doesn't want you, he wants your car.

She crouched there almost motionless while Bobby tried to wrestle the gun away from the bastard.

Another fifty feet . . . you can run fifty feet . . . you're out there every day pounding asphalt at the track . . . What the hell's wrong with you now?

He was running in slow motion. Years passed between each step. He ran and ran and somehow stayed in place.

Get the gun, Bobby, get the gun . . . Shit, don't let him back you up against the car . . .

Bobby met Conor's eyes across the yawning expanse that separated them. He angled his head in the direction of the woman. *Get her out of here,* his expression said. *Move her and I'll take care of this bastard.*

The bastard was sweating. He shoved Bobby onto his back. Bobby kneed him, and he grunted and fell off to the side.

Conor found his speed at that second. "Move!" he roared as he grabbed the woman by the arm and almost threw her across the parking lot toward safety. "Stay down! Stay down!"

Bobby's eyes. *It's okay now. It's okay.* Sun glinting from the barrel of the gun. The stench of terror. Move. Don't move. Talk him down. Talk him out of it. Don't talk at all. No time. No more time.

Bobby . . . the gun . . . do it . . . get the gun . . . do it now . . . the barrel against Bobby's temple . . . why are you standing there . . . don't fuck up . . . coward . . . movemovemove . . . why the hell aren't you moving . . . do it . . . do it before—

Bang.

THIRTEEN

On the O'Brien one to ten Scale of Domestic Disasters, Maggy figured they were at eight and climbing fast.

Conor was due in fifteen minutes, and unless a miracle occurred, he was about to meet her entire family in one fell swoop. Rita was overflowing with stories, photos, and gifts that absolutely positively had to be delivered that very night, and what better place for the Halloran girls to gather than at Maggy's house. Unfortunately, she forgot to tell Maggy until an hour before.

"I know what you're up to," Maggy said to her mother before Claire and Ellie arrived. "You want to inspect my date."

Rita was the picture of innocence. "You're very suspicious, honey."

"I should have known something was up when you refused to go home to your own beautiful, quiet, kid-free, pet-free, smoker-friendly condo."

"I'm enjoying your company."

"Right," Maggy muttered as she scurried around, searching for her favorite mascara. "Sure you are."

Claire and Ellie feigned surprise when Maggy told

them she wouldn't be around to enjoy the merriment.

"I had no idea," said Claire, straight-faced.

"Neither had I," said Ellie. She turned to Rita. "Mom, you should have told us."

"Oh, please," said Maggy, shaking her head. "You three are the worst actresses on earth. I know what this is all about." Claire and Ellie nudged each other while Rita made a show out of smoothing the front of her *Bahama Mama* T-shirt. "I hate to disappoint you, but if you think I'm going to put that man through a family inspection, you've got another think coming."

Nicole chose that moment to drift into the room. She wore a pink wool bathrobe, bright orange socks, and a dark blue towel wrapped around her wet purple hair. Somehow she managed to look so lovely that she took Maggy's breath away. "Who are we inspecting?"

"You're mother's new boyfriend," said Claire.

Nicole made an awful face, then threw herself into one of the kitchen chairs. She plucked a grape from the platter in front of Ellie. "I heard him on the phone," she said. "He sounds stupid."

"Nicole!" Maggy couldn't mask the irritation in her voice. "That's unfair."

Nicole shrugged her slender shoulders. "I can't help it if that's how he sounds."

Ellie and Claire pressed the girl for details, but they'd forgotten how quickly a fifteen-year-old could retreat into her adolescent shell. Their attempts at extracting gossip were met with monosyllabic responses that warmed Maggy's maternal heart. *That's my girl.*

She dragged out the ironing board and draped her favorite little black dress across it.

"You're wearing *that?*" Nicole asked, wrinkling her nose.

"That's the plan," Maggy said. "Why? Is there something wrong with it?"

Once again Nicole's answer was a shrug. This time

Maggy didn't find her response quite so amusing.

"It's a lovely dress, honey," said Rita in a tone of voice that made Maggy's teeth itch. "I'm sure it still looks fine."

"This dress is a classic," Maggy said, switching on the iron. "The kind that never goes out of style."

Ellie and Claire exchanged looks. It was all Maggy could do to keep from knocking their perfect heads together.

"That hemline is a little dated," Claire said gently.

"It reminds me of the time Sister Immaculata wore civilian clothes to the opera," Ellie said.

"Girls!" Rita sounded as though she was biting her tongue to keep from laughing. "Leave your sister alone."

"Oh, quit that, Ma!" Maggy poured some water into the iron and adjusted the thermostat. "I don't need you to protect me."

Rita got all huffy, and Maggy would have felt contrite if they'd given her even a micrometer of breathing room. Three generations of Halloran females watched her iron her dress, looking at her as if she'd announced she was running away with Sean Connery, Harrison Ford, and Mel Gibson to live in extremely happy sin. In fact, they'd probably find that less surprising than the fact that she had a dinner date.

"We'll get along fine," Claire said with a wink in Nicole's direction. "Order in some Chinese, gossip about you. We'll be fine."

Nicole looked sullen and annoyed. She focused her attention on the small television mounted under one of the kitchen counters.

". . . the jury has been chosen in the Detective Bobby DiCarlo murder trial set to begin next week in Somerville . . ."

"Turn that off, would you, Nic?" Ellie piped up. "The last thing I want to hear after a day in court is more courtroom gossip. I heard more than I care to today from one of the defense team members.''

Nicole aimed the remote at the set and clicked it off. Maggy looked up in time to see a photo of a handsome, dark-haired young father who was posed with a pair of beautiful little girls flare then fade away. *How terrible,* she thought, then pushed it from her mind. Her life was too wonderful right now to dwell on sadness.

''Where did you say you were going?'' her mother asked, all wide-eyed innocence in her Bahama Mama T-shirt.

You're a sly one, Ma, but I'm not falling for it. ''To dinner,'' she said.

''Where?''

''I don't know exactly.'' Which wasn't a lie since she didn't know his exact street address.

''What if there's an emergency?''

''I'll have my cell phone with me.''

''Your sister's being awfully secretive,'' her mother said, sipping her homemade margarita.

''She's been like this since her birthday trip to A.C.,'' Claire said, running a crescent of lime across her tongue. ''We knew she'd met somebody down there, but she tried to put us off the scent.''

''She's on the phone with him all the time,'' Nicole said, not meeting Maggy's eyes. ''That's why she got the second line.''

Three pairs of eyes zeroed in on Maggy.

''What?'' she said, feeling a lot like tiny Lichtenstein defending her borders against a NATO strike force. ''Am I such a loser you can't imagine that anybody would want to go out with me?''

''You're not a loser,'' said Claire, ''you're cheap. I want to meet the man who's special enough to make you spend your money on a second phone line.''

Rita and Ellie burst into laughter. Nicole remained

stony-faced, but it was quite clear she agreed with her aunt's assessment.

Maggy, who didn't find the lot of them remotely funny, looked at the clock over the kitchen sink. "Oh, my God!" she shrieked. "He'll be here in ten minutes!"

Oh, Conor, she thought as she grabbed her dress and ran for her room. *Whatever you do, don't be early.*

He was early.

Conor parked at the curb to the left of the mailbox. The mailbox was in the shape of an old barn. The previous owner's name was faintly visible through a wash of dark red paint. It now read O'Brien in little light-reflective stick-on letters.

He turned off the engine, then climbed out of the Jeep. The small ranch house was set far back on the property, giving the illusion of a sprawling front yard. The yard was neatly clipped, but the shrubs and hedges were beginning to look ragged and untended. Small yellow and orange flowers lined the walkway. A skateboard rested on its side beneath a window. A basketball nestled in the grass at the edge of the driveway, beneath a slightly tilted hoop. A little boy sat on the front step with two sleeping dogs of indeterminate lineage. He looked up as Conor approached. The boy had his mother's eyes, wide and blue, and her curly dark hair.

The dogs woke up, and the bigger of the two grumbled sleepily. " 'S'okay, girl," the boy said as he stroked her ear. He looked up at Conor. "You're the guy my mom's going out with." He also had his mother's direct manner.

"I'm Conor Riley." He thought about shaking the kid's hand, but he remembered how much he would have hated that gesture at his age and kept his own hands in the pockets of his leather jacket. "You must be Charlie."

The kid nodded, but he didn't say anything. He wasn't going to make it easy on Conor.

"So how come you and Tigger and Data are sitting outside?" Conor asked.

Charlie aimed his thumb toward the house and pulled a face. "They're all in there helping Mom get ready."

That wasn't what he wanted to hear. "Who's in there?" he asked.

"All of them," Charlie said. "Grandma Rita, Aunt Claire, Aunt Ellie, Mom, and my stupid sister."

"So you bailed out." *Don't blame you, pal. That sounds like a formidable crew in there.*

"Uh-huh." Charlie buried his face in a ruff of dog fur in a gesture that reminded him of Sean when he was a little boy. He'd missed so much of his son's growing up. It seemed as if one September he put a shy little boy on the plane home to California, and the next time he saw him, Sean was a self-confident young man. Charlie reminded him of all he'd missed, and he felt a sudden kinship with the man who had fathered him and now lived far away.

He heard laughter from inside, the kind of female laughter that usually meant some poor unsuspecting male was being raked over the coals. He had the feeling he was the unsuspecting male in question.

He crouched down and scratched the larger of the dogs behind her right ear. She leaned into his touch with a blissful expression on her canine face.

"So how are you at hoops?" he asked Charlie.

The boy peered over a ruff of sleeping dog. "Good."

"So am I," Conor said. "Feel like some one-on-one?"

"I guess."

Conor grinned. That was about as close as you got to a show of excitement from a nine-year-old boy who was intent on seeming nonchalant.

"Want me to spot you?"

The kid glowered at him. "No way."

"Okay," said Conor. "It's your funeral."

• • •

Nicole heard the sound of Charlie's laughter coming from out front and the heavy *thud-thud* of the basketball pounding against the driveway. The noise bugged her, like fingernails on a chalkboard.

"What's that noise?" Aunt Claire asked, tilting her head in that way she had.

"The moron's shooting hoops," Nicole said.

"Who's he playing with?" Aunt Ellie asked.

"I don't know," Nicole said with a shrug. "One of his moronic friends."

"Listen," said Grandma. "That doesn't sound like one of Charlie's friends, does it?"

They all leaped to their feet at once and ran for the front door. Grandma actually pushed Nicole aside so she could be the first one out onto the porch to see what was going on. Her aunts weren't much better. In fact, the next time one of them told her to act her age, she was going to point to this little episode.

"He's a big one," said Grandma. "Six-two, I'd say."

Aunt Claire peered over Grandma's shoulder. "Six-three or four's more like it."

"Great hair," said Aunt Ellie.

"Hair?" Aunt Claire hit her on the arm. "Look at that butt, will you? We're talking world-class."

Nicole couldn't see what the big fuss was. He looked like an old man to her. He wasn't half as handsome as Daddy, and that made her glad.

Conor was about to slam-dunk the ball when he saw them standing on the front porch. Three women, each one almost as tall as he was, each one exceptionally good-looking. Two of them looked to be in their late twenties; the loveliest of them was probably their mother. Behind them stood a stunning young girl with a bright orange towel wrapped around her head. She looked at him as if he were something that needed to be scraped off the bottom of her shoe. He didn't have to ask twice if that was Maggy's daughter.

The thought boggled the mind. They were a family of Amazons. He couldn't begin to figure out how Maggy fit in. She would look like a munchkin standing next to them. Adopted, he thought. She had to be.

The four of them stood there staring at him as if he were a sneak preview of the latest Star Wars prequel.

"Whaddya say we challenge them to a game?" he asked Charlie in a stage whisper.

"They stink," Charlie said with a big smile on his face. "We'd wipe them out."

"Sounds good to me," Conor said, and they slapped hands. He grinned at the assembled Halloran females. "Feel like a game?"

"You're kidding," said the one in a tailored business suit with a skirt the size of a postage stamp. She had to be Ellie the lawyer. "I'm wearing Manolo Blahniks." She pointed toward her skyscraper heels.

"You're on," said the one he figured was Claire. She was almost painfully beautiful, but she lacked the womanly softness that made Maggy so memorable. She joined Conor and Charlie on the driveway. "Want me to spot you?" she asked.

Charlie looked up at him, and they both cracked up laughing.

"Okay," said Claire, "be that way. You had your chance. Don't hold me accountable for crushed male ego."

"Count me in, too," said the knockout who was the matriarch of the family. "I was captain of my high school basketball team a thousand years ago."

He grinned at her, and she gave him an answering smile that reminded him of Maggy's. Okay, so maybe they were blood-related, even if Maggy would only come up to the woman's shoulder.

The daughter Nicole gave one of those teenage girl

sighs that amplified themselves through sheer force of will then flounced back into the house. Ellie the lawyer leaned against the porch railing and said, "I'll do the play-by-play." He liked the way they all joined into the spirit of things, even if it was just because they wanted to check him out.

The women played hard. It didn't take more than ten seconds to figure that out. They weren't afraid to get in there and block his shots. They were even tough on Charlie, and he was only nine years old. Rita was especially aggressive, and if he didn't know better, he'd think she was trying to send him a message behind that gleaming white smile.

Maggy blessed her short haircut as she made one more pass with the blow-dryer. How had she ever managed her time back when she had that waist-length ponytail? All of that combing and detangling and the endless wait for it to dry, and then when it finally did, the best she could do with it was pull it back with a coated rubber band. It seemed like a lifetime ago when she'd been dragged kicking and screaming into Andre's salon and agreed to being shorn like a sheep.

She clicked the switch to Off then ran her fingers through her hair. Best thing she ever did. She couldn't help smiling at her reflection. Who wouldn't smile at the woman looking back at her from the mirror? She looked happy enough for the entire state of New Jersey.

She plucked a pair of silver hoops from the tiny china cup she kept on the vanity and slid them into her ears. Her makeup wasn't quite the way she wanted it, but there wasn't time to be fussy. Right now, the most important thing was making sure the Halloran Harpies didn't get any alone time with Conor.

Her shoes and purse were in the bedroom. She moved quickly from the master bath, determined not to waste a second. She slid her feet into the perilously high heels and winced. To think she used to wear those things on a regular basis when she was an officer's wife. Okay, now where was her purse? She scanned the tops of her night-stands, the dresser, even the windowsill. There it was in the middle of the bed. She tucked the purse under her arm and hurried down the hallway, congratulating herself on getting ready in record time. She wasn't one of the Halloran girls for nothing. She'd wave good-bye to the throng and be waiting for Conor on the front porch, same way she used to wait for her dates when she was a teen-age girl. Funny how some things never changed no mat-ter how old you were.

"I'm out of here!" she called as she whipped past the kitchen. "Don't stay up too late, Nicole!"

Hmm. That was odd. They were being awfully quiet in there. She doubled back and peeked inside. No wonder they were quiet. There wasn't a soul in there. *Please, God, tell me you wouldn't play a trick like that on me. Tell me all those years of not eating meat on Friday bought me a few heavenly brownie points.*

That was when she heard shouting from the driveway and the rhythmic sound of a basketball bouncing against the blacktop, and she knew her worst fears had been re-alized.

Ellie was perched on the railing. "They won't be much longer," she said to Maggy. "The girls have them on the run."

"Oh, God," Maggy groaned. Her mother and sister were making mincemeat of the men in her life. The noise level was prodigious. Mostly male grunts and groans with the occasional counterpoint of a decidedly female cheer. Charlie's little face was screwed up in lines of intense and painful concentration. Conor didn't look too good himself. Maggy had to put a stop to it before Rita and Claire stomped them into the ground.

Conor was in the middle of setting up for a throw when Maggy stepped down from the porch. He turned, looked at her, and smiled a smile the likes of which she'd never seen in her entire life. He dropped the basketball to the ground and walked toward her. Her mother and sisters, even her beloved son, faded from view. She saw nothing but his wonderful face. She heard nothing but the sound of her name on his lips. She was standing there at the top of her suburban New Jersey driveway, but it could have been Paris.

His smile grew wider as he drew closer. Her own smile seemed to engulf her entire being. She felt like shouting with the sheer joy of it all. She ran toward him, and he swept her into his embrace.

"I missed you," he said.

"I missed you, too."

He tilted her chin with his index finger and kissed her right there in front of her family and her neighbors. The kiss was brief but so sweet she sighed with happiness, and it wasn't until she heard Charlie's pained "Ma-a-a!" that she floated back down to earth long enough to say good-bye.

"I don't like him," Claire said as Maggy and Conor drove away in his Jeep a few minutes later.

"Neither do I," Ellie said.

"But Maggy does," said Rita as she put her hand on her grandson's shoulder, "and that's the problem."

FOURTEEN

"I think it went well," Maggy said when they turned off Sycamore. "All things considered."

"You should've warned me," Conor said as they rolled to a stop at the traffic light. "They're an intimidating group of women."

"They're tall. I'll grant them that."

"Tall doesn't intimidate me. The way your mother shoots hoops scared the hell out of me."

"Don't you dare tell her that. She'd be even more impossible with that kind of ammunition."

"When I first saw them, I figured you were adopted."

"Nope," said Maggy as the light turned green. "The crazy Halloran blood flows through my veins, too."

"Crazy blood but great genes."

"They're a comely bunch." She shot him a look. "If you like them big and blond."

"I'm partial to petite brunettes myself."

"I was hoping you'd say that."

He leaned close, and his words made her dizzy.

She touched his cheek. "I was hoping you'd say that, too."

The air in the Jeep shimmered as they looked at each other. She loved watching him. He was the most deliciously tactile man she'd ever met.

"Do you know what you're doing?" she asked softly.

"Doing?" He seemed puzzled. "Driving."

"No, besides that."

"Thinking about how you look beneath that dress."

A voluptuous shiver rippled through her. For a second, she was tempted to do something wicked and out of character, but she reconsidered. There was also something to be said for anticipation, the deeply erotic satisfaction to be found in waiting for the right time and the right place.

"That's not what I mean," she said. "See? You're doing it right now. You stroke the wheel with your thumb." He slid the fleshy part of his thumb back and forth across the slick curve of wheel in an unconscious gesture of such deep sensuality that it made her burn. She knew how his hands felt against her body, the way those thumbs circled and caressed her naked skin, the magic that happened when she gave over to the impossible wonder of it all. Oh, yes, there was something to be said for anticipation.

They talked about the weather. *Lovely*. About basketball. *Fun*. About the traffic. *Moderate*.

Of course, they weren't really talking about any of those things. The words were blinds to hide the desire sizzling between them.

She wanted to take his right thumb into her mouth and bite down gently on the plump pad, then slide her tongue along the inner curve. Her lips would leave a deep red imprint along the base. Her teeth would leave just the slightest indentation in the soft flesh. The thought made her smile.

He'd never seen a smile like hers. The thought occurred to him fresh and new each time he saw her again. Her smile warmed him like summer sunshine in the dead of winter. When she smiled at him that way—eyes shadowed and mysterious, lips gently curved as if protecting a secret—he felt as if he'd won the lottery or scaled Everest. If he could make Maggy O'Brien smile that way, he could do anything.

When she talked, he heard music. She had a honeyed voice, supple and expressive. She spoke low and urgently, and he wanted to cup his hands and catch all of those beautiful sounds before they faded away. She asked him what they were having for dinner, and he heard the Hallelujah Chorus.

He had it all planned, right down to the dessert. He'd make her stand outside while he lit the candles he'd plopped down on every available surface. He'd switch on some soft music, have the champagne ready to pop, the broiler hot and ready for the steaks. He'd even scrubbed down the john and made sure his towels matched. The blue ones. When in doubt, always pick the blue ones.

He'd light a fire. They'd sit on the sofa and talk while the flames danced and the logs crackled. He'd casually sneak an arm around her shoulder when she wasn't looking, like a teenage boy at the movies with the girl of his dreams. Fake a yawn, a phony stretch, let your arm settle around her shoulders. Maybe while they were on their second glass of champagne, he'd lean over and kiss her, savoring the sweetness of her mouth and the sparkle of wine. Tonight they had time to tease and yearn and discover.

Slow and easy. That was how it would be this time.

He lived on an inlet south of Asbury Park in a small ranch house with an enormous garage. The grass was mowed clear to the ground. Mountains of leaves drifted across the flagstone pathway that led from the street. Bare lilac bushes and rhododendron fronted the door, but there wasn't a flower bed in sight. Somehow that didn't surprise her.

What did surprise her was how nervous she felt. Her
hands were trembling, and she held onto her purse tightly
to keep it from showing. *You're being an idiot,* she told
herself as he pulled into the driveway and clicked off the
engine. *It's not as if this is your first time with him.* There
wasn't an inch of his body she didn't know intimately
and well. His runner's thighs, long and well-muscled.
The way the mat of thick, dark hair on his chest tickled
her cheek when she rested her head against it. His smell.
Oh, God, the smell of his skin, warm and faintly peppery,
made her want to see if he tasted as wonderful as she
remembered. She knew all of those secrets, yet there she
was feeling as if this was the first time.

He walked around to the passenger side and helped
her from the truck. She made appreciative comments
about the house and the property, but nothing was reg-
istering on her. All she could think about was being alone
with him again. *Seduce me,* she thought as they walked
up the pathway. Wine her and dine her. Pour on the
charm the same way he poured champagne. Tease her
palate and her imagination. Make her forget that right
this very minute, her mother and sisters were analyzing
every single thing Conor did or didn't do and finding
him lacking.

"Stay here," he said as he unlocked the front door.

She looked up at him. "Out here on the porch?"

"For a second. I want to do something."

"If that's what you want." She was utterly charmed.
He dragged his hand through his hair in a nervous gesture
that left one tuft of shiny chestnut standing at attention.
She reached up and smoothed it down with her palm.
How silky and cool it felt against her skin. How excited
it made her feel.

"I won't be long."

She pretended to shiver. "I would hope not."

He vanished inside. She heard a thud, then a muttered
curse, and she smiled. She'd never been to a man's place

before, never had a man cook a romantic dinner for her. It was worth standing out there in the chilly dusk while he set the stage for seduction.

He dimmed the lights, lit the candles, started the fire, wrecked the roses. Only the first three were on his list. He was barreling through the hallway when his elbow knocked into the crystal vase on the hall table and sent everything flying. Glass and water flew everywhere. So did big, beautiful, deep-red roses, two dozen of them, scattered from one end of the room to the other. He grabbed for a shard of broken glass, then swore when a jagged edge scraped his finger.

"Oh, no!" She was standing next to him, her legs long and shapely in those dangerous heels. She bent down and picked up one American beauty. "Roses."

"They were for you," he said.

"I love them."

"You would've loved them more in the vase."

She bent down next to him. "They're awfully pretty on the floor."

He gestured toward the living room where the fireplace was ablaze with light. "At least I didn't set the house on fire."

"Yes," she said with great formality, "we should be grateful for that."

He looked at her, and all of his plans for a long, slow seduction incinerated. She touched her index finger to her mouth and then to his. Faintly wet. Very sweet. He slid her finger between his lips then bit down gently. His teeth pushed against the tender flesh. Her eyes widened. Her sigh of pleasure made him instantly hard.

"I was going to take all night to seduce you."

She leaned toward him. "I'd say you're way ahead of schedule."

Glass and water and roses were forgotten. So was din-ner. The only hunger that mattered was the hunger they felt for each other, the deep, almost savage need to be together in every way possible.

They made love standing up with her back against the wall and her beautiful legs wrapped tightly around his hips. He drove into her, and she matched him in intensity and excitement. She was the lover, the woman, he'd waited his whole life to find. Her round bottom settled neatly into his hands. He could feel her heat and juices spilling over his fingers as he stroked her at the point where they were joined. She sucked his tongue deep into her mouth, stroking him with her own tongue, teasing him with her teeth, while she rode him hard and fast. Her skirt was pulled up to her waist. The silky folds drifted across his forearms. She still wore her heels and the dark stockings attached to a lacy wisp of garter belt. He'd slipped his hand under her dress, trailed his fingers up her silky thighs, expecting to find a barrier of lace. Instead, his fingers slid through the soft tangle of curls between her legs. "Surprise," she said, looking shy and wild and achingly lovely. He would carry that image of her with him for the rest of his life.

Maggy cried out when she came. The sound seemed to spring from a part of her soul she'd never known existed before that moment, a place beyond words, without rules or boundaries or expectations. The sound of her own voice raised in ecstasy spilled over her like moonlight, and whatever remained of her inhibitions vanished in that moment. You made love silently when you had children. You swallowed cries of passion with kisses and feather pillows and behind strong hands. Squeaky box springs, the thump of a headboard against the wall, the sounds of love seemed magnified when you were a parent and you heard them through a child's curious and unknowing ears.

She used to dream that she was flying high above the clouds, soaring up and up and up toward the heavens.

She didn't need that dream anymore. Now she sailed through the stars with her eyes wide open every time he touched her.

"No pizza," Claire said when her mother offered her a slice of pepperoni. "I'll work on the salad." They were gathered around Maggy's kitchen table, gossiping about the new man in Maggy's life and eating.

Rita shook her head in dismay. "You're too skinny as it is," she said. "I hope you're not dieting." There was a question hidden in that statement, one her mother wouldn't ask, but it was there just the same.

"Maintenance," Claire said. "It's part of the business." *Don't worry, Ma. No drugs. Five years now and counting.*

"Some business," said Ellie. "Starvation isn't high up on my list of priorities."

"Well, unemployment isn't high up on my list of priorities either. If I want to work, I don't eat pizza."

Nicole looked over at her from the opposite side of the table. "Never?"

"Maybe once or twice a year," Claire said, noticing the horrified expression on her niece's face. "It's not so bad. After awhile you forget that you ever liked it."

"I don't *think* so," Nicole said, and everyone but Charlie laughed. He was too busy feeding strings of cheese to Tigger and Data who were lurking under the table. In two minutes, they'd already devoured Claire's entire fat content for a year.

She poured herself an inch of chianti and ignored her mother's arched brow. Rita knew she couldn't afford to drink more than a few sips, or it would all show up on her face in the morning. Or worse, but she wouldn't let herself think about that. Makeup artists could be brutal in their assessment of your raw material, something that wasn't easy to take before your first cup of coffee. Or any time, for that matter. She'd had a reminder of that fact this morning.

Sam Deloy was one of the best. Everybody said so. New York was beginning to sniff around, and it was clear that before too long he'd be saying good-bye to the Garden State and hello to the Big Apple. It was always that way with the great ones. You couldn't keep them on this side of the Hudson, no matter how hard you tried. Somehow word always got out, and the siren call of Manhattan lured them away. She'd been in the business for twelve years now, and nobody had tried to lure her beyond the Lincoln Tunnel.

She and Sam had greeted each other like long-lost friends this morning at the shoot on the old Onassis property in Peapack. They air-kissed each other's cheeks, made the requisite noises about it being way too long since they'd caught up, then Sam held her away from him and clucked his tongue against his teeth. "Going to need a magic wand this morning, darlin'," he said, shaking his head. "Father Time's been having his way with you."

She'd laughed as if he'd cracked an uproarious joke. What else could she do? If she let those words crawl inside her head, she'd burst into tears. "I need your magic touch, Sammy. You're better than my own personal airbrush."

"I'm not joking, darlin'," he said as she took her seat in the makeup chair where he draped her. Her hair was already in hot rollers. "You're going to need more than my magic." He inspected her face carefully, touching a spot next to her mouth, beneath her eyes, along her jawbone. "I hope you've been very kind to Freddy because, darlin', you need him today." Freddy was the photographer, a man known for his ability to light aging models to perfection.

"I'm only twenty-eight, Sammy," she said in a quiet voice very unlike her usual boisterous tone. "It shouldn't

be happening already." Hadn't Maggy said the same
words a week ago? Claire had found them funny then,
but she wasn't laughing anymore.

She'd endured a thoroughly miserable time in the
makeup chair, only to face Freddy and his miracle lights.
"Good thing I like a challenge," he said as he began
moving key lights and umbrellas around, searching for
the best configuration.

"I know I'm having a bad day," she snapped as he
positioned her in front of a white screen. "You don't
have to keep reminding me."

"Touchy, aren't we?" Freddy said as he shot a test
Polaroid. "The camera doesn't lie, babe. If I don't tell
you, it sure as hell will."

It was the first time she'd ever lost it on the job. She
lowered her head and began to cry and she kept on crying
until her makeup was shot and her eyes were too red and
swollen for any amount of magic to disguise. They canceled the shoot, and she knew there would be hell to pay
when her agency found out about it. She hated having to
answer to somebody for every move she made. She hated
even more being at their mercy for jobs. She gathered up
her belongings and was heading for the door when
Freddy waylaid her.

"Listen," he said, laying a slender hand on her shoulder, "you know I didn't mean to make you cry, don't
you? You're a pal, and I always shoot straight with
pals."

She moved slightly away, just enough so he knew she
was still hurt. "Maybe shooting straight isn't always the
kindest thing to do."

"Nothing kind about this business," he said, and she
knew he was right. "Don't ever make the mistake of
thinking we're about anything but externals. That's how
you end up spread-eagled in *Playboy* like Farrah and Si-
natra's girl."

"You should embroider that on one of your pillows."

She made to leave, but he wasn't quite finished. "Words for a young model to live by."

"So did you show the photos to your niece?"

Claire was instantly alert to the subtle change in his tone of voice. Freddy had enough work to keep a dozen stylists busy. He didn't have time to waste on anything but sure things. *I'm right,* she thought. *Nicole is everything I thought she was.* "Not yet," she said in as casual a tone as she could muster. "Life's been so busy . . ." She let her words trail idly away.

"It could get a whole lot busier if you bring her in to meet with a few people. They don't stay young and nubile for long, babe, in case you don't remember. I like to get them while they're still virgins."

Of course she remembered. It wasn't that long ago when Freddy found her standing in front of Saint Jude's High School and handed her a business card and her entire life changed.

"I'm trying to find the way to broach the topic with her mother."

"Her mother?" Freddy had laughed, exposing a set of very expensive, very white teeth. "Talk to the girl, dear heart, not her mother. That's how you get things done."

That's how you get things done.

She looked over at Nicole, who was finishing her second slice of pizza. The girl was exquisite. A beautifully clean jawline, delicate chin, even features that were regular without being bland, huge wide blue eyes very much like Maggy's, and a spill of thick wavy hair that, when it wasn't purple, was a rich shade of walnut brown. She was balanced on the spun-silk tightrope that formed the bridge between girlhood and womanhood, so lovely to look at that it hurt Claire's eyes.

Freddy was right. This magical time wouldn't last forever. Same as her own career. Everything was changing, faster than Claire could keep up with. If she was ever going to talk to Nicole about the photos, now was as good a time as any.

"Hey, Nic," she said, pushing back her chair and standing up. "How about we take the canines out for a walk?"

It was after nine o'clock by the time Conor left the bed.

"Déjà vu," Maggy said lazily from the center of the tangle of sheets and comforters. "I could get used to this very easily." In Cape May she'd stayed happily in bed while he went out into the storm in search of pizza.

"At least it's not raining," he said, inching his faded jeans up over his thighs.

"And you only have to walk as far as the kitchen."

He leaned over and kissed her. "Tired?"

"Yes, but it's a good tired." She nuzzled briefly against the side of his neck. "You're a very energetic man."

He grinned. "I aim to please."

"Let me say for the record that your aim is perfect."

He reminded her about something she'd done that was particularly memorable and it was her turn to grin. "There's a robe on the chair," he said, pointing to a wing chair near the floor-to-ceiling bookshelves. "And the kitchen's at the end of the hall if you feel like kibbitzing while I cook."

"Do you mind if I snoop for a while?" she asked. "I want to inspect your bookshelves."

"You're not going to find anything interesting," he said. "Just a lot of textbooks from when I went back to school."

"I want to see them," she said. She wanted to see them and touch them and skim the pages. She wanted to know everything there was to know about him. "You can tell a lot about a man by what he reads."

"Don't hold it against me if you're disappointed."

"I won't be disappointed," she said. "I promise."

He kissed her again then left to start dinner. She lay back against his pillows and listened to the sounds of cabinet doors opening and closing, pans rattling, Miles Davis playing softly. *Sketches of Spain*, the only Miles album she knew and liked. So he enjoyed jazz as well as Motown. Two seconds ago she hadn't known that very important fact. Suddenly she was overcome with the urge to snoop not only his bookshelves, but his CD rack as well. She leaped up from bed, used the bathroom, then wrapped herself in the robe he'd left on the wing chair. Soft, old flannel worn thin from a thousand washings. So old it held both his shape and the delicious smell of his skin. Sliding her arms into the sleeves was almost an erotic experience. How could everything about a man feel so right? If she were in her right mind, she'd be terrified by all of this perfection. His sheets, the feel of them, their smell, the way he angled the blinds, the soap in the bathroom, everything felt familiar to her. Familiar and right, as if she'd been part of each small decision.

She decided to start her snooping with the stack of books on the table next to the wing chair. Nothing terribly interesting there. Police procedure. Law. A book on the history of forensics. It startled her to be reminded that he was a cop. He never talked about his work. It didn't seem to play any part in the plans he made. How odd. So far, her part-time job at the rectory had had a greater impact on their time together than his very real job as a police detective.

Oh, wait. What was that over there? Pictures! How could she have missed them. Two small framed photos snuggled among the books on the third shelf from the top. This was even better than snooping through his books. She raised up on tiptoe and grabbed the first photo, the one in the black leather frame. It was standard graduation day fare. A young man in cap and gown clutched a diploma and smiled broadly into a faceful of sunshine. He was very tall and skinny, and she didn't have to look at it for more than a second to see the staggering resemblance he bore to Conor. His son Sean, of course. Who else could it possibly be? That meant the attractive blond woman on Sean's right was probably his mother. Conor's ex-wife. She had the slightly weepy-eyed look any mother worth her Huggies would have on such an important occasion. Maggy studied her face for a few moments, trying to imagine her with Conor, but she couldn't quite make the two of them fit together. Yet there was the handsome graduate, proof that once upon a time, they'd fit together very well indeed.

She reached up again and managed to snag the other photo with the crook of her index finger. This one was in a frame of dark, lustrous pine. It was a family photo of a handsome, dark-haired husband, his equally attractive dark-haired wife, and their two absolutely beautiful little girls. They were posed in front of Cinderella's castle at Disney World and smiling big wide smiles for the camera. The two little girls wore mouse ears.

"Salad's ready, and I'm looking to pop a bottle of champagne, so why—"

She spun around to find Conor standing in the doorway, looking adorably disheveled. "You said I could snoop," she said, smiling at him. She held up the Disney World photo. "What a handsome family." He didn't say a word, and a terrible feeling of dread scraped against her nerve endings. The silence grew deeper. "He looks so familiar," she went on, trying to fill the silence with chatter. "I'm sure I've seen him someplace."

"That's Bobby DiCarlo and his family," Conor said at last. "He was my partner."

"Was?" Her feeling of dread grew stronger. *Think hard, Maggy . . . where have you seen him before?* "You don't work together anymore?" Maybe Bobby DiCarlo retired or was fired or moved down to Florida. *A tragedy . . . you saw it on the news . . . a terrible tragedy that changed lives. . . .*

"Bobby was killed last year during a carjacking." He told her the day, the hour, the minute it happened. He told her where. He spewed facts the way a computer downloaded data. Only his eyes gave away the depth of his loss. "I held down the son of a bitch until the squad car showed up. His trial starts next month." His voice cracked, and he glanced away for a moment, the classic male gesture of camouflage that never worked. "I should've killed the bastard and saved the county the trouble."

Her eyes filled with tears that were as much for the man who stood before her as they were for Bobby DiCarlo and his family. That was why Bobby's photo seemed so familiar to her. She'd probably seen it a hundred times on the local news over the past year. She had only vague memories of the story itself. She'd been so busy with school and work and being a single parent that keeping up with the news had dropped way down on her list of priorities.

But this wasn't a news story to Conor. This was his life. His loss.

"Let the jury send him away forever," she said to him. "You did the right thing."

"There is no right thing," he said, turning away. "That's what they forget to tell you."

FIFTEEN

"No way!" Missy said, her high-pitched voice nipping at Nicole's eardrum. "A model?"

Nicole couldn't blame her best friend for sounding skeptical. She still couldn't believe it herself. "For real," she said, stretching her legs out in front of her and wiggling her toes. The blue nail polish was starting to look a little tired. "Aunt Claire said the photographer thinks I could be a big deal."

"Can you keep the purple hair?"

"Nuh-uh. The hair's gotta go . . . and ten pounds."

"Ten pounds! You're a size four, Nic! What do they want, a size zero?"

Nicole patiently explained that the camera added *beaucoup* pounds and inches and you had to be better than perfect to show off the designer's clothes the way they were meant to be displayed.

Missy had to think about that for a few seconds. "Did you see the pictures?"

She couldn't hold back a giggle as she looked at them spread across her lap. "You should see them, Missy. I looked twenty-five!" Like some stranger she met at a party and wouldn't recognize ten minutes later.

"Wow," said Missy. "You'll show them to me?"

"Tomorrow," she promised.

"So when do you get more pictures taken?"

"I dunno. Guess it depends."

"Uh-oh," said Missy. "You haven't told your mom yet."

"Can't," Nicole said. "She's out with that guy I told you about."

"The one from the phone?"

"Yeah." She told Missy about the way he'd treated Charlie like he was a relative or something.

"Bet Charlie hated that."

Nicole snorted. "The little worm can't wait for the jerk to come back again and play more basketball."

"Was he cute?"

"Yuck. He's way too old to be cute."

"What about your mom? Does she like him a lot?"

"She let him kiss her right there in the driveway," Nicole said. "I can't believe she'd do something that gross right in front of us."

Missy's voice got that dreamy, dopey sound it always got when she talked about romance. "Do you think they're in love?"

"Puh-leeze," Nicole said. "That's disgusting."

"Your dad's in love. Why not your mom?"

"Because she's not like that," Nicole said. Besides, she wasn't convinced her dad was really in love with Sally. "She's too busy to worry about stuff like that."

"Guess she found time somewhere." Missy started to speculate about her mom and that big jerk she was having dinner with, and it was all Nicole could do to keep from hanging up on her.

She felt like squeezing her hands over her ears so she didn't have to listen to Missy's dumb remarks. Missy didn't know what she was talking about. Her parents had been together forever and would probably be together until the end of the world. They'd lived in the same house since the day they were married, and her friend had done all of her growing up in the same room, the same house, the same town.

Missy didn't know what it was like to move every twelve months your whole life. Or how it felt to have divorced parents. Sometimes Nicole thought her heart had been torn into two big, jagged pieces that would never fit back together again, not in a million years. Everybody thought she was being so cool about Daddy and Sally, but they didn't know that just thinking about it made her cry herself to sleep. All these months she'd been thinking Daddy was just lonely and Sally was a good friend. Deep down in her heart, she'd believed that the divorce was just a big, fat, stupid mistake, and sooner or later both her Mom and her Dad would see things her way and they could all be together again the way it used to be.

Because it used to be really good, even if she was the only person in the world who remembered that fact. Even Charlie didn't seem to mind so much anymore. Why else would he act so happy with that jerk who'd come to take their mother out to dinner? Wouldn't you think he'd hate seeing her kiss a stranger? Nicole had wanted to kick the guy in the shins when he kissed her mom. You would think he had a right to do that or something, the way he just casually leaned down and planted one on her lips. Her mom should've told him to back off and pushed him away. Of course, maybe she didn't want him to back off, which was such a horrible prospect that Nicole almost cried just thinking about it.

She remembered the day her parents broke the big news to her and Charlie. Her parents called them into the living room and asked them to sit down on the sofa. Charlie had just turned seven, too little to pick up the vibes and figure out what was coming down, but Nicole knew. She'd heard the sadness in her mom's voice, seen the expression in her dad's eyes when he didn't know she was looking at him, and she knew. Charlie cried when they broke the news, but Nicole didn't shed a tear. She listened and nodded, and when they finished talking, she said, "Can I go to my room now?" They looked at each other, and finally her mom nodded and said yes. She lay on her bed for a very long time, looking up at the ceiling, and she didn't think one single thought.

"We're very proud of Nicole," they told the on-base family therapist who met with them once as part of the divorce proceedings. "She's been very grown-up about this." They worried about Charlie who seemed to cry every time you looked at him, but it was Charlie who got over it before the month was out.

Two years later, Nicole was still hoping for a miracle.

Maggy and Conor ate dinner in front of the fireplace, feeding each other long crispy spears of romaine dressed in lemon and olive oil, warm pieces of crusty bread, wine-sweet kisses. They drank big cups of cappuccino and ate chocolate-dipped biscotti. He licked the chocolate from her fingers, which led to a short but achingly wonderful encounter right there on the floor.

"Ouch," she said afterward, as she moved closer to him. "I'm not sure thirty-five-year old women can handle love on the rug." She was one very satisfied ache.

He enveloped her in one of those glorious, voluptuous full-body hugs that were almost as wonderful as making love. "You don't hear me talking about my bad knees, do you?"

She leaned up on her right elbow. "Your knees hurt?"

"Like hell," he said. "Too much football in college."

"Don't tell anybody," she said, "but my knees aren't the best, either." She told him about the time she went ice skating in Switzerland and was knocked off balance by the colonel's two-hundred-pound wife. "I landed on my knees. I tried to pretend I'd dropped down for a quick rosary, but nobody believed me." She'd spent the night in the hospital having emergency surgery on her right knee.

He made a show of kissing her behind each knee, sending ripples of pleasure through her. Oh, yes. Definitely a new erogenous zone to add to the list.

She pressed her lips to his shoulder and closed her eyes. "I should go home soon," she whispered.

"Stay."

"I can't."

"Your mother's with the kids."

"No," she said. "I don't feel right about it."

"I don't want you to leave."

"I don't want to leave either, but I have to."

Their silence was long and filled with kisses and touches that said more than words possibly could.

"I wasn't looking for you," he said. "I've been alone for almost twenty years. I thought I was happy without you."

"I've been alone for almost two," she said. "The kids and I have a good life. I didn't know anything was missing until I found you."

"You can do better," he said. "You could find yourself a handsome guy with a Mercedes and a big fat bank account."

"I don't want a guy with a Mercedes and a big fat bank account." She rained kisses on his eyelids and nose and lips. "You could find yourself somebody like my sister Claire: young and beautiful and unencumbered."

"I don't want your sister Claire. I want you, with all of your encumbrances."

She couldn't help laughing. "You barely know my encumbrances. Charlie is a sweetheart, but Nicole is the current poster child for adolescent angst."

"She'll grow out of it."

"Kids change everything," she said to him, struggling to retain her ability to think while he stroked her breast with large and gentle fingers. "They figure in every decision I make." Every breath she took. Every beat of her heart.

"That's the way it should be. I understand that."

"This all happened so fast," she said, shaking her head. "There's a right way to go about this, but we're so busy breaking sound barriers that I can't seem to get my bearings."

"Then we'll slow things down," he said. "Take it one step at a time."

One step at a time. One scary, wonderful, hopeful step at a time. She drew in a shaky breath. "So how would you feel about spending the day with us tomorrow?"

He held her close. "I'd say it was a good start."

"You're nuts." Conor's brother Matt threw the words across the pool table two weeks later. "Certifiable." He missed his shot and swore under his breath.

"Your brother's right," Frank, the Riley patriarch, said as he chalked up. "Why would you waste time with some divorced woman with kids? Believe you me, you don't need somebody else's troubles. Plenty of fish in the sea, that's what I say."

Conor nursed a beer at the bar and wondered why in hell he'd told his family anything about Maggy. First his mother gave him the pursed-lip look he'd hated since childhood and murmured a deadly "That's nice, dear." Then his two sisters exchanged looks over their sleeping babies and said they'd been hoping he would make them aunts again before their kids were on Social Security. Now his brother and their old man had spent the last hour ragging on him about his choice in women, and he was getting close to the breaking point. For the first time in over a year, he felt like his old self. For the first time since Bobby died, he felt he had the right to go on living.

"You get what I'm talking about," his brother said, gesturing for another Guinness. "You've got enough on your plate lately. I don't think you know what's good for you.''

"And you do?''

"Maybe,'' said Matt. Funny how he didn't hear the sound of the ice cracking beneath him. "I know you've spent the last year blaming yourself for Bobby's death. I've watched you kick yourself from one end of the state to the other. Now you show up and say you've met some single mother with two kids and you're ready to start playing house. That's transference, if you ask me. You're taking your guilt over Denise and Bobby's little girls and transferring it to this babe and her kids. Pretty easy to figure out if you know where to look.''

Conor stared at his kid brother in astonishment. "Do you really believe this crap or do you just like the way it sounds?''

"Hey,'' said Matt, clearly offended, "it wouldn't kill you to do a little couch time with a therapist. You could learn a lot about yourself if you'd open up.''

He'd done a few sessions with a counselor after Bobby's murder. *"I can't help you if you won't talk to me,''* the counselor had said after a particularly unproductive session. Conor had simply gathered up his jacket and walked out the door. He wasn't a talker. He worked out his pain with a speed bag and a pair of running shoes and found his soul again in Maggy's arms. He still didn't have answers to all the questions, and he probably never would, but he was moving forward again. A year ago, he wouldn't have believed that was possible.

"Don't get so touchy, big bro.'' Matt grabbed for the Guinness he'd left balanced on the windowsill. "I'm just looking out for your welfare. Taking on another man's kids is like taking on his bills. Who needs it?''

Conor took a long pull on his brew. "Yeah,'' he said, "you've got it all figured out. That's why you shoved Lisa aside for an ad exec with an overbite and a fat 401K.''

Matt glowered at him. "I told you there was nothing serious between Lisa and me."

"Tell it to somebody who believes you," Conor shot back. "I was there. I saw you two together. She was the best thing to happen to you in a hell of a long time, and you were too goddamn stupid to hang around." His brother had always been a man in a hurry. He wanted everything, and he wanted it now: money, prestige, power. Lisa was still in law school with a long road in front of her, and waiting wasn't in Matt's vocabulary. As far as he was concerned, she was nothing more than a cocktail waitress with a dream.

"Why ask for trouble?" Matt said, watching while Frank lined up his shot. "Why make your life any more complicated than it already is?"

Their old man sank two shots then scratched. "He's got a point," Frank said as he joined Conor at the bar. "Marriage isn't exactly a bed of roses. Why take on another man's kids if you don't have to?"

Conor found himself glad his ex-wife's husband hadn't felt that way years ago. Now that he was getting to know Maggy's kids, he had more respect for the guy than ever before. There was nothing easy about it, especially not with her daughter, but he wasn't about to tell that to his father and brother.

"You two are beginning to sound like something out of the dark ages." He slammed his can of Coors down on the shiny surface of the bar. "And who said anything about marriage, anyway? I mention that I'm seeing a woman named Maggy and that she happens to have two kids, and all holy hell breaks loose around here."

"You taken a look at your face lately?" his father asked him. "You're a marked man. The only thing missing is the marriage license."

"Listen," he said, "I'm bringing her down for the christening on Sunday, and if either one of you jokers starts up . . ." He let his words trail away ominously.

His father raised his hands in the air like a perp surrendering to authority. "Won't hear anything out of me."

"Do what you want," Matty said, racking up the balls for another game. "None of my business if you want to fuck up your life."

"Is *he* coming over again?" Nicole asked Maggy on Sunday over a late breakfast.

Maggy withheld a sigh. Her daughter had taken to speaking in italics whenever she spoke about Conor. "Yes, Conor is coming over," she said calmly. "We're going to his nephew's christening down in Absecon. Remember? I asked you to join us."

Nicole rolled her eyes. "There's a big deal."

"We'd still love it if you came with us."

"I don't think so."

"Charlie's coming along."

"Like he has a choice," Nicole muttered.

Let it go. Don't let her bait you. If you do, you'll never get through to her.

"You've been keeping to yourself a lot lately, Nic. I miss you." It seemed as if every spare second was filled with friends and school activities that kept her just beneath Maggy's radar screen. She felt a little guilty that she'd been so caught up in school and work and Conor that she hadn't tried harder to keep track of what her daughter had been up to. In truth, she had grown so accustomed to seeing her overtures rebuffed that there was great relief in letting go just a little bit. "I'd like us to spend some time together as a family."

The angry mask on her daughter's lovely face slipped for a moment, just long enough for Maggy to see that her little girl was still in there somewhere. It was enough to give her hope.

"Like you'd even notice if I'm not around," Nicole said.

"I noticed that you rinsed the purple out of your hair."

"No big deal," Nicole said with a shrug of her slender shoulders. "I got tired of it."

She reached out and drew a loving hand along her daughter's silky head. "I'm happy to see your own pretty hair again."

Nicole's eyes flashed. "I was thinking of going green."

Maggy drew back and folded her hands on the tabletop. "Nickel," she said, using an old pet name for her daughter, "what did I do to make you feel this way?"

Her little girl's rage spilled across the table in a torrent of tears and angry words. "Daddy called this morning. He *married* her! He went and married her last night, and he didn't even tell me first."

It took all of Maggy's self-control to keep from bursting into tears right along with her daughter. Only this time it had nothing to do with Charles and Sally and everything to do with her child. So much pain. How she wished she knew how to make it all disappear. "Oh, honey, I'm sorry you had to find out after the fact this way, but you knew your Daddy and Sally were in love and planning to get married. This isn't that big a surprise."

"Yes, it *is!*" Nicole cried. "This wasn't supposed to happen! He wasn't supposed to go and marry her. He was supposed to—" She stopped and buried her face in her hands and sobbed as if her heart were breaking.

Maggy's heart felt the same way. "You thought your daddy and I might get back together, didn't you?"

There was no response from Nicole, just the sound of steady sobbing.

"Oh, honey, even if your daddy hadn't married Sally, that never would have happened. We explained it all to you. Your daddy and I like and respect each other, but somewhere along the way, we stopped loving each other the way a husband and wife should love each other.

There was no way we were ever going to get that back again.''

"Maybe if you hadn't met *him*, it could've happened.''

"No,'' Maggy said softly, "not even then.''

"I don't understand,'' Nicole said, wiping her eyes with her sleeve. "I thought when you love somebody, you love them forever. How can you just stop like it meant nothing?''

Oh God. Help me say the right thing. Help me explain something I don't even understand myself. "Your daddy and I loved each other very much. In some ways we still do. It's just that the way we loved each other changed.''

"Why?'' Nicole demanded. "I don't understand why things have to change. Does that mean one day you'll wake up and you won't love me anymore either?''

"I'll always love you, honey. You're my little girl. My firstborn.''

"Why should I believe you? You said you'd love Daddy forever and you didn't. Why should it be any different with me?'' With that, Nicole kicked over her chair and ran from the room.

For a moment, a part of Maggy shut down. How many times had they replayed this scene? The angry teenage girl. The bewildered mother. The accompanying sounds of a slammed bedroom door and loud sobbing from within that invariably tore at Maggy's heart. She had always let the scene run its course in the past, but this time she leaped up from her own chair and raced down the hallway after Nicole.

"Honey, we need to talk,'' she said to the locked door. She heard the sound of muffled crying. "Nickel, please don't shut me out.'' How had it come to this? She'd carried that little girl inside her own body for nine months, nursed her, changed her diapers, dried her tears, and now all she could do was stand in front of her locked bedroom door and pray for a miracle. She heard the bedsprings squeak, soft footsteps, then the scratch of a lock being opened. Could it be her prayers were being answered?

She tested the door. It opened wide, and she saw her little girl sprawled diagonally across the bed with her face buried in the fluffy pink and white pillows. A splash of morning sunshine spilled through the big windows and picked up the golden highlights in her daughter's hair. All of the confusion and anger melted into a rush of love so intense it almost brought her to her knees.

"Oh, baby . . ." She sat down on the edge of the bed and placed a hand on Nicole's trembling shoulder. Suddenly she understood the tears. "I know how much you miss Daddy." She'd missed her father, too, all those years ago. She'd never stopped missing him, never would.

"I hate him!" Nicole's voice was muffled against the pillow. "How can he marry somebody I don't even know?"

"He wasn't trying to hurt you," she said, struggling to find the words that would heal her daughter's wounds. "He and Sally have been together a while now, and they're very much in love. The moment must have seemed right to get married." There. She'd said it and she was still alive, still breathing. Charles and Sally were married, and her world continued to turn despite that fact. How quickly things had changed for the better. "You have to remember how far away your Daddy is, Nic. He must be very lonely." How do you explain to a fifteen-year-old girl that time moves faster as you get older, and sometimes you have to close your eyes and jump in?

Nicole looked up at her, her face tear-streaked and filled with pain. "I could go live with him," she said. "Charlie could live here with you, and I could go live with Daddy."

"That's not a good idea," Maggy said carefully as she negotiated her way through a maternal minefield. "Your Daddy and I think it's better that you and Charlie stay with me and go to school in the States.'' They'd spent a lifetime on the road, or so it seemed. It was time for a little stability.

"You and Daddy think it's better if I stay here, but doesn't anybody care what I think?''

Maggy opened her mouth to refute that statement when she caught a glimpse of shiny paper poking out from beneath the frilly bedspread. She bent down and retrieved a half dozen eight-by-ten glossies. "What on earth—?'' They were all black and white, all beautiful, all of her very grown-up-looking daughter.

Nicole sat up, her blue eyes wide with a combination of pride and alarm. "They're mine,'' she said, trying to snatch them away from Maggy. "They have nothing to do with you.''

"Where did they come from?''

Nicole stared back at her, closed-mouthed.

"Nicole.'' Maggy managed to keep the tremor from her voice. "I asked you a question. Who took these pictures?'' They were provocative pictures. Sophisticated, just bordering on overtly sexy.

"Some guy.''

Some guy. The possibilities made Maggy feel physically ill. "What's his name?'' She took a deep, steadying breath. "Where did you meet him?'' This wasn't the first time Nicole had been approached by so-called talent agents who hung out around the high school, looking for exceptionally nubile and naïve young girls.

"I don't remember his name.''

"You don't remember his name?'' Her voice crept up an octave. "How can you—''

"He's one of Aunt Claire's friends.''

"Claire?'' Her head was spinning. "Claire had something to do with this?''

Nicole had that deer-in-the-headlights look she got whenever she was cornered by a direct question. "What do you care, anyway?'' she countered. "You're never

home to know what's going on. You're always at work
or at school or with *him*."

A daughter's aim was always deadly, but never more
so than when she sensed weakness. Guilt: the place every
mother called home.

"That's unfair, Nicole, and you know it."

Nicole stared back at her in open defiance, and Maggy
was torn between wanting to hug her until she came to
her senses and the desire to ground her for life.

"Get dressed," she said, tucking the photos under her
left arm. "That settles it. You're coming to the christening with us."

"No, I'm not."

"No arguments, Nic. We're going as a family."

"Why should I be punished because you're sleeping
with some jerk?"

Maggy had never struck her daughter in anger, but this
time she felt an ugly swell of something that frightened
her, and she stepped back. "Get dressed, Nic," she said
again, forcing herself to remain on topic. "I'll speak to
Claire about these photos when we get home."

"I want the pictures," Nicole said, holding out her
hand. "They're mine."

"Nonnegotiable," Maggy said. "Now, please get
dressed. Conor will be here in an hour, and we're not
going to keep him waiting."

SIXTEEN

"I'm so sorry," Maggy said for the tenth time. "I don't know what's keeping Nicole."

She looked worried, frazzled, and extremely lovely, and he couldn't keep his mouth shut any longer. "Yeah, you do," Conor said as he nursed a cup of coffee in her kitchen. "It's me, isn't it?"

She gazed out the window at Charlie, who was running the dogs in the backyard. "No, it isn't you. It's the concept of *us* that she's having trouble with."

"There's a lot of that going around."

She swung around and met his eyes. "Your family, too?"

"They're opinionated. I'm used to it, but I thought I should warn you."

"If you withstood the attack of the Halloran Harpies, I'm sure I can hold up under an attack of Rileys." She forced a smile, but it wasn't up to her Olympic standards. "We had a fight just before you got here."

"Anything you want to talk about?"

"Standard mother-daughter warfare." She tried to make light of it but failed. She told him how it had begun with her ex-husband's remarriage the other day and escalated into a confrontation over some photos.

"You just found out your ex was engaged, right?"

She nodded. "The day we met," she said, then laughed softly. "Endings and beginnings."

He knew all about both.

"How about you?" he asked, because he had to. "Are you having as tough a time as Nicole?" He and Linda had only been married a couple of years when they divorced, but her remarriage had still hit him like a two-by-four between the eyes.

No quick answers. Not from his Maggy. "It hurt," she admitted after a moment, "but it wasn't fatal. It's hard to imagine there's a new Mrs. Charles O'Brien on board."

There wasn't much he could say to that without revealing more of his own insecurities. He'd seen enough of them lately to last the rest of his life.

They sat together in silence for a few minutes more, then Maggy pushed back her chair. "That's it," she said. "I can't let you miss your own nephew's christening because my daughter is having a bad day."

"We have time," he said. "Give her a couple minutes more."

"What I'd like to give her is a piece of my mind."

"Why don't I talk to her?"

She looked at him and burst into laughter. "Oh, there's a great idea."

"Nicole and I have to get to know each other sometime."

"What if you make things worse?"

He winced. "You'll never fail a polygraph."

"You know I don't mean it quite the way it came out. She views you as a threat. I doubt if she'll open up." She kissed his shoulder. "I can't believe I'll be going through this again with Charlie in a few years."

He gripped her by the waist then pulled her onto his

lap. "I mean it about talking to Nicole. Sooner or later, we'll have to reach an accommodation. We might as well start working on it now."

She knew what he was saying. He could see it in her eyes, the tilt of her head, the way she held his hand just a little tighter. *I'm around for the long haul, Maggy. I'm in this for the duration.*

She kissed his mouth. "That's okay," she said. "She's my problem. I wouldn't wish this on anybody."

"I love Jeeps!" Charlie said as they pulled out of the driveway a little while later. "Did you always have a Jeep?"

Conor looked at him in the rearview mirror and grinned. "Pretty much."

"That's what I'm gonna drive when I'm old enough," Charlie said, tracing a design on the window with the tip of his index finger. "A black one with gold trim and my initials on the driver's side door."

"The man knows what he wants," Conor said to Maggy who was sitting next to him. "That's the first step."

Maggy started to say something but was interrupted by a loud sigh from the backseat. "You said something, Nic?" she asked politely.

"Not me," said the girl slumped in the corner against the door. "I don't have anything to say to anybody."

Conor shot Maggy a look, and she shrugged. "Pyrrhic," she said, "but it still counts." Nicole wasn't happy about it, but she was there. He had no idea what Maggy had said to her, what maternal pressures she'd brought to bear, but they must have been considerable.

"You're almost at driving age," he said to Nicole. "What kind of car would you buy?"

Another long sigh followed by silence. He could feel Maggy tense up next to him. "Forget it," he said quietly. "It doesn't matter."

He could barely see Nicole's golden hair in the rear-view mirror. He was surprised such a tall young girl could fold herself up into such a tiny ball of woe, but somehow she'd managed to do exactly that. She was almost a parody of teenage despair, but he found nothing humorous about her emotions. He'd only seen a little of that with Sean during a few adolescent summers, but he knew that Linda had experienced a full measure of what Maggy was going through now. Up until now, he hadn't really understood what it was all about. His admiration for his ex-wife and his new love skyrocketed.

He wished he felt some of that for Nicole, but he didn't. She was beautiful, difficult, disrespectful to her mother, and completely uncommunicative where he was concerned. He tried to find something of Maggy in her, some little mannerism or phrase he could focus on, but there was nothing. He flat-out couldn't find anything to like about the girl, but she was part of Maggy, and that made her important.

Maggy was fiddling with the CD player, riffling through his discs in search of the right peacekeeping music for the drive down to Deirdre's. Charlie peppered him with questions about the Jeep, and he fell easily into the same father-son groove he inhabited every time Sean came to town. It felt good being with Maggy's son. It felt right. Charlie was easy to love. He was bright and enthusiastic and joyful, same as his mother, and Conor felt a stab of regret that he'd missed out on this kind of day-to-day life with his own son. Maybe that's what second chances were all about.

"It'll happen for you one day," his dead partner used to tell him after one of those supper-and-a-video evenings with Denise and the kids. "A woman's gonna come along and *pow!* You'll be history same as me the first time I saw Deni."

Wouldn't Bobby be laughing his ass off if he could

see him now, driving a couple of kids around in his Jeep, same as his partner used to do once upon a time.

"I want to go home," Nicole said to Maggy about two hours into the christening party.

"So do I," Maggy whispered, "but we have to wait for Conor."

"He's over there," Nicole said, gesturing toward a knot of Rileys gathered in the corner. "Go get him and tell him we're going nuts."

"We're his guests," Maggy said, clinging to her best adult behavior. "We'll have to wait until he's ready to go."

Nicole muttered something, then said she was going off to find her brother, the surest sign of desperation Maggy had ever encountered.

Party: ten, she thought, looking around the beautifully decorated home. *Family: zero.*

Harsh? They were lucky she wasn't into rating in the negative. Everyone from Conor's mother to his baby nephew had been scrupulously polite, but that was all. If she'd been looking for warmth, she'd be better off crawling into the fridge.

She would never forget that first moment when they stepped into the room and everything stopped cold. Conversation. Laughter. Movement. Breathing, more than likely. Every blessed activity ground to a halt the moment they turned and saw her step into the room with Conor and her two children. For the first time she fully understood how he had felt when confronted with her own formidable family.

His sister Deirdre, mother of the infant being christened, was polite and friendly, but it was clear she was being a good hostess and nothing more. His mother made a few pointed comments about Nicole's advanced age until Maggy managed to work the fact that her daughter was only fifteen into the conversation. She managed to work that fact into a conversation with Conor's brothers as well, and wasn't above enjoying the looks of disappointment on their faces.

She wondered again what Claire had been thinking when she had those photos of Nicole made. If anyone knew the pitfalls involved in modeling, it was her sister. Claire had been modeling since seventh grade. She quit school at sixteen to pursue it full-time, much to their mother's dismay. "Look at this, Ma," Claire had said, waving a fat check under Rita's nose. "You can't earn this in a year, not even with overtime."

Rita had crumbled just as Claire had hoped. Money had been an issue all their lives. No matter how hard Rita worked, there was never enough to go around. Claire's amazing paychecks had shifted the balance of power in her direction, and Rita never managed to tilt it back in her favor. Claire ran wild for a few years after Maggy married and moved away, and Rita had blamed it all on her modeling career.

Bad influences, Rita had said, but Maggy wasn't so sure Claire was blameless. Give a wild child money and independence, and you were asking for trouble. She wasn't going to make that mistake with her own daughter, no matter how tight finances might occasionally be. She was disappointed that Claire would try to undermine her this way, and as soon as she got home she intended to place a phone call to her sister and tell her exactly that.

She walked over to the buffet to refill her glass of punch and was joined by one of Conor's younger brothers.

"I'm Matt," he said. "We almost met that night in Atlantic City."

She smiled and extended her right hand. "Maggy," she said, then glanced around. The beautiful young blond she remembered from the restaurant was nowhere in sight.

"If you're looking for Lisa, she isn't here. We were just friends." He gestured toward a studious-looking woman deep in conversation with a group of equally studious-looking other women. "I've been seeing her for a month now."

Maggy nodded. The use of the pronoun *her* jarred her, but she wasn't going to make an issue of it at a christening. Matt was the brother who wasn't a cop or a fireman, which made him stand out in this particular crowd. Conor's father was a retired cop; his uncles were firemen; most of his cousins were on the force in some capacity. It was pretty clear to Maggy that law enforcement was the family business.

They hung together in tight little groups, and she couldn't help but notice that none of those groups welcomed Conor into their midst. Only Matt, the budding hotel executive, seemed open and friendly.

"Your daughter's a beautiful kid," Matt said, helping himself to punch after Maggy finished refilling her glass.

"Emphasis on the word *kid*," she said. It didn't hurt to remind him.

"Must give you a few gray hairs, worrying about her."

"More than you'll ever know," she said. "I've considered building a moat around my house, but we don't have the right zoning."

Her joke flew right over his head. *Your brother would've laughed.* One of the many ways in which he differed from his family.

"She's pretty enough to be a model."

"I know," Maggy said. "Unfortunately, so does she."

Conor joined them. He placed a hand on her shoulder, a gesture that did not go unnoticed by the assembled Rileys in the room. "Enjoying yourself?" he asked.

She smiled up at him. "What do you think?"

He brushed her ear with his lips. "We'll split soon," he said. "Soon as they make the toast."

She made sure her smile didn't waver. She also made sure she didn't burst into applause.

They chatted casually with Matt, who had the amazing gift of being able to bring any conversation back around to himself and his ideas, and were soon joined by the matriarch of the clan. She was tall, rangy, and as tightly wound as her fiercely gray hair. "You're staying for dinner, aren't you?" she asked the group. "The family's going to Golden Dragon once the party winds down."

"Sorry, Ma," said Conor, "but we're heading out soon. Maggy's kids have school tomorrow."

"It's a special occasion," his mother said, giving Maggy a look that only another woman could interpret. "Surely you can make an exception."

"Not this time," Conor said.

"I know you're not family," his mother said to Maggy, "but if it wouldn't be too uncomfortable for you—"

"Conor's right," she said. "We need to leave soon."

"It must be difficult," his mother said, "bringing up two children on your own."

"Their father is a big help," Maggy said, biting back a sharp retort. "I just wish there were a few extra hours in every day."

"Have you been divorced long?"

"Two years," Maggy said.

"Does he live nearby, dear?"

"He's in London," Maggy said pleasantly. "With his new wife." *Take that, you nosy cow.*

Mrs. Riley was well trained in the fine art of verbal warfare, female style. She turned to Conor. "Joe and Angie Renaldi had their first last week. Eight pounds, twelve ounces."

"Huh," said Conor while Matt drifted away at the first mention of marriage and procreation. "Whaddya know."

"And here he never thought he'd have a family."

Conor turned to Maggy. "Joe's my age," he said. "His second wife is twenty-three."

"Ah," said Maggy. "I see." Breeding stock, Mrs. Riley was saying in her subtle way. *I have a few good years left in me,* Maggy thought as she smiled benignly at Conor's mother. *I'm not menopausal yet.*

One of the numerous cousins burst into the room. "You better get out there right now," he said to Maggy. His eyes were as wide as fried eggs on a plate. "They're fighting like cats and dogs."

"Oh, God!" Maggy was out the door in a flash, tearing across the back lawn toward the commotion near the swing set. Charlie was sweet but competitive, and he'd been known to get into more than his share of scrapes over any game that involved a ball. If he gave any of the Riley relatives a bloody nose, she would—

Nicole was standing in the middle of a group of angry Rileys, one of whom was holding her arms behind her back. For a second, Maggy saw her child the way a man might see her, and the revelation terrified her. Nicole looked wild and disheveled and impossibly beautiful. The Rileys looked just plain furious.

"Let go of my daughter!" Maggy commanded in a tone of voice that only a fool would ignore.

"She's crazy," one of the myriad Riley males said as he released his hold on Nicole's wrists. "She tried to break my nose."

Maggy stepped forward, hands clenched at her sides. Although the smallest Riley had at least six inches on her, they all backed away. Nobody in his or her right mind would get between a mother and her child. Not if they knew what was good for them.

"What's going on?" She addressed the question to everyone, but her eyes were locked on her daughter.

"She jumped him," said one of the Riley cousins. "They got into a fight, and the next thing we knew, she was all over him."

"Nicole." She willed her daughter to meet her eyes. "What happened?"

"Nothing," Nicole muttered. Her face was a mask of pure defiance.

"Are they telling the truth?"

She shrugged. "I guess."

Maggy forced herself to look back at the growing knot of Rileys. "Anyone want to tell me what happened?"

"It was her fault," said a girl with straight black hair. She pointed straight at Nicole. "We were talking about Uncle Conor, and she opened up her big mouth and—" The girl stopped abruptly. Her cheeks reddened, and she looked away.

Suddenly they all looked uncomfortable, almost sad, and began to drift away. She turned slightly and noticed Conor standing behind her. *I don't want to know,* she thought. *Whatever it is, I don't want to hear it.*

"Everything's under control," she said to him, "but I think it might be time for us to say good night and head home."

The ride home was dismal. Nicole cried from the moment she climbed into the back of the Jeep until they pulled into Maggy's driveway. At first Charlie tried to tease her out of her mood, but then something about the tension in the truck got to him. The next thing Maggy knew, he was crying, too. There was no point in trying to get the story out of Nicole right now. That would only lead to more hysteria, something that was in abundant supply at the moment.

Besides, Maggy wasn't sure she wanted to know what the fight was all about. She told herself it didn't matter, that it was nothing more than the push-and-pull dynamics between teenagers, but deep down she knew there was more to it than that.

Maggy and Conor soon gave up any pretense of making conversation and rode in silence.

Welcome to family life, she thought as he turned into her driveway. *Destroyer of romantic illusions.*

Her mother had said that nobody could love your children the way you could, and she was probably right. In fact, at that particular moment, as she watched Nicole run up the stairs and into the house followed by a wailing Charlie, Maggy wasn't so sure she was all that crazy about them either. Love, yes. Like? That was a whole other story.

"Run," she said, turning to Conor who was leaning against the hood of the Jeep. "Run for your life."

He didn't. Instead, he opened his arms wide, and she stepped into his embrace. She didn't much care if the entire neighborhood was watching.

"When worlds collide," she said, resting her forehead against his chest. "Bet you wish you'd left us all home."

He kissed the top of her head. Nobody had ever thought to kiss the top of her head before. It made her feel cherished, and she closed her eyes against a rush of longing that made her dizzy. If only it could be this simple.

"Bet you wish you'd stayed home," he said.

"It wasn't that bad."

He tilted her chin until she was looking him right in the eye. "Try looking at me when you say something like that."

"I can't," she said on a laughing sigh. "I lied. It was pretty grim."

"I gave my mother hell while you were talking to Nicole in the yard."

"You didn't have to do that."

"Yeah, I did."

"Why does this have to be so complicated?"

"Because we're not eighteen," he said, "and we don't travel light." They both came with histories trailing behind them like a chain of cabooses behind a locomotive.

"Your mother thinks I'm too old for you."

"My mother can be a jerk."

"I think she's looking for breeding stock."

His hands spanned her hips in a subtle but very effective gesture. "I don't see a problem."

"You know what she's talking about." Grandchildren, a whole bouquet of them, all with a fifty percent quota of sturdy Riley blood flowing through their veins.

"I quit taking my mother's opinion seriously about twenty years ago, Maggy. What she thinks doesn't matter."

"I'm glad," she said, but she knew firsthand the trouble family pressures could inflict upon a marriage. She and Charles had been fine when they were stationed overseas, but the second they came back within a two hours' drive of either family, the fireworks began. "I just wish the kids had made a better impression."

"What's the difference?" he said. "They already have a great family. They'll never miss mine."

"Single mothers are judged by how well their children are doing. I failed that test today with flying colors."

"Screw it," he said, then said it again more colorfully.

Maggy couldn't help laughing. "You make it sound so simple."

"This will work out," he said, holding her tight. "Once they see we're serious, they'll have no choice but to accept us."

"Do you remember how easy it was that weekend in Cape May?" She knew she sounded wistful, but she couldn't help it. She felt wistful. "We didn't even know each other's last names."

"We'll go back there again," he said, stroking her hair.

"Sure we will," she said, but she was afraid it wouldn't be the same. They knew too much now and, what was worse, they wanted even more.

SEVENTEEN

Nicole couldn't sleep. She tossed and turned and even went so far as to put one of the pillows over her face to block out the noise and light, but nothing helped. Finally she switched on the bedside lamp and tried to read the latest *Seventeen*, but she was too tired to concentrate. The words danced all over the page, and she couldn't seem to follow the story, no matter how hard she tried. She tossed down the magazine in disgust and just lay there, staring up at the cracks in her ceiling.

She could hear her mom and her aunt Claire arguing in the kitchen. They'd been at it for two hours now, and Nicole was ready to scream. At first she'd tried to sit there with them and plead her case—it *was* her life, after all, they were talking about—but her mom had turned on her and ordered her back to her room. She'd looked to Claire for support, but Claire just looked at her and said, "Listen to your mother," then turned away. Her aunt might as well have driven a stake through her heart. It couldn't have hurt any more than those words did.

You couldn't believe any of them. No matter what little thing they promised you, you'd better believe if you looked hard enough, you'd find the escape hatch they'd set up for themselves. *It's for your own good, honey. . . . I'm only thinking about you. . . . You'll thank me one day. . . . When you're my age, you'll understand. . . .*

Oh, she understood, all right. She understood just how unfair and selfish her mother had been every single step of the way. It was her mom's fault that they were no longer a family. All because she got tired of moving around, following Daddy from place to place. She said she wanted to settle down in one place, have a real home, get her college degree. She didn't give one single thought to what Nicole or Charlie wanted. She just didn't care.

It wasn't like they were rich or anything. Her mom couldn't afford an extra car or insurance or any of the great clothes Nicole spent hours mooning over at the mall with Melissa and Stacey on Saturday afternoons. Why not let her start working right now so she could buy all those things for herself? Besides, if Aunt Claire was right and she really could make it superbig as a model, she could afford to fly over and see Daddy any time she wanted to, no matter how far away he was stationed. First class, even, with free shrimp and room to stretch out and maybe even a movie actor or rock star sitting next to her.

He probably didn't even know how much she missed him, since every time he called there was so much other stuff to say that the important things kind of got pushed aside. She knew it wasn't his fault that he was so far away. His job with the Army was important, and sometimes they sent him to places where family couldn't go. That was why he and Sally had suddenly married, even though he'd said they wouldn't make any plans until Christmas. "I'll be spending some time in the Middle East," he'd told her while she tried real hard not to cry. "I wish you and Charlie could've been here, but Sally and I wanted to make it official before I shipped out, Nickel." Which told her that it was dangerous where he was going, even if he never said those words himself.

You couldn't put much over on an army brat, no matter how hard you tried. She knew that her dad was off someplace dangerous, same as she knew her mom was about to make a big fat mistake with that cop. Maybe if her mom got her head out of the clouds for a minute or two, she'd see what a worm he really was. She'd heard her aunts talking with Grandma about his dead partner and how it looked like that Riley guy had sacrificed his best friend to save his own ass, which was probably the worst thing a cop could ever do. Her aunt Ellie was a lawyer, and she'd heard all the gossip, how they'd put him on a sabbatical or something so he'd have a chance to get it together again. She'd mentioned that to those dickhead relatives of his at the party in a real casual sort of way, and they all went nuts on her, like she'd gone and told them Christmas had been canceled for lack of interest. Like it was her fault they couldn't handle the truth.

Who cared what they thought, anyway? Who cared what any of them thought about anything? So what if her father had married a woman she barely knew and her mother was dating the kind of guy who'd push his best friend into the line of fire. It didn't matter to her anymore.

She got up and switched on her computer then searched for the scanned business card she'd filed away, deep within folders within folders. She didn't need her parents' help. She didn't need her aunt Claire's help. She'd do just fine on her own.

"You stay out of my daughter's business," Maggy said to her sister near the end of Round Fourteen, "and I'll stay out of yours."

"You're making a mistake," Claire said, pouring herself another cup of coffee. "That girl is a gold mine."

"That girl is my daughter, and I don't want to see her ending up like—" She stopped dead, ashamed of what she'd been about to say.

"Like me," Claire said with a short laugh. "Go ahead. We've said everything else tonight. You might as well say it."

Maggy was torn between anger and embarrassment. "You've had a difficult life," she said carefully. "I want Nicole's road to be easier."

"Well put," said Claire, applauding. "Honest, but not cruel."

"I don't appreciate the sarcasm."

"I'm not being sarcastic. You said what you meant, and I appreciate it. I've had a shitty life for the most part, and you want to spare your daughter. Who can blame you?"

"I said difficult," Maggy repeated. "There's a difference."

"Shitty. Difficult." Claire laughed again. "It's all the same. Why would you want Nic to emulate her faded and failing Auntie Claire?"

Maggy blew out a loud breath and refilled her coffee mug. "Not that again," she said. "It's getting a little old, don't you think?"

"It's what we've been talking about all night," Claire shot back. "I'm sinking, Nicole's rising. I can help her. I can guide her. I can make sure she is treated the way she deserves to be treated, not the way I was treated coming up. I can make a difference."

"I understand that," Maggy said, "but the fact remains I'm not about to allow my fifteen-year-old daughter to become a model." *Or turn her over to your care, Claire, no matter how much I love you.*

"You're making a mistake."

"I don't think I am."

"You're very good at making mistakes," Claire observed, "but not so good at admitting to them. It's a flaw, Mags. You should work on it."

"We're not here to discuss my myriad flaws," Maggy

snapped. "We're here to agree that there will be no more secret photo sessions with my daughter."

Claire glared at her across the table. "You always make the safe and predictable decision, don't you, Mags? You leave Charles and a life of travel and come crawling back home to Nowhere, New Jersey, so you can live the way your mother lived thirty years ago. The way your mother *wanted* to live. I can see why your daughter's ambitions might not sit too well with you."

"You're being a bitch, Claire. I think it's time you went home."

"Just the truth, Mags. You're the one who's so in love with the truth. Why is it so hard to take when it's close to home? Nicole isn't you. She doesn't want what you want. She loved the traveling. She misses Charles. She wants more from life than a quarter acre and a mortgage."

Maggy pushed back her chair. "Talk to me when you get your own house in order. I'm not the one who wants to hitch a ride on a fifteen-year-old girl's fortunes."

"Maybe not," Claire said, pushing back her own chair and rising to her feet, "but at least I'm not fucking a loser."

The sound of the slap echoed in the quiet kitchen. Maggy's palm stung from the impact with Claire's perfect cheek.

"Nice," said Claire, touching the right side of her face with cautious fingers. "Something else for Nic to emulate. Maybe we're more alike than I thought."

"I'm sorry," Maggy said, reaching out to her sister. "I shouldn't have done that."

Claire took a step back. "Remember that wonderful guy Ma married not long after Daddy died?" Her words dripped with venom. "There's an example of a swell stepfather for you. Ever stop and wonder how good Mr. Wonderful would be at the job?"

"That's none of your business."

"Seems like it'll be everybody's business once that trial starts."

Maggy had to think for a second. Conor hadn't mentioned his partner since that evening at his house when she discovered the photo of Bobby and his family. She'd almost forgotten about the trial. Bobby's death had been a terrible accident, a heartbreaking tragedy, and there was no reason to dwell on it with Conor. If he wanted to talk about Bobby, she would be honored to listen. If not, that was fine, too. Last week he'd mentioned that the trial would begin the week before Thanksgiving and was expected to be finished by the end of the first week of December. He seemed unconcerned, and she took her cue from him.

"And your point is?"

Claire seemed taken aback. "That should be clear."

"It isn't."

"Ellie didn't tell you."

"Tell me what?"

"It's pretty much an open-and-shut case but the defense is going to try to throw some mud on your new boyfriend." Claire looked as if she was struggling between enjoyment and shame. Enjoyment was winning. "They say he could've saved Bobby DiCarlo's life, but he froze, stood there staring at the gun pointed at his partner's head and didn't do a thing to help him."

"Ridiculous," Maggy said. "That's not the man I know."

"You mean that's not the man you think you know. Your hormones are doing the thinking for you right now, Mags. You don't know the first thing about this guy. Not really."

"I know everything I need to know." He was kind and loving and smart and funny and he treated her like a goddess.

"You're thirty-five-years old and you've been single only two years of your adult life. You're making every mistake in the book, and you don't even know it. Open your eyes, Mags. You just might've picked yourself a loser.''

"You're going too far," Maggy warned her sister. "This isn't any of your business."

"You say you care about the kids, and I believe you. You're the best mother I know, but if you care so god-damn much, why don't you look for a better man to be their stepfather?''

"This conversation is over."

"Scared, Maggy? Afraid I just might stumble onto an ugly little piece of reality you can't pretty up the way you pretty up everything that doesn't work out quite the way you wanted it to?''

Maggy was trembling with anger. "Get out, Claire."

Claire gathered up her belongings. "Think about what I said. He might be great between the sheets, but is he good enough to sit at the table night after night with your kids? Our mother didn't ask that question, and look what it did to me."

"You can't blame Ma's marriage to Cal for your prob-lems, Claire. You brought most of them on yourself."

"How would you know?" Claire shot back. "You ran off the first chance you got and left the rest of us high and dry."

"You make it sound as if I ran away from home the way you did when you were fourteen. I got married, Claire, remember? White dress. Church. Flowers. I started a family of my own."

"You took the first escape route that came along," Claire said, not backing down an inch. "Charles was tall and handsome. He was off to see the world, and you wanted to go with him."

"I fell in love."

"And you wanted out."

"Yes, I wanted out!" Maggy shouted. "I wanted a home and family of my own, the kind with a house and a husband and two kids and a dog. I wanted to try on normal and see if it fit. Is that a crime?''

"I wanted out, too, Mags. I just found another way. Don't let that happen to Nic.''

In typical fashion, Charlie was his usual good-natured self the next morning, while Nicole nursed a healthy grudge against Maggy. The kitchen simmered with hostility.

"I advise you to get a move on," Maggy said to her daughter as she dawdled over her bowl of cereal, "because I'm not of a mind to drive you to school today if you miss your bus.''

The expected string of smart remarks was not forthcoming. Instead, Nicole gulped down a few spoonfuls of cereal, polished off her orange juice, then grabbed her books and raced out the back door without saying goodbye. Charlie was out a few minutes later, and Maggy found herself alone with Tigger, Data, and the rest of the menagerie.

She had an hour before she had to get ready for work. The house was in good shape. The breakfast dishes were neatly stacked in the dishwasher. Maybe she could use that time to do a little Web-surfing for information about Bobby DiCarlo's murder. She felt funny about going to the library and asking Karen the librarian to bring out all the articles pertaining to it, especially since Karen and everybody else in town seemed to know she was dating Conor. At least the Internet afforded her some privacy.

Yesterday had been such a complete and utter disaster that she had the hollow and exhausted feeling of a soldier on the verge of battle fatigue. No bombs had been dropped or bullets fired, but the sense of being in enemy territory had been too strong for Maggy to ignore during that happy Riley family get-together. Unfortunately, her family was no better. Each time they saw Conor, they'd made him feel like an escaped felon. His family had tried to cut her out from the herd. Her family had tried to annihilate him in a game of hoops. *Yeah*, she thought. *Tell us how you're really feeling.*

She turned on the computer and sipped coffee while she waited for Windows to load. No wonder sane people go to such great lengths to keep love affairs secret. They knew that once their families sank their fangs into the tender flesh of fantasy, they'd be doomed.

Doomed. Now there was an ugly word for you. They weren't doomed at all. Not a bit. It was just that those close encounters with familial disapproval had worked like twin splashes of ice water in the face of romantic bliss, a reminder that, whether they liked it or not, there were more than two people involved in their love affair.

Windows finished loading, and she clicked on the icon that would dial up the Internet. She liked to believe that everything happened for a purpose. Maybe they'd gone public too early. Their relationship had moved along at rocket speed. Perhaps this was reality's little way of slamming on the brakes. On more than one occasion she'd sensed that he was ready to take the next step and begin talking about a permanent future together, and each time she'd managed to deftly change the conversation as her mother's words of warning came back to her. *No man will ever love your children the way you do.* Once you brought a man into the life of your children, everything changed. She wasn't ready to do that. Not yet. Maybe not ever.

She clicked over to her favorite search engine and typed in "bobby dicarlo AND new jersey AND murder AND conor riley" then hit enter and waited for the system to amass the information. The results were disappointing. The DiCarlo story was a local one, and most of the local papers were still playing catch-up when it came to maintaining a sophisticated Web presence.

"This is stupid," she said out loud after twenty minutes of clicking and scrolling. She didn't know any more than she had when she started the search. The story still seemed much as Conor had told it to her: a tragic sequence of events that had cost a young man his life and left his family shattered. Yes, there did seem to be some speculation about how Conor had managed to escape without a scratch, but she chalked it up to an attempt to sensationalize the story. She had no doubt he'd done everything he could to save his partner's life. Hadn't he stepped right into the fray when that young man was hassling her on the boardwalk in Atlantic City? She'd been a total stranger to him, and he'd still seen fit to come between her and potential danger. That told her something very important about the kind of man he was.

Still, the notion of something not quite fitting into the puzzle lingered with Maggy as she went through her days. Midterms were approaching, and she spent a lot of time on Crisis Management with her study partner Janine while Conor was occupied with practice sessions with his attorney, preparing him for the grilling he was sure to face in court. Her mother had moved in for a few days to help with the kids, which gave Maggy the freedom to come and go as she pleased. She rented a motel room near the campus and pulled an all-nighter with her Principles of Modern Marketing study group. When they left, she took a long bath, slipped into the silky blue robe Conor had bought for her in Cape May, then fell asleep on top of the bed.

Two days later, she pulled an all-nighter at his house.

She'd put in a full day at the rectory then driven out to the campus for a three-hour practice test that scared her so much she figured the real thing would kill her. By the time she pulled her minivan into Conor's driveway, she was dead on her feet. It was nearly ten o'clock, and seduction was the last thing on her mind. She wasn't even sure she could manage conversation. He pulled into the driveway seconds after she turned off her ignition.

"You're early," he said, then kissed her.

"Am I?" she said groggily. "I'm too tired to tell time."

"I'm glad you're here."

"Pizza," she said, sniffing the air. "Please tell me you bought us a pizza."

"Two of them," he said. "And a bottle of Asti Cinzano."

She sighed. "If I weren't so tired, I'd show you how happy I am."

"Take a nap after supper," he said, grinning. "Then you can show me."

She was asleep before she finished her first slice of pizza.

Maggy woke up slowly, a languorous surfacing from warmth and darkness into a place more wonderful than her dreams.

"Hey, sleepyhead." She felt a kiss against her temple. "Feeling better?"

She smiled as the warmth of his voice seeped into her bones. "Much," she said. She stretched lazily within his embrace. "I'm sorry. I don't think this is what you had in mind when you asked me over."

"I had you in mind," he said. "However I could get you."

She curled closer to him on the sofa and watched the fire as it crackled and hissed in the grate. He poured her the rest of the Asti, and she took her time with it, savoring the sweet bubbles against her tongue, savoring his sweet kisses even more. "This is heaven. I wish things could stay this way forever."

"Not bad for starters."

"Starters?" She sighed deeply. "No families. No prying eyes and unsolicited opinions. No expectations. No commitments."

They were quiet for a while. He stroked her hair. She traced designs on his chest with the tip of her index finger and breathed in the intoxicating smell of his skin. There was nothing else she needed. Nothing she wanted. It was all right there within the span of her arms. Funny how you could spend your life looking for something but not know what it was until he found you.

"I don't mind commitments," he said, breaking the silence. "I've heard I'm pretty good at keeping them."

She wanted to kiss him quiet but knew that would be taking the coward's way out. "I'm not sure I'm ready," she said, hating the harsh sound of her words but knowing she had to say them. "I love what we have right here, right now, just the two of us with nobody else to answer to. No expectations. Why can't that be enough?"

"Because it isn't," he said. "Not for you and definitely not for me."

"Why rock the boat?" She sat up a little straighter so she could see his eyes. "You saw the way our families reacted to us. Let's keep what we have between the two of us a little while longer. Let them get used to the idea."

"You can't go back, Maggy. They know about us now. They'll learn to deal with it."

"It's easier for you," she said. "Your son lives with his mother on the other side of the continent. My kids are right here with me, and they've been drawn into this, too, right along with the rest of my family."

"You're talking about Nicole."

She nodded. Charlie was as easygoing and adaptable as his two lovable dogs. The world of adults was still of little interest to him. He was secure in his parents' love and comfortable with their geography. If only it had been half as simple with Nicole. "How can I ask you to love her when I'm not even sure I like her half the time?"

"How about asking me to respect her and love her mother instead? We'll let the rest happen when it happens."

If it happens, she thought but didn't say. Nicole was lovely and difficult and determined to make Maggy's life as complicated as she possibly could. There were times Maggy felt as if she was being repaid in spades for thinking she had managed to avoid the pitfalls her own mother had fallen into years ago. Nicole was Claire all over again, as if Maggy had done nothing more than carry Nicole. The genetic material seemed to belong entirely to her beautiful baby sister.

They talked some, kissed some, then Conor got up to toss a few more logs onto the fire.

"Let's sleep here tonight," she said, patting the oversized sofa. "That fire is too wonderful to waste."

He seemed distracted, as if her words reached him but not their meaning.

"Conor?" she asked. "What's wrong?" *What do you think is wrong, Maggy? You hurt him.*

"I'll be out of here early tomorrow morning," he said, rejoining her on the sofa.

"Oh," she said, swinging her feet to the floor. "Maybe I should go home."

He reached for her hand. "I'm taking the stand tomorrow."

"It's time," she said softly, wishing she had magical powers that could take away his pain. "Once this is finished, you'll be able to move forward."

She sensed him withdraw just the slightest bit, and it scared her.

"It's not that easy, Maggy."

"I know it will be hard to live through it again on the stand, but once it's over, you'll never have to do that again."

The look he gave her pierced her heart.

"You don't know the whole story," he said.

"You told me about Bobby," she reminded him. "And I've read some of the stories. I know all I need to know."

"I froze," he said. "Bet you didn't read that anywhere. I saw Bobby and that son of a bitch with the gun, and all the training, the friendship, every fucking thing dropped away from me. I just stood there and watched it all happen.''

She wanted to tell him he was wrong, but she couldn't. She'd seen the way the other cops in his family treated him, picked up on the judgmental tone in the newspaper articles. He was telling her the truth, and she had to sit there and listen to it, no matter how it made her feel. No matter how it changed things.

He told her how he stood still, his eyes pinned to the gun pointed at Bobby, how his brain shut down, and his muscles turned to stone, and even his heart seemed to stop beating. All he remembered was the way the sun hit the gun, the sound the gun made when that bullet tore straight into Bobby's heart.

''I let it happen,'' he said. ''I should've stopped him, done something—I just fucking let it happen.''

''Listen to what you're saying. The guy had a gun on Bobby. There was nothing you could do. If you made a move, he would've—''

''Killed him?'' he asked. ''Maybe that's not what I was worried about.''

She would give the world to erase that haunted look in his eyes. She said to him the things she would have said to her children or her sisters, the same things they would say to her. Meaningless things. Pointless things. Words meant to comfort, to ease, to obscure and erase.

''How can any of us know what we'd do in such a terrible situation?'' she asked him. ''Who can predict how you'd react when your life is on the line?''

The silence between them returned, but this time it had weight and dimension it didn't have before and a sadness she couldn't ignore. He had done the best he could, and it hadn't been enough.

She knew it was unfair, but she found herself wishing for more from the man she loved.

EIGHTEEN

Maggy sipped coffee as she watched Conor dress for court. The pillows were bunched behind her back. The dark gold blanket was tucked neatly around her. She did mornings very well, which was a good thing because his sartorial sense apparently didn't come to life before his third cup of coffee. She helped him pick out a tie, told him to wear the pale blue shirt and not the icy white one, and tried very hard to pretend it was just another morning in paradise when they both knew it was anything but.

"I don't know when they'll be calling me," he said as he shrugged into his coat. "If I'm finished by lunch, maybe we—"

"I'm afraid I'll be out of here within the hour," she said quickly. Maybe a tad too quickly if the look on his face was any indication.

"I wouldn't mind it if you were still here when I got back."

"I wish I could be, but I have a study group with Janine and a few others at nine-thirty and a test at one, and then I'm putting in a few hours at the rectory. Somewhere in there I have to remind my kids that I'm still their mother."

"You're a busy woman," he said and kissed her on the forehead. "I know that. I'm just glad you find time for me."

"So am I," she said. "Now off with you before you end up stuck in the worst of the rush-hour traffic. You don't want to be late."

He kissed her again, on the mouth this time, and she found herself pressing up against his body, suddenly hungry for his warmth and his scent and the feel of his hands against her bare skin.

"I don't want to lose you," he said. "We'll make this work. We'll find a way."

"You're not going to lose me," she said, but they both knew she was only saying what they both wanted to hear. Something had changed between them, and she wasn't at all sure what magic it would take to put it right.

His hands slid under her T-shirt and up her rib cage until he cupped her breasts. "This isn't enough," he said. "I want your heart."

After he left, she locked the door and leaned her forehead against the jamb. She closed her eyes and listened to the sound of the Jeep's engine turning over, then the crunch of wheels on gravel as he backed out to the street. "You have my heart," she whispered as he drove away. She just wasn't sure it made a difference. She'd spent her entire adult life as a mother, thinking maternal thoughts, worrying about what would make her children happy, what would keep them safe. It was only very recently that she'd begun to wonder about the things that would make her happy as well.

It felt strange being alone in his house. Except for the photos she'd noticed her first night there, he displayed very few personal items. Decor was restricted to the normal big-ticket items: television, couch, a couple of chairs, shelves everywhere. Not even the spare decor, however, could mask the intense sensuality of the man who lived there: Supple leather, soft as a woman's cheek. Warm wood that invited you to trace the grain with your tongue. Deep cushions, huge fireplace, curtainless windows that opened out onto the acres of woods behind the house.

Why couldn't this be enough for them? A place where they could be alone and explore each other, body and soul. A place where they could lock the door and pull the blinds against the real world and create a sanctuary that belonged only to them. And, since she was asking for the impossible, why couldn't she find a way to be daughter and sister and mother and friend and lover and not let the various threads of her life get all tangled up until the only way she could separate them was to cut them all free?

How easy it had been for Charles to bring Sally into his life, to create a cozy world for the two of them that floated far above the mundane daily concerns of family life. He was only able to see his children once or twice a year, and then only if the Army cooperated with their plans. Sure he wanted Nicole and Charlie to love Sally as much as he did, but the world wouldn't come to an end if they didn't. Sally was a minor addition to their lives, not a daily presence who had veto power over their comings and goings. And what difference did it make if your siblings and parents hated your new spouse when all of your annoying relatives lived on the other side of the Atlantic Ocean and not the other side of town?

She knew that none of this would matter if she only knew what was going on inside her very puzzling heart.

The train station at Princeton Junction was crowded with Manhattan-bound commuters. They clustered in small groups on the windswept platform. Some sipped coffee from Wawa or 7-Eleven. Some leaned forward to look down the endless length of track, as if glaring at the train would make it appear that much faster. They all looked old and tired to Nicole, and it wasn't even eight in the morning yet.

"My mom would *kill* me if she knew what I was up to!" Missy said for what had to be the jillionth time since they got off the school bus and hitched a ride to the station.

Nicole shot her best friend a withering look. "You're not up to anything, Missy. I am. If she wants to kill somebody, let her kill me."

"I'm not supposed to go into Manhattan alone." Missy's voice was beginning to get that trembly sound that meant she was this close to bursting into tears. "What if something happens?"

"Nothing's gonna happen," Nicole said. "We'll be back home before anybody knows what we were up to."

"What if the school calls and asks where we are?"

"Will you quit worrying? You sound like my mother."

Not that she remembered what her mom sounded like these days. Grandma Rita had been staying with Nicole and Charlie for what seemed like forever while her mom studied for midterms. Or something. Nicole wasn't entirely convinced her mom had only school on her mind.

Of course, she still had had time enough to completely screw up her dreams. Aunt Claire took her out for pizza the other night and told her that they wouldn't be doing anything with those pictures after all. She didn't say it was her mom's fault, but Nicole knew the score. She'd heard them screaming at each other on Sunday night. You'd have to be stupid not to know what it was all about, especially after the way her mom ragged on her when she found the photos sticking out from under the bed.

That was probably the dumbest thing she'd ever done. If she'd just taken an extra second to make sure she'd shoved them under far enough, none of this would've happened. Aunt Claire would've found her the dream job of a lifetime and made sure the contract was as good as it could get and Nicole would sign it with her favorite red pen, the one with the black and silver cap, and before she knew it she'd be rich and famous and living in London right around the corner from her dad and Sally. She wasn't too thrilled about the Sally part, but the rest of the fantasy was so terrific that she could put up with it.

But that was okay, she thought as she pushed Missy onto the train and toward the first pair of empty seats. Aunt Claire had given her the pictures as a kind of consolation prize, and now she was going to take those pictures into the city to show one of those hot-shot agents who'd given her his business card. They were having an open call at eleven o'clock, which meant she'd be up against lots of other pretty girls with ambition. If he didn't like her, there would be another agent who would. She was sure of it. She had almost a megabyte of scanned business cards tucked away in a file on her computer. Her mother would have a cow if she knew about them. She was always going on about how men sometimes liked to take advantage of beautiful girls who were young enough to be their daughters, while Nic just muttered "Yeah, yeah," and zoned out. Like anybody would take those old goats seriously. Sometimes her mother acted like she wasn't part of the real world.

"Those guys are staring at us," Missy whispered, giving Nicole a sharp nudge in the rib cage. "Old farts."

"Ignore them," Nicole said. She'd been doing that her whole life.

"The fat one's smiling at us. What should I do?"

"Don't smile back," Nicole said. "That's a good start." How dumb *was* Missy anyway?

Men had been staring at Nicole her whole life, it seemed, and she had ignoring them down to a science. Don't make eye contact. Don't give them any encouragement, and they'll go away soon enough like those seagulls at the beach who hover around you, looking for handouts. Ignore them, and pretty soon they'll be flying off in search of somebody else.

"You scared?" Missy asked.

"A little."

"I'm petrified," Missy said, "and I'm not the one who has the appointment."

"Listen," said Nicole, "we're still in the station. If you want to, you can get off. I won't be mad or anything."

"No." Missy shook her head. "No way. I can't let you go there by yourself. I mean, I'm the only other living person on the entire face of the earth who knows what you're doing today."

Nicole laughed at the look on her best friend's face. "It's not that big a deal," she said, lying just a little. "Besides, if they don't like my pictures, then it's all been a big waste of time, and I'll have to try somebody else."

Missy let out a huge sigh. "How could they not like them? You look like Sharon Stone."

"They might not be looking for Sharon Stone," she said with a little laugh. "They might want another Gwyneth Paltrow."

"You could be Gwyneth Paltrow," Missy said. "I can see that."

She gave Missy's arm a shove. "I don't look anything like Gwyneth Paltrow."

"You know what I mean," Missy said. "You look like you could be famous."

"Maybe one day I will be," she said as the doors slid shut and the train lurched out of the station. Rich and famous and able to do what she wanted without answering to anyone.

"You're late," said Glenn Matuszek. He was Conor's attorney.

"I'm five minutes early," Conor said. "Your watch is fast."

Glenn glanced up at the wall clock in the anteroom.

"Whatever." He shook Conor's hand. "So how're you doing?"

"Been better," he said. "I'll be glad when this is over."

Glenn dragged a manicured hand through his hair. "You and me both. Been a long time coming. We'll all breathe a lot easier when that bastard's behind bars."

Conor gestured in the direction of the courtroom. "Is she here?"

"Denise? Yeah. Front row with her mom and a sister or two." Glenn looked closely at Conor. "This gonna be a problem?"

He shook his head. "It's just been a long time since I've seen her." Or the kids. He lost so much when Bobby died. A partner. A friend. A family. Still, he knew that his loss couldn't compare to Denise's.

". . . just remember you're not on trial here," Glenn was saying. "Answer the questions they ask you, don't add anything, don't get defensive, don't let that son of a bitch psych you with that evil eye of his. Talk to the attorney. Talk to the jury. Don't acknowledge anything the bastard does, and you'll be fine."

"You're telling me not to lose it."

"Damn straight I'm telling you not to lose it. Judge Drymond is a tough customer. She'll hold you in contempt if you blow up at Walker. Simple Q and A," he said. "That's all it is. Don't make it more than that."

Good advice. Now the trick was to take it. He didn't know how it was going to feel to see the bastard who'd killed Bobby sitting in the same room with the woman who'd borne his two daughters, and not want to put an end to his fucking life. Simple Q and A, Glenn said. That's all it was. He told himself he could hang tough long enough to get through it. He was there as a witness, not a defendant. He had to remember that.

"Show time," Glenn said, straightening his tie.

Conor nodded. "Let's go."

The courtroom was smaller than he remembered. He'd been there once a few years before to give testimony on an extortion case he'd worked on. The soaring ceilings, ornate paneling, the aura of democratic majesty had all impressed him, just as they were supposed to do. Public buildings were designed to remind the private man and woman of their basic insignificance in the general scheme of things. Today none of it registered. He saw only Walker, who sat next to his attorney. Gone was the angry street punk with the shaved head and loaded gun; in his place was a clean-cut young man in a suit and tie. His well-manicured hands were folded pleasantly on the tabletop. The picture of innocence except for the look in his eyes.

Conor knew that look. He'd seen it too many times over the years not to recognize it, no matter how sly the packaging might be. *It's not over,* that look said. *It'll never be over.* In that moment, he knew he could commit murder. His only regret was that he hadn't last year when he had the chance.

"Easy," Glenn warned softly as they took their seats. "No eye contact. Don't let him know he's getting to you."

Conor tried to unclench his fists, but it wasn't happening, so he sucked in a lungful of air instead. The room smelled funny, like mothballs and wood soap. He felt the way he had the time he went flying with Matty. The pilot did a barrel roll at Matty's instigation, and Conor almost lost his breakfast. He'd waged war with evil every day for almost twenty years, and it hadn't seeped into his pores until today. That young man with the baby face and the flushed cheeks was a murderer. Not hearsay. Not speculation. Conor had been there, seen it, heard it, smelled it, touched it, done nothing to stop it. He knew there was nothing that would change that fact, no experience that would wipe it from his memory. He knew as he looked over at Bobby's widow that whatever punishment they handed out to the baby-faced murderer, half of that punishment belonged to him.

"Maggy!" Janine sounded exasperated. "How many times are you gonna look at your watch?"

Maggy ignored her study partner. "It's almost noon," she said. "I have a one o'clock exam. I think we'd better call it a day."

"I think we nailed the postbreakdown module, don't you?"

"Definitely," said Maggy, trying to calculate how quickly she could get to her car. "If Alex comes up with some great AVs, we should blow everyone away with the presentation."

"Why don't you come back after your one o'clock, and maybe we could drag Alex over and do some prep work over a pizza."

"Wish I could," Maggy said, gathering up her papers and books and stuffing them into her unwieldy tote bag, "but I'm working at the rectory this afternoon."

"I'm going to do a paper on you one day," Janine said. "The woman with the ninety-six-hour days."

Maggy laughed. "I wish I had ninety-six-hour days. Maybe then I could get something accomplished."

"What if I can get Alex here around six? An hour or two could make a difference."

Maggy reluctantly agreed. She knew she hadn't been the most reliable partner of late. They made plans for their next session, then she flew out the door and down the front path to her car. The radio was set to the local all-news station, so all she had to do was turn the ignition key.

"Traffic on Route 9 . . ." *Come on, come on. I don't care about the traffic.* "The Walker trial hit a snag this morning when one of the jurors was rushed to the hospital with chest pains. The trial will resume this afternoon with an alternate juror. The Dow Jones continues to—"

She switched off the radio. She wished she could switch off her emotions half as easily.

"Here's the address." The red-haired young woman pushed a slip of paper toward Nicole. "Tell him Benno at StarTrax sent you for a comp and a special."

Nicole took the slip of paper and turned it over. The address was some place in Fort Lee. Missy nudged her hard. "What's a special?" she asked, wondering how they were going to find their way around Fort Lee.

"He'll know," said the woman. "Just relax and let us do our job."

"We can't go to Fort Lee," Missy said when they stepped back out onto the busy city street. "We don't have enough money, Nic. You'd better call up and cancel the appointment."

"No!" Nicole grabbed Missy's arm. "I didn't come all this way to screw it up now. I'm going to Fort Lee."

"Nic! We only have five bucks plus our train tickets home. We can't do it."

"We'll hitch."

Missy shook her head. "I think we'd better go home."

"You go home," Nicole said, suddenly furious with her best friend. "I'm gonna do what I came here to do."

"I can't leave you alone."

"Sure you can. You can go home and cover for me if anyone asks where I am." Not that anybody would notice, but still . . .

Poor Missy. She looked so relieved that Nicole was afraid the girl was about to cry. Maybe that's how she'd be, too, if she'd lived her whole life in one little town, in one little house. Nicole wasn't afraid of new things, and she sure wasn't afraid of going to Fort Lee.

Jack Oliphant owned Jack's Pay-Less Shoe Store, which was situated diagonally across the parking lot from the

Toys "R" Us where Bobby DiCarlo had been headed the afternoon he was murdered.

Sonya Bernstein, the district attorney trying the case, stood quietly while Oliphant finished identifying himself for the court record. "And isn't it true, Mr. Oliphant," she said when the man finished, "that you were the person who placed the 911 call when Detective DiCarlo was shot?"

"Yes, I am," Oliphant said then shook his head. "I mean, yes, I did."

The guy was scared. Conor noted the twitch in his left eyelid, the way his right foot tapped the ground as if he couldn't wait to get out of there. Oliphant's eyes landed on Conor briefly then slid over to land on Walker who sat Boy Scout straight in his trust-me suit. Oliphant's face turned bright red, and he looked back at the DA. You'd expect nerves in a situation like this. Fear was something else entirely.

"Mr. Oliphant, tell us please what happened on the afternoon in question."

"I was putting through a credit—you know how slow computers can be—when I heard some yelling going on out there and—well, it's a nice neighborhood. You don't hear language like that, so I stopped what I was doing and went to the door. We don't want any trouble around here, you see, so the other owners and I try to watch out for what's going on. Like a neighborhood watch."

"And what did you see when you went to the door, Mr. Oliphant?"

"I saw him." He pointed toward Conor while the DA. supplied the necessary name and title for the court reporter.

"Did you see anyone else?"

"Detective Riley was holding Detective DiCarlo."

"What was Detective DiCarlo's condition?"

Oliphant looked as if he wished he could be anywhere else but in that courtroom. His eyes darted around like fireflies on a hot summer night. "I'm not a doctor, but I knew he was—I mean, the blood—" he shook his head sadly—"it was everywhere. Everywhere. He didn't look to be a big guy. You wouldn't think there'd be so much blood."

Denise's sob stopped everything. One sharp keening cry that sliced into Conor's heart and twisted. He had to go to her, put his hand on her shoulder, tell her it was his fault, all of it, that if he had any balls at all, her husband wouldn't be lying dead in his grave, and they wouldn't be here on a sunny autumn afternoon trying to make sense of tragedy. He shoved back his chair, but Glenn's restraining hand on his shoulder kept him from rising.

"No," Glenn said just loud enough for Conor to hear. "Don't do it."

The judge waited a few seconds then issued a gentle warning to Denise, whose face was buried against her mother Anne's shoulder. The last time Conor saw Anne was at Bobby's funeral. She'd turned away from him as if they'd never laughed together over Bobby's kitchen table after another christening.

"Mr. Oliphant," the DA said, "you said you heard a commotion."

"Yes."

"Did that commotion include a gunshot?"

Oliphant's gaze slid over Conor to Walker, then back once again to the DA. "I don't know."

"You don't know or you don't remember?"

"I don't remember."

"Who else was in the area?"

"I don't know. All I remember is the blood"—he turned slightly toward Denise then caught himself—"I mean, I was focused on what happened, and I ran back in to call 911."

"Did anyone tell you to call 911?"

"I don't know." Oliphant thought for a moment then

pointed in Conor's direction. "He might have yelled for somebody to get help."

Glenn looked at Conor, who shrugged. He had no recollection of doing anything.

"But you're not sure, Mr. Oliphant?" the DA asked.

"No," said Oliphant, "I'm not."

The questioning went on for fifteen more minutes, then Oliphant was excused.

"We'll take a ten-minute recess," the judge said from the bench, "then continue with the next witness."

They rose while the judge left the courtroom, then turned to file out themselves. Conor reached the door a few steps before Denise DiCarlo. He hesitated before holding it open for her. She looked at him for a moment and walked past him.

He called her name, but he supposed she didn't hear him because she kept on walking.

NINETEEN

Nicole made Missy swear she wouldn't tell anyone what she was up to. "Promise," she said. "You know you owe me one, Missy." She had covered for her friend the time Missy ditched school to see the *Star Wars* trailer.

"I promise," Missy said, her big brown eyes going all weepy. "You be careful, Nic."

Nicole made a face. "Of course I'll be careful. I wasn't born yesterday, was I?" Missy always seemed to forget that Nicole had lived all over the world. She knew the score. Nobody could put anything over on her.

"Here," Missy said, pushing her cash at Nicole. "You take this. I can walk home from the train station."

Nicole hugged her. "Just don't tell anybody, okay? I'll be home as soon as I can."

Missy nodded, then ran off to catch her train. Nicole had already returned her ticket for cash then bought herself a bus ticket for Fort Lee. Fort Lee was right across the Hudson from Manhattan. She used to have a cousin who lived in Fort Lee, and she remembered it was a pretty fancy neighborhood. Certainly fancier than the one she lived in with her mom. Although she would have died rather than admit it to Missy, Manhattan was a whole lot scarier.

There were only three seats left on the commuter bus when Nicole boarded. She chose one near the back, next to an old lady in a pretty blue coat. The old lady's hair was tinted the color of ginger ale, and her lap was piled high with shopping bags from Bloomingdale's. She smiled at Nicole, who smiled back, praying she wasn't one of those talky women like her Grandma Rita's friends, but the woman closed her eyes as soon as the bus left the terminal and didn't say a word.

The trip to Fort Lee was short but boring, and it gave Nicole a bit of time to think. If only her mom hadn't stepped in and put a stop to Aunt Claire's plan. It would have been so cool to have her aunt show her the ropes and introduce her to people, make sure that things were going the way they were supposed to. Aunt Claire was even smarter than she was beautiful, and Nicole knew that with Claire guiding her career, big things would have happened. Now her aunt and her mother weren't speaking, and Grandma Rita was all upset, and even Aunt Ellie was choosing sides. They acted as if they were masters of the universe and could make all the decisions for her, like she didn't even have the right to pick out what clothes to wear. They thought they were the bosses over her, and that wasn't true. Her dad had a right to an opinion, too, and Nicole knew he'd side with her. Daddy wasn't afraid of change. Wasn't he the one who always said that his little girl was as pretty as any of those girls on the magazine covers? She'd tried to call his apartment in London last night, but Sally had answered the phone. Nicole had been about to hang up when Sally, out of the blue, said, "Nicole? Is that you, dear?" and caught her dead to rights.

"It's me," Nicole had said, and then Sally had gone into some weirded-out explanation about ESP and lucky guesses when they both knew Daddy always had a caller

ID box attached to his telephones. "Is Daddy there?"

"He's TDY in Kuwait, sweetie. I'm not sure when he'll be back." Sally paused a moment. "Is it an emergency?"

Nicole thought about that. She really, really wanted to talk to her dad, but he'd be majorly pissed if they tracked him down in the desert for something that wasn't life-or-death. "No," she said. "It's not an emergency. Just tell him I called, okay?" Sally sounded a little disappointed, like maybe she would've liked to talk a little longer, but Nicole hung up. It wasn't like they were friends or anything. Sally was just the woman her father married, that's all, not really part of Nicole's life.

It was around one-thirty when the bus let her off in Fort Lee. Her appointment wasn't until two o'clock, so that gave her some time to figure out where the photographer's studio was. Fort Lee was bigger than she'd expected, and she started to worry that maybe the studio might be on the other side of town and she'd need to take another bus and end up without any money. But she lucked out when a passing mail carrier directed her to a building just four blocks over.

The Glo-Jon Studio was on the second floor of the three-story brick building. The place smelled kind of funny, like the inside of a musty freezer, and she found herself trying not to notice the way her footsteps sort of crunched a little as she walked up the stairs. Her mom would notice that kind of thing, and it irritated Nicole that she had become such a little suburban mall rat that a little dirt on the floor would bother her. This was exactly the kind of place where a photographer would live. Artists didn't care about stuff like dirty floors or smelly air. She wouldn't care about it either.

The door to Glo-Jon was made of frosted glass with the name scrawled across it in slashes of bright red. Nicole hugged herself with excitement. She wished her Aunt Claire was there, too, but that was the way it goes.

Wouldn't they all be surprised when they woke up one day and found out Nicole was famous?

Court reconvened at two P.M.

"The State calls Detective Conor Riley to the stand."

Slam. Slam. Slam. The doors inside him clanged shut. Guilt. Sorrow. Love. All locked away where they couldn't get out and hurt him. Only hatred remained: deep, gut-burning hatred. He passed in front of Walker, close enough to catch the smell of fear rising from the scumbag's body. No suit and tie or manicure on earth could hide what he really was. The bastard knew it. He knew Conor knew it as well. It was there in the bastard's empty eyes as he watched Conor approach the witness stand.

He was an arm's length away from pure evil. All he had to do was throw himself across that table and take him out. Nobody would care. The trial was a farce. It was only happening because the bastard recanted his confession, and a defense sprang up around him. He'd make sure justice was served. He'd sink his thumbs into the base of his throat and press deep into the windpipe, watch the bastard's eyes widen with fear, then the realization that he was going to die.

Conor walked slowly to where the bailiff was waiting for him.

"Put your right hand on the Bible and repeat after me . . ."

He took his seat on the witness stand. A small microphone jutted out near his right knee. He was being audiotaped, videotaped, and transcribed by the court reporter. None of that mattered to him.

Bobby's widow watched him from her seat. That mattered to him a lot.

He gave his name then slowly spelled it for the court reporter. He listed his rank, his years on the force, his current position, same as he'd listed them hundreds of times before in a hundred different cases. He'd taken the stand, recited the facts, then stepped back into his real life without letting any of it register on him. Somebody else's problem. Somebody else's tragedy. He never really got it until today.

Sonia had grown into a good DA. You'd never know to look at her that they'd dated a few times back in the '80s, when they were both young and lonely and newly divorced. Her expression betrayed none of the disappointment she must be feeling in him.

"Tell us, Detective Riley, what brought you to the Toys "R" Us parking lot on the afternoon in question."

He forced himself to stay focused on Sonia and let Denise's haunted eyes fade into the background. If he didn't, he'd go down for the count.

"Bobby—Detective DiCarlo—wanted to stop to pick up something."

"Do you remember what specifically he was there to pick up?"

"A—a Barbie doll for one of his daughters."

Denise bit back a sob. The judge rapped the gavel hard. Conor flinched but continued to stare straight at the DA. He owed that much to Bobby.

"Did you go into the store with him?"

"No."

"You stayed in the car?"

"Yes."

"Were you listening to the radio?"

"I don't remember."

"You don't remember if you were listening to the radio."

"No. I don't think I was."

"Did you see Detective DiCarlo enter the store?"

"No."

"What happened after Detective DiCarlo said he was going to go into Toys "R" Us to pick up the Barbie doll?"

"I saw him heading for the door. We'd spent the day at a horse farm on River Road. It was getting late and I was tired, so I closed my eyes."

"You closed your eyes?"

"We were in a good neighborhood. Everything looked quiet. I had no reason to—" *Shut up. Shut the fuck up.* "I was sitting there with my eyes closed. Not really thinking about anything. Just enjoying the quiet." *Half asleep. Drifting. Thinking it would always be this good.*

"And how long were you sitting like that?"

"I don't know. A minute. Maybe less." *Come on. What the hell's the matter with you? You can do better than this.* He felt Walker's dead eyes on him. Mocking him.

"And then what happened, Detective Riley?"

"There was a thump against the car. I opened my eyes and saw that Bobby was already halfway across the parking lot."

"And what did you do?"

Nothing. Not one fucking thing. Not when it mattered. "I got out of the car and started after him."

"And why was Detective DiCarlo running across the parking lot?"

"There was a carjacking in progress. A woman was down on the ground in front of a black Blazer. She was screaming."

"Is that woman in the courtroom?"

"Yes." He pointed to a dark-haired woman in her forties. "Mrs. Mills."

"Is the perpetrator in the courtroom?"

"Yes." His jaw locked. He could feel his body turning to stone. He stared down at the microphone bumped up against his knee.

"Can you point him out for me, Detective Riley?"

He turned toward the scumbag in the new suit and tie. He pointed his finger at the bastard. He wished it was a loaded gun. He wished he could do now what he hadn't been able to do when it could have made a difference.

"Let the record show that the witness indicated the defendant Allen Walker."

Walker's expression didn't change. He'd been well coached. No matter what happened, no matter what anyone said, his facade would never crack. When that was all that stood between you and life imprisonment, you could fucking act the lead in *Hamlet* if that was what you had to do to keep your ass out of prison.

"Tell us what happened next."

He told them. Simple declarative sentences, one following the other, until he reached the end of his story. The courtroom was quiet except for the soft sound of Denise's tears. They fell on his heart like drops of acid.

The DA leaned closer. "You saw the defendant pull the trigger."

"I'm not sure." *There's nothing there, Sonia. Nothing to tell you. I was there and then I wasn't.*

"You don't remember?"

"I don't know." *I'm not bullshitting you. It's like it never was. Never happened. One minute the guy had the gun pressed against Bobby's head, and the next they were calling a priest to administer last rites.*

"You were looking at him, weren't you?"

"Yes."

"And you didn't see the defendant pull the trigger?"

"I'm not clear on it." *Clear black. Nothing there.*

"Were you ever clear on it, Detective Riley?"

"No," he said. Not once. Not ever. He saw it all in bursts of sight and sound, scenes out of frame, moments from another man's life. Images scattered across a black canvas.

He told them about the look in Bobby's eyes. He told them about the blood he'd seen trickling from the corner of his mouth. He told them how Bobby had whispered "Denise" and squeezed his hand, and then nothing. He thought Bobby had paused for breath and he waited for the next word and was still waiting when the squad car arrived and then the ambulance and he was waiting when a guy with red hair and bad skin wrote "Time of Death: 4:38 P.M." on a sheet of paper and asked him to sign it.

And then it was over. They cuffed that scumbag Walker and took him away. "I'm sorry," he kept saying. "That wasn't supposed to happen." They loaded Bobby on a stretcher, covered him with a coarse white sheet, and then they took him away, too.

Sonia looked at him for a long while after he finished speaking. "That will be all, Detective Riley. You may step down."

By three o'clock, Maggy was on her way from school to the rectory to put in a few hours' work. She was reasonably sure she'd blown the test. Her mind had refused to stay focused on the neat row of questions, and so her answers had ended up with the vague, unformed look of yeast rising. She'd surfed the radio dial in search of news on the trial, but it was filled with weather reports. Heavy rains were expected later that evening, and the usual flood warnings were being issued for shore areas regularly plagued by such catastrophes.

Father Rourke greeted her when she arrived. "Your mother called," he said to her as she hung up her jacket and slid her tote bag under the desk. "No emergency, Margaret. Don't look like that. Call her back when you can."

Maggy was reaching for the telephone before he finished his sentence.

"The garage door is stuck," Rita said by way of hello. "Who do I call?"

"You called her," Maggy said. "I'll see what I can do when I get home. Make sure Tigger doesn't sneak out."

"He already did. Joann down the block found him on her front porch."

Maggy laughed. "Everything else okay?"

"Charlie's upstairs changing out of his school clothes. Nic isn't here yet."

Maggy checked her watch. "Not to worry. She's probably over at Missy's."

"I saw your friend on the television."

Maggy noticed the special emphasis on the word *friend*, but she forced herself to ignore it. "Did he testify yet?"

"They said—wait, I wrote it down. . . . Where did I put my glasses? There they are." Maggy heard the sound of papers rustling. "Okay. They said—and I'm quoting for you, Maggy, I wrote it down exactly—'Detective Conor Riley was unable to positively identify the defendant as the man who pulled the trigger.' "

Maggy said nothing. He'd told her about the gap in his memory, and she had assumed it was a way of protecting himself from his failure to save his friend's life.

"Maggy? Hello? Are you on the car phone?"

"No, Mom, I'm at work. Sorry. Something caught my attention." She quickly regrouped. "Did they say anything else about the trial?"

"No, but they showed your beau leaving the courthouse. He didn't look very happy."

"There's certainly no reason why he would be, Mother. Bobby was his partner and his best friend. This must be very difficult for him."

"I don't understand why he didn't just throw himself at that little Walker person. He's a big strapping man. He could have—"

"The guy had a gun," Maggy snapped. "Would you throw yourself in front of a loaded gun?"

"I'd do whatever I could for someone I loved. If one of you girls or the kids were in danger, I'd give my life. A machine gun couldn't stop me."

"How can you be sure?" Maggy asked. "Unless

you're in the situation, you can't possibly know what you'd do."

"It's not something you have to think about, sweetheart," said Rita. "It's either part of you or it isn't. It's not something you can fake."

"If you have something to say about Conor, why don't you just say it?"

"What could I possibly have to say about Conor? I barely know him."

"You think he screwed up, don't you? You think he's to blame for his partner's death."

"I didn't say that."

"You didn't have to. You've always managed to get your point across without actually saying anything."

"And what brought on this outburst?" Rita demanded, sounding quite huffy.

"I'm tired of everyone in this family taking cheap shots."

"Nobody's taking any cheap shots."

"Oh, you all are. You're always zinging me about Conor every damn chance you get, and I'm tired of it."

"I'm sorry you feel that way."

"So am I," Maggy said. "Isn't it enough that I'm trying to figure out where this is going without the bunch of you giving me a hard time?" With that she burst into tears and slammed down the phone.

She looked up to find Father Kevin, Father Roarke's young assistant, watching her from the doorway.

"I didn't mean to eavesdrop," he said, looking both concerned and uncomfortable.

She brushed her tears away with sharp, angry gestures. "I'm sorry," she said. "My mother—" She shrugged and tried to laugh, but fell far short. "It's an old story."

"The oldest," he said. "You were talking about the man you've been seeing."

"Either I'm louder than I thought, or you're the world's best eavesdropper."

He smiled gently. "Perhaps it's a little of both."

"Maybe."

"Your mother disapproves."

"My whole family disapproves, and so does his."

He sat down on the edge of her desk. "And how do you feel?"

"How in hell do you think I feel?" she shot back, then stopped, appalled. "I'm sorry, Father. This isn't one of my better days."

"No problem, Maggy. I still want to know how you feel about the man you're seeing."

She thought of the hours spent in his arms, delicious shimmering hours of pure heaven, and felt her pale Irish skin give her away once again. "He makes me very happy," she said, "but—" She shook her head. "It was so easy the first time around. I knew exactly what I wanted and I never looked back."

"You were younger then," Father Kevin said. "You didn't have two children in your care."

"Nicole is so unhappy," she said. "I've been blaming it on the fact that she's fifteen, but Claire says it's because she misses her father."

"Is there a way Nicole could spend more time with Charles?"

"Nicole is fine where she is." Maggy felt her hackles rise. Let him peddle his psychology degree somewhere else. "She'll spend two weeks with him this summer. Charles doesn't live a regular nine-to-five kind of life, Father. He lives in London and he's away half the time on TDY assignments." She shot him a look. "Did I mention that there's a new Mrs. O'Brien?"

The priest was quiet for a moment. "You know the Catholic position on divorce, Maggy, but life goes on. We're not meant, any of us, to be unhappy or alone."

"You don't understand," she said. "It's easy for him. He doesn't have to explain every decision he makes to his children."

"And you do?"

"It feels like it sometimes." If she wasn't explaining herself to her children, she was explaining herself to her mother and her sisters, and now to a priest barely old enough to shave.

"Charlie and Nicole don't care for your young man."

"Oh, Charlie's crazy about him." The very thought of the two of them shooting hoops or walking down to the canal and fishing made her feel warm and happy inside. "It's Nicole who doesn't."

"As you said, Nicole is fifteen. She isn't happy with much of anything at this point in her life."

Maggy couldn't help laughing. "Oh, Father, you don't know the half of it." The arguments about purple hair, Goth makeup, piercings, homework, music, and the latest blow-up over the photos Claire had arranged to have taken. "I've tried everything I can think of, but nothing is enough. She's unhappy, and I can't seem to change it."

"Maybe the best way to lead your daughter toward happiness is by being happy yourself."

"You sound like a Hallmark card." *A bad Hallmark card.* "Nothing about raising kids is that easy."

"It can be. The greatest gift you can give your children is a happy mother and a loving home. Everything else flows from that."

"You've never been married," she said. "You don't have children. You don't know what it's like, bringing somebody you—somebody you care deeply about home and having them rip him apart later."

"Did their criticisms change your opinion of him?"

"Of course not."

"Then why do the criticisms matter so much?"

"Because they do." She took a pair of deep breaths in an attempt to control her temper. "Because what kind of future can you have if your families feel you've made the wrong choice?"

''You can have whatever future you chose. You know that. You're not eighteen any longer. You make your own luck and build your own future. Your families will fall in line behind you, one way or the other.''

She shot him a look. ''This is why priests should be allowed to marry,'' she said. ''If you had any on-the-job experience, you wouldn't say that.''

''My parents divorced when I was eleven years old,'' he said, not taking his eyes off her. ''My mother remarried when I was thirteen.''

''Right,'' said Maggy, ''and you and your stepfather bonded over a pair of fishing poles and walked off into the sunset like Andy and Opie. I'm glad it worked out for you.''

He crossed his arms over his chest and continued to lock eyes with her. ''I ran away three times. I punctured the tires on his Camaro. He considered putting me in military school.''

''So that's how you ended up in the seminary.'' She couldn't help smiling at the thought of the serious Father Kevin poking holes in his stepfather's radials.

''In a manner of speaking, yes. Tom's a good man, and after I finally got tired of the chip on my shoulder, I was able to see just how good. He was the only one in my family who supported my decision to go into the priesthood.''

''That's a lovely story,'' she said, ''but I don't see what it has to do with me.''

''My mother loved him. She knew he was a good man, that he'd be a good father. She married him in the face of loud protest, and I thank God every day she did.''

''How did she know it was the right thing to do?'' Maggy whispered, as much to herself as to Father Kevin. ''How could she be so sure it would work out for all of you?

''She trusted her instincts and she listened to her

heart,'' Father Kevin said. ''Sometimes that's the best thing you can do.''

''See? That's what I'm talking about. She knew what she wanted.''

''You have your doubts.''

''Yes,'' she said after a moment. ''I have my doubts.'' There. She'd said it. She'd been dancing around the truth for days now and never had the guts to admit it, not even to herself. When Conor mentioned the future, something in her had taken a giant step backward, and she didn't want to look too closely for the reason why. Maybe she didn't really want to share her life with anybody. Maybe she wasn't sure he was the man she wanted him to be. Maybe she'd reached the point in her life when the questions made more sense than the answers.

She had told Conor that she liked things the way they were, that she wished they could stay lovers forever and never let reality intrude, but she'd been lying to him and to herself. She still wanted what she'd wanted when she was a little girl taking care of her baby sisters: she wanted a home and family of her own. A husband to stand beside her. A man who loved her for her flaws as well as her finer points. A man she could allow to be imperfect.

She longed for that one moment of crystal-clear certainty that, one way or the other, would drive all of these shadowy, unformed doubts away forever.

She figured the odds of finding that moment were about the same as picking a winning Lotto ticket: a million to one.

TWENTY

Nicole stared at the wisp of silk draped over the folding chair. "You want me to wear that?"

Guy, the photographer, laughed. "You're blushing, love. Quite charming. Careful, you might restore my faith in human nature."

"Nobody told me I'd have to pose in my underwear."

"Now that pains me," Guy said. He touched her chin with the tip of his index finger, and she tried very hard not to shudder. He had to be older than her father even. "Lingerie, little one. Surely you've seen the Victoria's Secret catalog. Every girlchild who walks through my door wants to be the next Stephanie Seymour."

She took another look at the bra and panties. They weren't all that much smaller than her bikini, but no matter what fancy name you gave to them, they were still underwear.

"My mom'll kill me," she said.

"You're eighteen," Guy said then looked deep into her eyes. "Aren't you?"

She nodded. If she'd told anyone she was only fifteen, she would have been turned away. "Of course I am," she said, then forced herself to laugh. "But that doesn't mean my mother likes what I'm doing."

"Love, if I were you, I'd be more concerned right now that the camera likes what you're doing. Now let me see that luscious bod of yours bedecked in lace, and we'll continue."

He told her he was going out for a smoke and to be ready when he came back in. She didn't want to disappoint him. Guy had been wonderful to her. For the last two hours he'd treated her like a princess, praising her beauty, posing her before the white sheet suspended from the ceiling, telling her about key lights and filters and angles.

"Your left, duchess," he'd said after turning her face this way and that. "That's your best side. If anyone asks you, and they will, it's your left." Pictures of beautiful women were pinned to every available surface. She even recognized a few of them. Some of the most famous models in the world had worked with Guy, so he must know what he was talking about when he said she needed to add some lingerie work to her portfolio. She had almost giggled when he said that. What portfolio? All she had were the photos Aunt Claire's friend had taken of her as a favor. "Amateurish," Guy had said, flipping through them as if they were a bad hand of poker, "but the subject is divine."

She unbuttoned her blouse and hung it from the hook behind the door. A second later she hung her jeans on top of it then slipped out of her own white cotton panties and stretchy white bra. A full-length mirror leaned up against the wall, and she caught a glimpse of herself as she reached for the lacy underwear. Her body looked as white as typing paper except for the red marks her jeans had left around her waistband. She rubbed at them with her hand, but that only seemed to make them worse. Maybe she should put some concealer on them. She reached for her tote bag, then remembered she'd stowed

it in the hall closet with her jacket. She'd never seen
Stephanie Seymour or any of those other models with
red marks on their waists, but then maybe that was what
the photographer was supposed to do. The good ones
probably had all sorts of tricks to make red marks and
blotches disappear.

Mostly her body looked long and skinny to her. Well,
except for the big boobs. She was the only female in her
family with big breasts, and sometimes it made her feel
weird, like she was showing off or something when she
really wasn't. "You'll never need implants," her aunt
Claire had said the last time they'd gone to the beach
together. "You're a lucky girl."

Maybe, she thought as she slipped her arms into the
flimsy bra and tied the front ribbons that held it all together. She'd never seen a bra that tied with ribbons. The
panties were made the same way. A pair of tiny ribbons
on either hip that tied into small bows. The bra and panties covered much more than she figured they would, but
for some reason she felt worse than naked, like she was
doing something wrong.

She wished her aunt Claire was there to tell her that it
was okay. Even having Missy around would help. It
wasn't like she was afraid of Guy or anything. It was just
that she'd never been alone before with a man who
wasn't a relative, and she knew that sometimes it was
better to be safe than sorry. But it was too late for that
now. Missy was probably lying on the bed in her room,
talking on the telephone with Stacey and telling her all
about her adventure in Manhattan. Just so long as she
didn't tell her mother.

"Darling girl!" Guy called out from the other side of
the door. "Time is money. Chop-chop!"

Chop-chop? Grandma Rita said things like *chop-chop.*
Maybe Guy was even older than she thought. That made
her feel a lot better.

"Just a sec!" she called back. "I'm almost ready."

She took one last look in the mirror. Her breasts looked gigantic in that tiny ribboned bra. The bikini bottom was cut so low and tight that it didn't leave much at all to the imagination. She easily looked like a woman in her twenties, and for the first time in her life she wasn't sure that was such a good thing.

"You told the truth," Glenn said to Conor as they stood on the courthouse steps. "You answered her questions to the best of your ability. Nobody can ask more of you than that."

"Bullshit," Conor said. "I could've made it easy for them. Given them what they wanted. It wouldn't have killed me." Who could say it would even be a lie? He didn't remember a goddamn thing as it was. A little creative storytelling, and that bastard Walker would be guaranteed life without parole. As it was, there was still enough doubt to make the outcome less than certain.

"I know where you're going with that, and forget about it. You did the right thing."

"Like I did the right thing the day Bobby died?"

"Let it go, pal. It's time to move on." He draped an arm across Conor's shoulders. "We'll catch a bite to eat. Hell, we can forget eating and get drunk, if that sounds better."

"Gimme a rain check on that, will you, Glenn? I'm not good company right now."

"You're on," Glenn said. "I'll call you tomorrow, and we'll set up a time."

He drove home on autopilot, just aimed the Jeep in the general direction and made sure he didn't hit anybody. He didn't want to think about Bobby or Denise or the kids or what the hell he would do with the rest of his life if he decided to stop being a cop. It would be hard to go back after this. He wasn't one of them anymore. The circle had closed, and he was on the outside.

He left the truck in the driveway and let himself in the

front door. Maggy had left a note for him on the desk.
Dark green ink on white paper. Her clear, Catholic-
schoolgirl handwriting angling toward the upper right-
hand corner of the page.

Miss you already. Maggy.

Just four words, and he felt his world right itself.

He picked up the telephone and hit her number on the
speed dial. Number one. There had been no doubt about
that from the first moment he saw her.

"Is that you, Maggy?" a woman said by way of greet-
ing.

Her mother, he thought. The killer basketball player.
"This is Conor Riley, Mrs. Halloran. I'm looking for
Maggy."

Her disappointment seeped through the wires. "I was
hoping she was with you. I was searching for your number, but I don't know what town you live in so I couldn't
call information."

"Is something wrong?"

She hesitated, her innate dislike battling with her obvious agitation. "I'm not sure," she said. "That's why
I'm trying to track down my daughter."

"You tried the rectory?"

"First place I called. And I'm not getting an answer
on her cell phone, either."

"What about her study partner?"

"She has a study partner?"

"Janine. They're working on a paper for the Crisis
Management course."

"Oh," said Rita.

Score one for the new guy.

"Is there something I can help you with?" he asked.
Might as well be magnanimous in victory.

Another silence heavy with maternal misgivings. "If
my daughter calls, tell her to phone home."

A quick good-bye, and the exchange was over. He
stared at the phone for a second after he hung up.

"What the hell was that all about?" he said out loud. Maggy's mother hadn't struck him as an alarmist, but there had very definitely been the sound of panic building in her voice. As far as he could see, he had two choices. He could either stay there and wonder what was going on or he could drive over to Maggy's place and find out for himself.

Maggy left the rectory a little after five o'clock and found herself smack in the middle of rush-hour traffic. The study group had opted for an early supper and brainstorming session at the Cadillac Diner where Maggy and Conor often met, and from the look of things on Route 18, she was going to be more than a little late. She reached for her cell phone to call Janine.

No dial tone. The battery was dead. She'd been meaning to stop at Radio Shack and pick up one of those battery chargers you plugged into the cigarette lighter, but it was just one of a thousand errands that kept getting pushed to the bottom of the list. She'd planned to call home to check up on things while she made her way to the diner, but now that would have to wait until she actually got there and could use the phones in the lobby.

For a moment, she was tempted to turn the car around and drive home, but she forced herself to continue on toward the diner. She'd been feeling vaguely uneasy for the last few hours. Nothing she could put her finger on, just the sense that all wasn't quite as it should be. Not with Conor or Nicole and most especially not with herself.

"Darling girl, relax," Guy said as he circled her with his camera. "Try to look like you're having a good time."

But I'm not having a good time, Nicole thought as she threw back her head and smiled widely. She was probably having the worst time of her life. So far, she'd posed in three different bra and panty sets, and each one made her feel more awful than the one before it.

"Unlock your knees, there's a love," he said, touching her right calf as he circled. "Sweetly trashy, that's what we're looking for . . . available, but not to just any-one . . ."

Tears sprang to her eyes. This wasn't how she'd imagined it would be. Not one single bit. She'd imagined a room swirling with hair stylists and assistants and hangers-on. So far, it was just Guy and his camera, and she was starting to hate both of them. The whole thing seemed to be taking forever, too. It was almost five o'clock, and he still wasn't finished.

"Is there much more?" she asked as he stopped to tilt her shoulders another way. "It's getting kind of late."

"He'll wait for you, darling girl, whoever he is. First you see to business, then you see to pleasure." His hand slid to her right knee, and he gave it a gentle nudge. "A tad too virginal. We want the eye to follow all the way up those gorgeous legs of yours, straight to the gates of paradise."

Oh, God. Did men really talk this way? It sounded like something from one of those awful cable movies her mom didn't know she watched. She wasn't exactly scared, but the creepy feeling was growing stronger.

He asked her to roll over onto her stomach and play to the camera, but she couldn't quit checking to make sure the bikini panties were where they were supposed to be. Finally, Guy lost patience.

"Give up the ghost, darling," he said. "Go change into the last set, and we'll put an end to your misery."

She felt so weird, walking past him in her underwear. It was so cold in the studio that her nipples popped right through the thin lace. She'd be glad when this was over and she had her portfolio and she never had to pose in her underwear again as long as she lived.

Her last outfit was draped over the chair in the changing room. She held the sheer, rose-colored teddy up and felt a blush flood her entire body. She might as well be naked for all the good this would do her. He'd be able to see everything, ab-so-lute-ly everything, and so would anyone who saw the pictures.

So why don't you just leave? Nobody's forcing you to stay here.

Of course she couldn't leave, not when the portfolio was almost finished. If she gave up now, she might never get another chance. Her aunt had told her all about how quickly a model could get a bad reputation in the business for being difficult to work with, and that bad rep could stop a new career cold. She'd gone this far. She wasn't stupid. She could handle this.

Mom and Daddy will kill you when they find out.

Big deal. Her mother was just as likely to kill her for skipping school as for having these pictures taken. Either way, she was already in trouble. And what difference did it make what Daddy thought when he and that new wife of his lived on the other side of the ocean?

She skimmed off the bikini panties and unfastened the bra. She stepped into the teddy and was straightening the straps when she heard voices from the studio and she stopped cold. There was another man out there, talking to Guy. She tiptoed to the door and pressed her ear against it and listened.

"... she's new and a little shy about her body ... great body ... tits you won't believe ... she'll be glad to do it ..." she heard Guy say. "She needs a portfolio. You need some test shots. I need the money." Male laughter. "Everybody's happy, dear boy."

Everyone except Nicole, who was suddenly so scared that she started to shake. Her knees felt like melted butter, and she wished she was anywhere else in the entire world but where she was. A weird prickling sensation crept up her spine, and she knew she had to get out of there. Her mother had always told her to listen to her hunches, that when you got that funny itchy feeling that something bad was coming, you were probably right.

You're being a big baby, Nicole. It's only a bunch of stupid pictures. If you want to be a model, you have to learn how to do these things.

"No," she whispered as she grabbed her clothes from the hook behind the door. Maybe she didn't want to be a model bad enough, because right now all she could think about was getting as far away from there as she could. She scrambled into her clothes, then looked for her bag and her—they were both jammed into the closet out front. No way was she going out there to get them.

What was it her mom always told her? *You can replace money and property, but you can't replace yourself.* She had two dollars in change jingling in the pocket of her jeans. She could call her Aunt Claire to come get her, and her mom would never know, and if Aunt Claire wasn't home, she'd think of something else. She'd noticed a back door at the end of the hallway that led to the bathroom. First she'd get out of there, then she'd worry about the rest of it.

By the time Conor reached Maggy's house, all hell had broken loose. The lawyer sister Ellie was shouting into her cell phone while a cluster of neighbors talked animatedly at the kitchen table. Rita leaped on him the moment she saw him.

"Nicole cut school to go into Manhattan with her friend," she said. "Missy came home without her."

"You're telling me Nicole's alone in Manhattan?"

"No, no!" Rita waved her hand in the air. "That's not the story."

He wouldn't want the woman on a witness stand. It would take a week to get to the story. "Where is she?"

"I don't know." Rita was on the verge of hysterical tears. "Fort something—Fort Lee? That's it. Fort Lee to see some photographer. Ellie's talking to Missy right now, trying to get the story.''

"Has anyone heard from Nicole?''

"Nothing. Not a word. Missy said she left her at the bus station in the city.''

"Listen,'' Conor said in his most comforting tone of voice, ''there's no reason to think Nicole is in any trouble. She's probably stuck on a bus somewhere on the turnpike and can't make a phone call.''

"You're a lousy liar,'' Rita said, blowing her nose into a crumpled tissue.

"You're right,'' he said. ''I am a lousy liar. That's why I don't do it. Let me make a few calls and see what I can find out.''

"Don't use our phone! We've got to keep it open in case Nicky calls.''

"No problem,'' he said and whipped out the cellular he'd been planning to use all along. She irritated the holy hell out of him, but that was okay. She was obviously scared to death and struggling to hold herself together, and it didn't much matter if the two of them weren't destined to be best friends.

"I didn't know you were here,'' Ellie said as she strode into the room. ''What do you know about Fort Lee?''

"Not much,'' he admitted, ''but I know the chief of police up in Bergen County. I was about to call him.''

Ellie looked down at the notepad in her hand. ''She was on her way to a photography studio called Glo-something. Missy couldn't remember if it was Glo-Dot or Glo-Bob.''

Rita's tears spilled freely down her cheeks. ''Call Claire! She knows everybody in the business. She'll be able to help.''

Claire had never heard of Glo-anything, which Conor right away took as a bad sign. If a woman who made her living working with tristate photographers hadn't heard of the place, there had to be a reason, and he'd bet the reason wasn't good.

He placed a call to the police chief. Don wasn't home, but he left a message and his cell phone number, along with Maggy's home phone number; then he placed a call to a female detective he knew who specialized in scams aimed at teenage girls. Patricia wasn't home, either. He left a message there, too. "It's drive time," he said, feeling goddamn useless. "Tough to get hold of people."

Ellie shot him a withering look. "Maybe you're not calling the right people."

"You have a better idea?" he shot back.

"Maybe somebody should get out there and look for Nic. Fort Lee isn't that big, you know."

"She could be anywhere," Rita said, reaching for a new tissue. "She could be on the train or on a bus or—" She buried her face in her hands and sobbed.

"Oh, Mom!" Ellie put an arm around Rita's shoulders and glared at Conor. "Everything's going to be fine."

Conor grabbed the notepad from Ellie and pulled a pen from his pocket. "Here," he said, shoving the pad back at the lawyer. "That's my cell phone number. Call me if you hear anything."

"You're leaving?" Rita asked. "How can you leave us?"

"You stay here," Ellie said to Conor. "I'll go look for Nic."

"You do what you do best," he said, "and let me do what I do best."

Maggy meant to call home the moment she got to the diner, but she bumped into Janine in the lobby.

"Where the hell have you been?" Janine demanded. "I've been calling your cell phone for the last half hour. Frank just dug up your home number and I was about to—"

"I'm sorry," Maggy said, "but the traffic was horrendous. Have I missed much?"

"Soup and salad," Janine said as she led the way back to their booth. "We couldn't start brainstorming the project until you arrived."

She told herself that there was no reason to call home right that second. Her mother had things under control, and she knew Claire and Ellie would pitch in if needed. Besides, it was a run-of-the-mill school night. The kids would be busy with their normal after-school activities and then an evening of homework after supper. They probably didn't even realize she wasn't there.

Nicole knew she couldn't stay hanging around Glo-Jon without coming face-to-face with Guy and his friend, so she hurried back toward the main street where the bus had let her off hours earlier. The street was crowded with commuters hurrying toward the parking lots and the huge condos that overlooked the river. She had her eyes open for a pay phone where she could stop and call her Aunt Claire to come and get her, and she finally found one next to a gas station adjacent to the bus stop.

"Please deposit an additional one dollar and seventy-five cents."

She looked at the coins in her hand. That was all she had. Reluctantly, she slid the coins into the slot and listened to the succession of dings as they registered.

"This is Claire. I'm not home right now. You know the drill."

"Aunt Claire, this is Nicole. I'm up in Fort Lee, and I need you to bring me home. My number is—" She read the number from the dial. "Call me!"

She paced up and down in front of the telephone for what seemed like forever, and when a man in a white Beemer drove up to use the phone, she almost had a fit.

"I'm waiting for a very important call," she pleaded with him. "Can't you use another phone?"

He ignored her and tied up the line for a good five minutes while she almost wept from frustration.

"You're lucky I don't call the cops," he said as he climbed back into his fancy car. "Young girl like you working the streets."

She wanted to die. This had been the worst day of her entire life. No wonder she'd been getting those looks from people driving by. She probably looked like a hooker waiting for business to heat up.

When the phone finally rang, she was on it instantly.

"Aunt Claire! Please hurry. I'm freezing and—"

"This is Conor Riley, Nicole."

"What are *you* doing calling me up?"

"We'll talk about that later. I'm a mile away from Fort Lee. Tell me exactly where you are, and I'll be there in a few minutes."

"I didn't leave a message for you." Instead of feeling happy, she was annoyed. "Where's my aunt?"

"Nicole, it's me or nothing. Now, where are you?"

A man in a dark green Lexus rolled to a stop at the foot of the gas station driveway. He grinned at Nicole through his open window, then winked. That did it. "I'm at the Getty gas station at the corner of—" She read the names from the street signs overhead. "And hurry!"

"Don't do anything stupid," Conor muttered as he clicked off with Nicole. All she had to do now was stay put for another three minutes, and they'd have themselves a happy ending before Maggy even knew her daughter had gone missing.

At least the girl picked a good neighborhood for her escapade. Fort Lee was hanging on to its upscale sensibilities despite urban sprawl and the proliferation of businesses fleeing Manhattan. If your kid was going to get herself into a mess, you couldn't pick a better place for it. Okay, maybe Disney World, but that was about it.

He punched in Maggy's number. Ellie answered.

"Mission accomplished," he said. "She's waiting up the block for me."

"Just get her in the car," Ellie said. "Then we'll celebrate."

"Tough crowd," he muttered as he clicked off.

He turned onto the main street and had to hit his brakes hard when a commuter whipped out of the Jersey Transit parking lot without looking. Up ahead he saw the bright lights of the Getty station, and then a moment later he saw Nicole standing under the streetlight. She looked young and weary and too damn sexy in her tight jeans and light T-shirt. No wonder that old son of a bitch in the black Miata was trying to get her attention. Too bad you couldn't arrest a guy for intent.

It was forty degrees out there. Where in hell was her jacket? Why wasn't she carrying a bag? He beeped the horn twice to signal his approach and felt bad when he saw the way her delicate shoulders stiffened, and she stared down at the ground. Poor kid. Must be tough to have the body of a woman and the heart of a little girl.

He rolled down the window. "Nicole!" he called out. "Over here."

She spun around, recognized him, and for a second that weary adolescent mask dropped, and he saw a flood of pure relief and happiness light up her lovely face. She ran toward the Jeep, but by the time she climbed inside, the mask was back in place. "What took you so long?" she demanded as she slammed the door shut. "I've been waiting forever." She wrapped her arms tightly around her chest. He noted she was shivering.

"Four minutes," he said, reminding himself that she was using aggression to hide her intense relief. "There's a sweatshirt in the back. Help yourself."

"N-no, thanks. I don't need one."

"Put it on," he said, in much the same tone of voice he'd used on his son Sean in the past.

She hesitated then reached back and grabbed for the

sweatshirt. The arms were the right length, but the rest of it swam on her, making her look even more delicate than she was.

"So where's your jacket?" he asked.

"Back there," she said, gesturing over her shoulder. "At the photographer's."

"Feel like telling me what it's doing there?"

She shrugged. "I got scared when I heard another man with him and I let myself out the back door."

"Smart girl," he said. Her mother's daughter. "What else did you leave back there?"

She looked at him, wide-eyed, as if she'd never seen him before. "My bag."

"You want them, don't you?"

"Sure," she said, "but I'm not going back in there."

"You don't have to," he said. "I'll go back in there for you."

He angled into a parking spot across the street from Glo-Jon Studio. "Stay here," he said. "I'll be right back."

Nicole sat in the truck and waited while Conor went off to retrieve her stuff from the creepy photographer's studio. The truck smelled like him, kind of spicy and soapy. It reminded her of the way her father used to smell when she kissed him good night. She wondered if all dads had that smell, kind of familiar and comforting. Funny thing. She hadn't ever really thought of Conor as being somebody's dad until tonight when he came to her rescue.

Sure, she knew that Conor had a son named Sean who lived in California. He'd shown her and Charlie a picture of a skinny, dark-haired kid with a big wide smile who looked a lot like him, but she'd never managed to connect the dots until she saw that look of angry relief in his eyes when she climbed into the Jeep and closed the door behind her. It was exactly the same look her dad had given her the time she wandered away from the mall in San

Diego and the security guys found her crying at the far end of the parking lot. Funny how seeing that look again made her feel protected, like she was part of a family.

"Jerk," she muttered as she watched a handful of cars exit the commuter parking lot at the corner. Sometimes she made herself sick. Who was she kidding, anyway? They weren't a family. He was just some guy her mother was seeing. He didn't care about her. He was only doing this to score points with her mom. Well, she'd show him. If he wanted her mom to know what a good guy he was, he'd have to tell her himself.

It took longer than Conor figured it would, but the sight of his badge and revolver finally won the photographer over to his way of thinking.

"Next time ask for a birth certificate," Conor said to the guy as he tucked the jacket and bag under his arm. "Safer that way."

Nicole was waiting for him out on the sidewalk.

He gave her the stern look that he saved for Sean's occasional transgression. "I thought I told you to stay in the Jeep."

Her back was to him, and she jumped at the sound of his voice. "You were taking forever," she said in that accusatory tone that reminded him of his son at fifteen.

He handed her the jacket and bag.

"You got my stuff!" she exclaimed, dropping the facade. "Thanks!"

"Our photographer isn't a happy camper. He said you copped out with one of his necklaces."

Her hand flew to the base of her throat. "Oh, no!"

"Don't worry about it," he said as they stepped off the curb. "You can mail the necklace to him."

"No! I'll go run back and stick it in his mailbox."

"Forget it, Nicole." They were halfway across the busy street. "Let's get out of here."

"It'll just take a second." She turned and darted in

the other direction just as he saw headlights swing around the corner.

She was halfway across when she stumbled over a small pothole. "My ankle!" she cried out, then bent down to look.

The headlights from the approaching car illuminated her face, and suddenly Conor realized the car was going too fast to stop in time.

"Nicole!" he roared. "Move!"

But she didn't. She couldn't. She was frozen in place, staring at him with eyes wide open and terrified.

His brain shut down, and he sprang into action.

He hurled himself at her, putting all of his weight and strength behind him. He heard the blare of a car's horn. The sickening screech of brakes. *No time. No time. Do it now!* He grabbed for her. He couldn't see past the glare from the headlights. She screamed as he lifted her from the ground, then threw her as far from danger as he could before the car slammed into him and everything went black.

TWENTY-ONE

"Now don't worry," her mother said when Maggy got home. "She's fine."

Maggy's entire body went on red alert. "Who's fine? What are you talking about?"

"Nicole. We found her, and your friend went out to bring her back."

"Slow down, please." Maggy threw her coat over a kitchen chair. "Found Nicole where?"

Ellie popped up in the doorway, looking all lawyerly in her Ally McBeal suit and serious glasses. "Nicole and Missy cut school and took the train into the city."

Maggy sagged into the chair with her coat. "Oh, God." She rested her head in her hands. "I should've known this would happen." She looked up at her sister. "Modeling, right?"

"What else?" Ellie said. "Sounds like she had an appointment with an agency midtown."

As far as Ellie and her mother could figure, Nicole went from there to a photographer's studio in Fort Lee.

"What about Missy?"

"She went home from Manhattan. Nic swore her to

secrecy, but when Nic didn't show up by five o'clock, Missy cracked and spilled the beans.''

"And who went to get Nic? Claire?"

"Your boyfriend," said her mother. "Not that he seemed all that thrilled."

"Be fair, Mother," Ellie said. "He was a big help."

Rita made a face. "He made some phone calls. Big deal."

"He really was a help," Ellie said to Maggy, who was beginning to brew a monster headache. "He didn't have to go find Nicole the way he did."

"You should've been the one, Eleanor." Rita shot her middle daughter a pointed look. "We should have kept this in the family."

Maggy whirled around to face her mother. "You should be grateful he was here and willing to help. Where's Claire? Where are Uncle Jack and Aunt Tina? I don't see them pitching in to help."

"He isn't family," Rita persisted. "Some things should be strictly family."

He is family, Maggy thought. *In every way that really matters.* The realization hit her like a bolt of lightning. It was all so simple, so perfectly clear, that she wondered why it had taken her so long.

"You're smiling," Rita said. "What are you smiling about?"

"I'm happy," Maggy said, dodging the question. "My daughter is safe and on her way home. That's something to be happy about."

"I hope you're going to punish her for pulling a stunt like this," Rita said.

"Mother, Nicole is my daughter. I'll take care of this."

They squabbled halfheartedly while Maggy started a pot of coffee. Ellie fielded business calls on her cell phone then set up her laptop on the kitchen table and got to work.

Maggy drank two cups of coffee then checked her

watch. "When did Conor call you from Fort Lee?"

"Around six-thirty," Rita said. "What time is it now?"

"After nine," Maggy said.

The two women looked at each other.

"I'm sure everything is okay," Rita said. "They probably hit traffic."

By ten o'clock, Maggy was pacing the length of the living room. She tried more than once to reach Conor's cell phone, but each time she was passed over to his voice mailbox. She walked the dogs, cleaned litterboxes, made sure Charlie was tucked in and sleeping peacefully. She was pulling things out of the hall closet in a vain attempt at straightening it up when the doorbell rang and she leaped to her feet.

"They're here!" she shouted out, unable to contain her excitement. She ran to the door and swung it open. "What on earth took you so—"

"Mrs. O'Brien?"

Two policemen stood on the front porch. Maggy felt her knees give way, and the younger of the men grabbed her by the arm to steady her.

"Yes," she said. "What is it? What happened?"

"There's been an accident, Mrs. O'Brien."

She listened over the rush of cold air flooding her brain and body. *An accident . . . struck by a car . . . unconscious . . . Nicole and Conor . . . oh, God . . . oh, Jesus, don't let this be true. . . .*

Behind her she heard her mother scream, then the sound of Ellie's crying, and she whirled around to face them. "Stop it!" she ordered. "Don't wake Charlie up!" Not yet. Not until they knew what was going on.

The policemen waited while she grabbed her coat and purse and car keys. "Somebody has to stay here with Charlie," she said to her mother and sister who had grabbed their coats as well.

"I'll stay," Ellie said then enveloped Maggy in a hug. "Everything will be okay. You'll see."

The roads were clear. Visibility was unlimited. No rain or ice or fog.

"What could have happened?" she whispered over and over as she followed the policemen north to Fort Lee.

Rita reached over and patted her hand. That act of kindness was almost Maggy's undoing. She had to swallow hard to keep her emotions in check. It would be so easy to let go, but she couldn't do that. Not yet. She'd let go when it was all over and everyone was safe and this was all nothing but a bad memory. A bad dream. A terrible dream but nothing more.

Her mother seemed to sense that she wasn't up to conversation. Maggy knew exactly what Rita was doing. The faint click of rosary beads hidden in her coat pocket gave her away.

"Say one for Conor, would you?" she asked in the quiet dark of the car.

They reached the hospital just before midnight. The cops pointed them to the emergency room where Maggy was assaulted by what seemed to be a score of nurses and technicians bearing charts and forms to sign and throwing information at her faster than she could take it in.

"Your daughter hit her head when she fell," one of the young doctors said while Maggy struggled to write down the information on a scrap of paper.

"I'm sorry," she said. "Would you mind repeating that?" Delayed reaction had set in, and her hands were shaking so badly she had trouble holding the pen.

"Your daughter hit her head. She was unconscious when she was brought in. We don't think there's any serious damage, but we want to run a complete series of tests on her, keep her here for a few days for observation." The more minor injuries included torn cartilage in Nicole's right knee, bruises, a separated shoulder. "She's in a great deal of pain,'' the doctor said, ''but we can't medicate her until we determine the extent of her head injury.''

''I understand,'' she said, but she didn't. That was her baby behind those doors, her little girl, and the thought that she was in pain and there was nothing anyone could do to help made her want to rip down the hospital walls with her bare hands.

The doctor turned to leave.

''Wait!'' Maggy touched the woman on the forearm. ''Conor Riley—he was with my daughter. How is he?''

''Are you a family member?''

''No,'' Maggy said. ''I'm a very close friend. Please, how is he?''

The doctor's expression slid from concerned to guarded. ''I'm sorry,'' she said, ''but I can't give you that information.'' She forced a professional smile. ''You can see your daughter as soon as she's down from X-ray.''

She found Rita at the bank of phones near the waiting room. She relayed the information to be passed on to Ellie and Claire then turned to find herself face-to-face with Conor's parents.

They looked devastated, and she felt the last of her strength begin to leave her body.

''Your daughter,'' Mrs. Riley said. ''How is she?''

''She's in X-ray. So far, it doesn't seem to be life-threatening.'' She drew in a long, shaky breath of courage. ''Conor?''

Mrs. Riley's face crumpled, and she turned into her husband's embrace. Conor's father met Maggy's eyes, and she saw the answer she'd feared.

''It's bad,'' his father said, then spewed a list of horror that ripped into her heart. Ruptured spleen. Multiple fractures of the right leg. Concussion.

''Where is he?'' Maggy whispered. If she spoke any louder she would howl her rage to the skies.

"He's in surgery," Mr. Riley said. "How in hell did this happen?"

"I don't know," Maggy said. "Were they on the highway?"

"No," said Conor's mother. "They were hit crossing a street. Crossing a street, can you imagine?"

Maggy couldn't. She couldn't imagine anything at all. Her mind was empty of everything but the white noise of fear.

She told the Rileys what little she knew, about Nicole and the photographer and how Conor had volunteered to drive up to Fort Lee to bring her back home. She felt her body tense as she waited for Mrs. Riley to turn on her, to heap blame on Nicole and on Maggy's mothering skills, but it didn't happen. Mrs. Riley had other things to worry about. That was her son in there, and she loved him every bit as much as Maggy loved Nicole. They locked eyes and knew the first moment of understanding between them.

The doors burst open, and a score of Rileys exploded into the waiting room. Maggy turned away and joined her mother near the telephones. She was an outsider. That was his family, his blood. No matter how deeply her feelings ran, they carried no weight here.

"I'm sorry," Rita said.

Maggy nodded.

"Nic will be fine."

"I know that," she managed. "I'm—I'm praying for Conor."

Maggy rested her head against her mother's chest and held back her tears.

The Rileys took over the far end of the waiting room. Maggy and Rita kept to themselves near the phones. Matt came over once to see how Nicole was doing, but other than that, they maintained separate camps. Finally, at a little after two in the morning, a nurse came for Maggy. "Your daughter is in ICU," she said with a big smile that worked on Maggy's heart like a shot of pure hope. "If you'd like to see her . . ."

ICU was on the second floor. She followed the nurse through a series of winding corridors, through two sets of double doors covered with warnings that would scare any sane person. Maggy saw none of it. All she saw was her little girl waiting at the end of it.

"You can only stay fifteen minutes," the nurse warned. "She's in a lot of pain, but we should be able to give her something very soon."

Maggy thanked her then stepped into the room. Nicole looked so fragile with those tubes and bandages and wires rigged up everywhere. A patch of hair had been shaved from her right temple, and the area under her eye was noticeably blackened. She looked almost unbearably beautiful to Maggy as she bent down to kiss her little girl. To touch her.

Nicole's eyes fluttered open at the first touch of her Maggy's lips.

"Mommy?"

Maggy's heart turned over. It had been a very long time since she'd been called Mommy by either of her children. How wonderful it sounded.

"How're you doing, sweetheart?"

"Conor . . ." Her voice was raspy from the tubes stuck down her throat. "How—?"

Oh, God. Forgive me this one lie. "He's fine, baby. He's in surgery, but he's going to be fine." *From my mouth to your ear.*

"I—I'm sorry."

"Shh." Maggy pushed back a lock of hair from her daughter's smooth forehead. "We'll talk about that some other time. Right now, all I want is for you to feel better." There would be time enough later to deal with everything else.

"He did it," Nicole whispered. "He saved me."

Maggy bent close to Nicole so she could make out the words. "Honey, what was that?"

"Conor s-saved me . . . pushed me out of . . . way . . ." Her words continued, broken and almost inaudible as Maggy tried to piece them together into their proper order.

"You were crossing the street," she repeated, "and a car came out of nowhere?"

Nicole's eyes closed then opened again in assent. "I tripped . . . the car was c-coming . . ." Tears welled up then trailed down her bruised cheeks. "He threw himself at m-me . . . I heard the car when it—" She stopped, obviously overcome, as Maggy stroked her cheek.

He saved your life, Maggy thought as she watched her daughter struggle to regain her composure. They were so much alike, more than she'd ever realized. Both of them unwilling to let their guard drop and show their soft underbellies to the world. She wouldn't have had the chance to learn that simple fact if it hadn't been for Conor. *You put your own life on the line so my little girl could live.* There could be no greater proof of love than that. She was overwhelmed with emotions so intense that they almost brought her to her knees. Love, fear, hope so fierce that it cut right through her heart. The connection between them was unbreakable. She knew it now, beyond doubt, straight through to her marrow. This was real, what they had found together, and it was powerful. It was about love and desire and family and loyalty and bravery and honor and, please, God, it was only just beginning. There had to be a happy ending for them all.

A nurse tapped on the door then entered the room. "I think that's enough for now, ladies. We want to let that BP settle down a bit."

"Rest," Maggy whispered to Nicole as she kissed her. "I'll be right outside." She touched her nose with the tip of her index finger. "Love you, Nickel."

"Love you, too, Mommy."

She carried those words with her back to the waiting room where she found Claire, Ellie, and a very sleepy Charlie sitting on a couch across from the Riley family. Claire stood up as Maggy approached. "Oh, Mags," she said, then her voice broke, and somehow Maggy found herself in her sister's arms.

"I'm so sorry," Claire said. "This was all my fault."

"I should have known she would do something like this," Maggy said, brushing away her little sister's tears. "I wish I'd let you oversee the whole thing."

"You were right about me," Claire said. "It was every bit as much about my own interests as it was about Nic's."

"And you were right about me," Maggy said. "I *am* jealous of you. I always have been. If I could come back as anyone, it would be you."

Claire's lovely face turned bright red. She'd never seen her sister embarrassed before, and the sight charmed Maggy. "I've made a lot of mistakes," she said.

"Oh, I wouldn't make any mistakes," Maggy said, and they both laughed. There was work to be done between them, but they'd taken the first step, and that meant the world.

"Good news?" Matt Riley appeared next to them. "I hope it's good news."

"Nicole's doing well," Maggy said, then introduced him to Claire. "Any news on Conor?" *You don't have to like me, but I love him and I want to be part of his life.*

"The surgeon said he'd come down when they're finished. We're hoping for the best."

Maggy nodded. She knew she was a stranger in their eyes, a passing fancy who had no right to ask for anything, not even information. They saw her as a woman with too many encumbrances, and they were probably right. Their son was lying in an operating room right now because he'd put his own life on the line to save her daughter. They deserved to know they'd raised a hero. "Is your mother up to talking?"

Matt shrugged. "When isn't she." He stayed behind to talk to her family.

She excused herself and approached the knot of Rileys gathered together on the other side of the room.

"I'm sorry to intrude," she said, meeting Mrs. Riley's eyes, "but I'd like to talk with you for a moment if you wouldn't mind." Woman to woman. Mother to mother.

Mrs. Riley handed her cup of coffee to her husband then stood up. "How is your daughter?" she asked Maggy as they moved toward a fairly secluded corner near the nurses' station. "Rita said you were able to see her in ICU."

"The test results aren't in yet, but it's looking good."

Mrs. Riley made the sign of the cross. "Thank God."

"Thank God," Maggy agreed, "and thank Conor."

"Conor?" Mrs. Riley frowned. "What does my son have to do with it?"

"He saved her life," Maggy said, unable to keep the quaver from her voice. She told his mother the story she'd heard from Nicole. "If he hadn't done that, I would have lost my daughter."

His mother's eyes glittered with tears. The woman tried to speak but couldn't.

"He's a hero," Maggy said, and his mother nodded. They both knew what that meant, how very much it mattered. When the time came to act, he did so without hesitation, without a thought to his own safety.

"Thank you," Mrs. Riley managed, then returned to her own family to share the news.

There was nothing Maggy could do but return to hers.

Charlie and Matt were engaged in a deep discussion about the Jets' Super Bowl chances. Charlie was bright-eyed and animated, and she couldn't help but notice that Matt was treating the child with a surprising degree of respect that won her heart.

"Don't judge his mother too harshly," Rita said, slipping her arm through Maggy's. "Her son is being operated on. She's scared out of her mind. Think of how you felt before you knew Nic was going to be all right."

"It's more than that, Ma. She feels about me the way you feel about Conor."

Her mother started with surprise. "I certainly don't act that way."

Maggy had to laugh. "Oh, don't you? You and your daughters have made your feelings perfectly clear."

"Only because I don't want you to make my mistakes. I want you to have a man who puts your happiness before his own, one who would lay down his life for you."

"I think I found him," she said.

"Maggy." The voice floated toward her from another galaxy. "Maggy, please wake up."

The sounds. The smells. Nicole so pale in that hospital bed with the tubes and the—

Conor.

She opened her eyes and found herself face-to-face with Matt Riley.

"He's out of recovery and he wants to see you." Matt inclined his head toward the Rileys at the other side of the room. "They're raising holy hell about it, but he told the nurses in ICU that it's you or nobody."

She scrambled to her feet and ran her hands through her hair. She wished she had a comb. Lipstick. A toothbrush.

The Rileys didn't look too pleased as she ran past them, but she didn't care. He was alive. He was awake. He wanted to see her. And, oh, God, how she wanted to see him. She wanted to hold him and breathe in his smell and tell him everything that was in her heart, spill all of that love and gratitude and hope over him like a healing balm.

She knew her way to ICU by now. She'd managed to

see Nicole twice more since the first brief visit, and now there was Conor just three beds away. Life sometimes moved in very mysterious ways.

His eyes opened at the sound of her footsteps, and it was the same as it had been the very first time she saw him. She felt blessed to have found him, as if the gods of good fortune had taken her under their wings.

"Nicole?" His voice was scratchy and weak, but the emotion came through loud and clear.

She knelt down on the floor next to him and took the hand that wasn't a mass of IV tubes. "She's banged up but nothing permanent." She gestured toward the other side of ICU. "She's three beds away."

His eyes closed for a moment, but not before she distinctly saw the glitter of tears. "She's a good kid, Maggy."

"I know," she whispered. "Thank you for saving my daughter's life."

He squeezed her hand, and she marveled that such a simple gesture could signify so much. She squeezed back. They had explored each other's bodies, made passionate love, but no touch had ever meant more. This was how you built a family, she thought. This was how it was done. You built it with love and trust and courage and tenderness, and you kept on building even when others tried to tear it down, because inside that shelter you were safe from harm. Inside that shelter, the ones you loved would live forever.

With a man like this, nothing was impossible.

She wanted to tell him all of that and more, but his painkillers finally kicked in, and he was drifting in and out of consciousness.

"I'd better give your mother a chance to see you," she said after a few minutes, "but I'll be back."

The smile he gave her was pure gold.

To her surprise she found his mother standing in front of Nicole's bed.

"He's pretty groggy," she said to Mrs. Riley, "but he'd like to see you."

His mother nodded. Maggy could see the hurt on her face and the puzzlement and maybe the tiniest glimmer of acceptance. She would settle for resignation.

"She looks so young," his mother said as they watched Nicole sleep.

"She *is* young," Maggy said. "I tend to forget that sometimes."

"Mine were a handful at that age. There were nights I cried myself to sleep, wondering why I ever wanted to have a family."

"I've done the same thing," Maggy said. "I even considered joining a convent just to get away."

His mother looked at her and laughed tiredly. "Now, I wouldn't go that far."

Maggy smiled back at her. "For a good night's sleep, there were times I would have done just about anything. Celibacy seemed a small price to pay."

His mother considered that for a second then chuckled. "She'll grow out of this. I know you probably don't believe me right now, but in a few years she'll seem human again."

"That's what they tell me," Maggy said, "but you're right. I don't think I believe it."

"If you want to go home and get some sleep, I'll keep my eye on her."

"Thank you," she said, startled by the offer. "I'd be happy to do the same for you."

Neither of them moved.

"You're not going anywhere, are you?" said his mother.

"Not on your life," said Maggy. "You're not either, are you?"

"You couldn't drag me away from here."

They looked at each other then broke into quiet laughter. For a little while they were just two mothers with a lot in common.

TWENTY-TWO

"Look at them," Maggy said to Nicole as they paused in the doorway to Conor's hospital room three days later. "They're thick as thieves."

"I can't believe the twerp's making him play Go Fish," Nicole said. She was dressed in her favorite sweater and a pair of leggings stretchy enough to accommodate the brace around her knee. Her hair was pulled back into a ponytail, and for the first time in ages she looked like a fifteen-year-old girl who still had a lot to learn about life. "I'd tell him to take a hike."

She was back to hating her little brother. Maggy wouldn't have believed it possible, but the sound of sibling rivalry was music to her ears.

"Conor's good with kids," Maggy said.

"Yeah," Nicole said. "I guess he's not bad."

Maggy shot her daughter a look. "High praise," she said, arching a brow in her best Mr. Spock fashion.

Nicole ducked her head in embarrassment, but it was too late. Maggy had seen the look in her daughter's eyes, and it warmed her heart.

Small miracles.

She'd take them wherever she found them. She and Nic still had so far to go. She couldn't hide any longer from the truth. Nic missed her father more than Maggy had wanted to admit, and maybe it was time to rethink the decisions they'd made when they divorced. Her daughter wasn't a little girl any longer whose every need could be met by Mommy. If she was going to keep her place in Nicole's heart, she would have to learn how to let go.

Just a little bit.

"Hey, you two," Maggy said as she navigated Nicole's wheelchair into the room. "Aunt Ellie's waiting to take you home, Charlie, and you know she hates to be kept waiting."

Conor looked up, and her heart sank. He smiled, but it wasn't a real smile, not the smile she had fallen in love with. *Don't go reading anything into it,* she told herself. *He's recovering from surgery. He's pumped full of pain-killers. This has nothing to do with you.*

"Go fish." Charlie slammed his cards down on the hospital bed, barely missing the cast on Conor's leg. He totally ignored Maggy and Nicole.

"Again?" Conor glared at his own cards, then tossed them down next to Charlie's. "Are you using marked cards?"

Charlie grinned. "I'm just better than you, that's all."

"Think so, do you?"

Charlie's grin widened. "Know so."

"Better go get your jacket," Maggy said to her son. "Ellie said she'd take you to McDonald's if you help her get a head start on rush-hour traffic."

"You stay," Conor said, ruffling Charlie's hair. "I'll grab your jacket and leave."

Charlie thought that was hilarious, and Conor looked quite pleased with himself. Even Nicole couldn't manage to withhold a grin.

"C'mon, twerp," said Nicole. "You can push me back to my room."

That was all Charlie needed to hear. He gathered up his cards then pushed a shrieking Nicole full speed down the hall.

"Look under the bed for your football!" Maggy called after him.

"Sean was like that," Conor said as Maggy lingered in the doorway. "Perpetual motion."

Look at me, Conor. You haven't really looked at me since the accident.

"You made two more headlines," she said, tossing a pair of local newspapers on the nightstand. "Hero cop saves teenager from certain death." Just saying the words made her shudder.

"Toss them," he said, his voice tightly controlled. "I don't need to see them."

"Maybe your mother—"

"Toss them."

"Okay." They hit the wastebasket with a loud thud.

There was a long silence.

"Charlie said your ex and his new wife are on their way over from London."

Maggy nodded. "Compassionate leave," she said. "They'll be here tomorrow morning for a long weekend. The kids are thrilled."

"And you?"

"I'm happy for them," she said after a moment. "Beyond that, it's ancient history." And it was. She'd had a lovely telephone chat with Sally the morning after the accident. Sally was warm and funny and extremely bright, and when Maggy wished her well, she found she meant every word. That chapter of her life was over.

It was time to move on.

Maggy excused herself a few minutes later to say good-bye to her sister and Charlie. She hesitated for a moment, then bent down, and kissed him lightly on the mouth. "I'll be back in a little while," she said. "I'm meeting your mother in the coffee shop at six."

"When did hell freeze over?" he asked, but she didn't hear him. She was already out the door.

He leaned back against the pillows and tried not to notice the bouquets of flowers, the sprays of balloons bobbing near the ceiling. He tried very hard to ignore the newspapers sticking up from the white metal wastebasket to the left of his nightstand, but that was a tough one. He was sure the headlines glowed in the dark.

"My dad said you're a real hero," Charlie had said to him that morning while they were playing Monopoly. "He's coming to visit, and he said he wants to shake your hand."

"That's great," Conor had managed, even though the idea made him feel like even more of a fraud than before.

They filled his room with flowers and balloons. They wrote about him in the local papers. *Eyewitness News* ran a story on the accident during their six o'clock broadcast.

His parents were so proud they marched up and down the hospital corridor like visiting royalty, accepting accolades from one and all. His brothers thought his celebrity was a cool way for them to meet women. His married sisters fussed over him as if he was one of their kids.

The Halloran women set out to make amends. They showered him with chocolates and cushy feather pillows and a splashy rainbow comforter to cheer up his hospital room. Claire had even bought a fistful of Day-Glo markers that she used to decorate his cast. He wasn't sure how he felt about all of the yellow daisies and fat red hearts trailing up his leg, but everyone else seemed to love it. He'd been accepted as one of their own, and he could feel the circle of family protection closing around him. *You're one of us now,* their actions said. *You proved yourself when you saved Nicole.*

Nicole had wheeled herself into his room to thank him

yesterday. She had looked so young and vulnerable with her hair scraped back into a ponytail and those ugly bruises marring her lovely face that his heart actually twisted at the thought that all of her potential could have been so easily lost. She blushed bright red as she stumbled through her speech, and he'd felt every bit as embarrassed as she did.

"Forget it," he said, coughing to hide the catch in his voice. "I did what anybody would have done in the situation."

"Nobody in the whole world but my mom and dad would've done that for me," Nicole said. "I-I'm sorry for the way I treated you."

"Change is scary," he said. "For all of us." New dreams. New lives. New family patterns emerging every time you turn around. All of that and being fifteen.

She'd stayed with him for an hour. They hadn't talked about anything important, but they'd talked. She was a good kid. She loved both of her parents and wished they'd stayed together. He couldn't fault her for that. What kid didn't wish his parents would somehow get back together and start all over again? She was making peace with her father's remarriage, and Conor was sure she would have found a way to accept her mother and him if only the lady was still willing.

He'd seen the way Maggy had withdrawn once she heard the story of the day Bobby died. He'd seen the disappointment in her eyes, the dimming of wonder. When the excitement over Nicole faded away, that disappointment would remain, and it would overshadow everything else.

A hero wouldn't have stood there and watched his partner die without doing something to save him. It didn't matter what else he did in this life; he would always be defined by the one thing he didn't do, and there was nothing in the world that could change that simple fact.

•   •   •

Maggy and Conor's mother had fallen into the surprisingly agreeable habit of meeting in the cafeteria for coffee during the day. Both of them had put the rest of their lives on hold to be there for their children. It formed a bond between them that was undeniable.

Maggy had told Kathleen about Nicole and how much Nicole missed her father. "I would suggest she go live with him for a while, but he's in the army and—" She shrugged her shoulders. "Besides, he's a newlywed. He and Sally need some time."

"What about you?" Kathleen asked as she poured two blue packets of sweetener into her coffee. "Maybe you need some time, too."

"For what?" Maggy asked. She was genuinely puzzled.

"To be a newlywed yourself maybe. Anyone with eyes can see that my son loves you, although I'll admit I wasn't crazy about the idea at first."

"There's a surprise," Maggy said, softening her words with a smile. They had come a long way. When you were dealing with issues of life and death, you didn't waste time on nonsense.

"There's no excuse for the way I behaved at the christening."

"I don't suppose there is."

"I can apologize, though, and hope you'll accept it."

"Gladly." Maggy pushed aside her cup and leaned across the table. "How would you feel if I told you I'm in love with your son?"

"I'd say you were crazy if you weren't."

She took a deep breath. "Something's changed, Kathleen. He looks right through me, as if we'd never met."

Kathleen frowned, then pressed her forefinger to the furrows above the bridge of her nose, ironing them flat and smooth. "He's hurting, Margaret, that's all." She stood up and rested a hand on Maggy's shoulder. "He isn't always easy, but he's worth the trouble. It's been a long time since we've seen him this happy, and we have you to thank.'' With that, Kathleen slipped out the side door to smoke a cigarette.

Didn't that beat all? His mother's blessing when there was nothing there to bless. Less than a week ago everything had seemed so complicated. Family issues had overwhelmed her. The murder trial had raised questions she wasn't sure she wanted answered. Nicole had been spinning out of control. When Conor spoke about a future together, Maggy had taken ten giant steps back from it, unable to see how the disparate bits and pieces of their lives could ever come together.

Now none of it seemed important. What had she been thinking, anyway? Had she been thinking at all? Love was the only important thing. How bland that sounded. How miraculous it truly was. She had planned to say that and more to Conor when he brought Nicole home from her adventure. She had planned to sit him down in her kitchen and tell him everything that was in her heart, but she never had the chance. The accident happened, and by the time the dust had settled, something fundamental had changed between them. She could see it in his eyes whenever he looked at her. He was moving away from her, and she couldn't understand why.

He should be on cloud nine, like everyone else in their families.

Both he and Nicole were going to make full recoveries. His recovery would take longer, but the doctors had said there was no doubt he would be as good as new in a few months. There were so many reasons to be happy and grateful and optimistic that she couldn't begin to count them all. He'd even made the six o'clock news, an accomplishment that elevated him to superstar status in Charlie's book. It seemed as if everyone in the hospital wanted to meet him and shake his hand.

He should be bursting with pride and happiness. She'd been there when his son Sean called, and she'd had the pleasure of telling the young man about his father's bravery. There were local politicians who would sell their souls to get the ink Conor had received from the local newspapers over the last few days. Kathleen had left behind a copy of today's *Star-Ledger*. His picture and Nicole's were on the front page of the second section, right next to a story about the DiCarlo trial. The irony of it all suddenly grabbed her by the throat.

His greatest loss and his greatest triumph, linked together on that page for everyone to see. He was hurting. How on earth could she have missed that? Hurting not just physically, but deep in his soul. She'd thought he was turning away from her, but it wasn't that at all. He was turning inward, thinking only about the life he'd lost and not the one he'd saved. She believed he needed her right now, more than he'd ever needed anyone.

Almost as much as she needed him.

So what was she waiting for?

She was out of there like a shot. She raced through the lobby, punched the button for the elevator, then when it was too slow, she ran up the stairs to the fourth floor. Nurses stopped and stared at her as she careened down the corridor toward Conor's room, but she didn't care. All she cared about was telling him everything that was in her heart.

"I love you, Conor," she said as she burst into his room. "I know this isn't the way to—" Her words died abruptly. He wasn't alone. A pretty, dark-haired woman sat on the edge of the bed, holding Conor's hand. Her eyes were red, and she clutched a crumpled tissue in her other hand. Conor's eyes were suspiciously moist.

"I'm sorry," Maggy said, wishing she could blink her eyes and disappear. "I didn't realize you had a visitor." She might have thought twice about the *I love you* if she'd looked before she leaped. She turned to leave.

"Don't go, Maggy."

"Really," she said, inching toward the door. "No

problem. I should have knocked or something. I'll just—''

''Come here, Maggy.'' He didn't sound like a man who'd been through major surgery seventy-two hours ago. He sounded like the man she'd met that rainy day in Atlantic City. The dark-haired woman sitting next to him must be extremely pleasant company to manage that.

''If you insist.'' She tried to sound bright and breezy but fell far short of the mark. Mostly she found herself focused on the fact that Conor and the mystery woman were still holding hands.

''This is Denise DiCarlo, Maggy.''

Denise gave her a gentle smile, then released her hand from Conor's. ''I've heard a lot about you, Maggy.''

They shook hands. Maggy's head was spinning. Bobby's widow. She remembered Conor saying that he had lost more than a friend and partner, he'd lost an entire family. The DiCarlos hadn't been part of his life since the funeral.

''It's good to meet you, Denise.''

They took each other's measure, then Denise turned toward Conor. ''Mom is home taking care of the kids. I'd better run.'' She bent down and kissed his cheek. ''Call me when you get home.''

''Thanks, Deni.'' Maggy watched as his eyes misted over. ''I—'' His voice cracked, and Denise patted his hand.

''I know,'' Denise whispered. ''I wish I'd let myself believe it sooner.''

Denise said good-bye to them both, then left.

''I guess she watches *Eyewitness News*,'' Maggy said as she kissed Conor lightly on the mouth. ''I'm glad she came to see you.''

''So am I,'' he said. He pointed toward a stack of photos on the nightstand. ''The kids have grown.''

''They're sneaky that way,'' she said. ''Did you have a nice visit?'' She sounded like Queen Victoria at high tea. What happened to the woman who'd burst into the room screaming *"I love you"*?

He met her eyes. "You could say that."

She sat down on the bed next to him. "Listen," she said, "I haven't slept more than four hours in the last three days. In the best of times, patience isn't my strong suit. Something happened between you and Denise. I can see it in your eyes. Now, are you going to tell me what it was, or do I have to drag it out of you?"

"It's over," he said, reaching for her hand. "It's finished."

"What's over? The trial? Your estrangement? What?"

"We have a witness," he said. "Somebody who saw what happened and can fill in the blanks."

"Conor!" She clutched his hand. It could only be good news. She was *sure* it was good news. "Who? What? Tell me!"

"Jack Oliphant from the shoe store across the parking lot."

"The guy who made the 911 call?"

"The same."

"But didn't he testify that he didn't see anything?"

"He was being threatened," Conor said. Apparently, Walker's friends or family had hired some thugs to apply pressure on Oliphant to keep his mouth shut. Conor was no threat because of the gap in his memory. Oliphant represented real danger. A witness to the actual shooting would make life in prison without parole a certainty. "He was scared. He has a family to worry about. He caved."

"He's a coward."

"Yes," said Conor, "but he's also a man with three kids he wanted to keep safe from harm. You do what you have to do."

"Even if it means a guilty man gets off easy?"

"Welcome to the world," he said.

"So why is he talking now?"

"Conscience. Compassion. I don't know." He told her

the basics of the story Denise had supplied. It seemed
Jack Oliphant had seen the media coverage of Nicole's
accident and Conor's bravery, and apparently that trig-
gered a surprising response in him. He showed up on
Denise's doorstep the next morning and spilled his guts
to her, and then Denise had gone with him to see Sonya
Bernstein, the DA on the case, to come clean.

"He committed perjury," Maggy said. "They'll throw
the book at him."

"I don't think so," Conor said. "I'm sure Sonya will
find a way to make it go easy for him."

She took a deep breath. *Please, God. Help him see
what a fine man he is.* "You didn't freeze, did you? You
didn't just let Walker shoot Bobby."

"No," he said, his expression one of deep sorrow and
great relief. "I didn't let Bobby die."

The details were sketchy as he related them to Maggy.
He still needed to hear the entire story from Oliphant
himself, to ask questions, so he could finally put together
the pieces of that terrible afternoon, but what he knew
changed everything for him.

She heard the sound of his world clicking back into
place.

"Oliphant saw Walker holding the gun to Bobby's
head. He said I was trying to talk to Walker, that the
bastard said he'd blow Bobby's brains out if I didn't put
down my gun." His recitation was quick and without
inflection, as if he were relating somebody else's story.
She supposed that in a way it was, since he had no direct
memory of it. "The gun was on the ground, about three
feet away. Oliphant remembered it because the sunlight
bounced off it and into his eyes."

Maggy's eyes brimmed with tears. "That's the same
thing you noticed about Walker's gun."

"Oliphant told Denise that he hid behind a Mazda and
saw the whole thing. He heard me trying to work things
out before they went too far. He said I told Walker that

if he put down the gun, we'd go light on him, that his
cooperation would be taken into account. Oliphant said
it was working. Walker was talking, sounding like a
scared kid looking for a way out. Oliphant was sure we
had him, that we'd finally gotten through to him. He said
the kid lowered the gun like he was going to put it down,
and Bobby twisted to his left and went for it.'' He
stopped, and it was quite a few seconds before he continued. ''Oliphant says I grabbed for my gun, lunged forward, but they were all over each other—I couldn't have
gotten a clear shot or maybe I wasn't fast enough. The
next thing Oliphant knew, he heard the gunshot and saw
Bobby fall against Walker, and it was all over.''

She held him as close as she could, watching out for
the cast and the incision and the tubes and wires sprout-
ing everywhere. She stroked his hair and listened to the
ragged sound of his breathing and wondered how it was
she had ever lived without the other half of her heart.

Pain left, and in its place came acceptance and peace. It
had been so long since he'd known either of those emotions that Conor didn't recognize them at first. This was
how it felt to be whole again.

This was how it felt to be loved.

She'd burst into the room and said those words loud
and clear for the world to hear, and she'd said them before she knew he hadn't let Bobby die.

''Maggy.''

She leaned back slightly and looked at him. Her china
blue eyes were wide with concern. ''Is something wrong?
Do you need—''

''You,'' he said. ''I need you.''

Those beautiful eyes filled with tears. ''Would you
mind saying that again? I want to make sure I heard
you.''

''I love you, Maggy O'Brien. I've loved you from the
first moment I saw you.''

"Across the parking lot," she said, smiling through a haze of happy tears. "What a silly place to fall in love."

"When I saw you the next morning on the boardwalk with your hair curling in the rain, I knew you had my heart forever."

"You cops sure know how to sweet-talk." She radiated joy, and he found himself thanking God for the choices that had brought them to this point.

'So what about you, lady?" He felt young and filled with promise. "Got anything to say for yourself?"

Her laughter filled his heart and soul with the purest happiness he had ever known. The kind of happiness he'd thought beyond his reach.

"Me?" she asked. "Not a thing."

"You love me," he said, unable to wipe the smile off his face. He couldn't pretend to be anything but what he was: deliriously in love, dangerously lucky, and damned glad of it all. "I have witnesses, O'Brien. You might as well come clean."

"I've heard you guys have a way to make people talk."

"Wait until I'm out of this bed," he said, grinning like a lovestruck teenager. "I'll show you a thing or two."

"I love you." She took his hand between hers, then bent her head to kiss his fingers. "I love your body and your heart and your soul and your mind and your courage."

"You know what this means."

"We're getting married, aren't we?"

"Damn right," he said, "and the sooner the better."

"We should probably tell the kids before we walk down the aisle."

"I'll get Sean on the phone right now," he said. "You round up Nic and Charlie and a priest."

"Father Roarke will be thrilled, but the kids might need a little convincing."

"If we love them enough, they'll come around. I think they're halfway there already."

There was that smile he loved, the one he planned on seeing every day for the rest of his life and even longer. "You don't waste time, do you?"

"I've already wasted thirty-eight years without you," he said. "I don't intend to waste another minute."

And that was when the woman he loved kissed him and their life together began.

National Bestselling Author
Katherine Sutcliffe

❏ **HOPE AND GLORY**   0-515-12476-1/$6.99
*Nations tremble before mercenary Roland Gallienne. Now, weary of war, he
seeks peace at the healing hands of the Chateauroux monastery healer.*

*The lovely woman is child of his enemies, and tries to kill him—but to everyone's
surprise he shows her mercy and takes her with him.*

*Their attraction can't be denied, and now, at the brink of a new battle, they must
both struggle with an inner war—of the heart....*

❏ **DESIRE AND SURRENDER**   0-515-12383-8/$6.99
*Her father murdered, her home burned to the ground, Angelique DuHon left
New Orleans with her mother—fleeing to the home of wealthy relatives in Texas,
hoping for sanctuary and peace.*

*But against all odds, Angelique would do anything to save the greatest
happiness she had ever known—even at the risk of her own life....*

❏ **JEZEBEL**   0-515-12172-X/$6.50
*Widowed by the town preacher and denounced by her neighbors, Charity Bell is
a marked woman. But beneath her misery and scorn is a lady of refinement—with
a past of privilege that left her unprepared for life's cruel twists of fate.*

❏ **DEVOTION**   0-515-11801-X/$6.50
❏ **MIRACLE**   0-515-11546-0/$6.50
❏ **MY ONLY LOVE**   0-515-11074-4/$5.99
❏ **ONCE A HERO**   0-515-11387-5/$5.99